CONSIGNED TO OBLIVION

EMILEE BREANNE WARD

First Edition: July 2024
Owensboro, KY

For Uncle Mike—

You were one of my biggest fans and knew I would write a book one day. I wish you were here to see it finally come to fruition.

"For God has consigned all to disobedience, that he may have mercy on all."
- Romans 11:32 (ESV)

PROLOGUE

Pat did not believe in magic but he did believe in monsters. This fear of monsters started at a young age. His father Owen Sherwood would find him rocking back and forth in his bed, shaking uncontrollably because of a nightmare he could not wake from. This pained Owen, who had spent his life creating technology to make peoples' lives better. The summer before Pat's 12th birthday, his father had begun experimenting with a new technology meant to free his son from his mental suffering.

He had always been obsessive, but when it came to his son he was maniacal. Pat was Owen's world after his wife died. When Pat turned 13, his father was ready to try out what he had created. Money was no object and resources were not hard to come by in the city of Kimber, which contained over 300,000 people and 10 different hospitals. Owen selected Mercy Research Hospital because it was smaller and designed in such a way that it was easier to keep the procedure private from the public. He also took great pains to secure Dr. Everett Winston to perform the surgery on Pat. He was known for his steady hands and the ability to successfully implement experimental treatments.

The surgery was completed with no complications and Pat awoke to his father standing over him with a slightly crazed smile.

His eyes danced as if watching his child walk for the first time, except that Pat's father had never been present for that particular milestone.

"Hey there, Jobs." Owen said huskily, using the nickname he had chosen for his son when he first showed an aptitude for technology. "How do you feel?" Instead of reaching for his son's hand as most parents would, Owen wrung his hands in slow motion as if to distract himself from his intrusive thoughts.

Pat did not speak immediately, but instead looked around the room. He took in the pale peach walls, picture windows looking out onto a sleepless city, and the beeping machines that proved he was alive. Then his eyes fell back on his nervous father. "I am not sure." He paused. "I am thirsty."

Owen was not deterred by this uncertainty. His son had been mentally ill for so long that it made sense that he was still unsure. The operations of the technology were rather clunky at first. Pat had to use his phone's Internet browser to run the program, but soon enough an app was developed. The microchip implanted directly on the surface of Pat's brain was able to eliminate any electrical impulses that were "wrong" or negatively affecting his quality of life. All he had to do was click "resolve" on his app and the Thought Conductor microchip would do its job. Six months passed and it became apparent that the technology was working. An entire year passed and Pat was using the new technology proficiently and starting high school feeling like a new kid. This was a glowing time in Pat's life because after the surgery he finally was able to tell the difference between reality and nightmares. He basked in the feeling of being a "normal" teen at last.

Instead of living in his imagination, high school became a time when he was consumed with thoughts about girls, cliques, and finding himself. Shortly into his sophomore year, a new girl started in his grade and seemed to take a shine to him. This sent his thoughts spiraling. He could think only of her. She mothered him and seemed to understand his spirit more than his father who had been tracking his moods and thoughts for two years. Pat could not deny that he liked being cared for by her and felt a sense of wholeness with her.

When they both graduated high school, they got married and moved into a home that Owen had bought for them as a wedding present. This was around the same time when Owen's technology truly began to take off when he designed a portal that he believed would allow people to interact with the human mind as if it were a physical place. Owen wanted to test this advancement on his son since he was the first patient to use the Thought Conductor to manage his mental illness.

A huge party was planned to showcase this new technology. Company stakeholders, friends, and family all gathered at the young Pat Sherwood's estate for cocktails, shrimp, low-fat pretzels, and chocolate. It was the first big event the young couple had hosted and Pat's wife was beside herself with pride in her husband and excitement at her home being full of important people.

After Owen had shared his crazed excitement with all the guests, it was time to show off what the Sherwood family was capable of. They all gathered around a stainless steel triangle standing upright at about 7 feet tall and glowing with golden light. Nothing was behind it except the glass windows looking out onto Mr. and Mrs. Sherwood's rolling green pastures in the backyard. Once Pat's microchip was connected to the system and the portal turned on, the guests waited with bated breath as an image began to flicker in the opening. Owen asked Pat to step inside but before he could something went very wrong. Like feedback from a microphone too close to a speaker, Pat's brain buzzed. It felt as though the microchip in his brain was burning a hole through his head and he wailed in agony. Barely being able to see through tears, he realized an unknown monster had come through the portal. Chaos reigned at the party and the last image Pat had was of his father being torn to pieces and a woman with bright red hair disappearing into the blackness beyond the portal.

CHAPTER 1

THE NUMBER OF PEOPLE SUFFERING FROM mental illness increased exponentially during the twenty-first century. As more things became automated and society spent more time in isolation, it was fairly normal for children as young as 9 years old to have generalized anxiety disorder or severe depression. The world had been holding its breath for some sort of savior. They looked to the government, teachers, healthcare workers, and celebrities for insight, but all had failed. The majority of society's heroes had been outed as pedophiles and rapists, but Dr. Clive Evers perfectly filled the void left by corruption. Only "radical conspiracy theorists" thought his achievements regarding mental health were Satanic and questionable. Everybody else could not praise him enough. It had been a horrific three years full of suffering, but now in the year 2040, the majority of the country was happy and that was a miracle.

Clive took pride in what he was doing for his community and the country. The goal of perfection was always at the forefront of his mind and, unlike other religious individuals, he did not think this was an unattainable goal. With Christ, all things were possible.

These thoughts buzzed through his mind as he pulled into his reserved spot at Healing Touch Hospital. He pressed the ignition button and his car powered down. Electric was no longer the future but the present. Those with the most money and influence were expected to have electric vehicles, and car manufacturers were nearly at the point where they were able to offer more cost-effective options for lower-income families.

Dr. Evers took one glance in the mirror to confirm that his hair was still in place, there was not any food in his teeth, and that every hair from his chin and upper lip had been shaved off. He then put on a surgical mask over the lower half of his face and slipped out the driver's side door. At this point, the continual mask-wearing was more for public appearances and less about safety. Since most of society was vaccinated, there wasn't a need to wear them except in a surgery or in labor and delivery. However, wearing a mask had become a universal gesture of goodwill towards others and, as a medical professional and good Catholic, that is what he was all about.

Clive shivered slightly as a crisp breeze blew through the parking lot. The last remaining brown leaves rustled in the half-naked tree branches as if cold as well. The sky was completely clear of clouds but it still felt dim outside due to all the tall hospital buildings. His gait was self-assured and smooth as he made his way to the front entrance. The automatic doors whooshed open to admit him and a security guard was poised to take his temperature. "Good morning, Doc."

The man's name tag read "Dill" but Clive was certain he hadn't had a full conversation with him before. He seemed to just refer to everybody in a white coat as "Doc". Dr. Evers dipped his head forward in greeting but also so he was close enough for Dill to wave the contact-free thermometer over his forehead. "Thanks, Dill."

"Going to save humanity from themselves today?" Dill teased.

"Of course." Clive saluted in place of a handshake. Nobody seemed to shake hands anymore. Dill returned the gesture and turned to temperature check the next person entering the hospital.

The surroundings had ceased to be magnificent to Clive over the past 2 years he had been working at Healing Touch Hospital. The lobby had several blue sparkling tiles cutting a path through white marble tiles over the larger parts of the floor and leading to a fountain in the center. Streams of clear water squirted into the air and landed in a pool lapping lazily against the tiled barriers. Above this magnificent 12-foot-tall water display was a domed glass ceiling. Some of the pieces of glass were clear and others were stained. One of Clive's main reasons for deciding to work at Healing Touch was because of the beautiful architecture, but unfortunately its beauty was something easily taken for granted. Dr. Evers craved lovely things since his job continually exposed him to the sickness of the world.

As he continued to his floor, people recognized him. Civilians waved to him sheepishly in the hall and Clive's heart would swell with pride. If he hadn't been wearing a mask, his signature crooked smile would have shone brightly. He was a beautiful man and worked very hard to keep it that way. His tailored white coat gave hints of his chiseled physique. His eyes were brown like a vat of melted chocolate and his short hair the color of wheat. He always was clean-shaven but even when he let his facial hair grow out, he still looked good.

Upon entering the elevator, Clive selected the third floor with his elbow. A sweet automated female voice said, "Going up." The back of the elevator was all glass and, as it surpassed the second floor, he could see out to the courtyard behind the hospital. He let himself zone out to mentally prepare for the day ahead. He was tired but that didn't mean he could stop to rest. Too many people were relying on him.

The ding alerted him to his arrival on the third floor and he rushed out. His work had always been busy but since he had become head of the chip implementation project, he had even more tasks to tend to. Even so, he always began the start of his shift by doing a pass-on with the previous attending.

"Nothing terribly unusual last night. The treatment seems to be working well on the new patients and hasn't dipped yet in the long-term ones." Dr. Shepherd informed Clive when he arrived.

"And no signs of high blood pressure in Ophelia?"

"None at all except when she missed the toilet sitting down to pee."

Clive tried not to smile but that was typical. No matter how mentally sound she became, she would never achieve normalcy. There were certain things about Ophelia that society would always think were atypical.

Dr. Shepherd continued, "One of the nurses does want to speak to you about a shipment of new microchips. She was approached by somebody but she wasn't certain if he was at the right hospital. It was a whole ordeal…Libby!" He waved at a nurse with a tall statuesque body and bouncy brunette hair bound in a tight ponytail. "Tell Dr. Evers what you told me."

While she spoke, Clive could not see her lips move due to the double masks on the lower half of her face. She did pay specific care to doing her eye makeup and Clive noted that he liked the shade of blue she had used.

"So, I didn't know if the chips were authorized." She finished.

"I will check into that." He said simply as he pulled out his phone from his pocket to input a reminder.

Dr. Shepherd smiled and said, "Well, that's all I had. Do you have any questions?"

Clive shook his head and the two professionals parted ways. His first stop was to meet with Ophelia to see her progress for himself. He also liked to get her out of the way at the beginning of the day because she was the hardest case. He passed through several checkpoints, waving the QR code on his badge across the camera by each. He finally arrived outside a hospital room with a one-way window. He looked in and could see a young woman sitting on the bed twiddling her thumbs. Her stringy red hair looked as if it hadn't been brushed yet and she chewed at her left ring finger knuckle with crooked teeth. She wasn't easy to look at but this was the calmest Clive had seen her in a long time.

With a gentle knock on the hospital door, he let himself in and quickly nodded at a nurse nearby to follow him. A few beeping machines sat in the far corner of the room closest to the window which looked out onto several tall office buildings. Ophelia stopped chewing on her finger and looked at Dr. Evers as if she had never seen him before.

"How are you feeling today, Ophelia?" Clive asked, flashing a smile she couldn't see.

"Lonely. Empty. I want people to like me but I need to like me… you know? I used to like me…" She trailed off and glanced back out the window.

"You liked hallucinating?"

"I had friends."

"They weren't real." Clive corrected gently.

"I don't have real friends now either."

"You will, Ophelia! Your brain will be able to process things neurotypically so you can make friends, get a job, and enjoy your downtime at home. That's why you volunteered for this trial."

"But I haven't stopped seeing things."

Clive's breath caught in his throat and he blinked a few times to try to organize his thoughts. This was the first he had heard of this happening. Up to this point, Ophelia's hallucinations had become nonexistent and she wasn't experiencing night terrors.

"I thought they were gone."

"No!" She rolled her head back and forth and hummed softly to herself. "They have been visiting me."

"When and where?"

"Well, just one. He is a snake that visits me in my dreams. His eyes are like my cat's and he has a hook for a tail."

Clive sighed internally. She was getting off subject like she did most days when he checked in on her.

"Could I get some water?"

"Yes…but the hallucinations?" Clive persisted as he signaled for the nurse to get some water.

"Would you want to go see a movie?" Ophelia asked sweetly as she swung her eyes back onto Clive.

"I can't date my patients. You know that!" He said, trying to regain back some of his charismatic charm. He was concerned at what she let slip but he could tell she had already mentally moved on and he wasn't going to be getting anything else out of her.

After Ophelia got her water, Clive proceeded to the other patient rooms. Every other patient seemed to be taking to the treatment very well and didn't have any alarming relapses. It was beginning to look like the hospital would be able to offer this sort of treatment to more people suffering from mental illness just as planned. People would be clamoring for the chip when they heard what it was capable of. If Clive had struggled with mental illness himself, he would've gladly gotten it.

The rest of the day soared by but he didn't get any downtime. His lunchtime came and went without a morsel of food. As he neared the end of the day, he figured he should make a call to the technology company manufacturing the chip implants. With the pending mass manufacturing of the chip to larger populations, it wouldn't be good to have a poor relationship with the manufacturers. Whatever had happened with the nurse earlier in the morning seemed odd to him and he wanted to get to the bottom of the situation.

Miraculously, he made it to his office with no detours or nurses stopping him to demand that he deal with their issue first. He shut the door behind him and was greeted by the smell of cinnamon and cloves. Sitting in his chair was Tonya.

"Clive, you're right on time." Her voice was dark and velvety. Nothing she said ever sounded like it was full of good intentions.

"Of course. People are waiting on me." His eyes flickered over the parts of her that were visible. Shoulder pads. A silky curtain of straight black hair. Eyes the color of the river of Styx. Tanned skin. Elegant, perfectly shaped brows. A long pointed nose over lips painted red. Those lips curved into a knowing smile and she stood to loop her way around the desk. As she rounded the sharp corner, she took his breath away with how beautiful she was. This was a path he kept going down.

"Of course. You're their savior."

The use of the word "savior" made the Catholic part of him cringe. Saying it out loud made him have to face the fact that he thought he was doing far more good in the world than the Lord.

"God has gifted me in this area. People are happy for the first time in years."

"Which God?" She cooed as her arms wrapped themselves around his neck.

She untied his mask and leaned over to sit it in a wooden chair in the corner of the room. He liked when she spoke about things he didn't agree with. It felt forbidden. He also felt alive when with her.

***

Clive tried to regain enough focus to make the call to the microchip manufacturers. After his encounter with Tonya, he was distracted and not in the mood to work. He placed his thumb over the home button and the screen flashed to life with an audible "click". His long, skilled fingers navigated through the device until he found the main line for Sherwood Servers.

"Theresa Clark, how may I direct your call?"

Sherwood Servers always surprised Clive with their personal touch to doing business. While most advanced technology companies were moving to 100% automation, Owen Sherwood's company legacy continued to employ live humans to handle day-to-day operations.

"Hello, Theresa." Clive responded warmly, a smile accompanying his phone voice. "This is Dr. Clive Evers…I…"

"Oh, wonderful! It's an honor, Doctor." Her tone went from sounding slightly bored to absolutely glowing in a matter of seconds.

"Thank you." He was most comfortable listening to people sing his praises. He had worked hard to reach this point in his life and it encouraged him that he was doing well. "You're too kind. Truly."

"What can I help you with, Dr. Evers?"

Clive explained the situation to Theresa and requested to speak with whoever had visited the hospital. "So, we think there might be a mix-up."

"Oh no." She breathed. There was a significant pause then she said, "Can I do some digging and reach back out to you? Currently, none of our sales or delivery staff are in the office. They are finishing up for the day so I will need to call them."

"Certainly." Clive sounded kind but he was put out by the delay. *"If I had called earlier."* The image of Tonya flashed into his mind and he ran his left hand through his hair as if to erase the thought from his mind. "Thank you for all your help."

"Of course, Doctor. Have a great day!"

"You as well." Clive ended the call and then felt the heaviness of his thoughts rest over him like a weighted blanket. He knew he would have to go to confession before heading home.

To finish out the day, he completed some dictation notes and by 6 pm he was mentally tapped out. He then locked up his office, did pass-on for the night shift doctor, then left the hospital in his fully charged car.

Not too far from the hospital was the Immaculate Heart Cathedral. Dr. Clive Evers attended most Sundays, tithed once a month, and regularly went to confession. Being a good Catholic was a full-time job but it was all that he knew. In such an uncertain world, Catholicism was certain. His faith was the only thing that was beautiful and perfect consistently.

Taking a deep maskless breath as he walked into the sanctuary, he felt the prick of tears beginning when he looked at Mother Mary in her stained-glass form bowing at the feet of an angel. A few sisters sat scattered throughout the pews. What was lovely is that the Catholic Church just accepted whoever you were, which took away some of the pressure to appear virtuous by always wearing a mask.

Each step he made down the aisle echoed eerily yet nobody turned around to look since they were deep in prayer. The confessional stood off-set from the pulpit looking ominous in the semi-darkness. As Clive wrapped his fingers around the door handle it felt cool to the touch and he could almost taste the metal at the back of his throat. That was possibly just his schoolboy nerves coming back to haunt him.

As the door clicked behind him, he said, "Bless me, Father, for I have sinned. My last confession was a week ago today." As he listed each sin, the shame disappeared. "Thank you, Father." Clive finished. Barely perceptible, the figure on the other side of the confessional seemed to shift slightly in acknowledgment.

A self-satisfied smile blossomed across his face as he left the confessional. It was a wonder to him why everybody didn't convert to Catholicism. There was so much beauty in the grace and forgiveness that permeated his beliefs.

On the drive home, the exhaustion tugged at the corner of his eyes tempting him to close them. This was the first night in a week that he had time in the evening, which was a relief since he was so tired. Most of his drive kept him alert because of traffic and the bright lights of downtown Kimber. It was truly magnificent as you drove through tunnels well-lit with LEDs and quickly rose over a bridge that was level with skyscrapers and perfect rows of maple trees lining quaint city streets.

The second half of the drive is when he tended to get distracted after a long day. Once off the main highway, each street that passed by organized subdivisions looked nearly identical to one another. His home was down a road called Dermont Lane which only had a couple of large Craftsmen style homes and a long gravel driveway leading to Dr. Evers' farmhouse-style home. Behind it was two acres of apple orchards. He parked his car in the two-car garage and unlocked the door leading from the garage to the kitchen. The light over the range was on as well as a lamp in the corner of the living room. Sitting on the counter next to the sink was Mayre. Her legs were crossed and her torso leaned forward to peer into his face with pursed lips.

"Hello, honey." He whispered.

CHAPTER 2

Sometimes the screaming in Pat Sherwood's mind stopped long enough for him to feel human again. These were moments he treasured like a perfect cup of coffee or a stimulating conversation, which were also rare because the coffee at work tasted like muddy water filtered through a bag of pennies, and the people he worked with were about as socially adept as logs. Pat did not always have a low opinion of his peers or work environment, but something had changed in him since he took over Sherwood Servers at nineteen years old. This was the same year in which he had become a widower.

On this particular day mid-autumn, Pat was feeling very human. He had no idea how long this feeling would last and he did not want to try to guess. He was afraid that if he thought too much about it, the screaming would start again. Or worse; that he would see his wife.

He untangled himself from the layers of blankets and the copper frame king-sized bed squeaked as all 120 pounds of him left the mattress and landed barefoot on the cherry wood floors. He couldn't figure out why this type of cold flooring was in style now.

"The point of being technologically advanced is to keep

advancing and not go backward." Pat muttered to himself as his feet padded to the on-suite master bathroom.

Even more rustic decor peppered this room. The vanity was covered in white paint that had been sanded to appear as though it was much older. The round mirrors were framed with plastic but spray-painted gold to appear more ornate than they were. The sink basins were copper to match the bed frame. The intentionally distressed pieces were supposed to mesh with the modern walk-in shower, top-of-the-line toilet, and perfectly sealed second-floor windows but to Pat, it seemed like society was trying too hard to appear like salt of the earth without callouses to show for it.

Pat wasn't a humble man by any stretch but he also wasn't self-impressed. Lately, he didn't think about himself much at all. He rarely felt insecure about how he looked. His tired face stared out at him from one of the mirrors and he thought about how futile it was to care. This body of his was merely passing through this world and he would cease to exist once he was dead. How he looked was the least of his worries. The only striking aspect of him was just how skinny he was. It didn't matter how much he ate, he continued to look like a white sheet pulled taught over a skeleton. His brown hair fell in messy waves all over his heart-shaped face and his eyes looked like pools of dark chocolate that rippled when he found something amusing. He wasn't necessarily attractive to most people, but it was his family's money and his intellect that set him apart.

He ran his thin fingers through his hair to loosen the tangles and proceeded to his walk-in closet to select an outfit for the day. After choosing a dark brown t-shirt, jeans, and blue Converse, he proceeded downstairs to his freshly brewed coffee. The old-fashioned, rustic warmth continued in the downstairs part of the house, but the open-concept kitchen was truly modern. Every room in the house was filled with light. Pat had never taken an interest in interior design but now that his wife was gone, every decoration, paint color, and light fixture was a reminder of what he had lost.

After taking a moment to try to enjoy the wind rustling through the trees and drinking his coffee, it was time to go to the office. Sherwood Servers was on the cusp of a nationwide rollout of their product the Thought Conductor so the day would be busy. He hoped that the relaxing start to his day would help him manage himself. Even on his best mental health days, he had the nagging feeling that a dam was about to break and spill out over his whole brain. If only he was able to articulate what that feeling was, he could properly deal with it in his father's app, but how to describe what he felt evaded description.

Off the kitchen was a mudroom that led to the garage. As he poked his fluffy head out, he felt the distinct temperature shift. The smell of motor oil and dust filled his nostrils in the cool stagnant air. He quickly grabbed a black windbreaker from the hooks in the mudroom and slipped out the door with a click.

His car hummed to life and immediately connected to his phone which started playing some ethereal-sounding classical music. Usually, this was where the state of his mind was, but today he was feeling more upbeat so he changed the music to something faster-paced with singing. In a familiar motion, he pressed the reverse button and began to back up. The garage door sensed the car's movement and began to open steadily revealing the gray light of a rainy morning. Pat had such a savage pleasure about rain especially when the leaves began to change.

His morning commute was longer than most, but his father had gifted him this home, and Pat felt it was a perfect distance from the city. He had worked hard to be a more social person, but nothing could change his deeply introverted roots. Additionally, people seemed to treat him differently than others which automatically made him more reclusive. Being able to go home and get a break from human interaction is how he survived being the CEO of Sherwood Servers. Unlike most people, Pat enjoyed the constant stimulation from devices. The more whirring of devices in his life, the less time he had to dwell on himself.

As Sherwood Servers came into view, it had the appearance of a greenhouse. Flora and fauna filled the entirety of the glass building making it look like a forest captured in a cage. Instead of a physical barrier in front of the entrance to the parking lot, there was a scanner continually scanning vehicles as they passed through. Each authorized vehicle had a QR code placed in an inconspicuous place on the bumper and if it wasn't present the computer inside the dash would turn on the parking brakes and power down the engine.

His car drove through the invisible barrier easily and he parked in his labeled parking spot around the back entrance. The Sherwood Servers app gave him continual access to the building while his phone was on. Pat didn't pause at all as he reached for the door and swung it open.

Coming in through the back way, there was a short hallway and a few restrooms, but you could see the rest of the first floor very clearly. It was an open space which was deceptive. This design was meant to curate the feeling of transparency and creativity. Sherwood Servers took privacy very seriously, however, and kept their most secret work in the lower levels of the company. All three of the above-ground floors were where upper management, PR, and marketing resided.

As he was carefully instructed to do, Pat made his way to the most visible part of the lobby to show he cared about his employees. It was a lie, but he had gotten good at faking consideration for people. He didn't see a reason to care about anybody else since the accident.

When he had completed the mundane interactions with the front desk intern, the director of marketing, and a delivery driver, Theresa Clark led him to his first meeting of the day. In her normal fashion, she jiggled her way up to him and adjusted her glasses as if annoyed at his lateness even though she had advised him to speak with the lower-level employees every morning. This reaction seemed to be a leftover habit she had developed when Owen was in charge. She had loved Pat's father and showed that love by bossing Owen around. Whether she admitted it or not, she seemed to regard Pat as her son and he did not like it.

"Your first meeting today will be with some of the medical supply salespeople. You will need to explain to them about the new features of the chips and how to properly educate the doctors, nurses, and hospital managers about them."

"Great."

"You must do all the talking. I'm not allowed."

"Great."

"They are expecting professionalism."

"I suppose I can manage."

"Don't mess this up."

"You mean, do not be crazy."

Theresa stopped walking and looked him in the eyes. "I didn't say that. I don't think that word is politically correct anymore."

"It is if I am using it to describe myself." Pat lifted his left-hand palm side up under his chin to highlight the sarcastic smile plastered on his face.

"You're no more 'crazy' than Owen." She said signing air quotes around the word "crazy" as she continued their progress to the meeting.

"He was a bit much." Pat muttered.

She glared at him out of the corner of her swampy green eyes and seamlessly rounded another corner. The strong smell of honeysuckle assaulted his nostrils when they reached the elevators. The rest of their journey to the meeting was in silence, but Pat could feel Theresa's disapproval wafting over to him. The more he irritated her, the more aware he was of the screaming in the depths of his mind. It gnawed at him. Like an itch he couldn't scratch. He rolled his left shoulder a couple of times and then laid his head on it to distract from the panic welling in his spirit.

When they reached the third floor, Theresa glided out first and Pat followed close behind. Pulling out his phone from his right pocket, he scrolled to his company's app and clicked on an alert that had popped up stating that his anxiety levels were high. He selected the option that said "resolve" and could immediately feel a cooling sensation in his mind. The screaming was still there in the distance, but he no longer was afraid of it…instead, he was merely an observer of his own suffering.

Instead of entering the conference room and looking for the exits, he appreciated the lush plants, distressed maple conference table, and six floor-to-ceiling windows creating a "u" around the furthest end of the room. All these things pleased him and he knew he would conquer this presentation.

"Good afternoon, Theydies and Gentlethems. I am Patrick Sherwood, the late Owen Sherwood's son."

"I'm Theresa Clark. I've been the one speaking to you all by email." Theresa interjected.

"Thank you for that clarification, Theresa, but I can manage." Pat said pointedly.

The disapproval then became a heat wave. Pat could imagine her eyes turning red and cutting the maple table in half out of anger.

"Yes, sir." She flounced out letting the door click behind her.

"Anyway, I suppose you have questions." Pat continued to stand to keep himself distracted.

A nervous-looking man in his 30's with brown hair and beard spoke up and said, "I am Clinton Briggs…"

"Nice to meet you."

"Thanks, sir, Pat." He ducked his head. "We have a basic understanding of what we are selling but we'd love to know more details about how it truly works."

"Well, we've come a long way since my Father's first chip." Pat tapped his skull. "My father installed the very first chip directly on my brain. It works but there can potentially be complications if it malfunctions. Surgically operating on the area when it is on the brain is highly dangerous and there is not a very good success rate with these invasive procedures."

"We've heard that the chip is placed in your arm now. How does that affect things going on in the brain from all the way down there?" A very pretty red-headed woman in a blue body-hugging dress asked this question. Pat was momentarily distracted by how similar she was to somebody he knew.

"We have fixed that by installing a barely detectable chip to the base of the skull on the outside. It communicates with the arm chip and can easily be worked on if it malfunctions."

"Was this discovered in the human trials?" The woman followed up quickly. Her eager face was so familiar his heart ached.

"This was discovered when my father experimented on me." Pat then placed both pointer fingers on the sides of his neck, made a zapping noise, and fluttered his eyelashes. To show it was a joke he then laughed loudly. The laugh was not enough to conceal the anxiety that was ramping up inside as the screaming began to reach normal levels again. For whatever reason, this was his fate. No amount of treatment seemed to be able to silence the screaming.

"Oh." Breathed the girl as she wrote on a notepad.

"I was the first human trial and when some errors occurred in the functions of the chip, it was a lot harder to operate on the brain than at the base of the neck. My father had the money to hire surgeons to handle this but not everybody has this privilege. We want the chips to be accessible to all. Especially those that most need it." Pride welled up inside him as he said this. Despite how messed up he was, he was doing good for humanity. He at least would make a mark on society before he dissolved into nothingness.

"Is it easy to operate, then? You don't have to understand

advanced technological systems to use the chip?" Clinton asked.

"No, of course not. It simply connects to an app on your phone or tablet. The majority of the filtering the chip does is automatic, but some mental illnesses require more training."

"Such as?"

"Anxiety and depression are tricky. We want people to have their normal range of emotions still. Some amount of anxiety, fear, and depression is normal. The client must work in conjunction with their therapist to determine which emotions are being experienced at unnatural levels or are causing issues for the client in their daily life. However, we do have safeguards set to prevent people from numbing themselves completely. They cannot simply delete emotions of grief, depression over the ups and downs of life, or fight or flight in a truly dangerous situation."

"What about the controversy?" The third man who had been silent up to that point piped in.

"Controversy?" Pat asked.

"When Owen Sherwood first introduced the chip, some hacked into the chip and managed to take down the safeguards. What happened with that?"

Pat ran his fingers through his fluffy hair and sighed. "Unfortunate cases, truly. Several of the perpetrators were caught and arrested. We also increased security measures on the chips so that it is highly unlikely this will ever occur again."

"Were the victims compensated?"

"Yes," Pat said reluctantly. "Sadly, they will not be able to come back from the state they are in. When you numb every feeling long enough, you become a vegetable."

An oppressive silence filled the room at this pronouncement. Pat had longed to be somebody who didn't feel anything for the majority of his life, but when his dad explained what had happened to those people, he realized that he was one of the lucky ones.

Those people had been suffering for so long that they resorted to taking away all the pain to live in a numb purgatory.

"And with that…do you have any other questions for me?"

Clinton relieved the heavy silence by asking a few traditional questions about the cost of the device, installation, and packaging. When this was done, the salespeople seemed to not have any more questions.

"Thank you for coming." Out of habit, Pat bumped elbows with each of them in a gesture of goodwill. Shaking hands was long forgotten. When Pat reached the young woman he paused.

"Thank you, Mr. Sherwood." She bumped his elbow.

"I did not hear your name."

"Janice May." She flashed a bright smile.

"Lovely." He looked down at his shoes and said nothing else.

Janice took this as her cue to leave and walked out the door. As soon as she was gone Theresa bustled in and asked how it went. Pat didn't respond, but instead proceeded to his office. He needed to do something to distract him from thoughts of Janice.

Realizing he wasn't going to answer her, Theresa started a new topic of conversation as she bounced down the hallway after him. "Dr. Clive Evers is currently heading up the human trials for the newest version of the chip."

When this registered in Pat's brain, he uttered a few choice profanities under his breath.

"He's the best surgeon in the state and nationally recognized in the top 10." Theresa argued.

"Rather than worshiping God, I think he believes he IS God."

"It doesn't matter who he is as long as he does a good job."

Pat snorted as he opened his office door. The shelves spilled over with green leafy plants and the walls were entirely made of windows and let in a lot of natural light. He sat down on his ergonomic chair and immediately straightened up his posture. It was very noticeable because he tended to always hunch. He usually made himself smaller than others because he didn't like all the attention on him. This was such a contradiction from how he acted at work. His self-deprecating humor and sarcasm made it seem like he was impervious to criticism or embarrassment.

"Okay. As long as I don't have to interact with that peacock." Pat said simply.

Theresa nodded and said, "I emailed you the list of messages you received over the weekend. When you have time, could you return those calls?"

"What if I decide to shoot myself instead?"

Theresa glared at him and he returned the glare with a jovial smile. "I'll leave you to it." She conceded.

"I will cry endlessly while you are away."

She didn't acknowledge the jab with any kind of smile. When she was gone, he started his work playlist right away and began filtering through the emails. When he had dreamed about what he wanted to do when he grew up, it never included checking emails, PR, or creating presentations. Sadly, since his father had died, nobody but Pat was able to take over the company.

"Tale as old as time…" He sighed to himself.

A good chunk of his day turned into writing emails, making calls, checking the lab, and more meetings. It was 7 pm before he left and he was ready for his comforts. The first stop was Lucky Smith's Gastro Pub. He loved it because the backs on the booths were high and the music loud. Not only was the atmosphere perfect but the food and drinks were excellent. The hostess took him to his usual booth which was out of the way from the general traffic of the restaurant, but in view enough where he could observe the comings and goings of everybody.

As he sipped on a rum and coke, his eyes gazed over at the live band. He tried to let the notes wrap him in noisy peace. The lights were dim and autumnal. They dangled from the ceiling on long black cords. The exposed black pipes on the ceiling zigzagged every which way. The bar took up half of the restaurant with floor-to-ceiling glass shelves holding decanters of all kinds of alcohol. Shallow baskets were nailed to the walls every few feet above the tables which looked like they were poured concrete. Outside, the small trees were covered in twinkling lights that illuminated the cars pushing through. Traffic was heavy tonight and Pat was glad he had gotten here when he did.

"Mr. Sherwood! I mean…Pat."

Pat tore his eyes from the music and saw his wife walking towards him. His heart skipped a beat and he wasn't sure if he was still breathing. She was just as he remembered. Long red hair parted down the middle, aquamarine eyes, beautiful hourglass figure.

"Seeing you again is serendipitous!"

It wasn't Justice. His love wasn't here.

"Janice, good to see you again." Pat lied.

"May I sit?"

"Of course." It wasn't what he wanted, but he was now in a position where professionalism was of the utmost importance.

"This is a great place." She said, starting in on the small talk.

Pat unintentionally gritted his teeth. "Yes, indeed."

"I'm glad we got to speak this morning. There has been so much controversy surrounding mental health lately but I think you are doing great things for people. What happened to those people that numbed themselves too much is not your fault."

"Thank you. I appreciate it."

"So, what are you drinking?"

"Rum and coke."

Just then, a waitress came by to take Janice's drink order. She ordered an Irish Coffee.

"What kind of movies do you like?" She asked suddenly.

"Japanese horror." He took a long sip from his drink, hoping that she would notice his disinterest and leave.

"You're joking! Me too!"

Pat was skeptical but played along anyway. "Oh, really?"

But when she began listing off several of his favorite movies and describing them in detail, he perked up a little. For the first time in months, he felt engaged in a conversation and intellectually stimulated.

The waitress sat down Janice's drink and then asked if they wanted food. They both ordered appetizers and proceeded to continue talking about their shared love of movies. Pat was unexpectedly enjoying himself. When the evening was winding down and their food and drinks were nearly gone an intrusive thought came into his head. *"Take her home."* The voice didn't feel like his own but he agreed that's what he wanted to do.

Looking down slightly he said, "Janice, would you like to get out of here?"

Her eyes sparkled like the gems that they were and she said, "Yes."

Warning signals were going off in his brain too but they weren't louder than the screaming or the insistent voice saying, *"Take her home. Take her home. She'll right the wrongs. Take her."*

He drove her to his house and he could tell she was excited by the privilege that this was. She was getting to see The Pat Sherwood's home. When he had parked, he walked around to the passenger's side of the car to let her out. Janice giggled as he bowed slightly and offered his elbow to lead her inside.

"Your home is beautiful." She gushed when they entered the dining room.

"Thanks."

"Is this your dad?" She asked, pointing to the picture that hung just inside.

The portrait was meant to be unassuming but the distressed wood frame was much larger than average. It was a 10-year-old photo taken just outside by the fence. Pat had been laughing and hanging on his dad's sweater-covered arm. Owen had suffered from eczema for as long as Pat could remember so he primarily wore sweaters, but it had gotten worse over time. He was a stocky man with shoulder-length black hair and black sparkly eyes that seemed to be amused by a private joke. The glasses that sat firmly on the bridge of his nose were thick, black square frames and he wore a black turtleneck tucked into jeans. He kept things simple because of his OCD. It was easier to manage that way, but Pat was his chaos.

"Yes, it is."

She smiled fondly at the image for a moment. "I've heard a lot about him." Janice paused and Pat guessed what was coming next. "What happened to your mom?"

Pat never knew how he would react when people asked this question. He had no particular feelings about her, but he was too young to have any memories of her. He was only two years old when she took her own life. His father seemed to be the only one broken up about it.

"She died when I was young." He said with finality.

Janice's eyebrows lowered sympathetically and she muttered something about being sorry for his loss. As Pat gazed at her, he began to feel a warmth in his heart. She genuinely seemed sad on his behalf. She was beautiful and seemed very interested in him. It was like his love had returned to him in a new form.

"Show her. Take her to the portal." The unbidden voice demanded.

"Would you like something to drink?" Pat shuffled into the kitchen and began searching for a glass.

"Water would be great." Janice said simply, moving on to the next set of portraits on the opposite wall of the dining room.

He filled both glasses under the special tap for filtered water. As he rounded the corner to give Janice a glass, his heart skipped a beat as he saw her fingering a frame that had been hiding behind the china cabinet.

The happy feeling that had been with him was no longer there. There was no comparison between the girl in the photo and this impostor in his dining room. The screaming started up again and the demanding inner voice was yelling instructions at him too fast to be able to follow. Both cups crashed to the floor and the glass spun out all over.

"Take her."

"Pat!" Janice laid the portrait on the table and hurried to his side, being careful to avoid the large glass shards. She placed an unwelcome hand on his shoulder to try to comfort him. "Are you okay?"

He looked down at the mess and his soaked pant bottoms. Silently, he went to the pantry and grabbed a broom. Janice was still gazing at him intently but she didn't speak. He allowed her a moment to be uncomfortable before he decided to answer.

"I'm sorry. I have not seen that picture in a long time." As he swept the accumulated pile of glass into the dustpan, Janice nodded solemnly. Pat figured that to get some peace he would have to be honest. "My late wife, Justice…it still haunts me. It was an accident."

"Oh, Pat." She cooed. "How do you handle so much loss?" Pat cringed internally at this. As time went on, she definitely was nothing like Justice.

"Would you like to see where it all happened?" His eyes gleamed.

"Yes, I would." She said, trying not to let her eagerness show.

Pat could tell now that she was simply nosy and not interested in him at all. She was just like all the others and nobody would miss her.

He emptied the dustpan into the trash, put up the broom, and gestured at Janice to follow him.

When Owen Sherwood had gifted this home to Pat and Justice, he had been most excited to show them the conservatory. Up until that point, Pat had only heard of conservatories when playing the board game Clue. However, seeing it in person for the first time was a totally different experience. As he led Janice inside, intense humidity and the smell of wet Earth and rose water filled the air. Several small trees, bushes, leafy plants, and flowers were sprawled around the perimeter of the space. In the center was a small pond with unkempt leafy grasses spilling up and out of the pool and a cobblestone path circling around. Above the ceiling was domed transparent glass that hadn't been cleaned in a long time. When they were on the backside of the pond, Janice gasped audibly at what was before her. A 10-foot-tall white, metallic triangle sat amongst the greenery. It glowed orange within the frame and a faint hum could be heard coming from it.

"What is it?" A hint of fear was in her voice, but Pat ignored it.

"This is where it all began." He spun on his heel to look at her and began walking backward towards the device as he continued to speak. "As I get closer…" The orange glow faded and you could see the faint outline of some kind of hallway, "…a new way appears."

She allowed herself to be led like a sheep through a doorway that opened up into a narrow high-ceilinged foyer with crown molding. The benches on the left and right walls had cracks in the wood and were dusty from lack of use. In the corner was a tired coat rack holding unwanted suit jackets. The floor was dusty too, but within the dust were little footprints from small animals and bigger footprints from when Pat had been here before. Paintings hung on the walls that depicted dreams and desires. Janice gazed at them with confusion.

"Do you trust me?" Pat asked in a husky voice full of emotion.

"Yes." She breathed.

He led her into the next room. It was much wider than the first with a dusty marble staircase branching off in two directions. The floor had a design on it that was hard to distinguish under all the turned-over furniture, dried leaves, and fabric. On both sides of the space were doorways and in the middle of the ceiling was a chandelier that mysteriously had several bulbs still lit. Along the sides of the staircase were paintings of women looking very solemn. They weren't nearly as old as everything else and the women appeared to be wearing clothes from the 21st century. Pat approached the portrait closest to the wall. This woman had blue eyes, red hair down to her butt, a gray v-neck sweater, jeans, black boots, and a green pair of horn-rimmed glasses. Instead of looking afraid like the other women she looked slightly amused.

"That's your wife!" Janice sounded surprised.

"It is."

They continued between the staircases and through a set of double doors. A disheveled galley kitchen rested in this darkened room and sickly green light streamed in through a set of French doors. The look in Janice's eyes appeared skeptical but Pat mustered up one last dose of charm to get her to her final destination. His cold hand slipped into hers and he rubbed his thumb on the inside of her wrist. As he drew her close to him, he smiled wide and she looked away bashfully. Wordlessly, he opened the doors and walked down to the stone porch. There were a few steps leading down to a path that wound its way up to a weeping willow tree draped over a prominent gray stone seat.

"So, why are we here?"

Pat knew he was starting to lose her. He had to act fast. "Trust me."

He pulled her around and shoved her into the stone seat. When she protested and tried to stand, he gripped her wrists and forced them down onto the armrests. In the distance, there was a rumbling like a stampede of horses. Dark clouds rolled towards them at breakneck speed. It surrounded the spot where they were and Janice shrieked.

Before it could be stopped though, Janice was swallowed up in the unforgiving darkness. His legs automatically picked up and ran back from where he had come. When Pat became aware of what was happening, he found himself outside the humming portal. He looked around and didn't see her anywhere. He ventured back into the portal again and when he reached the paintings, Justice was still there but now a new painting was hung on the wall beside it. There, looking terrified out of her mind, was Janice. Pat's long fingers traced the outline of her face as he tried to drown out the new screams in his head.

CHAPTER 3

Harmony never got coffee when she was at the office. Her reasons for preparing her beverage at home were because it was easier to disguise that she didn't drink coffee and secondly, she wasn't a fan of the morning chit-chat by the Keurig. It was harder to keep her secret when Glenda was going on and on about needing a caffeine fix and Romilda despairing over the lack of all-natural sweetener options.

Once Harmony had found a treatment that worked for her depression and anxiety, she was allowed to incorporate caffeine back into her routine. Despite this, she preferred to go without since she had been away from it for so long. She had found a mint tea she was growing fond of and her morning routine usually included her savoring the rhythm of steeping the tea leaves with a tea infuser and mixing a few squirts of honey in the brew. Once she had made the beverage perfect, she would pour it into a reusable Starbucks cup. This saved her from facing the shame of realizing how different she was compared to her coworkers. Her skin was the wrong color, her heritage was boring, her sexuality was all wrong, and her inclinations were merely tolerated by others. It felt unbearable to add one more thing to the list of differences.

As these thoughts buzzed in her mind while driving to work, she instinctively traced the spot on her right wrist where her surgeon had slipped a Thought Conductor. This little device had transformed her life.

As she pulled into the familiar parking space, the feeling of dread she used to have when going to work was no longer there. She turned off the car, slipped the lanyard with her keys and ID badge over her head full of tight brown curls, grasped her decoy cup, and slipped on a face mask that said "Mucho Gusto" on the front. She was trying to beat the crowd but, no matter how hard she tried, she always got to work during the rush. It felt like a Mardi Gras parade as the diverse crowd scanned their keycards upon entry. Not much talking went on but as soon as they were inside, the chatter began as everyone separated into their cliques.

The building was made entirely of one-way glass so there was no place that natural light didn't shine in. The atrium connected to four different hallways for each of the departments and several large leafy plants graced the corners. It was a truly beautiful place but unfortunately, the employees were still separated by cubicles. These cubicles weren't the old-fashioned tan color but instead a pearly white with black trim.

Harmony made her way down the third hallway from the left where the mortgage processing department was. She adjusted the cup in her hand so the Starbucks logo was visible. As she passed the break room she saw Glenda preparing her coffee for the day. Her beautiful curly black hair flowed down her back and to her waist. Her eyelashes were the same velvety black and stretched out like flower petals. Her skin was a flawless deep brown color that Harmony could still not figure out how she kept so perfect. As she did every day, her outfit was a work of art and included a matching face mask. Harmony greeted her with her Starbucks cup.

"What did you get, girl?"

"Caramel Macchiato!" She lied easily.

"Good choice, chica."

The warmth of being accepted flowed over her. "Thanks. Catch you later!"

"You can't get rid of me. I'll see you later for sure!"

Harmony would be basking in the glow of that encounter all day. Glenda was one of the few people who could truly make her feel like she had friends at work.

One minute until her shift started, she sat down at her computer. As soon as the computer flared to life, the webcam scanned her features and she was clocked in. Since Hackney Corp had upgraded their systems, the clock-in and clock-out systems only activated when her face was staring at the screen and her butt in the chair. They were allowed two 10-minute breaks a day and a 30-minute lunch but the times for those never fluctuated no matter how early she got hungry or tired.

Thirty minutes into her shift, she suddenly received a calendar notification on the bottom right-hand corner of her screen. Her boss had called an impromptu meeting in 60 minutes. According to the description of the event, the topic was about more efficient practices for getting through mortgage paperwork faster and free programs to help with productivity. When a calendar event was sent to an employee, it automatically adjusted the clock-in feature on the computer so she was allowed to be away from her desk during the designated meeting time. This could be difficult to stick to sometimes because Lyric Elrod liked to talk which meant the meetings went too long.

Harmony had been sensing she was developing feelings for him over the last few weeks but she had been tamping those urges down. This meeting brought those feelings bubbling back to the surface of her mind. It wasn't that her workplace didn't allow workplace relationships, but socially it seemed completely taboo. She wasn't the right kind of person for him and he was in such a strong social position compared to her.

When it was time for the meeting, the entire department made their way to the conference room and chatted freely with one another while Harmony simply observed. Normally, crowds made her anxious, but her treatment was working so well that she felt nothing. She seated herself in the very back of the room and hoped this meeting ended on time. If it didn't, Lyric would need to manually go to each computer and input the override code so the late alarms wouldn't go off. Being that close in proximity to him would not help keep her romantic feelings in check.

She quickly found out that proximity wasn't the issue. Amongst the vibrant staff of 15 that encompassed the mortgage department, Lyric still stood out. He was beautiful. His skin was a smooth, warm brown and his eyes looked like the color of tiger's eye gemstone. His hair and goatee were black and curly and kept very neat. Finally, his fashion sense was understated and yet so well put together. The gold, tan, and red polo shirt he wore looked like a tapestry tucked into deep blue trousers. To bring the ensemble together, his shoes were gold. Harmony held her breath as she watched him make his way to the front of the room.

"Perfect." He clasped his perfectly manicured hands together and surveyed the room. "You all look great." He then smiled a smile that could surely be seen from space.

Harmony felt her phone buzz and was almost certain it must be notifying her that her heart rate had gotten too high and that she should do something about it. Harmony wasn't the only one who noticed Lyric. All the gay, lesbian, non-binary, pansexual, and asexual beings in this office were equal-opportunity rubberneckers when he walked by. He was like a cat with cool unrushed confidence and it was very attractive to Harmony. She identified as heterosexual, but even though Lyric seemed to reflect femininity at times, she didn't care.

"Of course, we have plenty of resources available if anybody needs extra support through their mental health journey."

Lyric finished.

Since the Thought Conductors were becoming much more mainstream, Harmony's office had started offering workshops on how to utilize them in the workplace and coping skills in case your chip was being repaired. Even though the chip had mostly managed her symptoms, she still went to the coping skills workshop. The occasional times when she had a panic attack, reminded her of how she never wanted to have one again.

"Do you have to go to these events if you don't have a chip?" Asked Romilda right on queue. She always asked questions that Harmony deemed unnecessary and it was very annoying.

"Of course not." Harmony quickly covered her mouth when she realized that she had spoken out of turn.

Everybody turned to look at her. Some were stunned and others looked worried. Romilda glanced up at Lyric as he walked around the table so he was closer to Harmony. Despite herself, Harmony's heart leapt in her throat when she smelled his musky cologne.

"I'll excuse it for today," Lyric said as if he was a benevolent ruler absolving Harmony of her debts. The entire room seemed to breathe a collective sigh. "But, remember to check yourself before you interrupt your Latinx queer peer. Even though whiteness isn't your entire identity, it is partially there and will come out at inopportune moments."

Even though this was normal procedure when something like this occurred, Harmony always had to reign in her feelings. She wanted to argue that part of her was also Latinx but she knew that would get her nowhere. Besides, she knew she was in the wrong.

"I'm sorry for not allowing you to express yourself uninhibited, Romilda."

Romilda didn't seem completely satisfied with the

apology but knew that nothing else had to be done to make the situation right. Lyric nodded, satisfied, and then turned to answer Romilda. "No, you do not have to attend. I would highly encourage you to speak to our health insurance representative so you can see the ways that you can have the chip completely covered under your plan. It is an outpatient procedure so you would only have to take one sick day."

After the rough beginning of the meeting, the rest of the time passed without incident. Harmony found herself obsessing on and off about the mistake and barely remembered all that was said. When they were dismissed, she was so distracted, that she realized she had gotten turned around. It wasn't that far of a walk to her cubicle but she knew she would be late. As she expected, her computer was locked when she arrived and Lyric received a notification about it.

He rounded the corner a few moments later and insisted she sit down. Wordlessly, she slid into her chair and he reached over her left shoulder to type in the password. He left as quickly as he had arrived, but she still felt the warmth of his presence.

***

Harmony finished out her workday like any other day. When she sat quietly in the stillness of her car she allowed herself to cry. She used to cry nearly every day after work before she got the Thought Conductor, but once she was eligible for implantation, she was so excited. The rumors she had heard about the chip's effectiveness gave her so much hope. Most of her crying, panic attacks, and spirals were gone. There were only certain moments, like today, where a new circumstance cropped up and the chip wasn't programmed to handle it. The occasional dissatisfaction with her mundane office job and loneliness seemed to be something that would never resolve no matter how much therapy or medical interventions she had.

By the time she left the parking lot, most of the cars had gone. She pulled out onto the road and drove to the outskirts of Kimber where her home was in a little subdivision. Since her workplace and home were on the eastern side of town, she rarely drove downtown for anything. Everything she needed was within a 5-mile radius and keeping to smaller roads helped keep her anxiety down as well. When she reached the cul de sac at the end of Evergreen Drive, her house was nestled between a cluster of evergreen trees down a slight incline. The house was an A-frame made with dark wood siding and brown shingles. The door was bright red and in the very center. The pathway leading up to the door was made of stones, and a detached garage sat a little further down the hill.

She had tried to decorate the inside of the house rustically. All the colors were earth tones and the floors were all hardwood. A very excited Sheepdog bounded up to Harmony and licked every inch of bare skin he could reach.

"Rufus...who's a good boy? Who is a good boy? Yoooou are. Do you gotta pee?" She raked her hands all over his fur and talked in an excited, high-pitched voice.

He bounded for the screen doors and barked as if to say, "Yes!". She slid it open for him and he bounded into the fenced backyard. She shut the door behind him and started making dinner. Tonight it was just leftovers. She didn't feel like cooking, but that was how she felt on most nights. As the food rotated in the microwave, she went to her bedroom to undress. Every article of clothing came off and a giant t-shirt and shorts went on. The food was beeping as soon as she stepped out of her bedroom. In a quick motion, she grabbed utensils, the bowl, and napkins and swung around to plop on the loveseat. She was very invested in a show called Non-Binary Inquiry and hoped that Quincy would give the red rose to Jayden.

A few minutes into the reality show, she suddenly heard Rufus barking very loudly and persistently. Confused by his aggravation, she set her food down and proceeded to the back porch. Before stepping into the cold, she grabbed her windbreaker hanging from a hook near the sliding doors and slipped her shoes on. Her yard was dotted with more evergreen trees, a few blackberry bushes, and a neglected garden. The brisk air cleared her mind to where her aggravation subsided to be replaced by curiosity.

"What is it, boy?" She peered intently at him for some kind of answer.

Her gaze followed his and her breath caught in her throat. On the ground was a body. It appeared to be a child. She cautiously moved closer and looked down at the form. It was a child around 8 years old. Blood had poured from the child's nose and right eye down her neck and all over her chest where it had dried. She wasn't breathing.

Tears welled up in Harmony's eyes and she felt her chest tighten. Wanting more excitement in her life seemed like a bad idea to her now. She couldn't catch her breath. She put her hand on the tree to steady herself. She closed her eyes and focused on her coping skills. Breathe in and out. In and out. When she opened her eyes she braced herself for the horrific sight, but the child was no longer there! Her eyes scanned the area around the place where the child had been and beyond for some clue as to what was happening. She felt like she was losing her mind.

Rufus continued to bark and Harmony petted him absently to try to calm him down. Her brain was frantically trying to piece together the situation so she didn't lose complete control. This was not the reality she knew and she could not understand what she had seen. She then pulled out her phone and turned on the flashlight. Nothing was on the ground to show the body had been there. There was no indentation in the dry grass, no blood...no nothing.

When she had walked about four yards away she suddenly felt cold all over. Before her was a darkness that could not be illuminated by her flashlight. It remained dark and out from the depths white flecks floated out into the world. Between beats of her heart, she thought she could hear distant screaming from within this blackness. She was too afraid to step any closer for fear of being sucked into the void.

Rufus had followed behind her and began to sniff out the darkness. "Stay back!" She grabbed his collar and led him back inside the house. "I don't know what to do, Rufus." She turned off her phone flashlight and stood in her kitchen, still shivering from whatever that darkness was. One of her biggest fears was losing her sanity and this seemed to be something crazy. But she knew she wasn't crazy and that she needed to do something about it. She dialed 911 and waited with bated breath.

CHAPTER 4

Harmony's anxiety was easily dispelled after she called the police. Dispatch seemed very concerned with what she had said and told her that the police were headed her way. She made an executive decision to resolve this particular anxiety. The reverberations of fear that were going through her body were unnecessary now because the police were on their way. She clicked the notification on her phone stating that her anxiety levels were high and selected the "resolve" feature. There was a warmth that spread from the chip in her left forearm to the base of her skull. Having to "resolve" anxiety in this way had been less frequent because the treatment had been successful for over a year. Most of her stressors were predictable.

Before the knock was heard at the door, Rufus went bounding from the back door to the front door. Harmony followed, trying to keep pace with her furry friend. When she swung the door open, there stood two police. She could not identify their gender just by looking at them because of the nondescript double-breasted black suits and full metal face masks. She had only ever interacted with law enforcement when she was parked illegally and usually their identities were not concealed during those interactions. She had heard that their identities were only kept secret in dangerous cases.

To Harmony's dismay, new fears vied for attention in her brain. *"Was she a threat? Did a serial killer stumble into her yard? Was she unintentionally an accomplice?"*

Wordlessly, the taller of the two cops held out a tablet and it said, "Show us."

"Okay, sure." Harmony was a ball of nerves but she scrambled to her back door and flitted around trying to decide if it was polite to let them go out first or if she should. Rufus decided for her by barreling out ahead of everybody. She hurried behind but the police were in no rush.

When they all finally reached the place where the darkness was they didn't say anything. They waved their high-powered flashlights across the dark patch but no light could penetrate it. Harmony held her breath. It was bizarre and she hated that she couldn't see the expressions on the officer's faces. She needed validation that she wasn't crazy.

After what seemed like an hour, the taller officer held out the tablet again for her to read the screen. "Do you have anywhere you can stay tonight?"

"Stay?" The last thing she expected was to be kicked out of her house. Both officers nodded mechanically. "I guess. Let me make a call." She stepped to the side and pulled out her cellphone. She ignored the notification telling her she was stressed and decided to call the one person who made her even more stressed. "Hi, Mom."

***

Her blue GMC turned left into the Woody Pines subdivision and down a mile before reaching her mom's cookie-cutter home. Wendy Latham lived on the exact opposite end of town from her daughter, but that's how Harmony liked it. With traffic, it took 30 minutes to get across town, but since it was so late at night, the trip was closer to 20 minutes.

Woody Pines was predominately populated by people in their

mid to late 50's. The Home Owners Association was very strict about residents keeping the lawn perfectly manicured, only planting certain types of plants, cleaning out the gutters regularly, and not making loud noises after 10 pm. Harmony hated it, but her Mom claimed that it was much better to live in a new home with fewer repairs than an old home. Wendy had needed to call a repairman more times than Harmony did for her 1970s home, however, so this argument seemed to have holes in it.

Once in the driveway, Harmony exited her vehicle with her personal belongings and Rufus. The house was built in a brick Farmhouse style and pink azalea bushes flanked the small front patio. Inside, it smelled like gingerbread and coffee. Her mother rarely baked, but she liked buying gingerbread candles and burned them frequently. Her mother dropped heavy hints all the time about Harmony birthing her grandchildren so they could come to the house to bake. She insisted that the addition of grandchildren would inspire her to bake more.

Her mother appeared from the hallway looking disgruntled. "You can have your old bedroom." She said simply.

"Okay. Thanks." She gave her mom a hug and a kiss.

"What happened? You never explained."

Harmony was already leaving her mother's voice behind to unload her personal items in her bedroom and Rufus padded along behind. He began sniffing everything in sight but seemed satisfied with the familiar smells. Her mother followed and peered around the corner expectantly.

"I'm not sure. There was an injured child in my back yard but she disappeared. The police were very weird though. They were in full gear and insisted I find somewhere to stay."

"Did you ask them why?"

"I didn't, Mom. I was frazzled." Harmony rolled her eyes.

"Isn't that chip supposed to fix that?"

Harmony didn't want to waste her breath explaining that the chip didn't cure 100% of all anxiety. Having a half-dead child in your backyard would fall under the category of "unexpected" so it was impossible to prepare for that kind of occurrence.

"Do you work tomorrow?"

"Yes. I can't stop working."

"I would think that this would be an exception." Wendy Latham held out her hands, palm side up in a pleading gesture.

"I'm going to bed now."

"Are you sure you don't need any dinner?" Her mom's critical tone softened as she said this and so did Harmony's heart.

"No, thank you, Mom. I just need sleep." She reluctantly hugged her mother but knew that was the only way she would get some alone time.

"I hope you sleep well." Wendy peered into her daughter's face as she ran her fingers through her daughter's unruly curls and smiled softly.

Harmony returned the smile. "Thanks. I plan on it." Her mom walked down the hall to her own room and Harmony shut her door.

Harmony's childhood room should have felt familiar but it didn't. She had always assumed her memory was worse than other people's. The room had all the things a girl's room should have, but she couldn't bring back memories of sleepovers, doing homework, playing, or having her first kiss in this room. She walked to the bed without turning on the light and ran her fingers over the pink comforter.

Weariness radiated across her whole body and she knew she needed sleep. It had been a terrible day. Reluctantly, she pulled back the blanket and a whiff of vanilla reached her nose as she did so. She removed her jeans and bra and snuggled under the covers. Rufus joined her at the base of the bed.

She hoped that the mother of that little girl had found her. She hoped the girl was merely injured and hadn't lost her life. She hoped the mom wasn't up late worried about where her precious daughter was. Harmony wasn't a natural with kids, but she could imagine how it felt to be a scared parent. She'd been scared her whole life.

When Harmony finally did sleep, her mind was fraught with nightmares that she woke with no recollection of. Waking at 7 am as groggy as ever, Rufus barked at her demanding to be fed. She pulled her pants on and wobbled to the kitchen. In a sleepy haze, she let Rufus into the backyard to pee. As he bounded around outside, she filled a bowl with dog food and a separate bowl for water. When that was done, she turned around to survey the dining table where her mother usually sat drinking coffee. To her disbelief, Lyric was sitting there as handsome as ever, drinking coffee with her mother.

"Harmony," Lyric said silkily as he inclined his head towards her.

"Good morning." She mustered and glanced over at her mom. "Did you call my job?"

Wendy looked shocked that Harmony would even assume she would do something like that. "No, I didn't. He graciously came over to check in."

Harmony wondered how he had found out. She hadn't called or notified him of anything. She was planning to go to work like she was supposed to. She also didn't know how he knew where her mom lived.

"I'm still coming in to work today."

"I'm here to let you know that you don't need to come in today. I think after something so traumatic, you should take time off." Curling his pointer finger, he directed her to join them at the table.

She joined but still kept her arms crossed over her chest defensively. She was examining her mother's face. *"Had he threatened her? Was he controlling her?"* She couldn't figure out why her mother was so calm. She usually hated unexpected company.

A sudden surge of courage overtook her and she blurted out, "If this is about what happened in the meeting yesterday," Lyric was already shaking his head as she finished, "it won't happen again."

"Of course not. That was only one infraction. You are a valuable and unique employee. We would not be able to lose you."

While the words mollified Wendy Latham, Harmony was digesting what had been said very carefully. It would have made much more sense for him to have said "we wouldn't want to lose you" or "our office wouldn't be the same without you" but the words he had chosen sounded perfectly curated to absolve him from being called an outright "liar". Something was being omitted. The thing that Harmony couldn't figure out was what. She had never been this suspicious before, but Lyric's presence seemed too coincidental to be an accident.

"Well, this is where I leave you." Lyric stood and flashed a smile at her mother which was received with a giggle and a duck of the head. He then turned to Harmony. "Rest. We will see you Monday."

"Okay. Thanks." Harmony did not dare ask any more questions for fear of truly losing her job to somebody more intersectional. She knew she was on a tightrope even if Lyric did not say so.

"Do you need any breakfast for the road?" Wendy asked, rushing to open the door for him.

"No thank you." His canines winked beneath his dark red lips and he stared meaningfully over Wendy's shoulder at her daughter. "I am satisfied."

He left and the heaviness evaporated. Harmony stood immediately and opened the back door to let Rufus in. She then rushed back to her bedroom where she still had her phone plugged in. Rufus whipped his head around and began to bark and follow her.

"Some good you are. You didn't even bark at the stranger." Harmony muttered as she unplugged the device and rushed back into the living area.

"He seemed very nice." Wendy said pointedly.

Harmony didn't answer but simply nodded her head as she began to research.

"He's not at all how you described him."

"Mom, I'm busy."

"You should go out with him."

This cut into Harmony's thoughts and she glared at her mother. "That's not going to work." As so often happened when she thought of Lyric in a work setting, her heartbeat quickened and her upper lip began to sweat. This was a type of anxiety in her life that was more of a rush and she didn't want to resolve it. It was the only fun work had to offer anymore. The forbidden romance was still going strong in the modern era.

Wendy crossed her arms and said, "Why?"

"I'm not the right kind of person." To signal the end of the conversation, Harmony plopped down on the couch and Rufus joined her by jumping up beside her and laying his head in her lap.

Wendy's exasperation could be felt, but Harmony was able to tune it out easily after years of therapy and chip treatment. She couldn't pinpoint why she was feeling so uneasy, but it all seemed to be connected to last night.

She Googled information about "dark black patches" which only brought up information about skin conditions. She then looked up information about mysterious murders in Kimber but no results populated. A couple of armed robberies and a missing person's report for a woman about her age, but no missing children. Finally, she looked up information about black holes. This gave her much more information to look at but it was mostly about outer space and some man named Zion Jones who studied the stars. From what she could tell, he sounded crazy. He was a creationist and that alone made her doubt his credibility. Despite this, Zion was celebrated by scientists like Dr. Preston Winston who was somebody Harmony had heard of. He had donated several millions to the chip project and he was why she was able to afford to get the chip implant for her anxiety.

"I'm leaving, Harmony." Wendy said. Concern lined her Mother's face but she was respectfully refusing to talk about Lyric. "Will you be okay?"

"You don't have to worry. I'll be fine."

"If you need anything, just call."

Harmony nodded and stood to hug her mother. When the house was perfectly quiet, Harmony proceeded to make some breakfast and turn on cable news. There were still no reports about a possible murder or a missing child. They continued to report on the missing young woman though.

The day was rather uneventful and she hadn't received a call from the police station by the time dinner rolled around. Nobody from work had checked in on her and she was starting to run out of things to keep her busy. She sent a text to her mom letting her know she was taking Rufus for a walk.

Night had already fallen as she walked around the gated community. The LED street lamps provided more than enough light for her to feel safe and she knew for a fact the majority of the people in this neighborhood were middle-aged or older.

When she had made her way halfway around the block, she noticed a heavily wooded area at the end of the stretch of sidewalk. She hadn't remembered this being a dead end. She had been under the impression that the whole neighborhood was one big circle. Rufus's curiosity sparked and he trotted towards the dark.

"Hey, buddy, we need to head back home." Harmony pulled

gently on his leash. Normally he was obedient, but as she pulled he began to bark at the darkness beyond. "No squirrels today, Rufus." She laughed but her laugh was cut short by her surprise to see something emerging from the woods.

All the noise seemed to quiet and dirty fog curled behind the figure that approached. She had blond dreadlocks down to her waist with beads woven throughout. Her eyes were rimmed in thick black eyeliner and her lips were painted crimson with a cigarette hanging from them. A faded tattoo crept up her neck and she was wearing all black. Harmony could not speak. She simply stared. Despite some of the woman's harshness, there was an ethereal quality to her as if she was not truly part of this world.

Harmony held up a hand in greeting but the woman did not respond. She simply stared. Her eyes were ambiguous and her posture closed off. She looked like she did not want to be bothered.

"Are you okay?" Harmony asked.

After a few more seconds, the woman took a couple of puffs on her cigarette and turned around to walk back into the fog. It looked as though she had disappeared in the smoke she created. Harmony realized she had been holding her breath, so she sucked in a sharp breath making her head spin. Crickets chimed in after the women disappeared and in the distance, she could hear cars driving on the highway. She shivered and wondered why the woman seemed so familiar.

CHAPTER 5

PAT WOKE IN THE DIRT PATCH in front of the portal. The muggy heaviness inside the conservatory pressed in on him which didn't help calm his nerves. Carefully, he wiped the drool from the corner of his mouth with one hand and tousled his hair with the other. As he stood, he could see that his decent outfit was now covered in patches of dust and leaves.

Robotically, he made his way back to his house and went through his normal morning routine. Silently, he watched as the dirt flecks ran down the shower drain. Silently, he fried an egg in a skillet and sweetened a cup of coffee. Silently, he watched the news as they covered a story about a missing girl.

Pat was taking all this in but refusing to be bothered by it. All fear, anxiety, and depression surrounding last night was gone. Janice was simply a stepping stone to where he wanted to be and unfortunately, she paid the ultimate price. Even if he hadn't led her to her own demise, she was destined to be lost like his mother. Even as a baby, he must have been unbearable to be around for her to take her own life. Janice would have learned the same lesson sooner or later.

Once his morning routine was complete, he loaded up his car and began backing out of the garage. As he was driving away from his house, he happened to glance over and see somebody unfamiliar standing at his front door. During the split-second pause it took for him to evaluate who the person was, they caught him staring and began to run down the sidewalk to stop him. He then saw the news van parked next to the curb.

Slamming his foot into the gas pedal he screeched down the driveway and nearly missed a pickup truck as he careened onto the highway. He didn't dare look back, but he knew the reporter must have already corrected their course and made a beeline for their vehicle.

Pat's heart rate sped up as he flew around curves and through yellow lights like he was late for work. When he reached the office, he saw a heavy crowd by the front entrance. Several security guards had taken their posts out front to form a human barricade and just then, Theresa was calling Pat's phone.

"Are you here yet?" She asked in a desperate whisper. No greeting.

"I'm parking now. What's going on?"

"The police are here to speak with you."

Pat didn't respond. The car continued to move forward as he neared his usual spot. When he was fully parked he said, "I'm parked. Be right up."

Unlike the day before, he didn't make his usual stops at each department. He ignored anybody who approached and headed straight for the elevators.

"Mr. Sherwood!" Came a shout from his right shoulder. "Mr. Sherwood. Do you have anything to say about Janice May? You were the last one to see her before she disappeared."

Without missing a beat, Pat turned away from the elevator and rushed to the stairwell instead. With his long legs, he took the stairs two at a time until he reached the 3rd floor breathless and alone. He took a few calming breaths, then marched to his office where he was confronted by one police officer and Theresa.

"Mr. Sherwood." The officer inclined his head towards Pat.

"Who are you?" Pat asked. "Why was there a reporter at my house this morning? Why are people crawling all over my company?"

"I'm Officer Greenwald. I'm investigating Janice May's disappearance. An eyewitness testified to you being the last one to see her."

"I have a right to a lawyer, correct?"

"Yes, but if you're innocent I don't think you need one. Let's just talk man to man."

Pat tilted his head to the right and rolled his eyes up to the ceiling. "I can't do that. I need to have my lawyer present."

As much as Officer Greenwald tried to remain emotionless, it was easy to see the exasperation on his face. Pat knew that having a lawyer present would be much more difficult for law enforcement than just chatting.

"It is your prerogative." Officer Greenwald said finally. "Don't leave town."

They exchanged contact information and then the officer left the room. Pat could feel Theresa's judgmental gaze boring holes through the back of his head.

"You had dinner with one of our pharmaceutical reps?"

Pat did not respond but instead began to set up his workspace and start his computer. He then picked up the telephone went to the entry for his lawyer's office number and made a quick call. Once that was done, Theresa was still standing before him with her arms crossed.

"I'm taking care of it."

"What am I supposed to do with all the reporters, Pat?"

"Give them your best evil face and they'll go away." For effect, Pat snarled and squinted his eyes.

"Do you want to talk to any of them?"

"Not at all." Pat returned his gaze to his computer and began responding to emails.

Theresa knew this was the end of the conversation so she left in a huff. Pat heard the screaming at the very edge of his mind. It hadn't superseded other exterior noises, but it sounded like it was trying to overtake him. He wasn't sure why this continued to haunt him. The chip did nothing to solve this and it had arguably been the worst side effect of his schizophrenia to date.

Nothing provided him with the relief that he so desperately needed.

***

To his despair, going out to dinner like he usually did was not an option. The press had been hounding him whenever he was in public spaces and it had become too much for his senses. As he drove home, he glanced at the sad bag of Chinese takeout in his front passenger seat.

"You will have to do for now." He said to the bag as he turned into his driveway.

He didn't see any media vans which was a big relief. Once parked, he walked up into the house to drop off his dinner and then proceeded back outside to the mailbox. Usually, all of the mail he received at his personal address was spam mail and bills. He scanned through the stack and realized there was nothing interesting.

"Pat Sherwood?" Breathed a voice ahead of him.

His ducked head whipped up and he could see the white outline of teeth and shining, eager eyes. As Pat's eyes adjusted to the dim streetlight-lit yard, he saw it was a tan-skinned young man with a tablet and stylus in hand. Possibly another reporter.

"Excuse me." Pat muttered and tried to shoulder his way around the man.

He was stopped, however, by a surprisingly strong grip. Pat could hear his heartbeat in his ears and feel the beat in his throat. If he had to, he would punch this guy out.

"This could be my big break. Nobody else has gotten a statement from you but if I did, my whole world would open up. Please?"

"No." Pat said simply and continued to try to shove past him. When he pushed past the reporter's grasp, he stumbled towards his front patio. In a rush, he righted himself and began his way up the couple of steps leading to the doorway, but as his right leg raised to climb the first step, the young reporter grabbed Pat's left ankle. With no time to catch himself, Pat's head slammed down hard onto the concrete patio and everything went black.

CHAPTER 6

Clive had always prided himself in being an optimist. He was able to smile and socialize with others even when his life was falling apart. That's why he was able to get up from the formal couch in his living room where he had slept the night before and manufacture excitement about the day ahead. He knew that he would be able to tune out his wife's angry face from his mind while he presented to the board at Kimber University.

As expected, he and his wife did not cross paths as he went about his morning routine. He did not seek her out because he knew it would just start the fighting again and he couldn't handle that.

An hour later, he was driving up to the university and parked on the top floor of the parking garage. The city of Kimber took every opportunity to brag about their university's 40,012 students, moving planetarium, and expansive selection of medical majors. If he nailed this presentation, the university's support could be invaluable for getting more young doctors to take up residencies at Healing Touch Hospital and possibly become the next generation of doctors and nurses to champion treatment for mental health.

In a tan, textured two-piece suit and brown shoes, Clive strutted to the Administrative Building. His presentation was all on a flash drive in his pocket and his phone in the other. A nearby fountain splashed and a gaggle of college girls giggled just ahead of him. One of them had particularly tan legs that seemed to go on forever and Clive glanced back at her as she passed.

His wife's words wafted over him. "How did I become second best?" With great effort, he tore his eyes away from the beautiful girl and pushed the front door open into the breezeway of the building. The cold outside air mixed with the warm indoor air in the space. As he pushed open the next set of doors he was inside the heated space. Students were walking all over and several sitting on chairs studying or sitting on surfaces not intended to be seats. There was a welcome desk in the center of the room and everything in the space was colored either tan or white. Hanging from the vaulted ceiling were blue glass baubles in an asymmetrical curtain design which created blue polka dots of light on every surface.

"May I help you?" Asked the woman behind the welcome desk.

Clive realized he had been stopped in the middle of the floor just staring while confused students brushed past him.

"Oh, yes. I'm looking for conference room B." He said hurriedly as he walked to stand level with the desk.

She gave him quick and concise directions and he thanked her. There was a set of stairs to the right of the desk that led to a balcony overlooking the lobby. On this level, there were several rooms which must have been the conference rooms. When he had located the room with a "B" label next to the doorway, he entered the space.

There was already a handful of impressive-looking people sitting in comfortable black armchairs in front of a large oval cherry wood table. Each space at the table had a computer monitor that could be popped up, and in the front of the room was a large screen for presenting.

"Dr. Evers!" Dr. Preston Winston made his way around the table to greet Clive as soon as he saw him.

Preston's smile was gentle and his eyes a calming olive green. He almost looked as though he didn't have any eyelashes or eyebrows, however, which was unsettling for some people. Finally, his styled graham cracker brown hair was the only indicator of his status due to how perfect it was. His clothes on the other hand were simple but well put together.

"Dr. Winston." Clive flashed his crooked smile and the pair bumped elbows in greeting. "I'm so glad to finally be here. This is a gorgeous campus."

"Thank you. You are too kind. I can't praise our community here enough. I simply enjoy getting to use my privilege to enable others to succeed." Preston said modestly.

Clive nodded but was unsure how to respond. Dr. Winston had always been very giving but Clive found himself intimidated by the fact that this man seemed to truly give of himself to help others in a way that Clive was not sure he did himself.

"Will you be using the screen?" Preston asked, ignoring the awkward silence.

"Yes, please!"

Preston proceeded to help Clive set up for his presentation. As the pair hovered over the computer, more professors and university board members filtered into the room and began to chatter. The noise steadily became louder until it was just a continual humming noise.

"Thank you, Theybies and Gentlethems," Preston interjected, cutting through the noise perfectly. "I hope you all are ready for a treat. We have the extreme honor of hearing from one of the most renowned surgeons in Kimber as well as the leading expert on microchips used to manage mental illness in partnership with Sherwood Servers…Dr. Clive Evers."

Everybody applauded politely and Clive looked out into the diverse group. The representation in the room covered nearly every race, religion, gender, sexuality, and ability. Clive beamed with pride knowing that this is what society had been trying to achieve for over a century and he was honored to be able to bring his technology to such a group. They were the future.

"You all are very kind." Dr. Evers said. "I am so honored to be here." The last word stuck in his throat as he remembered the hard work on the road to his success. "It's been a long time getting here, but I am so excited to be rolling out this treatment to all those who suffer from mental illness." He rubbed the back of his neck to ease some of the tension in his muscles and continued. "The numbers of those struggling with anxiety and depression are growing by the day and the treatments available to us right now are not always effective."

All eyes were on him as he crossed the front of the room to address everyone and also point to things on the main screen. Now and then people referred to their own screens, but otherwise, they were hanging on his every word. This was Dr. Clive Evers in his element and he loved it. He was proud of who he was and what he had accomplished.

"You wouldn't be here if it wasn't for me. I worked two jobs while you went to school full-time." The harsh words from his wife Mayre intruded into his brain and he paused momentarily to get his bearings.

"Does anyone have any questions so far?" He said finally, unsure which direction to take his presentation in next.

"Will we simply be promoting the chip on campus or will we be able to actually research its effectiveness and gather data from it?" Asked an unnamed student sitting midway down the right side of the table.

"That's a great question, Edith." Preston encouraged.

"This will open up avenues for studying its effectiveness, with consent of course. However, we do not catalog any of the data that a client chooses to resolve. For instance, if somebody has anxiety, we are not privy to those personal anxieties. Only their counselor has that access. Any other…"

Clive was immediately cut off by what looked to be a board member of the university. "That's a shame because we could learn much more about why people struggle with certain mental illnesses if we were able to track thought patterns."

"Yes, but people have the right to their privacy." Clive said, his tone a little more firm than before. He still wore a smile but he didn't like the direction that this was going.

"But what if the person is dangerous?" Asked the youngest-looking person in the room.

"What do you mean, Dallas?" Preston asked.

"If somebody has a mental illness that makes them prone to violence, shouldn't we be able to monitor what is going on in their brain? It could be effective for identifying others that have this tendency and preventing violence before it happens." Dallas insisted.

Dallas seemed more than prepared for this presentation and Clive found himself thrown off balance. Up to this point, he had enjoyed his presentations and everybody seemed to just be in awe of the technology. However, these academics were delving into realms of the technology that he didn't intend for it to be taken.

Clive had personally never dealt with mental illness. He had always been pretty happy and confident. Mental illness did not run in his family and overall he was privileged. However, due to his confidence in the technology, he had considered receiving a chip implant just to prove how confident he was in the treatment. But when he thought about people he didn't know having access to his fears and sad thoughts, he shriveled up on the inside. Anybody knowing his weaknesses was too much.

"Privacy is paramount for us." Clive cut in. "When a client chooses to 'resolve' a particular mental health issue, that electrical impulse in the brain is deleted. It is not channeled into a database somewhere."

He hoped that would be the end of it, but Edith spoke up again. "Could it be channeled into a database?"

"In theory, yes, but it has never been tried." Dr. Evers was feeling the control of this meeting slipping through his fingers like sand.

"That might be worth looking into." Preston said kindly. His smile was reassuring, but Clive did not return the expression. "Thank you all for your good questions. Let's hear what else Dr. Evers has to say."

Clive appreciated the lifeline. While he had the confidence, Preston seemed to be able to handle people better. He knew just what to say.

"Thank you, Dr. Winston." The rest of the presentation proceeded without a hitch, but the unsettling conversation sat with Clive like a rock in his stomach.

He had always believed the best of humanity, but there were moments when he wondered if everything was destined to be tainted. He believed that the privacy of his patients was critically important to maintain. At this time, there was a medical board that had his back along with Tonya.

Tonya.

He was going to have to speak with her about their secret rendezvous. If Clive ended it, he may no longer have the support he needed. She was a lawyer, but even lawyers could become unprofessional. The more he thought about it, the more he felt like he was entrapped in a spider's web that he could not escape.

***

The drive back to the hospital was uneventful besides stopping to pick up a bite to eat. He ate while navigating through traffic and finished the last bite as he parked in his spot. He went through his usual routine and pulled on his mask as he approached the hospital entrance. Dill took his temperature and he rode the elevator to the 3rd floor. When he arrived, Tonya was already waiting for him.

"Hey, you." She purred. "You're late."

"I don't have any other meetings today." Was all he could muster under the circumstances. She was beautiful and it captivated him.

"Well, now you do. The hospital board has gathered to discuss some details about chip implementation." Tonya grabbed his wrist and pulled him from the elevator. He silently twisted his wrist out of her grasp and pretended not to notice the surprise in her eyes. Even so, she continued speaking without missing a beat. "It's really important. Can you do pass-on afterward?"

"Wait, Tonya." Clive flapped his right hand to signal to her to stop in case she couldn't understand what he was saying through his mask. "Stop bossing me around. I'm a grown man and can make my own decisions."

"Don't you trust me? My judgment?"

Clive pulled his face mask away from his face slightly to scratch the prickly growth of facial hair on his chin and said carefully, "I trust that what you're telling me is true." Just then, a pair of nurses shuffled by and Clive lowered his voice. "But you have to stop treating me like a boyfriend."

"Did you talk with Mayre?" Tonya sighed, exasperated understanding lighting up her sharp eyes.

"We fought, yes." He grasped her elbow and began steering her down the hallway. They were beginning to get stares. "Where is this meeting?"

"The next hallway over." He could hear the smirk in her voice even without seeing it. "This is cliche, but...she doesn't know you like I do, honey." She pulled her elbow free and marched ahead of him to push aside the double door leading to a hall that connected to an administrative hallway.

He wasn't ready to give Tonya up, but what happened between him and Mayre last night was something he never wanted to go through again. Seeing his wife reminded him of all they had been through and it pained him to know he had hurt her. When at work, it was easier to forget his commitments.

"Here we are." Tonya said, snapping Clive out of his musings.

They walked in together and several of the powerful people running the hospital were chatting amongst themselves. As soon as they saw Clive, they quieted down. He made his way to a seat and sat down expectantly.

"We received a call about your meeting at the university." Spoke the chairman of the board. She was very short but had a very commanding presence about her and severe lines to even her nose and hairline. "It sounded very fruitful."

"That's fantastic to hear." Dr. Evers was pleasantly surprised but waited for the other shoe to drop.

"Dr. Winston specifically reached out to us to share some of the ideas that students and faculty had brought up. We think they are worth exploring."

"Which ones?"

"We could be protecting the general public with this technology. Is it possible to give the hospital access to the data from the chips of those who are suffering under more violent mental health conditions?"

Feeling comfortable in his workplace he found himself saying, "You thought *that* was a good idea?" Disbelief radiated out of every syllable and everyone present looked affronted.

"Is that so surprising?"

"Yes! People deserve to have their privacy."

"Not if they are being treated by us. It is reasonable to want to protect our reputation and to protect others if possible."

"I don't believe this." Anger was licking at his body like flames. "We are making progress with our patients. We are rolling this out to a wider patient base and you want to suddenly use this to peep into people's private lives?"

"People already have a lack of privacy due to smartphones." Tonya interjected unhelpfully.

"That's different." Clive stood. "I do not agree with the direction you want to take this. I can't get behind it."

"While we respect your viewpoint, we weren't asking permission. The vote has been taken. We had just hoped that you would be on board."

The room filled with a heavy silence. Clive's heart skipped a beat. All eyes were boring into his body creating holes for all the anger to escape and leaving despair behind. "You decided this before I got here today, didn't you?" The truth of this was confirmed when the board chair averted her eyes.

"Clive...don't." Tonya warned.

"Will I be required to perform surgeries on people still knowing that their private thoughts are being collected?"

"No, of course not. We're letting you go."

CHAPTER 7

Harmony was allowed to return home with no fanfare. She was simply informed that the property had been scoured for evidence and no clues of the girl's location were discovered. She was deemed as still "missing" and possibly deceased. The authorities couldn't give Harmony any more information to go off of and continued to avoid any questions about the girl's parents.

When Harmony finally returned home, she did her own investigation around the yard. No matter how hard she looked, the impenetrable darkness was nowhere to be found. Harmony knew that her mental health was the best that it had been in years, so it was not possible that she was seeing hallucinations or burnt out. Besides, she had never had a history of seeing things.

In addition to her suspicions, she had a strong desire to see Lyric again. She had questions for him but, strangely enough, she missed him. Despite logic speaking loudly in her brain, she took extra time to doll herself up for her first day back at work. She also decided to wear her transparent face mask instead of one that would cover up her lips. When she passed the break room and received several compliments, she knew she had succeeded in going above and beyond her usual workplace attire.

Self-satisfied, she sat down at her desk and clocked in as she took a sip of her fake coffee drink. The screen came to life and took a moment to load all the applications. She could hear Romilda making a fuss about something a few cubicles over and somebody had decided this would be a good morning to warm up broccoli in the microwave. Harmony felt content despite the terrible food smell.

"Harmony?" Lyric had appeared behind her and, instead of the dread she usually felt, her heart lifted in anticipation.

As she spun her chair around, she looked into his beautiful face. "Good morning, Lyric."

"How are you feeling?" He inquired warmly.

"Wonderful. I'm glad to be back."

"What did they ever make of the incident?" He lowered his voice so that any nosy coworkers wouldn't know precisely what they were discussing.

"They said it was nothing. No leads." She said flatly.

"Well, that's good." Lyric smiled, unconcerned that there was no official resolution or answer about what had happened.

Harmony was disappointed. For some reason, she had expected Lyric to have some special knowledge that she didn't. She had always been taught that her "whiteness" was a barrier to her having a complete understanding of certain deep truths. This is what made her pause. Perhaps this whole situation was something beyond what she was able to understand.

"I will let you get back to your work." A smile tugged at the corners of Lyric's perfect lips and fluttered in his eyes as he turned to disappear.

"Thanks." Harmony whispered, certain he hadn't heard.

When she went home later, her usual evening routine was not disrupted by visions of a horrific murder. However, when it was past 10 pm, Rufus began barking at the back door incessantly. This was unusual, so Harmony felt her stomach drop.

"Rufie, what is it, boy?" She asked as she tried to remain calm.

The dog bounced up and down and directed his barks at Harmony as if to say, "Let me out!"

Hoping he simply had to pee, Harmony slipped her feet into her shoes and pulled on a cardigan. She slid the sliding door open and stepped through. The air was cold and crisp, which was more reminiscent of winter than fall. She was dismayed to see Rufus sniffing at the spot where the girl had been.

"What is it, buddy?" His voice quivered as with each step she braced herself for blood and for the terror that might grip her. "Is it a squirrel?" She asked hopefully, knowing Rufus wouldn't answer.

He continued to sniff and Harmony felt relief as she saw that nothing was there, but before she had time to bask in that feeling, Rufus's head snapped up and he began to howl. Three long howls that pierced the night. In one quick motion, he turned to run left then corrected himself and ran right which was towards the fence.

"Rufus! Stop!" He went barreling through a weak point in the wood fence and was through to the other side. He usually was such a good-natured dog, but this Rufus seemed to have lost himself. "No! Come back!"

Harmony pulled herself through the hole he had made and ran after him as her curls bounced beside her ears and her cardigan flapped. Pins and needles began to prick her cheeks and her breaths came in sharp gasps. She had never been very athletic and was regretting passing up the workplace exercise accountability program. When she could no longer see Rufus in front of her, she slowed and collapsed onto her knees in breathless despair.

***

After Rufus had run off, Harmony didn't know what to do and ended up calling her mom. Wendy asked for all the details and insisted she would handle it. As much as Harmony loved her dog, she was exhausted and very thankful that somebody else was taking the burden away from her. Even so, she still woke up more tired than she had been in a long time. This made a cup of coffee sound very appealing.

Harmony was thankful she already had an appointment lined up with her therapist. During this monthly visit, it usually was all about calibrating the chip and programming it to handle any new anxieties that had cropped up since the last time. This time she immediately began talking about what had happened with Rufus, the strange feelings for Lyric, the woman with the dreadlocks, and the girl she saw in her yard.

When Dr. Rigby had completed a scan of Harmony's chip and its functionality, she looked up with concern on her face. "Have you been using, Harmony?"

Harmony's face turned white and she said, "No, of course not."

"There are traces of hacker codes on your chip. These codes are typically only used when people attempt to override the firewalls that protect them from becoming numb."

"I would never do that. My treatment has been working. I haven't needed anything extra."

Dr. Rigby studied Harmony's face for a moment then said, "I believe you, which makes this situation even more concerning."

"Why?"

"The only thing I can imagine would be occurring is that somebody has hacked your account. That would explain all the weird experiences you've been having. As for Rufus though, that would be the only thing that has been real."

Harmony gritted her teeth and closed her eyes. "What can we do?"

"Until we figure this out, we will have to deactivate your chip and rebuild the firewalls. It should only take a few days to repair the damage."

A familiar fluttering began at her bellybutton and traveled to her sternum where it spread tingling all over her body. Her chest tightened and she could barely get a full breath. When her upper lip began to quiver, she knew she was quickly heading for a panic attack.

"Breathe, Harmony." Her therapist reminded her compassionately. "Lay back and breathe. Use your coping skills."

She began to try to identify 5 things she could see, 4 she could hear, 3 she could touch, 2 she could smell, and 1 she could taste. Each shuddering breath was a reminder that she felt like she was dying and that her life was over.

"We will fix this. It is okay." Dr. Rigby said reassuringly.

After 10 minutes of focused energy, Harmony was able to come down from her anxiety and calmly discuss the next steps with Dr. Rigby. When a game plan had been decided, her therapist deactivated her chip and sent her home for the first time without any new treatments. Stepping outside of her therapist's office felt like the sky was crushing her skull and her chest. It had been over a year since she experienced this feeling, but it was as familiar to her as the phone in her hand.

"It isn't real." She whispered as her legs carried her quickly to her car.

When she had shut the door and started the engine, she blasted her face with cool air to try and calm herself down. It took her some time, but when she was calm enough to focus she began to drive to work. Thankfully, her therapy appointments were part of her workdays so she did not lose out on any of her hours for the week. Despite the negatives at her job, this was a positive. Nobody ever questioned where you were when it was time to go to therapy. It has been shown that employees were more committed to the workplace when they had an outlet for mental health. It became even more imperative that Harmony seek out therapy because of her anxiety.

Even though she had started her day with therapy, she realized very quickly why the chip was necessary. The mind-numbing work before her was nearly impossible to complete as her brain whirred with questions. One minute she would be filling out forms and the next she would be hearkening back to the encounter she had with the smoking woman, the hurt child, her interactions with Lyric, and Rufus running away.

She didn't think her anxiety could get much worse, but then a meeting notification popped up on her screen. Normally, meetings weren't held at the end of the day, but Harmony was relieved to have the break. Five minutes before the meeting, she made her way to the conference room and picked out a seat. Nobody else had arrived yet and she breathed a sigh of relief at her luck.

She pulled her mask slightly down under her nose as she checked her phone and waited. The minutes ticked by and 2 minutes after the scheduled time, she glanced up at the doorway to see Lyric just gazing at her.

"You are beautiful." He said simply. This was not an uncommon thing to hear from a coworker. When you were surrounded by gay, lesbian, trans, and queer peers it was expected to receive positive affirmations. However, hearing it from a boss was a different feeling.

"Where is everybody?" Harmony asked, disregarding the compliment and pulling her mask up over her nose. She suddenly realized how secluded this conference room felt. No windows and only one door in and out.

"This is just a meeting for us." He said and sat in the chair directly next to her. "You don't need to wear that mask."

She then pulled the mask completely off. She had so much anxiety, that she wasn't feeling elated to see him like she had been earlier.

"Am I getting fired?" The words flew from her mouth before she could stop them.

Lyric laughed and shook his head as his large dark hand squeezed her knee firmly. "Of course not." The hand sat there much longer than Harmony felt comfortable and she uncrossed her legs so the hand slipped off and she was able to subtly move the direction of her knees.

Lyric laughed. "You've loved me since you got here." Harmony tried not to let her true feelings slip but she averted her gaze.

"Why so shy all of a sudden? Are you seeing someone else?" He still was so close to her that she could smell his cologne and the coffee he had drank a few hours ago.

"No…I'm not." She whispered honestly.

"Is it that woman with the blond dreadlocks?" He demanded.

Harmony's fear then transitioned into disbelief when she realized what he had said. "I never told anybody about that woman."

Lyric backed up slightly. "You mentioned her when I visited you at your Mom's house." He shrugged it off.

"You hacked my chip, didn't you? You are the only one that has access to our files." Harmony carefully stood up and pushed her chair up against the conference table. She didn't release her grip on the back of the chair though because she was shaking hard. "Tell me the truth!" She squeaked.

Lyric stood. "I noticed you shut off my access to you. It made me sad." Lyric said simply. "You are everything I want. All of that old, traditional charm. Nobody else here has that."

Harmony was struggling to form words amidst her panic. Lyric's intoxicating cologne hit her nostrils again and she remembered why she had liked him. But now that he was showing explicit interest, she realized she was not enjoying it at all and was not attracted to him. She could see who he truly was and it was nothing more than a snake that had been injected with Botox and steroids.

"Please, don't hurt me."

"Why would you think that I would hurt you?" Lyric seemed

offended by the accusation.

"I don't want this. I'm sorry."

Lyric's eyes flashed. "It makes sense why you're alone."

"I'm not alone." She whispered, but she didn't quite believe it.

"Who hurt you to make you go into hiding?"

"Hiding?"

"Don't play dumb. I saw the witness protection block on your chip." Lyric said nonchalantly. "I friggin' always seem to go for the damaged ones." He then left Harmony alone with her thoughts.

CHAPTER 8

Pat never enjoyed being the center of attention and especially in high school. He had spent most of his time there alone, and when people did come over to speak with him they went away confused and uncomfortable. Even with the microchip to help alleviate the worst of his schizophrenia symptoms, he still looked at the world differently than others.

Teachers were concerned with the path he was going down and did everything in their power to include him when his peers didn't. Even so, one day he accidentally heard some boys talking about how Pat "looked like a school shooter". The statement settled in his stomach like a boulder and he carried it with him for months. He knew he would have sooner committed suicide than take another person's life so violently and wished others understood.

A lot of kids at his school grew up in religious families and, from what he could see, that didn't make them better people. Pat worked hard to be good to others and didn't need a belief system to fall back on. He was content knowing that he was a good person even if others thought he was odd.

Then he met Justice. He happened to notice her tall hourglass figure and curtain of red hair shimmering under the fluorescents in the cafeteria. He had been convinced he had never gone through puberty, but that all changed when he saw Justice. What was strange was that she saw him too. When she caught him staring, she took it upon herself to pull him from the darkness. Nobody questioned it. Nobody made fun of her for it. She was so popular that people just assumed Pat had become better because of her. Their friendship drifted seamlessly into a romantic relationship, and they ended up marrying directly after high school graduation. Owen Sherwood bought them a home and there they lived until the accident.

Justice had brought Pat out of despair and it was his turn to rescue her. His body was present as she was ripped from him. His body was present at her memorial service. His body was present when he went to bed alone for the first time since getting married. His heart wasn't present. His heart was with Justice and knew she couldn't be gone forever.

***

When he woke the next morning, the first person to greet him was his wife.

"Justice." He sighed. It was like his dreams had drifted into reality and he didn't question it.

"Patty." She sat beside him in the king bed and gazed into his eyes. "You look exhausted."

"I am." His hand reached for hers and he was certain he felt her warmth.

But this couldn't be real.

"I am real." She insisted as if reading his thoughts.

Pat grabbed his phone from his bedside table and quickly pulled up his app for the Thought Conductor. It was registering that the chip was off-line and his heart sank.

"You are not. I am hallucinating."

"Darling, why would you say that?" Justice's voice was filled with emotion and sounded as if her heart was about to break.

"You are not real and something is wrong. I must have…I must have…" A light bulb went off in his brain and he remembered suddenly how he had fallen last night.

Kicking his sheets aside and letting go of Justice's hand, he slid off the bed and rushed to his bathroom. He looked in his mirror at his thin haggard face. He was in his early 20s, but the few lines his face did have were very pronounced. Under his eyes were dark circles and dried drool was crusted on the right corner of his mouth. He ran his fingers across the place where they had inserted the microchip and he could feel a raised bump the size of a golf ball a few inches behind his right ear.

The demonic humming started up in his ears and below that the sound of women screaming for their lives. He could see Justice behind him in the doorway. She looked real, but he had to remind himself that she wasn't. He would know when she was real and this wasn't it.

"Excuse me." He said to the hallucination as he shoved past her and went downstairs.

He forced himself to walk through his morning routine and eat a bowl of cereal as she watched him quizzically from every doorway. As he tried to ignore her, a dog walked through his living room, but he knew he had no dog. Even though this was frightening, he kept telling himself that when he got to work, he would be able to figure out what to do.

As he was leaving, Justice smiled in amusement as she said, "I will make you believe, my love."

***

"There's the prodigal!" Theresa shouted whenever Pat was within earshot.

"Please. Shhh…" Pat held up a long bony finger to his lips to shush her. The noise he was experiencing in his head was enough without her screeching.

"We have been dealing with the media all day. One reporter is claiming that you nearly assaulted him when he asked for the truth. Is that true?"

Pat slowly shook his head. "Of course not. He ambushed me at my own home, knocked me over, and deactivated my chip."

Theresa held her breath. Even though she had always loved Owen Sherwood despite his flaws, there was something about Pat having schizophrenia that obviously bothered her. She seemed to be a holdover from the past when it was unacceptable for people to be different than the majority. As much as she tried to hide this from others, Pat could recognize the expression on her face as mild disgust and fear.

"Oh, is that so? Are you having…trouble now?" She asked cautiously.

"Yes. I need a list of all the microchip surgeons in the area immediately so I can get it fixed."

"Of course, but…"

"Now, please." He knew if he didn't act quickly, he would revert to his old self. The chip's effects would only last until the brain figured out what was happening.

Pat turned on his heel and headed to his office so Theresa wouldn't have space to complain about the task he had given her to do. When he was in the comfort of his office, he pressed his knuckles firmly into his eyes so that when he pulled them away he saw fuzzy purple dots.

A few emails later, Theresa brought him a list of the doctors to whom they supplied the microchips. Many of the calls he made ended in leaving messages with secretaries or having to leave a voicemail. When his calls resulted in nothing, he pulled open his desk drawer and dug around through the contents until his hand landed on a pill bottle. When he had been first diagnosed, they prescribed him a medication that gave him horrible tremors and nausea. Even so, he continued to refill the medicine just in case. Tentatively, he swallowed a pill and washed it down with lukewarm coffee.

Even though he had come to work at 10 am, he left for an early lunch at 11:30 am. It felt like he was walking in a fishbowl everywhere he went. He was amongst people but didn't feel part of humanity. It took all his energy to not let things overtake him.

His body took him to his favorite dinner place and he sat in the same booth he had shared with Janice a few nights before. At one time, he thought he was a good person to others, but that wasn't a certainty anymore. He knew he would hurt so many people just to bring Justice back.

"Patrick Sherwood, right?" A scruffy but handsome man in his late twenties approached the booth and broke through the fog of Pat's musings. His smile was bright and he seemed to be riding on a cloud of confidence.

"Yes." Pat wanted to respond sarcastically, but he was emptied of witty responses.

"Do you mind if I sit?" Pat nodded and the man sat across from him. "I'm Dr. Clive Evers." Pat did not say anything, but he recognized the name. That was one of the voicemails he had left despite his better judgment. "It's great to finally meet you."

"I don't get that often." Pat laughed derisively.

"I doubt that. You are widely recognized for all you've done to advance mental health treatments."

"What my father has done." Pat took a long sip from his drink and raised his eyebrows.

"Well, of course. He was a great man." Dr. Evers flashed a crooked smile that would certainly kill Theresa on the spot.

"Did you want to talk about something specific?" Pat was starting to get a headache and wanted Dr. Evers to leave as soon as possible.

"What was your intent with the microchip technology? What did you think should be done with them?"

Pat took another long sip from his drink while Clive flagged over a waitress to place a drink order.

"I don't understand." Pat didn't want to deal with this at the moment. He wanted to go home and sleep in his bed.

"Do you have a mission statement?"

"I don't know."

"Do you strive to help others because it helped you?"

"I guess…?"

"Are you aware patient privacy is at stake?" Clive's smile faltered slightly as he asked this and Pat looked confused.

"I was not aware, but if that is the case we will increase our microchip security features." Pat moved to leave and Clive's eyes flashed a momentary expression of panic. "Thank you for this enthralling chat and I appreciate you taking the time to meet with me, but if you have any complaints about the product, please contact the quality control office at Sherwood Servers."

"Of course. I'm sorry to have bothered you, but it was good to meet you." Clive said helplessly. Despite looking very lost, he was still extremely polite.

Pat knew he was being rude, but he had no time to deal with complaints about the product when there were more important things going on. He didn't want to go back to the office. That was the good thing about being the CEO. He could go home after lunch and not get in trouble.

***

Even though he knew what would happen when he went to the conservatory, he still wanted to check. As he reached the portal, he could tell that it was inactive. No manor within and no beast roaming the halls. Pat then went through the triangle frame of the entrance but he appeared on the other side in the same glass-encased greenery bubble.

He ran his fingers over the metal frame. Parts of the portal had vines wrapping around and poisonous-looking berries hanging from it tantalizing him. Pat couldn't be sure if the sounds in the conservatory were things he was really hearing or auditory hallucinations. It sounded as though rain was hitting the glass panes above, but his skin was wet. Birds sang, but it was going to be winter soon. Children laughed and played at a park nearby that didn't exist.

All was peaceful, which typically was not something that could be said for his imaginings. He usually thought about horrific things that made him curl into a ball and cry for them to go away. These nightmares haunted him during waking hours and he felt so lost being unable to do anything about it.

When the chip had been installed the first time, the procedure was done by a surgeon handpicked by his father. Pat wished his father was here to help. He knew things about the business like the product quality, mission statements, goals, and best business practices. That was something he never had time to explain to Pat in detail, and that was why Theresa took such a big part in the company. She had hung on Owen Sherwood's every word and this made her an extreme asset to the company. It also made Pat worried that eventually the board would decide he was unnecessary and give her free rein over everything. That was a shuddering thought.

As a teenager, he had always wanted to do something creative. His inclinations to write poetry, play instruments, and build things were deeply ingrained. While computer programming involved stringing together lines of code that flowed together, playing with technical instruments, and building fantastical virtual worlds, the career field didn't scratch that itch Pat had. He also seemed to bear the burdens of an artist by being mostly anxious and thoroughly depressed.

As he stood before his portal shivering, he realized he was currently depressed because of the loss of what he built with his imagination. At least, he thought he had built it. The place beyond the portal seemed to have popped into existence after the chip was implanted in his brain and he had the nagging feeling that all the things he saw within the portal were things he had seen before.

CHAPTER 9

Clive truly believed that everything happened for a reason. Without this belief, he would have already fallen into despair at the fate of his life. It also didn't hurt that he sincerely thought he was not at fault for any of his problems. The people who did not agree with his vision were simply challenges to his eventual victory. He was disappointed in how Patrick Sherwood had received him at the restaurant, but he had heard some credible rumors about how odd the boy was. Pat was not the sociable motivator that Owen Sherwood had been.

Clive chewed on these thoughts as he drove home. The radio played softly and his car easily rode up the incline onto the interstate. As he shifted into cruise, he fell deeper into his thoughts. He became so consumed that when he pulled into his driveway he startled slightly.

As he stepped out of the car, he instantly knew that something was wrong. He hurried inside the house calling out for Mayre as he went. All the lights were on and the ceiling fans whipped around silently. In the kitchen, a fresh pot of coffee sat undisturbed and a bag of chips was lying open on the table.

"Mayre?" He tried again. His heartbeat quickened when he

received no response. He knew he should have taken the day off to resolve things with her. He shouldn't have gone to work just to get fired and not have a wife to come home to.

He pulled his cell phone out of his pocket and called Mayre's parents. Her mother answered right away and dispelled the idea that Mayre was with them. Clive reassured his in-laws with his sturdy confidence that Mayre was okay and probably just had her phone on silent while at the grocery store.

"She wouldn't move out without letting her parents know." Clive said aloud. Mayre was very close with her family.

Taking a deep breath, he then dialed Mayre's number. It rang several times and then ended. No voicemail box, no recorded greeting, no nothing. He dialed again and this time it went straight to voicemail. It then felt like his heart stopped beating and dropped out of his chest. He had to hold a hand up to his chest to ensure he was still breathing. Something was really wrong.

Suddenly, there was a knock at the door. Clive knew it had to be Mayre. She must have lost her key. That would explain everything.

As he swung the door wide open, it was Tonya. Before she could speak, Clive shook his head slowly. "This is the worst time you could be here." He said, forgetting his charm in his disappointment and renewed fear.

"Please let me in, Clive." Tonya said seriously. Her outfit was still very flashy, but her posture wasn't intended to call attention to herself and her tone was normal. Clive could tell it must be serious.

Even so, his wife was the most important. "Mayre will be home any minute. You CAN'T be here." He moved to shut the door and Tonya shoved her foot in the gap.

"No. She won't."

He pursed his lips and allowed Tonya to walk past him and into the living room. She sat where Mayre had sat the previous night when she had told him he was a bad husband.

"She's gone, Clive, and you should leave too."

"Gone? Where? Do you know where she's at?"

"No."

Clive threw his hands in the air. "That's so helpful."

"I know she is safe though. You aren't."

"What are you talking about?"

Tonya folded her hands together over her right knee and crossed her legs. "There are things coming. Firing you was only the beginning. You have to find a safe place to hide until this all blows over."

"What kind of things?" Clive slowly lowered himself into the recliner and leaned in to gaze intently at Tonya. "Tell me. NOW." Clive had never gotten this aggressive about anything, but since Mayre and himself were hanging in the balance, he was not willing to be nice to keep up appearances.

Tonya seemed surprised at this new side of Clive, but she didn't make any comment about it. "I can't tell you. It is confidential between me and my client."

His beautiful face twisted in anger and anguish. "For the lips of the adulterous woman drip honey, and her speech is smoother than oil."

Tonya stood, her demeanor businesslike, "Leave, now. They're coming soon." She made a beeline for the door.

"What, no kiss goodnight?" He spat, sarcasm dripping off every word.

She looked back one more time, "I do love you. That's the only reason why I'm here."

When she was gone, the heaviness of the empty house descended. Clive proceeded to warm up leftovers and eat hardly any of them as he scrolled through social media. Despite what Tonya and he had shared, he did not trust her. Clive knew that she was just trying to get him out of the way so that the hospital could start mining patient's mental health data for profit. Somehow, his wife was also wrapped up in this mess. He couldn't just stand aside.

Not 20 minutes after Tonya had left, Clive heard knocking at his front door again. This time, he was more level-headed and looked at the security app on his phone first to see who was at the door. To his surprise, there were five police officers.

Still thinking he could charm anybody, he walked to the front door and swung it open.

"Officers?" Clive smiled jovially. "Can I help you?"

Three of the police were wearing full metal face coverings but the other two weren't completely covered. The officer in the middle with no distinguishable features held out a small screen for Clive to read. One quick scan was all he needed to realize that he was being arrested.

"What have I done?" He took an involuntary step backward.

"Please freeze." Said the automated voice box attached just below the chin of the officer.

"What am I being arrested for?"

"You have the right to remain silent." Continued the robotic voice.

Clive continued to back up as the officers advanced on him. "I won't be silent until I know what is going on." Clive still spoke cordially despite his body being flooded with fear.

The officer droned on as if Clive had said nothing. Dr. Evers realized that his natural charisma was of no use. Over the years, poor policing had driven society to seek out solutions for better law enforcement. The solution was much harder training and uniforms that made officers hardly human. The end result was now hollow, heartless robots.

Clive was backed into his kitchen as he had been read all of his rights. The ceiling fan whipped around rhythmically and the fridge hummed, oblivious to the fear raging in Clive's body. He wished he had gotten the chip installed so he'd have the option of dulling this feeling. He always had what he wanted and more than enough of what he needed, but this was the first time he felt his life slipping through his fingers.

If his senses hadn't been on high alert like they were, he was unsure he would have noticed the creeping thing that had seeped under his back door and made its way around the breakfast nook. It was snakelike and rippled like water. Its eyes looked more like a cat's and the tail curled up into a sharp metal hook. Before Clive had time to think, it made its first move on the lead officer. Despite the reinforced uniforms and Kevlar vests, the hook came down fast and stuck deep in the officer's thigh.

The distraction was enough for Clive to rush out his back door. He thanked Mother Mary that he still had his wallet and phone in his pocket and that his keys had been hanging nearby. He had barely made it into his car when he saw the officers flooding out the back door. Their guns were aimed in his direction and he floored the gas pedal. The car fishtailed, but when it gained some traction he rocketed forward towards the officers. They dove out of the way and he found himself flying across an open field. In a few minutes, he soared over a ditch and landed roughly on the highway behind his home, feeling a jolt start in his tailbone and radiate up his spine. That was going to hurt tomorrow.

He was certain that the snake-like creature in his home had been exactly what his patient Ophelia had described to him days before. This left Clive with questions and made him wonder if she was truly more sane than he had given her credit for.

CHAPTER 10

Harmony realized that she kept her conversations mostly surface-level at work. She barely interacted with others and when she did interact she only seemed to make small talk. The few times she had tried getting deep with anybody, they were patronizing about things that were ingrained aspects of her life such as her sexuality, race, or religious views.

"Oh, you're heterosexual? How classic of you."

"Of all the identities you could have chosen and you're straight? Isn't that boring?"

"I'm sorry you're half white. Is the privilege awareness training as bad as they say?"

"There's nothing out there. Agnostic isn't really a thing anymore since we know most everything now."

These were all things that had been said to her at one time or another and it generally didn't bother her until now. There was nothing keeping her anxiety in check at the moment and her insecurities returned like a toxic ex-partner. Her appointment with her therapist was a week away and every time she called the office the secretary stated there weren't any earlier appointments.

"I'm sorry, I know your anxiety has increased since your Thought

Conductor was turned off, but Dr. Rigby said to continue taking the medicine and she will see you in person next week. Do not hesitate to go to the hospital if symptoms become unmanageable."

Harmony already felt like her symptoms were unmanageable, but she didn't want to come across as dramatic so she didn't argue with the secretary. She was just doing her job.

She had spent the days after her meeting with Lyric avoiding him to the best of her ability. However, it was difficult to do in a small office. She sensed that he still was interested in her and she wasn't sure how to handle the situation. She felt paranoid that people were whispering behind her back even though there was no reason for anybody to know what had gone on between her and Lyric.

At one point, during midday on Wednesday, she was at the copier making copies when Lyric brushed past her under the guise of retrieving more coffee. Out of the corner of her eye, she saw him bustling around the counter gathering all the necessary things to make a cup. Harmony realized that this was the first time they had been alone in a room together since their meeting. The hairs on the back of her neck prickled and her shoulder muscles tensed. Every noise he made felt like a warning signal.

Her fight-or-flight response kicked in and she took what she had copied so far and went back to her cubicle as fast as her legs would carry her. The odor of the coffee burned in her nostrils through her mask and she felt the burning of tears starting at the corners of her eyes. He hadn't violated her body, but he had violated the privacy of her mind and it made her feel so exposed in the worst ways.

When she slid into her car at the end of another long workday, her phone began to ring. It was her therapist so she answered the call quickly. "Hello?"

"Hello, Harmony?" Dr. Rigby confirmed.

"Yes, it's me."

"Hi, good. How are you?"

Harmony's mind spiraled as she tried to find a suitable answer to that question. If it had been anybody other than her therapist, she would have simply said "fine" but this was the same woman who had listened to stories about her overly controlling mother, feeling isolated at work, and her deep fear of being forgotten.

"Fine. What's up." She said finally.

"Just wondered if you could make time to come in Friday morning instead? I think I've figured out what's wrong with your chip." Her tone was even, but Harmony could sense that Dr. Rigby was holding herself back somehow.

"Oh, okay? Is something wrong?"

"No! It was just a more complicated bug than what I originally thought. I figured you'd want to be back to your normal self sooner rather than later." She laughed lightly.

Even though there was no need to be anxious, Harmony could feel discomfort bubbling in her stomach as the last 3 cars in the parking lot began making their way to the main road. "Yes, I really appreciate that. What time?"

"10 am!"

"10 am, got it. Thanks."

They said their goodbyes and Harmony started her car so she could drive home. When she opened the door to her A-frame house not a few minutes later, the reminder that Rufus was gone hit her again. She decided that before anything else, she would walk around the neighborhood again to look for him. Grabbing the leash, she walked out her front door and made her way to the sidewalk. The sun had already set but it was surprisingly comfortable outside. The wind blew gently lifting a few small curls from her forehead and causing her pant legs to stick to her thighs. A group of preteens rode their bikes past her laughing and playing music on their phones which temporarily distracted her. She forced herself to focus on finding Rufus.

"Hello!"

Harmony glanced over where the greeting came from and saw a young girl staring up at her, bright-eyed.

"Hello?" Harmony responded uncertainly.

"Can you help me find my mom?" Her speech sounded as though her tongue was putting in a lot of extra work but her smile melted Harmony's heart and all she could do was nod.

"I can definitely do that. Is your family in this neighborhood?"

The young girl didn't respond but instead asked, "Where is your doggie?"

The girl had beautiful wavy white blond hair that reached her shoulders and her almond-shaped eyes were deep brown. She looked to be eight years old and Harmony wondered briefly what kind of parents would let their eight-year-old wander the neighborhood at night.

"He's missing. Can you help me look for him while we look for your Mommy?"

She nodded vigorously.

"Well, let's walk around the block." Harmony bent down and cocked her head to the side to peer down sweetly into the girl's face. The girl turned her face up towards Harmony's and flashed her a goofy smile.

"What is your name?"

"Harmony."

"That's the most beautiful name I have ever heard."

They began to walk together and Harmony said, "Thank you. What is yours?"

"Haven."

"Your name is also beautiful."

"Thanks." Haven hung her head bashfully and giggled.

Harmony continued to be the adult and glanced around for a woman frantically looking for her baby girl. Haven filled the silence by talking about some of her favorite things. When it seemed like Haven had listed everything as her "favorite", Harmony began to get concerned that she hadn't seen anybody yet.

As she peered down the sidewalk and glanced over at the house to her left she asked, "Where was the last place you saw your mom?" Silence. "Haven?" She glanced over and there was nobody beside her. "Haven?" She looked behind and there was still nothing. A chill ran down her spine and she cried out louder. "Haven?!"

Nothing greeted her but the rustling of autumn leaves.

CHAPTER 11

Something wasn't right. Pat could feel the difference. His brain had spent years being conditioned to function normally with aid from the microchip, but now that it had been jostled around, he was dissolving into darkness. When he woke the next morning, he could clearly hear Justice going through her getting-ready routine in the bathroom.

On his nightstand, Dr. Clive Evers' business card sat glaring at him. "I will not be calling that pompous…"

"Patty!" Came the lilting voice of Justice as she slipped into the room in all her glory. She was wearing just a long-sleeve shirt and jeans, but it was everything he wanted. To his shame, the tears came quick and fast. It was like every moment he was breaking and he didn't like it. "Oh, Patty." Justice swept in and wrapped her arms around his small frame and squeezed the life out of him.

"Please. Please." He sobbed uncontrollably, unable to communicate what he wanted.

"I'm here." She cooed.

That was exactly the problem. She persisted and it continued to make him feel unsettled. He couldn't move on because she still existed, but he couldn't find her real form because the beast had taken her. This hallucination he kept having was barely keeping her memory alive and tormenting him in the process. She was all he could think about and, whenever the opportunity presented itself, he had used vulnerable women in the hopes of bringing her back.

Justice backed up just then, holding his shoulders at arm's length. She studied his face as she wiped his tears away in a very motherly way. She was the only person that had ever cared for him like that. He barely knew anything about his real mother.

"I just need a moment." Pat said simply.

Justice let go of him and continued to examine his face for deceit. When she found nothing, she said, "Okay, Patty. I love you."

"I l-love you too." He gave a long shuddering breath as Justice disappeared from the room reluctantly.

As he disentangled himself from the sheets, he reached for the business card on his nightstand and unplugged his phone from the charger. Dialing the number before he lost his nerve, he placed the phone to his ear as it rang. His heart quickened and his breathing became shallow the more times it rang. He was torn between being terrified about having to speak with Dr. Evers or possibly not getting ahold of him at all.

As he was about to lose all hope, the phone clicked and he heard a jovial voice say, "Hello? This is Dr. Clive Evers."

"Pat...this is Patrick Sherwood." He cleared his throat realizing how hoarse he sounded from all the crying.

There was a long pause. It sounded like the doctor was driving. "Oh, Pat! What a surprise."

"I need your help."

Pat explained his symptoms and what was happening. He kept his voice low when talking about Justice just in case she still was hanging around.

"We're going to need to meet." Clive said when he had listened to everything Pat had said. "I can't explain everything on the phone but I am heading to a safe place. I will be at the boat ramp at German Park. Meet me there as soon as you can and we can figure out a treatment plan for you."

Pat didn't like the uncertainty. He already thought Clive was a pompous snob and Pat had to swallow all of his pride just to reach out to this man for help. Now this "professional" was asking him to meet at a boat ramp.

"Why are we not meeting at the hospital?" Pat pressed.

There was another long pause and all Pat could hear was the whooshing of the car. "I am meeting a man at German Park who I think has the resources we may need. I want to be able to get you the best and safest care."

"Okay." Pat suddenly heard rustling in the other room and realized that Justice might have returned. He was still skeptical of Dr. Evers but it was his only chance right now for immediate help. "See you soon." Pat hung up quickly and quietly gathered himself together to leave.

***

Before Pat had called, Clive had been racking his brain for a safe place to go. Most of his colleagues were connected to the hospital or law enforcement in some way. It never entered his mind that he would be on the wrong side of those establishments someday. Now he wasn't even sure how much longer he'd be safe in his car or using his phone. Each device had GPS trackers embedded. Maybe he had seen too many cop shows, but he was almost certain they would be able to track his movements if they tried.

That's when he was reminded of Arrow Tzur. Back when Clive had first begun shadowing doctors at the hospital, he became fast friends with a pharmaceutical salesman. He had been informed Arrow was the best man to work with. He was charismatic, thoughtful, and always able to get samples of medicines that had just hit the market. Unfortunately, he ended up on the wrong side of the law, which made everybody wonder if he was only good at his job because he was cutting corners and manipulating the system. After that time they lost touch, but Clive still remembered Arrow had transitioned into the life of a sailor. Clive had been one of Arrow's many calls he had made once he got out of prison. If anybody knew about being on the wrong side of the law, it was Arrow.

The number of residential buildings became fewer and fewer as Clive neared German Park. The pine trees were thick and clustered together along the road which made everything appear darker and gloomier with the oppressive gray sky above. It didn't feel like fall in this part of Kimber; it felt like the deepest part of winter.

As he turned down the drive to German Park, he could see several boat masts crowding each other against the dark sky. The wooden docks stretched out to cradle each boat. Some boats were covered by tarps, while others were still being used for fishing. Clive breathed a sigh of relief when he could see the top of a houseboat with peeling white paint and the name "Straight as an Arrow" written on the side. When he parked and glanced into the car beside him on the left, he was pleased to see an exhausted-looking Patrick Sherwood. Clive raised his hand in greeting, but Pat merely returned it with a jerk of the head.

The two men exited their cars. It didn't seem possible for two people to be more different. Despite running from the cops, losing his job, and being estranged from his wife, Clive's eyes sparkled. His hair and facial hair were perfectly groomed and his clothes were exactly what was fashionable for the time. Pat, on the other hand, had dark circles under his eyes, a noticeable bed-head, and simple jeans under a black t-shirt that had seen better days.

"I'm glad you could make it." Clive said, flashing a crooked smile. "We're going to that houseboat down there." Clive inclined his head to "Straight as an Arrow". He hoped that his charm would enable him to get both him and Pat on board.

Without access to the hospital, it would be harder to get Pat the help he needed, but Clive figured that would simply be a small bump in the road. If he could figure out a way of helping Pat, he just might be able to get his job back and convince Mayre about what a good man he was.

"Let's go!" Clive rubbed his hands together and smiled.

Pat had a very tired and unfathomable expression and Clive had no idea how to interpret how Pat felt, but Pat didn't argue as they trudged down the gravel hill until they were walking across the sand. There was a ladder that led up to the dock which they climbed and walked to the very end where the houseboat rocked gently. With no hesitation, Clive knocked.

"Whaddayouwant?" Came a gruff voice from inside the boat.

"Arrow?" Clive ventured, raising his voice a few octaves to be heard above the water lapping against the side of the hull.

The door swung open and in the small entrance stood a very tall man. His arms were covered in tattoos and curving with muscle. His hair was short and pitch black, framing a face that wasn't ugly, but asymmetrical. His nose looked like it had been broken multiple times. Paired with watery eyes that were struggling to focus, he was quite a sight to behold. "Yeah, whose askin'?"

"Dr. Clive Evers. From the hospital? This is Pat Sherwood, CEO of Sherwood Servers." He gestured to Pat who seemed very small in comparison. "You look…well. Can we come in?"

"Oh...yeeeeeaaaah. Hey, buddy! C'min." Arrow staggered out of the way and gestured for Clive and Pat to come inside. "You wanna beer?"

"Oh, no thank you." Clive waved the idea away and Pat stood awkwardly in the middle of the sitting room.

Clive was disappointed by the happy drunk residing in

the houseboat. His confidence in his poorly constructed runaway plans was starting to ebb away. A happy drunk might be fun to socialize with, but was not somebody who could guarantee your safety or security.

"It's been forever, man." Arrow said genially as he sat down. "I'm so glad you guys came over." His smile revealed a missing molar on the left side of his mouth.

"Well, we're glad to be here." Clive started, glancing at Pat who looked like he was not happy to be present.

"Sit down, guys!" Arrow insisted, flapping his hands up and down.

Pat reluctantly sat on the fuzzy brown couch under the window and Clive made a beeline to the kitchen. After taking a moment to locate cups, he found one and filled it with water. As he came back around the corner, he shoved the glass into the inebriated man's hand and insisted he drink deeply. Arrow obliged.

Pat's eyes nervously surveyed the whole room and seemed to startle every time the boat rocked. "Why are we here?" He said finally, looking as if he was going to snap in half.

"Right." Clive grimaced. He was hoping that his one hope for salvation from the law wasn't drunk, but beggars couldn't be choosers. "Arrow..."

"Yes, Doctor?" Arrow smiled and cocked his head to the side mockingly.

Clive gritted his teeth. He had forgotten how annoying Arrow could be. Taking a calming breath he started again. "Arrow, I am in danger."

Pat whipped around, his eyes boring into Clive's temple.

"What kind?" Arrow asked, trying to keep his eyes focused, but it was a struggle.

"I have been let go from my position at the hospital and

now the police are after me. I don't know all the reasons, but I think it is a philosophical difference about microchip care."

"The privacy issue?" Pat chimed in.

"Yes." Clive turned to meet Pat's critical gaze.

"They cannot hack anybody's chip." Pat ran thin fingers through his messy hair thoughtfully. "There are procedures in place to ensure each customer's privacy." This was a rehearsed phrase Pat had to throw around quite often because he didn't even pause to draw breath.

"Several of the people I spoke with were on board with instituting new policies to protect society as a whole. The ability to hack chips is already out there." Clive glanced over at Arrow meaningfully but he did not meet the gaze. He was peering at the tip of his left foot intently. He was either ashamed of something or sick to his stomach. Clive couldn't tell which.

"I need another beer." Arrow muttered and rocked himself forward to a standing position.

"No. No. No." Clive said rising quickly and closing the gap between them. He was much shorter than Arrow and not nearly as strong, but he reached out anyway to grip both shoulders and force Arrow to a seated position again.

"Getoff." Arrow shrugged Clive's helpful grip away and glared daggers at him. "This is my home. If you want my help, you gotta let me do what I want."

"I need you sober." Clive said, still trying to use his persuasion skills. He flashed a crooked smile and said, "I want you to remember this tomorrow."

"I don't." Arrow growled, rising to a standing position again.

Clive could smell the sweat, fish, and beer wafting off of him and it wasn't pleasant. He took an automatic step backward to alleviate his senses, but this signaled to Arrow that he was free to go get a beer. He lumbered up the single step and into the small kitchen.

"Please, if you would just listen to me…" Clive tried one last time to be polite but Arrow wasn't having any of it.

"Leave if yur gonna cause me this headache."

Pat sat unhelpfully on the couch with his hands folded and spindly legs looking too long to be comfortable. He also didn't even seem to be paying attention to the conflict brewing.

Clive's brain began to whir. He watched as Arrow opened his fridge and grabbed a single bottle of beer. Clive was so used to being able to coax people into doing what he wanted, he didn't know how to behave when they didn't listen.

But he knew he didn't want to go to jail even more.

In his panic, his right arm shot out and nudged the bottle from Arrow's loose grip. The bottle went crashing to the tile floor and glass spewed everywhere. Profanities flew from Arrow's mouth in a garbled mess and his left foot lurched forward in his surprise. Unfortunately, the foot landed hard on the biggest shard of glass, and his tirade was cut short by a cry of pain. He hopped a few times on his right leg and leaned over to sit at his breakfast table. He called Clive another few choice words and wiped his brow with the back of his hand.

"I'm going." Pat announced to the room as he stood.

"No, Pat!"

"Thanks anyway." Pat was leaving and Clive wanted to go after him.

"Get this out of my foot! Yur the doctor!"

Clive's attention was forcibly pulled away to the injured sailor. Mercifully, Arrow did have a first aid kit so Clive was able to remove the glass, dress the wound, and get the bleeding to stop. It wasn't as deep of a cut as it had first appeared. Once Clive had swept up the glass and given Arrow the all-clear, he stood gingerly on the injured foot and nodded in approval. He limped to his armchair and sat down.

"Was that your last beer?"

"Yes." Arrow said bitterly.

"Oh." Clive tried to hide his pleasure but it was difficult.

"You're lucky I need help on the boat. I'll make you work, but you can ride with me." Arrow conceded.

"Thank you, friend."

Arrow waved away the word "friend" with a strong hand and sat in a thoughtful silence. Then he said, "Where's the skinny boy?"

CHAPTER 12

Pᴀᴛ ᴛᴄᴛᴀᴍʙᴇᴅ ᴜᴘ ᴛɢᴇ ɢᴇᴀᴠᴇʟ ʜɪʟʟ. His head began to spin and the screaming got louder.

"You should've stayed home with me." Justice said, but he couldn't see her to his left or right.

As he nearly crested the hill he lost his balance and landed hard on his hands and knees. He felt the skin on his left palm tear. The world appeared to tilt sideways and he held himself up on wobbly arms to try to stay present. He desperately just wanted to lay face down on the rocks and sleep. After taking a few deep breaths and closing his eyes he was able to push himself to a standing position. The world had stopped spinning but the screaming was still there.

"Pat." Theresa was approaching him as he made the way up to his car. He was shocked to even see her, so he didn't bother to hide himself. "Where have you been all day?"

"Is it really you or am I seeing things?" His ears rang unnaturally loud.

"It's me. I found your car by turning on the GPS tracker. You never showed up at the office so I was CONCERNED." She stopped a few feet from him and put her hands on her hips in frustration.

"I had something I was looking into."

"Well, I hope it wasn't anything illegal." Theresa's tone was teasing but Pat knew that Theresa never joked. She genuinely thought he was up to no good. "The police stopped by again to speak with you. They still haven't found that girl." She squinted at Pat as if she knew he was guilty.

"You were never going to be my mother you know." Pat said harshly as he cut past her to his car. He knew this was a low blow but the selfish part of him didn't want to deal with her anymore.

He already had the door unlocked and was stepping inside when Theresa snapped back, "Someone has to be your mother! What has gotten into you lately?"

"Well, the previous employee for that job retired early so I wouldn't recommend applying."

Pat was about to close the door in her face, but she used her wide hips as a door stopper and was 4 inches from his face. Pat could have shared all that was on his mind. He could have told her that he was feeling claustrophobic dressing up and going to an office every day to do a job he wasn't passionate about. He could have said that he felt like he was in a fog and forgetting portions of his life. He could have shared that he reached out to Clive and realized it was a mistake. He could tell her that screams were always at the back of his mind and he wasn't sure where they were coming from. He could have told her that he had seen Justice. He could have said that missing Justice was the hardest thing he had ever experienced.

But Theresa didn't deserve that kind of transparency from him. Her motives were nothing but transparent and none of them had his best interest.

"Owen never loved you. Helping me is not going to make you feel better about that." He regretted the words as soon as they left his mouth.

Theresa's eyes sparkled with the precursor to tears and her lips pressed together tightly. She backed up and allowed Pat to shut the car door and he turned his gaze to the backup camera so he would not have to absorb the weight of the grief he had dredged up. The fact that Owen had not loved Theresa the way she wanted was true, but hearing it said out loud wouldn't ease her pain. Pat didn't necessarily like her but she had stayed by his side despite it all.

He backed up the car and caught a brief glimpse of Theresa frozen in place as he pulled away from the boat dock.

***

The more Pat researched, the more he realized how difficult it was to find a surgeon he felt comfortable with to fix his Thought Conductor. He was too embarrassed to go back to Clive but he was running out of options. He had been sitting in his car outside a McDonald's for an hour googling "surgeons in my area". Finally, he landed on one result that seemed exactly what he needed. This surgeon had trained under the surgeon that Owen had hired to perform Pat's surgery.

Relief melted over him as he realized that he might be able to get things taken care of and not continue dissolving into madness. It had been a long time since he had lived treatment-free as a schizophrenic. His symptoms had been so severe that he wasn't able to live normally. He couldn't go back to that place.

Since the accident, his goal had been to see Justice. Now his goal was to not see her. This wasn't because he didn't want her in his life but, having her back needed to be real and not just a hallucination.

To his dismay, the hospital where the doctor was based only took appointments over the phone. Pat grudgingly called their office and talked with the secretary about his situation. If Pat had believed in god, he would have said it was a miracle they had any openings. But what was even crazier was that they had an opening in a few hours.

"We actually had a cancellation today. Can you make that?"

"Yes. Indeed!" Pat had never been so excited on the phone in his life.

The woman on the line could tell and she laughed lightly. "Well, okay. I have you down as Patrick Sherwood for 2 pm."

"That isn't a good idea." Justice chimed in as Pat ended the call.

Pat's heart skipped a beat even though on the outside he was still composed. He looked beside him and Justice sat in the passenger's seat. Her beautiful red hair cascaded over her shoulder, the tips touching the middle console of the car. Her eyes were bright and sharp as she examined him.

"I need to be sane. I need to be able to see you for real. This is not the real you." Pat stammered.

"It is the real me." She said.

"You say that every time." He closed his eyes and laid his head on the driver's side window. "I'm trying to understand. I want to believe."

"I know, love." Justice's voice was caring and genuine.

Pat could feel the familiar longing in his heart for things to be back to normal. "Is my Dad with you? Wherever you are?"

"I don't know." Justice said sadly.

"Is there an afterlife like the Christians say?"

"I'm not dead, Patty. I'm right here." There was an edge to her voice that hadn't been there before.

He didn't say anything as he buckled his seatbelt but internally he wasn't convinced this woman beside him was his actual wife. He knew it would be no use arguing with her though. It was basically arguing with his messed-up mind.

Despite Justice's warnings and complaints, he drove to the doctor's office. This was going to be the first step to getting things taken care of. He just needed to be able to think rationally again. He knew he would never be able to fully enjoy Justice's presence because he knew she wasn't real.

When he parked the car outside Winston Wellness, Justice was gone. A tear escaped from his eye and raced down the side of his face. He hoped Justice would understand someday, but today it hurt him knowing she was upset even if she was a figment of his imagination. He wiped his face and roughly opened the car door. Ahead of him were glass doors leading into the place.

"Mask, sir." Said the receptionist at the front desk. Pat realized he had forgotten to put his mask on so he quickly obliged. He imagined the woman must be smiling because her voice sounded warm and kind. "Can I help you?"

"Yes. I'm Patrick Sherwood."

"Yes! I just spoke with you." She began to type and her eyes quickly scanned the screen through thick-rimmed glasses.

"Could I see your ID and insurance?"

As she plugged in all the necessary information, she asked him to be seated. Once his ID and insurance card were returned, it was only a few minutes later that the nurse came and retrieved him.

His shoulders rounded slightly as he walked through the doorway and he barely listened as the nurse asked him how he was doing and explained what would be happening next. She did all of this while getting his weight, checking his vitals, and asking for a basic rundown of what was going on.

"My microchip has been knocked out of alignment." Pat said simply. "I have schizophrenia." He preferred to refer to his condition as separate from him. He never referred to himself as a schizophrenic. Pat was so much more than his illness.

"Okay! The doctor will be in with you soon." Pat figured that this woman was also smiling. Everybody in this office seemed very friendly.

There was something that felt very juvenile about sitting on the parchment paper-covered exam table, so Pat chose to sit in the uncomfortable pink plastic chair instead. Three narrow windows were on the opposite wall right next to each other. Nobody would be able to escape out the windows in the event of a fire, but they let in some natural light without totally exposing the patients. The walls were light blue and blinking devices were scattered around the space. Some looked like security devices and others medical. Even though Pat worked in technology, he was not very familiar with these devices.

As he let his mind drift, he realized that he was drifting too far. It started as a roaring in his ears and then his vision began swimming. He touched his eyes but they were dry. He closed them and rubbed vigorously which did nothing but make them ache.

"Patty, sweetie. Come for me, please." Justice returned and she was far different than he had ever imagined.

A long black dress hugged her willowy frame and tattered black lace hung from her bell sleeves and melded into a train of the same material. Her red hair hung heavy under a black thorny crown and dark circles bloomed under her eyes. The LED lighting seemed to flicker and dim upon her arrival.

He had never seen her in this way and that was the moment he knew something was breaking inside him. He could feel half of his mind cracking and slipping into an abyss. Screams enveloped him but he quickly realized they were his own screams. Dark wisps of fog oozed from the corners of the room and windows. The taste of blood was on his tongue and his chest burned with fear.

"Mr. Sherwood!" The words seemed to fall from Justice's lips, but a part of him knew that it couldn't be. "Patty!" She crouched gracefully beside his writhing form on the floor and pulled him into her arms.

Her body was cold like peppermint oil. Everywhere her skin touched his the cold spread and would not wash away, but he clung to her anyway. Darkness fell at his feet and wrapped around his ankles. It seeped through every opening in his clothes and began constricting each breath he took.

"I can't. I can't. I can't." He sobbed hysterically and began to hyperventilate. When he felt like his body couldn't take it anymore, Justice let go of him and he continued to fall into the everlasting darkness below.

CHAPTER 13

In all of the days of her life, Harmony had never felt insane. Even in the depths of her anxiety and depression she still felt wholly in control of her actions. That grip on reality changed when she lost Haven. In her panic, she had knocked on a few doors in her neighborhood, but nobody had any idea of what she was talking about. When one of the neighbors offered to call the police, Harmony waved this idea away and muttered something about handling it herself. She didn't want the police to think she was crazy.

At work the next day Harmony spent every free moment checking the news. She was beginning to feel like an accomplice to murder and kidnapping despite being innocent of either action. Her anxiety was barely staying in check and her productivity times were dipping. Ten minutes before clocking out, she began to feel the fear crawling up her throat and, when she swallowed, her throat was completely dry. Each breath was intentional. Each minute was focused on keeping herself from dissolving into panic.

When she was free from her workplace prison, she collapsed into her car with a big sigh of relief. She had already decided to make a trip to the gas station to pick up a movie and a snack that wasn't good for her. For some reason, the gas station near her house had a collection of old DVDs so it was entertaining to find the craziest looking one. This was something she used to do all the time when her anxiety got severe. It comforted her like nothing else and would get her through until the following morning when she could see her therapist.

It was already twilight when she entered the gas station. A middle-aged, white male with a beer belly watched movies behind a counter framed by lottery tickets, expired candy, and condoms. She barely made eye contact with the man as she went to look for a tasty snack.

As she looked, she noticed a tattooed man in the corner of the convenience store eying the beer as if he couldn't make up his mind about what he wanted. She tried to be as discreet as possible but her fingertips brushed his leg as she tried to go past him. He whipped around. His eyes were bloodshot from drinking and she noticed that one of his feet was wrapped up in a bandage. He didn't look angry but she knew she had startled him.

"Sorry." Harmony said quickly and began to retreat.

"Is 'kay." He slurred. "Whater you doin'?"

She looked him straight in the face. She wasn't scared of this man. He was simply drunk and asking nosy questions.

"I'm hungry." Harmony offered up a slight smile like she was humoring a small child.

"I 'ave food on my boat. And drinks." He hiccuped and opened a refrigerator to grab a six-pack of beer. "I will 'ave drinks." He corrected himself.

"Thank you, but no. My husband is waiting for me." Harmony lied. She was used to this routine. Romilda had taught her the technique for discouraging men you weren't interested in.

Before he could respond, a low growling started from the hallway where the restrooms were. Her paranoia came back with a jolt and she froze. The drunk man even stopped speaking to listen. It was a growling that tickled the ears as the sound rolled across the floor.

The gas station employee was still watching TV and hadn't noticed the change.

The tattooed stranger was alert enough to step in front of Harmony without question and pull a gun from his belt. Black smoky tendrils began to slither across the turquoise tile as a rattling began. The freezers sprung open of their own accord and products from the shelves began jangling.

Replacing the strong fear in her soul was a sudden, bloodthirsty desire to rip the gun from the man's hand and watch his brains splatter onto the freezer doors. This intrusive thought seemed perfectly natural and welled up until she felt almost powerless to resist. Indistinguishable whispers filled the air and she slid to the floor covering her ears with her palms.

Despite the man being drunk, his hands appeared steady on the gun while his legs swayed slightly. Just then out of the strange fog came a horrifying creature. It had the body of a human woman with trailing blue filmy fabric. Her neck was long and stately underneath a disturbing face. The eyes flitted back and forth as if trying to read something under threat of death. Her mouth was replaced by a blank space of paper-white skin and sharp breaths were being drawn into her nostrils. The ears were the most horrific because out of both bleeding eardrums, two stakes protruded out. Her beautifully styled blond hair that fell around the nightmarish sight was almost comical if it hadn't been so terrifying.

She walked slowly, but not inhibited like a zombie. She seemed almost unaffected by the torture she was going through. Her arms then reached out as if to embrace the tattooed man but without deliberation, he fired three times into the girl's chest. She fell to her knees and her eyelids slowly closed as if what little life she had left had drained out of her. The growling sound continued, but before Harmony could deliberate any further on it the man grabbed her hand and they began racing from the gas station. As they flew out the front door, they briefly saw the gas station employee calling 911 and trying to flag them down. They had no intention of stopping, however. They both seemed to be channeling the same idea and that was to run.

When they neared her car she shouted, "Get in!" and pointed to the passenger door.

The tattooed stranger was not very fast with his injured foot, but his drunken state must have dulled the pain enough to where he was moving better than she expected. He managed to fling open the door and fall inside as she started the engine. Before he had time to buckle, she was pealing out of the parking lot.

"Go to the marina." He commanded. "My houseboat is there."

Harmony nodded, ignoring the voice of reason in her head and feeling the adrenaline pumping through her veins. She would decide where to go after they were as far away from that thing as possible. She made a sharp right when she saw the sign for the docks and the tattooed stranger's body fell hard on her. She caught a whiff of booze and musky cologne. Her heart flipped inside her chest but quickly calmed down when the man cursed under his breath and muttered something about female drivers.

When she was in a parking spot, she leaned back into her seat and took a few calming breaths.

"It felt...evil." The man said. "That woman."

"Yes." Harmony agreed. She paused then admitted, "When she appeared, I felt like the worst version of myself. Like I was going to do something terrible."

The man's eyes widened and he nodded. "Same."

"I'm Harmony."

"Arrow." It was silent between them then he said, "I thought I was seein' things." He gestured vaguely out the window and waved a hand over himself to imply he wasn't sure he could be trusted on his eyewitness account.

When the man let his hand drop into his lap, she took a good look at him for the first time. He didn't look old but simply worn out. His skin was dark from sun exposure. Tattoos covered his collarbone, disappeared into his stained white t-shirt, and curled down both arms in intricate sleeves. His hair fell below his earlobes and in a dark greasy mess. Lastly, gray stubble spread over the lower half of his face at the start of a beard. His eyes were denim blue but the whites were streaked with red. She expected to see a beer belly, but his torso was very trim and she could see a slight bulge under his sleeves where his toned arms hid.

"Me too…" Harmony knew this man was drunk and that he might not be very reliable, but the way he had shot that woman three times convinced her that he wasn't completely delirious. His aim had been true. "That's not the first time that kind of thing has happened to me." Harmony said, making a gamble that this stranger wouldn't think she was crazy.

It was hard to tell behind the watery eyes, but it appeared as though he was thinking seriously about what she had said. Before he could answer though, a rapping sounded at the passenger window and the fuzzy outline of a man could be seen.

Arrow buzzed down the window and barked, "Whaddayawant?"

"We have to go." The other man said tersely. "You can pick up women another time."

Everything about this man was perfect. His hair was dirty blond and perfectly styled. His eyes were deep-set and milk chocolate brown. His firm jawline was covered in stubble. His body looked like he made a concerted effort to work out. Nothing was out of place on him and she found herself staring a little too long. Arrow didn't notice. He was too busy glaring daggers at the man.

"I need a beer."

"I thought that's what you were getting!" The man said exasperated. "We can't stay in one place too long and we can't draw attention to ourselves."

"About that…" Arrow began. He then explained what had happened at the gas station.

When Arrow finished, his friend looked like he was about to pull his hair out. "Okay, I'm sorry for assuming you were looking for a hookup but, whether we like it or not, things have become much more complicated."

"I accept your apology." Harmony said sourly. "If it wasn't for me, your friend would've been walking back here." Harmony knew this man's perfection was too good to be true. He was obviously a pompous jerk.

Arrow gave her an appreciative smile then said, "Yeah, Doc, I would've been up a creek without a paddle."

"Get out here." The man Arrow called "Doc" grumbled.

Arrow rolled his eyes but obediently began shuffling around to leave. "Are you comin'? My invite still stands."

Harmony hadn't intended to take Arrow up on his offer in the first place. She figured that once she had dropped him off she would head home and go to bed. She still had her appointment the next day and a full day of office work before the weekend. There were so many questions about what was happening to her that she had hoped to answer.

On the other hand, the rush she had felt when running from the strange female apparition was unlike anything she had experienced before. It left no room inside her mind for worry or despair. She had also found another person who believed her. Maybe they could find the answers to her problems together. The secret part of her that craved adventure and excitement gnawed at her. While her work colleagues were creating their own drama and experimenting with drugs to create meaning in their lives, she would actually be doing something spontaneous. She also wasn't truly leaving anything behind. Rufus was gone, her mother and she weren't close, and her job was awful. This felt like her moment to take a risk.

"Yeah, sure." She said smiling.

A noise of complaint came from Doc, but Arrow seemed pleased by her response. The pair of them exited the car and Harmony made sure to grab her phone, keys, and wallet. She locked the car and followed the two men down to a small houseboat. When they were inside, she shut the door behind herself. Arrow slid unceremoniously into a recliner and let out a low whistle.

Doc didn't seem interested in relaxing because he continued to study Harmony.

"So, your name is Doc?" She ventured.

"To you."

"Aw, c'mon, Doc. Tell the girl who you are. She ain't goin' to the police."

Arrow had her pegged. She didn't plan on calling the police for anything at this point.

"I am Dr. Clive Evers."

"Harmony Latham. I think we met before but you were wearing a mask." Dr. Evers looked confused until she pointed to the scar on her forearm and his eyes lit up. "You did well."

"I am ashamed to say that I don't remember your specific surgery but I am glad that it was successful. I have been doing so many lately." He flashed a crooked smile that was whiter than his shirt. Clive glanced at Arrow who was nodding off in his recliner. A flash of revulsion crossed Clive's features, twisting them into an unpleasant mask which was quickly replaced by a practiced smile. "I guess I'll shove off."

Clive turned on his heel and went back out on deck. For an awkward few moments, she stood in the cabin alone with a man she had just met who was snoring as another man she just met pulled up the anchor. When the clock hanging above the window had ticked off 3 minutes, she approached the fuzzy brown couch, lowered herself down onto it, and shoved her hands under her thighs for added security.

This was the most interesting her life had been lately. She wasn't sure how much more of it she could handle. Her anxiety was still somewhat distant but she could feel it creeping at the edges of her awareness. It just wanted her to know it was there and ready to overtake her.

With a gentle scraping sound and the slapping of water against the hull, the boat began to move away from the shore. She could hear the "thunk" of Clive jumping back on board presumably after pushing the boat. These sounds triggered her fear and she had to bite her tongue to keep from breathing too fast and too heavy.

"What am I doing?" She muttered. Regrets were building but it was too late now.

"I'll be up top driving if you need anything." Clive said poking his head in through the door again.

"O-okay." Harmony said shyly.

He smiled again and shut the door. She heard his fading footsteps and the sound of the motor start shortly after. They weren't going fast but she could feel that they picked up speed. She turned around on the couch and peeked out between the blinds. She couldn't see much besides the moon casting silver light on the tips of the fir trees and peaks of the small waves of the water.

"You're going to be okay." She whispered to herself.

With a sigh, she stood and walked over to a door that led to a small bedroom. She went inside and locked the door behind her. As she cautiously laid back across the bed, the weight of what was happening fell on her. She pulled her phone from her pocket and wasn't surprised to see no notifications. While she was tempted to check all her social media accounts, she knew that would only increase her anxiety. Doubling down on her decision, she powered down her phone and pocketed it.

She was breathing in the damp and salty surroundings while

letting Arrow's snores from the other room lull her into a half-dreaming, half-waking state. The place in her mind drifted to Haven and the dead child in her yard. The strange woman with the dreadlocks. The woman in the gas station. Why were these apparitions following her? She had never believed in ghosts, but all these experiences were beginning to make her feel like she would need to believe in them soon or they would do something much worse. The last face she saw before drifting into a deep sleep was Lyric mocking her.

CHAPTER 14

PAT'S SENSE OF SECURITY HAD LEFT him. Everything he knew and everything that gave him comfort was gone and his paranoia was going into overdrive. The darkness he had been sucked into had taken him completely, so when he woke up in a white room it was an unsettling contrast. His body felt heavy as if he had been sleeping for weeks. He could hear the humming of machinery punctuated by occasional beeping. The ceiling that he looked up at was domed and came to a point in the middle where the housing for a security camera resided.

As he tried to move so he could see more, he realized he was strapped down on the uncomfortable bed. He moved his head barely an inch and could feel throbbing at the back of his skull. He had only ever had that kind of pain on his head when he had had the chip installed the first time. The first time he wasn't strapped down, though.

"Are you awake?" Said a soft feminine voice.

"Yes." His voice cracked as he forced the single word out of his mouth.

"I can't move either." She said simply.

"Why are we strapped down?"

"They don't want us getting away."

The statement caused Pat's heart to twinge. "What did they do to us?"

"I'm assuming we both had the microchip surgery." She said an edge of bitterness to her tone.

"Are we still at Winston Wellness?"

There was silence. He could hear the sound of the woman trying to move around but she did not answer right away. Then she said, "I don't know where I am."

Just then a door clicked and swung open into the room. Pat strained against his restraints to try to see anything that would give him an idea of where he was, but the straps were too tight. Because of this, his ears perked up to try to catch every sound. Footsteps. The clink of metal against metal. Beeping.

Just then a young woman in a white coat and white mask came into view. She jiggled his restraints to make sure they were still fastened. She then slipped a cold hand under his head to feel the place where his head throbbed. He winced and her beautiful blue eyes crinkled in sympathy.

"Sorry."

"Where am I?"

"In the recovery room. You have to stay absolutely still." She warned in low tones. She quickly moved to the woman next to him.

Before Pat was able to ask more questions, the clicks of the door opening and closing could be heard again.

"She refuses to explain. She just comes in to make sure our vitals are good." The female patient said.

"This doesn't feel right. I just came in to have my chip reinstalled." Pat said.

"I never even had a chip." The woman said mournfully. "I never felt like I needed one."

"That's nice." Pat said. "To not need one, I mean." He clarified.

He wanted a moment to think. As much as he appreciated the company, he desperately wanted to be free. Being stuck in an unfamiliar place was starting to wear down his nerves. The chip managed a lot of things, but whenever there was an unfamiliar situation that brought about new challenges, it needed to be recalibrated by a therapist. If he allowed himself to be overcome by this new situation, he was unsure how he would manage his feelings.

"What is your name?" The woman asked suddenly.

"Pat."

"I love that. Short for Patrick? That's a good Catholic name."

"What is your name?" Pat asked.

"Mayre."

"That is beautiful." Normally Pat didn't compliment people, but he already liked this woman even though he couldn't see her. She seemed genuinely caring. Like what he imagined an older sister would be like.

"Thanks." Her voice strained with emotion.

Suddenly the door swung wide and several voices were talking over one another and the room felt as if it was shrinking as the space filled. Pat could hear the sound of several carts being wheeled into the room and something much larger being pushed across the floor. Pat still couldn't see anything but shadows bouncing across the ceiling. He also couldn't understand the voices in the background due to the echoing of the room.

"Let me out of here!" Mayre shouted suddenly, cutting through the din.

Some of the voices quieted and one woman close to Pat's right shoulder said, "We can't do that just yet. Please stay still or we will have to put you to sleep."

Pat hadn't realized that Mayre was trying to escape her restraints until she stopped moving. The shuffling had all blended in with the other noises. More machine noise, more beeping, more metal clinks against other metal.

"Can I speak to the surgeon?" Pat asked the woman.

"He's unavailable at the moment." She said abruptly.

"When will he be available?"

"I'm uncertain."

"Tell him he has a terrible bedside manner. I didn't even know I was having surgery today."

The silence that followed was so thick. In a moment, the woman he had been speaking to leaned her head into his line of sight and shook her head from side to side almost imperceptibly.

"It's so funny what medicine can do to the memory sometimes." The woman laughed lightly but continued to glare at Pat. "The doctor will debrief you on everything once he is available." She then walked over to Mayre.

Pat kept quiet. The fear in the woman's eyes was enough of a warning. Even though he could not see her mouth under the mask, he knew she was no longer smiling.

Suddenly, the door burst open again but this time the response from the staff was shock.

"You're not allowed in here!"

"How did you gain access…?"

"Put your weapons down!"

The nurse who had spoken to Pat used her body as a human shield over his head. Pat could smell a distinct floral scent along with rubbing alcohol. Her warmth reassured him even though he barely knew her.

"We don't want to hurt anybody." Said a muffled voice. "We are here for your patients."

"We can't do that. They are under our care." The nurse said. Pat was certain he was the only one who could hear the quaver in her voice.

"You can continue caring for them if you come with us." The

stranger said.

"How do I know you won't kill us if we go with you?" The nurse demanded.

"I guarantee that going with us is more safe than staying here. Your life is on the line every day you clock in at this place."

"Our boss will kill us if we leave with you."

"No harm will come to you. Where we are going is safe. However, if you try to stop us from taking these patients, we will have to fight you."

Pat held his breath hoping that the nurse would comply. Pat was a skeptical person by nature but he trusted the armed stranger. Nothing they had said caused him any doubt that they would do what they said.

"Ameena, wheel her out." Commanded the nurse, easing up on her human shield over Pat.

"Sirona…" The other nurse began to argue.

"I am your superior. Listen to me now."

"With all due respect, I don't think this is a good idea." Ameena said quietly, but Pat could hear her shuffling to do as she was told.

"Can we be released?" Pat asked.

Sirona undid his straps quickly with shaky fingers. She helped him stand and he assessed the situation. Mayre was still strapped down but he could see why. Her entire torso was wrapped in a hard cast. Whatever had happened with her must've been severe. A small, timid nurse stood behind Mayre ready to wheel her out. Three individuals in dark, nondescript clothes stood in a V shape, each holding large guns across their torsos.

Two of the strangers went out first followed by Sirona, Pat, Mayre, Ameena, and the stranger who appeared to be in charge brought up the rear. Silent alarms flashed in the hallway casting flashing white light across the gray walls. Pat's legs were already tired at the swift pace down the halls. Despite their speed, hardly any noise disrupted the eerie quiet. Occasionally a wheel on the hospital bed creaked or someone panted as they tried to catch their breath.

After 5 minutes of a straight stretch, they reached a set of double doors. One of the two strangers in the front of the group pulled a white card from a hidden pocket and swiped it along the wall which gained them access through the doors.

"I can't do it." Ameena said suddenly. She was standing a few feet from the rest of the group frozen in place by her fear. Her eyes were wide and her hands were visibly shaking.

"You're going to have to do it. We have moments before they will be able to track us down." Said the armed stranger who had opened the doors.

"Sirona…I can't." She pleaded with her superior, completely ignoring the warnings.

Sirona approached her coworker and said earnestly, "It's okay. We'll figure this out. We have to go."

"I can't risk it. My son. He needs me. I don't want to be a vegetable. I-I-I…" She broke down into hysterical sobbing

"Breathe…it's okay. We will take you to our safe house. We can retrieve your son later." The man in charge said rapidly. "We. Must. Go. Now."

Pat's ears perked up and he could hear the sound of hurried footsteps making the way down the hall. They sounded heavy. They sounded numerous. They sounded unfriendly. Those assertions were confirmed when several armed guards with hospital ID badges came into view a few moments later.

"GO!" All the mysterious rescuers were shouting now and everybody obeyed.

Ameena was still sobbing but she pushed the bed as fast as she could. The locked doors did not slow the guards down so they were quickly gaining on the group. As they rounded a corner, Pat could see automatic double doors ahead and wondered if it was where they were headed.

It seemed as though they were going to cross the threshold and escape, but then Ameena began to crumble. She had glimpsed the officers behind her and froze like a rabbit. Before the head of the rescue team or Sirona had time to react, the guards were upon them. The two strangers leading the pack, Sirona, and Pat were already through one set of double doors and about to exit the final set of doors leading outside to a waiting car. They saw the man in charge of the group fighting valiantly to escape and Ameena and Mayre were easily subdued. The two armed strangers did not allow Sirona or Pat one moment to hesitate. They grasped their upper arms and dragged them out into the sun and then into a black car with tinted windows.

The taller of the two started the engine quickly and went careening out of the parking lot. Out of habit, Pat began buckling his seatbelt while Sirona sat in stunned silence.

***

The entire ride to the safe house was silent. Neither man explained what was going on. They also refused to turn on the radio. When they arrived at their destination, Pat had even more questions than before.

The place was secured by an iron fence that surrounded the property. The only opening was a gate at the very front that was opened by a code. As the gates opened, the first sight was a beautiful fountain splashing amidst drooping flowers. While trees were dotting the property, they weren't oppressive. There was a sense that you were in a wide open space upon entering. The main building was a three-story Victorian home as wide as it was tall. Multiple windows broke up the vast lines of brick. On either side of the place were other smaller buildings that mirrored the design of the main house except in miniature. A few young men milled around the property maintaining the landscaping, reading, and playing sports.

Pat imagined that this place would be much more brilliant in the spring and summer months when the trees were in bloom and the gardens spilled over with fresh fruit and vegetables. Today there was a chill in the air and the flowers seemed to be on the last leg of their annual journey.

Pat glanced over at Sirona and could see that she was still stricken with shock. She wasn't examining her surroundings or marveling like Pat. Instead, she was obviously processing something, and Pat assumed it must be guilt. The only movement that indicated she was alive was her hands grasped tightly in her lap and her right thumb running over the side of her left hand.

As the car pulled around the fountain to the front entrance, Pat could see two people step out of the double doors of the home. It was apparent that they were a couple and genuinely pleased to see the car. The man was shorter than average with caramel hair and gentle eyes. His wife grasped his elbow and was a few inches shorter. She had straight, long white-blond hair down to her waist and a beautiful porcelain face.

When the vehicle came to a complete stop, Pat and Sirona reluctantly exited. The rescuers made no move to follow but instead drove the car away to park.

The man quickly moved forward with his hand outstretched, "I am Zion Jones. This is Rachel, my wife." She tilted her head to the side to acknowledge the introduction.

"Y'all must be tired. Food first, then we will explain everything." Rachel said. Her voice was as smooth as a Prius and almost as quiet.

"Physical needs are always met and then we get into the nitty-gritty." Zion agreed and began walking inside.

Pat was first to follow and Sirona brought up the rear. Rachel noticed this right away and slowed down to walk beside the grieving nurse. They began speaking in low tones and Pat could tell that Rachel was offering comfort. Simply the way she spoke was comforting.

Listening closely to the women, Pat hadn't noticed Zion slowing down to come beside him. They walked beside each other through the spacious hallways until Zion finally asked, "You're Patrick Sherwood, correct?"

Pat was taken aback. He knew he was well-known thanks to his father, but it still always surprised him when somebody knew his name. "Yes, I am."

"It is an honor to have you in our home." Zion said.

Pat was used to things like this being said to make him feel better, but when he looked over at Zion's crinkled light blue eyes, he knew the sentiment was real. Zion was opposite from his father which is why Pat felt much more at ease.

"I appreciate you freeing me from that place, but I will not trespass on your hospitality for long. I have to go home." Pat said insisted.

"That may be harder than you think." Zion said solemnly and they turned the corner into a vast dining room. The table looked like three picnic tables lined up in a row. A handful of people ate at the table and an arched double doorway led into a commercial-grade kitchen. Rachel led Sirona to the kitchen and began showing her around.

"Is that a threat?" Pat demanded of Zion.

"No it isn't, but the circumstances aren't ideal for you to leave. Once we get some food in you, I'll explain the situation we have on our hands."

Pat gritted his teeth and followed Zion into the kitchen to select items from the buffet. Before he had time to complain, a man about the same height as Zion approached with a wide toothless grin.

"Howdy, stranger!" He pulled Pat into an unwilling hug and

aggressively slapped his back. "Welcome to New Creation Rehab. I'm Serrill."

When Serrill let go of him, it was obvious to Pat that this man had prematurely aged from whatever his addictive substance of choice had been. His eyes were sober and bright, but the rest of his face was wrinkled and dry. His clothes hung off his body like he had lost a lot of weight very quickly.

"I'm Pat." Pat said finally.

That seemed to be all Serrill cared about because he said, "Pat, so glad to have you! Hey, Terrence!" And he was off hugging somebody else.

"Serrill has been with us for a while. I think he just likes it here. He could've left months ago." Zion whispered. "Anyway, let's get something to eat."

There was pot roast, mashed potatoes, country-style green beans, yeast rolls, fruit salad, pigs in a blanket, corn on the cob, brownies, and cherry tarts littering the buffet. Pat wasn't obsessive about food so this did not mystify him, but Sirona seemed stunned. They both tentatively placed food on their plates and looked at each other as if doubting it was safe to indulge.

Pat picked out a few rolls and some pot roast, then began to head for the dining room. Zion silently waved him through a doorway directly off the dining room which led into a den. Once all four of them were present, they sat and Zion prayed a blessing over the food. Pat didn't believe in God but he bowed his head respectfully.

When Zion finished his prayer, he looked at Pat and Sirona solemnly. "Today was a bittersweet day. I was informed we didn't rescue everybody."

"Mayre was left behind." Pat said simply.

"Yes." Zion's hands were still folded in prayer and he pressed them to his lips thoughtfully.

"There is something sinister occurring with people who have the microchip." Rachel said, looking at Sirona.

"What do you mean?" Sirona asked with some defensiveness in her tone.

Zion responded, taking extra care to be kind. "Winston Wellness, along with some other medical facilities, have been using the microchip technology to conduct unlawful experimentation on patients."

"We were just studying patients who had had the chip implants." Sirona said. "They all agreed to the testing."

"I didn't agree to any testing." Pat chimed in. "I just came in to have my Thought Conductor reinstalled."

Sirona seemed shocked at this pronouncement. "That's not possible."

"Unfortunately, this has been happening. Some patients aren't informed about what they are volunteering for and others are debriefed on the risks but end up getting more than they bargained for." Zion said. "We have been sending in evacuation teams to get patients out." Zion then noticed Pat and Sirona still weren't eating. "Dig in! Please."

"How do we know you are who you say you are?" Pat demanded. He looked at Sirona and could see that she was wondering the same thing. "What is this place?" Pat asked, referring to their current location.

"Feel free to talk to anybody here. They will affirm what I'm telling you. This is a halfway house. People that served prison time for addiction or dealing have the option of coming here to be rehabilitated." Zion smiled mischievously for the first time. "What most people here won't tell you is that is a front for what we really do."

"People that don't have anywhere to go are given a purpose here. God has certainly given us a much heavier calling than we ever expected." Rachel smiled wistfully.

"How do you know that microchip patients are being mistreated?" Pat was beginning to realize he knew much less than he thought he did about his own product.

"I once had a chip." Zion said. "I suffered from night terrors which were unbearable. My doctor recommended I use the chip. I prayed heavily for wisdom and ended up feeling led to having the surgery."

Pat scoffed inwardly.

"It took a long time for us to figure it out." Rachel said. "But his dreams were becoming real."

"My night terrors weren't being resolved. They were simply being put somewhere else. I began to see them in the real world." Zion shot a meaningful look towards Rachel and she bit her lip.

"I don't understand." Sirona admitted. Pat was glad she admitted it because he was not willing to look foolish in front of strangers.

"My worst fears were being played out in the real world as if they were really happening."

Pat thought on that for a moment. When he was suffering from the worst hallucinations he had ever had, it was unbearable. But if he suddenly found out that everything he had been seeing was real, he wouldn't know what to do.

"Was this just your experience?" Pat asked.

"Not from what we can tell. People have been experiencing things like this all over but have been afraid to speak about it." Zion then looked directly at Pat. "I was hoping you might help us figure out what's going on since it's your Father's technology. As long as you don't mind of course."

Pat wasn't sure how he felt about the offer. All of this new information was whirring in his mind but he wasn't certain how much of it he believed. When Justice had been taken from him, he clung to her memories like a security blanket. Nothing of her memory was ever deleted and yet he continued to see her hallucination. He doubted this was a side effect of his microchip and thought it was simply a side effect of his schizophrenia. What if Zion and all the others were just hallucinating as well?

It suddenly occurred to him that since leaving Winston Wellness, he was no longer seeing Justice or having intense screaming. His brain was mostly quiet. Whatever the surgeon did at Winston Wellness must have fixed the problems he was having, which made him much more confident in his decision-making abilities.

To make sure he could trust Zion and Rachel, he took a chance on the food and took a bite of roll. When nothing happened he said, "I think that is a wise idea." Even though Zion seemed like a religious nut, he was also highly informed. Pat knew it would be advantageous for him to learn as much as he could about their operation and potentially improve the technology for everybody. Also, if people were being used for unlawful experiments, he couldn't let that stand. Especially if they were conducting unlawful experiments on Mayre.

"What can I do?" Sirona said suddenly, her eyes bright with the moisture from the few tears slipping from her eyes. Pat suddenly realized that she had removed her facemask. She had a very pointed chin and her mouth was wide and thin. She was surprisingly elegant looking.

"I think the best course of action is for you to help us evacuate the rest of your colleagues and Mayre out of that hospital." Zion said. "But we need more intel before we go barging in. There were far more complexities to the hospital than we first planned on so we will need more detail. We aren't professionals but the professionals aren't doing anything about it. We already tried to involve the police and hospital management but they won't listen to anything we have to say."

"Security has probably increased since we escaped." Sirona said miserably.

"Don't lose heart." Rachel said, resting a comforting hand on her arm and looking into her face lovingly. "The Lord is guiding our path."

Pat doubted her words but appreciated her confidence. It took much more confidence than Pat had to believe in an old man in the sky to get them out of danger. Any time he had even attempted to pray, he had been met with silence.

"I can't wait to pick your brain." Zion said to Pat suddenly. "You must have a lot of useful information about what is going on."

"Of a kind. You do not want to pick my brain though." Pat ran his spider-like fingers through his hair and raised his eyebrows.

Zion said nothing but looked at Pat with soft, kind eyes. Pat wasn't comfortable with this look because it was a cross between pity and understanding. Pat didn't want anybody to try to understand him.

"Well, let me take you to your room." Zion said finally, standing and smiling broadly. "Rachel, would you show Sirona to her room?"

Rachel nodded and gestured to the nurse. The two women left and Zion then led Pat back into the dining room and out into the hallway again. They walked up to the very top of the home and down to the very end of the hall where a 6-foot-tall window looked out onto the brown gardens getting ready to settle into a winter slumber. Zion then took an immediate left and they were in a small alcove. This space had a small table topped by a vase spilling over with fake flowers and a maroon door with a gold handle on the far wall.

Zion pulled a ring of keys from his pocket and selected one towards the middle and opened the door. Inside the walls were a cream color with white trim. Two twin beds sat to the left side of the room and a doorway to a bathroom was in the gap between the beds. There was a window straight ahead and a window to the right which let in tons of natural light. Finally, the floors were dark-stained wood that looked cold to the touch. Not much decor was in the room, but it was cozy.

"It's just you in here currently, but if we start to fill up extensively we may need to pair you with a roommate. I hope that is okay?" Zion glanced over at Pat to gauge his reaction, but his expression was passive.

He did not like the idea of having a roommate but he was here at Zion's home and didn't think it would be polite to protest.

"It will be fine." Pat said simply.

"Okay." Zion clapped his hands together and began explaining schedules and hospitality bags. "Meals are always at the same time every day. Breakfast at 7 am, Lunch at 11 am, and dinner at 5 pm. Any food between meals will typically be out on the table such as fruit and granola bars." Zion walked over to a thermostat and explained that it was for this room only. "The bathroom is controlled by the main thermostat. Also, in the linen closet is a hospitality bag with basic essentials. If you need something we don't have, let Rachel know and she will get it. Any questions?"

Pat had several questions. He wanted to know what was next. He wanted to know more about what they did here. He wanted to know how he went from being at the doctor to being strapped to an operating table. He was curious about where Justice had gone. He wanted to know more about Mayre and hoped she was doing okay. These were all things that he didn't know how to articulate and was scared he'd find out too soon. Zion knew a lot more than Pat expected, but he wasn't going to be able to answer all of Pat's burning questions.

Pat shook his head and said, "Thank you for everything. How much do I owe you?" The phrase came easily and was something he had always heard his dad say. The Sherwood men never liked to owe people anything so they paid all their debts immediately. Money was no object.

"You do not need to pay me. We give all we have here out of our abundance and all we ask is that you help us with things around the house." Zion smiled again. "You'll be helping me get to the root of this mystery and that is payment enough."

"Of course." Pat conceded.

"Good deal. I'll leave you to it. Let me know if you need anything." Zion then left Pat alone with his thoughts.

CHAPTER 15

Harmony and Clive walked off the houseboat as Arrow tied it to the dock and lowered the anchor. A large green sign sat propped up by the steps leading from the dock to the shore which said, "Welcome to Quincy!" and a picture of a guitar surrounded by wavy musical notes.

"It's not too far from here." Arrow said knowingly. "We'll take a bus."

"A BUS??" Clive exclaimed, his voice raising a few octaves. "Isn't that too exposed?" After a wearying journey with just the three of them, Clive was losing a bit of his charisma. Lines stood out on his forehead and dark circles framed his eyes. His hair was also losing some of its luster.

Arrow stared at Clive for a long, penetrating moment. His sober gaze was much more intimidating and Clive almost missed drunk Arrow. "Trust me. We will be the least noticeable bunch at this particular stop." He then glanced over at Harmony and smirked slightly. She returned the amusement by smiling back.

"What?" Clive demanded. "Are you laughing at me?"

"You're in rare form, mate." Arrow said in a fake Australian accent and popped him on the shoulder. "It'll be okay."

Arrow then began trudging across the deck to the gravel parking lot. Clive was not far behind demanding Arrow define what he meant by his statements. Harmony trailed behind the men. It was a chilly day with a slight breeze that was telling secrets to the pines. In a gap was a road only just large enough to let a single car pass comfortably. They walked alongside it and up the hill to a bus stop encased in glass. The only occupant of this stop was an older woman in black leggings, a large orange sweater, and a baseball cap. She didn't look up as they approached but continued gazing into her phone.

"How far is the place from here?" Harmony asked.

"Shh…" Clive hissed.

She stared at him in shock and then looked back at Arrow.

"Simmer down." Arrow snapped at Clive. "About 20 minutes." He said in response to Harmony's question.

"This isn't safe. I could be on every news outlet. I'm going to get reported." Clive whispered.

"Or maybe not. Don't get a big head now." Arrow snorted.

Just then, a gray bus came trundling around the corner and down the quiet street. The old woman stood and walked near the curb. She was the first to climb up the bus steps. She waved her phone screen across the doors and they opened for her. Arrow pulled out his phone and started it up. Pulling up the app for the bus station he was able to purchase three passes for each of them.

"How did you already have the app?" Clive asked as they boarded the bus and took a few seats towards the middle.

Arrow waved the question away with his hand as he sat beside Harmony and powered down his phone again. The trio rode in relative silence with Clive interjecting random comments occasionally to calm his nerves. The old woman had taken a seat close to the driver and at the very back of the bus was a construction worker sleeping under the shade of his hard hat. The only suspicious-looking person was a haggard, hairy man sitting directly behind them. He had nothing with him except the clothes on his back and seemed most alert to what was going on around him which made Clive nervous.

After a mostly silent 20-minute drive, the bus pulled up in front of a stop near a gated driveway. The sign beside the place read "New Creation Rehab" and it suddenly clicked in Clive's brain. This is where Arrow had been after being in prison. Clive looked over at Harmony, but her face was twisted up in confusion.

Arrow led the way off the bus and they approached a speaker. Arrow pressed the button, said his name and the gates opened. They walked inside and before them was a beautiful enclosed property with several brick buildings all surrounding a fountain and beautiful flowers reaching the end of their season. People milled around the property working, playing, and reading. It had the feel of a private university by how long the walk was from the gate to the front of the largest brick building. As they approached the steps to the entrance, a stocky man with caramel hair came rushing from the place and embraced Arrow warmly.

"Arrow." The man sounded like he was about to cry. "It is so good to see you again." The man held him at arm's length and the height difference was striking. Arrow towered over the man who now had tears running down his cheeks.

"It's good to see you, Zion. These are my friends." Arrow gestured over to Clive and Harmony.

"Lovely to have you." Zion said letting go of Arrow and approaching Clive first to shake hands.

"I am Dr…" Clive began then stopped. He glanced over at Arrow for reassurance to continue.

"He's good people, buddy."

"I'm Dr. Clive Evers." He said finally.

"Dr. Evers. It is a distinct honor. You have made so many great strides in science and medicine." He smiled a genuine smile that flashed in his eyes and Clive knew he was trustworthy.

Then he turned to Harmony. "And you?"

"I'm Harmony Latham." She said softly. "Not a doctor, but I'm here."

"No worries. Everybody is welcome here." Zion said warmly. "Will you need to stay here overnight or are you just planning to visit?"

Arrow looked at Harmony then at Clive. When neither of them volunteered to speak, Arrow said, "Clive is in some trouble. I told him this was a safe place. On our way here we met Harmony. We hadn't planned much further ahead than that."

"I don't need rehab." Clive said a little louder than he meant to.

"I don't either." Harmony interjected.

"Of course." Zion laughed good-naturedly. "You don't have the hallmarks of somebody struggling with addiction."

"We'll probably at least need to stay one night though." Arrow said looking at Harmony. "A storm is rolling in tonight and it might not be safe to be on the open water when that happens."

"I don't want to impose." Harmony said softly.

"It isn't an imposition. Our home is your home. Let me get you two men settled into rooms and, Harmony," Zion was able to calm anybody with that smile of his and those kind eyes. It seemed to work even on Harmony, as her discomfort gradually dissipated. "my wife Rachel will take you to the women's wing."

Harmony and Clive mirrored a skeptical expression, but they followed Zion inside anyway where the decor was warm and open. Every wall was filled with gallery walls of oil paintings and photographs. Behind these hangings was textured tan wallpaper and each room was trimmed with intricate-looking crown molding and baseboards. Everything felt truly antique.

Clive assumed Rachel was the lovely woman at the end of the

hallway because she mirrored Zion's joy and light coloring. Dr. Evers never missed a beautiful woman, so he immediately noticed her. This woman was exactly who Mayre had been when they first were married, but she had become too comfortable with mediocrity. This reminder pricked his heart. He was torn between being justified in his anger and disappointment while simultaneously missing her. He was so worried but he knew that his being in prison would be much worse for her safety.

"Rachel, this is Harmony. She will be staying with us tonight. Would you show her to a room?"

"Yes, of course." Rachel led Harmony away from the men and began to talk to her about how lovely her hair was.

"Dr. Evers."

Clive snapped to attention. "Yes?"

"I hope you don't mind, but, we have a young man staying here that could use a roommate. Would you be comfortable with that?"

"I don't think so." Dr. Evers said bluntly. "I have never had a roommate before besides…" He trailed off before saying "wife".

"Of course. I understand."

"I wouldn't mind. I've had to share rooms here before." Arrow offered.

"Thank you." Zion said clapping his hands together. "Let's go there first then we will find you somewhere to stay, Doctor."

"You can call me, Clive." Dr. Evers said with an unintentional edge to his tone. He didn't want to admit that Arrow showing him up in kindness bothered him. In this environment, he was an outsider and did not like the feeling.

Zion nodded without even seeming to pick up on the tone shift and led the men to the third floor of the house. He made an immediate left and at the very end of the hallway was a seemingly forgotten red door. As they approached to knock, it swung open and a man in his early twenties with arms and legs that seemed too long for his body walked out.

"Well, you beat us here." Arrow said wryly.

Pat looked mildly startled. His eyes went from Arrow to Zion and then Clive. The discomfort spread to his shoulders as he seemed to shrink a little.

"You all already know each other?" Zion asked excitement in his tone.

"We were going to travel together but that never happened." Clive said pointedly.

"Pat has been through a lot, Clive. You should hear his story." Zion insisted.

"We're going to be roomies." Arrow said, smacking the young man on the bony shoulder and shoving past him. As Pat, Zion, and Clive peered into the room they saw Arrow had commandeered one of the twin beds.

"That's my bed." Pat said softly.

"What?" Arrow slipped off his shoes and rubbed his dirty socks on the comforter.

"Never mind. I'm going outside for some fresh air." Pat said simply and left them.

"How did you all meet?" Zion asked, still oblivious to the tension.

"It's a long story." Clive said.

"That's a cop-out." Arrow shouted across the room. "You have time, outlaw."

"We can discuss it over dinner. I think we should all talk." Zion said cheerfully. "Let's find you a room, Clive."

They let the door shut on Arrow and proceeded down the opposite side of the building. The furthest room from Arrow is where they found themselves. The room was much smaller, but the bed was king-size and directly under a slanted part of the ceiling. The windows also were floor-to-ceiling and had heavy red velvet curtains drooping down the sides. A very small half bath sat in the far right-hand corner.

"Where do I shower?"

"You will have to visit Pat and Arrow for a shower. I am sorry about this. When we bought the property, the architect did not seem to have a mind for practicality." Zion said sadly. "Here is your key." He handed him a key and then said, "I have to tend to a few things but I will see you all at dinner."

"Thanks."

Zion left and the silence crept its way into Clive's bones. He had so many questions. It still surprised him that Pat was here and the mystery of his presence wouldn't be answered at that exact moment, so Clive had to content himself with exploring the room and relieving himself in the bathroom. When that was done, only 5 minutes had passed.

With a sigh, he plopped onto the bed and realized it was a water bed. It took him a solid minute to gain his balance, and when he had managed that he pulled his cellphone from his pocket. Fingering it he debated powering it on just to check his messages and see if Mayre had texted or called. As soon he was about to hold the home button down, a knock sounded on his door.

He stood and walked over to answer it. When he swung it open, Arrow was standing there.

"I'm going to get some beer from the store. Do you want anything?"

"This is a rehab facility." Clive said incredulously.

"Yes, Captain Obvious."

"You can't have alcohol here."

"I'm not a patient here anymore. Living my life how I want to live it is perfectly fine." Arrow said defensively. "I'm taking it that you don't want anything? Cool." He began to back away and bounced his hands up and down in the shape of finger guns.

"I don't think…"

"I don't need your negativity, Doc. See you soon." He turned on his heel and made a beeline for the stairs.

"I wasn't done talking!" Clive shouted exasperatedly. Arrow raised a hand in nonchalant disregard and continued to walk away with his head down.

Clive didn't bother going after him. He wasn't his babysitter and he was not in charge of medically caring for him. Not at this time anyway.

Before Clive moved from the hall to go back to his room, he noticed Pat was making his way into view from the staircase. He glanced at Clive with silent confusion.

"Where is Arrow going?" Pat asked.

"To the store."

"Oh." Pat responded simply. Clive noticed more strongly how gangly Pat looked and just how young he was. When they had first met in person and the times he had seen him on TV, he seemed so mature. Clive was quickly learning that was just a front.

"So, from the sound of things, Zion might have us working together."

"That is what he seems to think." Pat said.

"What happened after you left us?" Clive said, trying to look into the young man's downcast eyes.

"I have still been trying to sort it out."

Clive was hoping Pat would elaborate, but he said nothing else. "Sort…what out?"

"I don't want to have to rehash it twice. Zion wants me to cover everything tonight, so I should be ready then." Pat said.

"Oh, right." Clive nodded. "That's fine." An overly friendly smile spread across his face to mask his temporary offense. Clive was accustomed to people opening up to him, but Pat seemed to be reserved and he couldn't figure out why. "If you need somebody to talk to though, I'm right down the hall."

"I appreciate it but your room is such a long walk away from my room. Thanks anyway." Pat was smirking, so Clive sensed it might have been meant as a joke. Even so, Clive had to manage his hurt emotions again when Pat walked away signaling the end of the conversation.

"I'm nice." Clive reassured himself. "Everybody likes me."

CHAPTER 16

HARMONY COULD ALREADY SENSE THE PATRIARCHAL nature of this establishment when she arrived. It didn't help that she had seen articles describing how Zion was a hardcore creationist. Because of this, she naturally distrusted him. She typically spent her days with very open-minded people, but these people were Christians.

"It's wonderful to have another woman stay with us." Rachel said. "Majority of our adults here are men. While most of them are very nice, I enjoy getting to speak to other women."

"Do you have any non-binary folks here?" Harmony demanded, an edge to her voice. She didn't know why she was being so critical of Rachel, but she suddenly felt like she needed to show how inclusive she was by comparison.

Rachel didn't seem bothered by the question. "Not any that have said as much. Most of the clients we receive are so strung out on drugs or recovering from the trauma of prison, that they do not speak about those things readily."

This humbled Harmony significantly. Asking about diversity seemed a trivial question compared to questions like, "How is the quality of life for these traumatized individuals?" or "Is there a high success rate for adapting to life in the outside world after this program?"

"That's so sad." Harmony mumbled.

"It is." Rachel nodded solemnly as she took Harmony up a flight of stairs to the second floor. Rachel's eyes sparkled with the beginning of tears. "This can be some of the most terrible and most fulfilling work."

As soon as they were on the landing, Rachel led Harmony to the first room off of the right-hand hallway.

"Here is your key." Rachel said. "You have your own room. We'll all talk together about the next steps at dinnertime, so I'll see you then. If you need anything, the phones in the room have a directory."

Harmony nodded. "Thank you, Rachel."

Once Rachel had left, Harmony unlocked the door and walked into a room that was painted pale pink with white filmy curtains covering the blinds over the windows. A white canopy bed sat in the right corner closest to the wall facing the staircase. On the left was a narrow doorway leading to a bathroom.

Harmony wandered around the room examining everything. As she pulled open the dresser drawers, she noticed clean women's clothes folded lovingly in the two top drawers. Gingerly, she pulled out an outfit that had caught her attention. It was a cheetah print sweater and a pair of black leggings. There were even packs of unworn underwear and bras. They had thought of everything.

Harmony took the clothes with her to the bathroom and quickly managed to find a towel and toiletries. She relieved herself and then started up the shower. The water pressure was poor, but the temperature was piping hot. She stripped off her clothes and climbed in.

She let her thoughts wander as the steam hypnotized her into a sleepy daze. She grasped the bar of soap and rubbed it on the loofah until it bubbled up. She scrubbed her body on autopilot and felt her body relax. She hadn't realized how tense she was. Muscles she didn't even know existed were stiff. After being in the shower for more than 30 minutes, she turned off the water and grabbed the towel to dry herself. Once she was bone-dry she slipped on the new clothes and left her curls to air dry.

She stopped mid-stride as she stepped out into her room. She saw the woman in blond dreadlocks sitting on her bed. Every inch of visible skin was covered in tattoos. The woman looked like she was made of water floating within a womanly form. Harmony barely dared to breathe.

The mysterious woman raised her bowed head and looked at Harmony with glowing eyes. The seconds stretched into minutes as the two women stared at one another. Harmony's pulse was beating in her ears and her throat was drying out.

Then the woman stood and began walking towards her. If Harmony hadn't been so afraid she would have moved out of the way, but instead, she remained glued to the spot. The mystery woman didn't stop either and passed completely through Harmony's body. She felt as though bursts of static electricity were passing through her. Then the woman was gone. She had walked easily through the solid wood door.

Defrosted from her panic she spun around, flung the door open, and rushed out into the hall. One woman stood in the hallway in awkward confusion, but she was not the woman with the dreads. Harmony took a few tentative steps forward and looked again. There was no sign of the mystery woman— and that's when the fear set in.

"Are you okay, sweetie?" The random woman in the hall asked.

Harmony nodded and returned to her room. Cautiously, she examined the entire room for intruders. Under the bed, in the cabinets, behind doors, in closets. Nobody was there, but the room still felt like it was crackling with the strange electricity.

CHAPTER 17

The evening was crisp and cool. Trees rattled with one or two remaining autumn leaves about to forsake their home in the branches. All the people that had been working, playing, and relaxing across New Creation Rehab facility were inside eating dinner, in class, or settling into bed. While these tasks were being handled by other volunteers and employees of the facility, Zion and Rachel hosted the newest guests in their conference room deep in the building. On the buffet table in a far corner of the room were supplies to create a delicious meal of one's choosing.

Everybody within the room was nibbling on what they had selected and awaiting Zion to start discussing the next steps. It was one of the most homey and cozy places that Pat had ever been to. Even so, he felt a strong feeling that he was not supposed to be here. It wasn't that he had done anything truly horrible, but he just didn't feel like he was a good person in comparison to everybody else. Except maybe Arrow. Arrow was purely himself, which wasn't always pleasant.

And Clive. Clive was an arrogant pig.

"This is very exciting for us." Zion said finally. "We are glad that you all are here and we know there are a lot of aspects we need to discuss."

Zion stood and placed his empty plate of food on the table in front of him. Rachel gazed at her husband lovingly and Pat felt a pang in his chest remembering that Justice used to look at him that way. That gaze was burned into his memory in the form of one of their wedding pictures, which was a permanent reminder of his loss.

"I agree with that." Clive said a little too loudly, followed by his arrogant smirk and brushing his hair back with his fingers.

Pat used all his willpower to resist making a sarcastic comment. He was not among friends here.

"As I stated earlier, apparitions are being seen that seem to be based on private thoughts. These private thoughts are things that have previously been 'resolved' by the Thought Conductor technology."

"Why is this not making national news?" Arrow asked.

"Because somebody is snuffing out the stories." Zion said.

Harmony made an astonished noise where she sat and everybody turned to look at her. Quietly she said, "I think I was one of those stories."

"What do you mean?" Rachel asked, trying to coax Harmony to continue.

"I saw a girl that appeared to be fatally wounded in my backyard but then she disappeared. The whole situation was very odd and then it never made the news. Since then I have been seeing other apparitions, too."

"You have a chip, right?" Clive asked even though it seemed like he already knew the answer.

"Yes, I do."

"If you're comfortable with it, we may do more investigating on what is going on in your case." Zion said. "That's where Clive and Pat come in." Zion looked at the pair of them and Pat felt a lump drop into his stomach at the thought of having to work with Clive.

"You two have the inside scoop on how the chip works and what to do to install one. This information will be critical for our research."

"Of course." Clive agreed.

"We have always been a rehab facility, but we have been moonlighting as rescuers. Some of our clients have been victims of chip hacking by various doctors' offices in Kimber. Somebody has been installing microchips into the brains of addicts and deactivating the safety features, which has the potential to turn people into glorified vegetables."

"That's awful." Clive said. "We have had a few patients come into the hospital after using hacking codes they got from dealers."

"How does that turn people into vegetables?" Harmony asked.

"Each chip has security features which prevent users from deleting what is considered 'baseline emotions', or expected levels of reactions to everyday experiences. Some people will override those security features and enable their chips to delete any and all emotions." Pat said.

Clive bowed his head slightly. Pat assumed it was meant out of respect for the victims of these tragedies, but to Pat, it seemed like false piety.

"Are they turning those people into vegetables purposely?" Pat asked Zion.

Zion shook his head slowly, "We don't know. They are doing some kind of experiments on vulnerable people, though. That's why we had to get you out of there."

Sirona stirred for the first time since arriving in the conference room. A small sob escaped from her lips and she curled her legs underneath her where she sat in a far corner.

Pat's heart went out to her, which is what prompted him to say, "When are we going back for Mayre?"

At this, Clive stopped bowing his head in piety and snapped to attention. His eyes sparkled brightly and all the color drained from his cheeks. He looked like he was about to vomit across the floor. "Mayre? My wife?" Pat didn't answer. "You left. My. Wife???" Clive stood and stormed over to him. He was about to grab Pat by the shoulders, but he managed to duck under Clive's outstretched hands and back away closer to Zion, who was also standing now.

"Dr. Evers, we weren't able to get her out safely." Zion's voice was calm, but firm.

Clive seemed to teeter between throwing a punch and striving to rise above petty fights.

"Where. Is. She?" Clive spoke slowly but his voice shook. His control was breaking.

"I don't believe it would be wise…" Zion began.

"I'm getting my wife, you sack of…"

Zion stopped Clive from continuing by placing the palm of his hand over Clive's heart. "Clive." Zion's voice was calm, kind, and soothing as it always was. "I know you're scared. We intend to rescue your wife. Do not do anything rash."

Clive's shoulders began to shake with the tension he was holding, but he finally released it by swinging his right fist against the drywall behind Zion. He walked away cradling his wrist and his wounded pride. The tension within the room seemed to loosen slightly.

"We are doing our best to be cautious, but are also striving to rescue as many people as we can from these clinics. There could be more places than the ones we have identified." Rachel said.

"I want to help rescue Mayre." Sirona interjected.

"We'd love to have your help." Zion said sincerely. "We need your intel."

Clive continued to face the opposite wall. Pat figured he was trying to fix his face so it looked pretty again.

"For however long you all decide to be with us, we'd love to have you serve alongside us. Just know that none of these jobs are permanent and you are allowed to leave whenever you want. But we understand how hard it is to simply accept charity." Zion said glancing at Harmony, who seemed mildly surprised at the statement. Zion pulled out some note cards from his pocket and began to pass them out to everybody. "These cards contain information about which volunteer jobs we have open along with times and locations. Pat and Clive, your job is already set. I hope you don't mind."

Pat accepted his card from Zion and glanced at it. As he had figured, his job title was Micro-Chip Technology Consultant and he would be working directly with Clive.

"If you do not feel comfortable with the work, let us know, but we think that this is the most important thing we could be doing right now." Zion handed the last card to Clive. "We believe God brings people together for a reason." Pat wasn't sure about that, but he did believe it was an odd coincidence that he had ended up here with this particular group. "We also respectfully ask that, while on campus, you refrain from engaging in vaping, pre-marital sex, drinking, swearing, or utilizing recreational drugs. We have many people here not working for us that are recovering from various addictions and we do not want to tempt them."

Pat caught Clive giving Arrow the side-eye and a silent conversation seemed to pass between them. Pat was beginning to feel the weight of isolation from the others. He had spent the majority of his time going on annoying dates, talking to Theresa, and pretending to be social with clients of his father's business. Now that he was in a group that was trying to be friends with him, he was unsure what to do.

"Arrow, you know better than to have any substances on campus, so, if we find anything in your room, it will get thrown away. We do room checks before bed every night." Zion was kind when he said it, but his eyes were focused on Arrow.

"Gosh dangit, Zion. I haven't had a good drink in nearly 24 hours." Arrow grumbled.

"You are welcome to partake of anything you like after you're done working for the day and off campus." Zion said. "I just don't want you doing it here. However, as your friend, Arrow, I don't think you need it period."

"Yes, thank you!" Clive said with emphasis. He was still riled up and Arrow misbehaving seemed to be the distraction he needed at that moment.

"Are the bad people able to track us down if we have a chip?" Harmony said suddenly.

"They shouldn't be able to. Thought Conductors are specifically designed for mental health and not to work as a GPS tracker." Pat interjected, reciting a very familiar spiel.

"Oh, okay." She whispered.

"Why do you ask?" Rachel persisted, looking into Harmony's concerned face.

"Somebody was in my room."

For a moment, the room went radio silent.

"We need more details than that, girl." Arrow encouraged, relieved the attention was off him.

"She's a woman I saw once before. But she can walk through walls. Is she an apparition?"

"I think so." Zion affirmed. "I don't think they can hurt anybody, though. We have no proof that these apparitions are violent or even solid enough to do damage."

"It's still creepy." Harmony said. "I'm not sure I'll be able to sleep. I don't know if I can use my app to manage it because my chip was deactivated before I came here. I don't want m-m-more apparitions…" She trailed off into sobs and began to hyperventilate.

The panic seemed to grip her quickly, but Pat knew that it had been building. He had been watching Harmony on and off all night. She had been observing everybody apathetically, but he could tell that inside her mind there was a storm raging. It was the same for him.

Rachel swooped in beside Harmony and began to rub her back. "Breathe, dear." She said soothingly. "Could you get her some water?" She addressed Arrow who was closest to the buffet table.

He stood obediently and poured a glass. When the cup was half full he took her the cup, bending down slightly. He was already much taller and bigger than anybody in the room, but he dwarfed Harmony as she sat. Tears were creating paths on her cheeks and she sniffed aggressively. Pat tried not to stare, but he was fascinated by somebody else dissolving into chaos beside him.

"We will adjourn for the night. Since it is the weekend, we won't be doing much, but your job assignments will begin on Monday if you decide to stay. If you have any questions, feel free to reach out." Zion said tactfully. He was so good at being a host.

Pat stood and left along with Sirona and Zion. Arrow stayed behind awkwardly as if he expected to be asked to get Harmony more water. Clive also stayed behind, seemingly to not be outdone by a recovering alcoholic.

"Arrogance, thy name is Clive…" Pat muttered.

"What?" Zion asked.

"Nothing."

"You sure?" The warmth from Zion's smile made Pat feel the pressure to open up.

"I…I've been better." He offered.

"Do you want to talk?" The two men stopped in the hallway and Sirona went on to her room. Zion waved politely to her then looked back at Pat. "I have time."

"No, thanks." Pat tore himself from the kind offer and walked up the stairs to his room. He actually was disappointed in his choice. Zion seemed like a genuinely kind person, but Pat didn't want to get attached to anybody. His mission was still to find Justice, and once he had found her he'd be leaving.

CHAPTER 18

ALL HARMONY COULD FEEL WAS SHAME. The two people she most didn't want to melt down in front of were Clive and Arrow. Clive was a doctor and Arrow just seemed like he had never had a vulnerable moment in his life.

"You don't have to stay with me." Harmony mumbled to no one in particular.

"We'll leave together." Rachel insisted. "C'mon. I'll take you back to your room where you can decompress. Too much stimulation for one day."

"Are you sure you're fine?" Clive interjected. He seemed very upset that there was nothing he could do.

"I will be fine." She half-lied. In truth, she wasn't sure if she would be fine. After finding out about what the apparitions were, she was afraid.

Clive was the first to lead the group out of the conference room. Rachel linked her arm with Harmony's and they walked together with Arrow bringing up the rear. Rachel chatted, but Harmony didn't pay full attention to what she said. She knew that Rachel was trying to distract her but, truthfully it wasn't typically what helped her when she was struggling with anxiety.

"Rachel!" Came a shout from the other side of the hall and an unfamiliar woman rounded the corner. She was in a t-shirt and pajama bottoms and had long, scraggly blond hair down to her waist.

"Yes, Lelly?" Rachel said, her arm coming unhooked from Harmony's.

"Deb is seizing. I think she overdosed!"

"Did you call 911?"

"No, I…"

Rachel did not listen any further but instead flapped her arms at Lelly to show her where the girl was. As Lelly led the way, Rachel was pulling out her cell phone from her pocket to call 911. Harmony stood behind completely forgotten. Clive was already rushing after Rachel to assist.

Deflated, Harmony stood in the hallway for a moment. She was emotionally exhausted and couldn't worry about this girl Deb whom she didn't know.

"Do you want me to walk you to your room?" Arrow asked, stepping up beside her.

Normally she would've said no, but she was feeling scared and wanted the company. Besides, Arrow was the one who had protected her from the apparition at the gas station.

"Yes, that would be nice."

He smiled and said, "Well, show me the way, miss."

Harmony nodded and began walking up the stairs with Arrow alongside. "So, Zion said the apparitions aren't violent and can't hurt us, but that one at the gas station seemed pretty solid." Harmony ventured.

The realization of this fact dawned on Arrow's face and he said, "Yes! You're right. How does that work?"

"I don't know." She bit her lip thoughtfully and they walked in silence the rest of the way to her room. Both seemed to be lost in thought about everything that was going on.

"Is this it?" Arrow asked when they stopped in front of her door.

"Yes, it is." She looked up into his scruffy face. He wasn't beautiful, but his face was interesting to look at. It seemed like every time she spoke to him, she saw a new line, freckle, or secret in his face. "I'm not sure I feel safe."

"I'll scope it out and make sure it's safe." Arrow said as he rubbed his hands together. She unlocked the door and let him go in first. He marched in with an over-exaggerated gait and whipped his head around left and right. "A'right, apparitions! Git!" He then started to flail his arms. Harmony lost her composure and began to laugh. Encouraged by her reaction, he began to play it up even more by checking under the bed, army crawling across the floor, and diving onto the couch screaming "Come out, come out wherever you are!"

"Shhh…" Harmony walked into the room and pushed the door until it almost shut and flapped her hands at him. "Men aren't allowed to be in here. You are gonna get us kicked out on day one."

"Oh, right." He said from his lounging position on the couch. "Well, I'll sneak out." With a grunt, he sat up and approached her. "In all seriousness, are you sure you're okay?"

"I…" She was having a good time and didn't want him to leave. "I like you better sober." She said finally.

Arrow's face dropped the smile and was replaced by a blank mask. She immediately regretted mentioning it. She felt stuck in that moment and was afraid he was going to leave her after she said something so silly.

"I don't like me at all." He said quietly. "Speaking of which, I better dispose of some of my drinks before they check the rooms."

"Okay."

"You take care of yourself." Arrow saluted and made his way around her.

She didn't turn to watch him go. She stayed frozen until she heard the door click.

***

Harmony barely slept and woke to a sinus headache and throbbing behind her right eye. Even though she wasn't a fan of coffee, her mom had told her that caffeine sometimes helped alleviate headaches. Once she was showered and dressed for the day she proceeded downstairs. Several other women with unfamiliar faces were also heading the same way, but everybody seemed to be half asleep.

When she walked into the dining and kitchen space, she went to the coffee machine. It felt like she had woken up at a hotel and was now taking advantage of the continental breakfast.

Rachel stood nearby greeting everybody. When she noticed Harmony, she bustled over and began to apologize. "I am so sorry for abandoning you last night. One of our rehab patients had a seizure. She is going to be okay, but it was a lot of back and forth and paperwork."

"It's fine." Harmony said sincerely. "Arrow walked me back to my room."

Rachel said nothing even though she looked like she had more questions. Harmony was relieved that she didn't pry though. She was still feeling the shame from embarrassing Arrow. She hadn't meant to hurt his feelings.

"How did you sleep last night?" Rachel asked, her eyes wandering around the room trying to keep track of everything.

Harmony attempted a sip of her coffee before speaking and was shocked by how bitter it was. She reached for the sugar packets and said, "It's hard falling asleep in a new place, but I finally managed it." One, two, three, four, five packets of sugar later she took another sip.

"You like sweet coffee?" Rachel asked, chuckling.

"I don't like coffee at all but I thought it might help get rid of my headache."

"Well, no pressure to do any heavy lifting today. If all you want is to rest up, you can do that."

Harmony nodded. "Thank you." She then grabbed a few more things for breakfast and casually glanced around the room for an empty seat. She saw Clive by himself near the window. Sitting with Clive was better than nothing so she joined him across the table.

"Good morning." He said joyfully. He picked up his mug and took a long sip. "Doing better today?"

"Mostly." She said and began stabbing at the scrambled eggs on her plate. "How about you?" She asked, trying to be polite.

"Great!" The glint of an extra sharp canine tooth flashed behind his crooked smile.

Harmony couldn't tell if he was being sarcastic or if he was usually this chipper in the morning. "Where are the other guys?"

Clive shrugged, but this insufficient answer wasn't as annoying as it could have been since Pat chose that exact moment to make an appearance. Both Clive and Pat were in the public eye, but Pat seemed to try to make himself as small as possible in the large space. His shoulders rolled forward and his head bent down. A few of the residents tried to make small talk with him but he was obviously uncomfortable. After rebuffing several people as he prepared a bowl of cereal, he came over to Harmony and sat next to her.

"Where's Arrow?" Harmony asked without bothering to wish Pat good morning.

"Upstairs. Drunk." Pat took a bite of Cheerios without a concern in the world.

Harmony's breakfast caught in her throat and her stomach swirled. She tried to swallow but the lump remained in her esophagus and she could feel her chest tighten as her breathing became more labored. Everybody around her was behaving normally, but the turmoil inside her was slowly escalating.

"W-what?" She managed to breathe out. She was determined to calm down. She didn't want to have another panic attack.

"He was drinking pretty heavily last night."

"Why didn't you tell Zion?" Harmony demanded.

"It's not any of my business." Pat said simply.

Dr. Evers was oddly silent. He had stopped eating and seemed to be thinking deeply. When he realized that Harmony was looking at him he said, "I think we should tell Zion. It sounds like Arrow needs help."

Her anxiety evaporated into sadness as the lump in her throat turned into tears in her eyes. "Oh…" Her voice shook and she couldn't say anything else.

"I'll go tell him." Clive declared. He stood up with his tray, deposited it in its proper location, and rushed out of the dining hall.

Harmony took one more look at Pat's unconcerned face and decided to follow Clive. "I'm going, too." She stood, dropped off her tray, and hurried to keep pace with Clive.

It wasn't too long before they found Zion walking down the hall towards them. "Good morning, Dr. Evers and Harmony. How are you both?" Clive explained to Zion what Pat had told them and Zion's face went from jovial to concerned. He nodded solemnly when Clive had finished. "Let's go check on him."

It almost seemed like the two men hadn't noticed Harmony's presence, so she continued to trail along behind them. In a few minutes, they were facing the door to Pat and Arrow's room. Zion pulled out his set of master keys and used one to unlock the door. As they entered, the smell of beer wafted out. She couldn't see anything at first, but as they all walked into the dimly lit room she felt fear rising in her throat again. On the couch under the window was Arrow. A threadbare blanket covered his stomach and legs but his scarred and tattooed shoulders were exposed. On each shoulder blade was an intricately designed tattoo of folded angel wings that covered his entire back. His face was turned away but you could tell he was sleeping. A couple of bottles sat on the floor beside the couch, but there were far more piled up in the trash can. He hadn't bothered to hide the evidence.

Clive kneeled beside his friend and checked his pulse. "It might be a good idea to get him to the hospital. His breathing is very shallow and his skin color doesn't look good."

Zion was already pulling out his cell phone and making the 911 call. "Harmony, please go inform Rachel." Zion whispered.

"But…" Harmony didn't want to leave. She wanted to make sure that Arrow would be okay. She didn't want to lose sight of him in case this was the last time she would see him.

"Please." Zion insisted.

Harmony didn't want to make things worse, so she did as she was told. She had been on the fence about staying longer than a few days, but with Arrow being unwell she knew she couldn't go home. As she took one last look at Arrow she wondered why this felt like deja vu.

CHAPTER 19

Clive was beginning to think that no matter how good of a person you were, people would not appreciate it. When Arrow regained consciousness, he began fighting off Clive and the paramedics like a scared animal. Clive had felt a twinge of anger as he was remembering Arrow's foot injury on the boat. No matter what Clive did, Arrow fought him.

Once the paramedics had secured Arrow in the ambulance, Clive slipped away to change his clothes. He intended to check with Zion about possibly going to the hospital together to check on Arrow, but at the moment Clive needed to cool off. He was angry.

As Clive entered his room, he removed the wrinkly stained shirt and threw it in the hamper on the way to the sink to rinse off his hair. Once he had gotten his hair back to its perfect shape, he walked in front of the full-length mirror and looked everything over. He had always had confidence in himself. He knew he was attractive, healthy, and intelligent, but he longed for other people to affirm it.

As he pulled a borrowed shirt over his torso, his eyes caught a glimpse of his cell phone sitting on the bedside table. He had powered it off days ago for fear that he would be tracked. He was suddenly overwhelmed with the temptation to turn it on and see what was happening in the outside world. Did people miss him? Was the chip program suffering? He imagined that his phone would be full of new text messages and social media notifications from concerned family, friends, and patients.

Before he could give in to his curiosity, a knock sounded at his door. He answered it and was surprised to see Zion standing there.

"Mind if I come in?" He asked.

"Of course not." Clive said enthusiastically as he stepped aside.

"Thank you." Zion stepped past Clive and sat down in the nearest straight-backed chair. Clive followed suit by sitting on the cedar chest at the end of the bed. "I realized I had never asked you the nature of your fleeing the police." His face turned serious and Clive realized that there was a hint of distrust in his tone.

Clive became defensive. "I don't know. I didn't do anything."

"I'm not saying you did." Zion said patiently.

Clive expected Zion to say more but when he didn't Clive answered. "I was fired from my job and then informed by the hospital lawyer that I should run. I didn't believe her but the police visited me before I escaped."

Zion's eyebrows knitted together in deep concern. "Did you do anything to cause them to fire you?"

"They are planning to take away the privacy of the patients in the microchip program. I didn't like that. That's all I can think."

"I see." Zion's eyebrows were still knit together in concern.

"I'm a good person, Zion. We are commanded by Jesus Christ to serve one another. That's what I do for my patients." Clive insisted.

Zion did not comment but instead asked a question. "Are you aware of what's going on now?"

A heavy weight fell into Clive's stomach. "No…"

"The news has announced that Dr. Shepherd has become the

new head of the microchip program. Are you familiar with him?"

"Yes, he was our night shift doctor. He doesn't know the first thing about microchip implantation. He just knows enough to monitor the patients while I'm sleeping." Clive scoffed. "That's ridiculous. Healing Touch Hospital has always had poor management, but this…"

"He's already given a press conference and stated that they will be utilizing the new technology to help make our world a more peaceful place but, it is the humble opinion of Rachel and I, that he is helping powerful people use the chip for some kind of societal control." Zion rubbed the stubble on his chin. "He also stated that 'chip technology can give us insight into the disordered brain and reorganize it' but my concern is that he did not define 'disordered brain'. I have a bad feeling about the future of this technology."

"Dr. Shepherd is more like a sheep. He doesn't have any of his own ideas." Clive said bitterly. "It makes me wonder who is pulling the strings."

Zion sighed. "Kimber University is involved. They claim it is to help med students and psychology students. They will be allowed to observe some of the patients who have received the chip and analyze data retrieved from it."

"That's where I first heard about this idea. I spoke with Preston Winston and he seemed to be heavily advocating for lack of privacy."

"Preston is with us." Zion said definitively. "He's the one that told me about the university partnership with the hospital."

Clive was unable to conceal the surprise from his features. "Oh?"

"We go way back and that's why I felt like I could entrust him to scope out what was going on at the college. He was probably just playing devil's advocate when you were there."

"Good to know. He really ticked me off." Clive laughed out of relief and to conceal his embarrassment.

There was silence then Zion changed the subject. "There is much more to this calling than I ever imagined." Zion sighed. "If you had told me when I got into ministry that I would be like a Christian spy, I would have laughed."

"The good Lord doesn't give us much choice on what we are called to do." Clive said reverently.

"True, but I wouldn't have it any other way." Zion then stood. "I am honored to have such an intelligent and god-fearing man on my team like you."

Clive's heart warmed at the praise. "Thank you for letting me seek refuge." Clive stood as well and realized even more strongly how much taller he was than Zion.

"It is a pleasure." Zion held out his right hand to shake. The doctor Clive was not used to this gesture, but Clive trusted Zion so he shook his hand gratefully. "I recommend you keep your cell phone off and that you only use the internet over our secure network. The police have become much more advanced with their tracking technology. I will do all I can to keep you safe until you plan to leave, but I can only do so much. I believe you are innocent of any crimes."

"Thank you." Clive smiled a genuine smile this time as he let go of Zion's hand.

Zion nodded and then said, "Are you ready to go check on Arrow, Doc?"

"Yes, I would love to." Clive insisted.

***

"So, my thought is that if we can somehow open up a portal into wherever our data is going, we might be able to discover what is happening." Zion said on Monday night.

Pat was sitting incorrectly on an ergonomic swivel chair, his gangly legs touching at the knees and calves creating a triangle shape. He was wearing borrowed black slacks, an untucked white button-up shirt, and a thin black tie. His hair still hadn't been brushed.

"Sounds very sciencey." Pat said.

"Of course it is." Zion laughed good-naturedly. Pat marveled at how Zion was able to just take things in stride and continued to be happy.

"How do you propose we do that?" Clive asked, taking the responsibility for moving forward.

"Well, in each chip there is a feature that dissolves the feelings and memories that are causing the mental health issue. However, it doesn't seem that they are being dissolved, but instead are being sent somewhere. We need to figure out what command is sending this data and where it is sending it so we can prevent that from happening."

"When we make the microchips, there isn't a secret command we use to send this stuff elsewhere." Pat said dismissively.

"Right, that you know of anyway." Zion clapped his hands together and rubbed them excitedly. "But I think I found the place where some of these apparitions are coming from."

"Where?" Pat's demeanor visibly changed. He shuffled in his seat and leaned forward, interest in his eyes.

"Follow me."

Zion led the men to a back door of the main building where a small carport sat with a few golf carts parked inside. He sat in the driver's seat of one and gestured for them to join him. As they did, he started it up and began driving further into the backyard. There were pine trees everywhere and a gravel road leading from the carport down a hill. As they exited the trees and crested another hill, Pat could see a brick building in the distance. It looked like a short squat silo with a slit down the center. When they were level with it, it was about as tall as an average one-story home.

Zion unlocked the single door and let them inside. The interior looked like a spaceship command center. Keyboards encircled the space and wires hung down from monitors suspended around the walls. In the very center of the room was a huge telescope that pointed up and out of a slit in the roof. Up close Pat could tell that it wasn't open to the elements but covered by thick, crystal-clear glass.

"This is my observatory." Zion said proudly.

"It's beautiful." Clive gushed.

"Thank you. That's high praise coming from a doctor."

If it had been anybody else, Pat would have assumed it was a sarcastic comment, but Zion never said anything he didn't mean.

"So, what are we looking at?" Pat asked.

Zion strolled over to a keyboard across the room and began punching in commands for the telescope. It made no sound as it moved itself into the programmed position and stopped after a minute. Zion looked into the eyepiece and a moment later he was smiling like a cat with a canary. He backed up and gestured at Pat to take a look.

Pat obliged and peered into the eyepiece. It took a moment for his eyes to adjust. Because of the daylight, he was unable to see much in the way of constellations and planets, but he saw the tips of a few trees and clouds.

"I'm not sure I see anything."

"Do you see a thin line?" Zion asked.

Pat peered even harder. He was about to give up when he saw what looked like a crack in the sky.

"I see it." Pat leaned back and jerked his head to signal Clive to look next.

Clive came over and looked in the eyepiece as well. In a moment he leaned back and nodded.

"I suspect that anomaly in the sky will give us some clues about what has been going on. It doesn't look like anything I've ever seen before and I've been studying the skies since I was in high school." Zion said firmly. "There have also been some news reports about some odd sightings out that way."

"When do we check it out?" Clive asked, leaning against an empty wall and crossing his arms.

"Soon. I want to observe it for another week and then we can go that way. For now, I want us to do some research on the codes for where these things are being sent." Zion continued to gesture wildly.

"You really like this stuff, don't you?" Pat let out a small chuckle.

"It is amazing what the Good Lord has given us to learn about and explore." Zion's smile was blinding and Pat looked away.

"Truly." Clive agreed. "Our God is a masterful artist."

Pat said nothing in response. While he could agree that the world around them was fascinating and marvelous, he didn't think some higher power was responsible for it, and if there was a higher power then he must have been pretty sadistic. Pat's mind felt more like a creation of Pablo Picasso where nothing was where you expected it to be and sometimes didn't make sense.

CHAPTER 20

Harmony showed up to her job assignment on Monday morning and was unsurprised to see Rachel waiting for her.

"Harmony." Rachel greeted warmly. "I'm so glad you're here. We get to start right away."

"Sounds good." Harmony smiled.

Her job description was housekeeper/quality control officer. She knew what housekeeping was but she had no idea what quality control officers did. Even though she wanted to be with Arrow at the hospital, she was pleased to be doing meaningful work. After he had been rushed to the ER, Clive and Zion followed behind to check on the status of his health. Rachel, Harmony, and Pat were later updated that Arrow had alcohol poisoning and would need to stay in the hospital for a few more days to detox and take in nutrients. While she was relieved, it was hard to feel completely at peace when he wasn't nearby. She realized she was torn between missing him and being completely disappointed in his behavior.

Thankfully, she started training in housekeeping first, which was the perfect job to distract her from her conflicting thoughts. Rachel brought her into the rooms that had been recently vacated and taught her how to clean them. The majority of the rooms were similar in layout, but there were a few that were unusual and not intuitive to clean.

When that was done, Rachel explained that quality control was simply choosing a few jobs, classes, or people to observe and make sure they were following the guidelines. While this was not something that Harmony enjoyed, she understood the necessity. Thankfully, she didn't have to confront anybody unless they were being a danger to themselves or others. Rachel and Zion did all the follow-up if it was necessary to be confrontational. Also, she only had to do this with the women's programs so she wouldn't stick out like a sore thumb in a room full of men.

Rachel explained that she wouldn't need to do this part of the job during the first week because there was a lot of training involved, but for now, she would primarily do housekeeping. While residents were milling around the campus, Harmony would be doing some basic upkeep to the rooms that had occupants, but the hope was that no one would be in those rooms so she could get things done uninterrupted.

She learned her cleaning duties quickly so Rachel felt comfortable leaving Harmony on her own after lunch. She found that she enjoyed the work. It was satisfying because it was easy to do, but time-consuming so it didn't give her much time to think. She only had run into a few women who were resting due to a headache or because of a break between scheduled things. These interactions weren't as bad as she expected. The women were friendly and one of them talked about the progress she had made in her recovery. Harmony enjoyed celebrating with other women.

As she completed the women's rooms, it was time to clean the men's. She hoped she wouldn't have to deal with any weirdos, but Rachel assured her that she shouldn't have any issues.

By the time Thursday rolled around, Harmony was in a routine and felt confident in her abilities. While her anxiety wasn't cured, she found herself enjoying the slower pace of life and the manual labor. It kept her busy and gave her less time to lose herself in her thoughts.

Once her morning was complete, she decided to take her break outside because it was a surprisingly sunny day for the fall. She grabbed a jacket and proceeded outside to the steadily dying gardens. The stone pathways weaving in and out of the gardening plots were so chilled by the cool in the air that she could feel it through the soles of her cheap shoes. She made her way past spindly sticks and browning grass, reading each of the labels to see what the plants used to be. Since everything was dying, you could easily see all the spaces that were meant to be shaded by foliage including a black bench designed to look like starched lace. She brushed off the leaves from the seat and sat down, startled by the chill from what turned out to be iron.

Her nose was pink and she shivered slightly as the breeze picked up. She pulled the jacket tighter and gazed across the wide expanse of lawn. The majority of the residents were inside now and it felt even lonelier than the inside. She imagined it was much more beautiful to be placed here in the spring or the summer.

"Mind if I sit?" Arrow walked up and the only thing announcing his presence was a couple of seconds of crunching leaves.

"Where did you come from?" Harmony asked, her eyebrows knit together in confusion.

Arrow pointed and she noticed the patio halfway behind the main house with chairs and a table. She hadn't noticed that before. He looked tired, but his eyes were alert.

"I thought you were still at the hospital detoxing." Her tone came out harsher than she had intended, but she realized right away that she was feeling angry at him and disappointed instead of excited as she expected.

For the first time, Arrow looked ashamed. "I just got back this morning. I'm sorry if I scared you."

Her heart softened at the apology. She scooted over and patted the empty seat beside her.

"Thanks." He sat down. There wasn't much space on the bench, so they both looked straight ahead at the garden in silence for a moment. "I took what you said too personally." Arrow said finally.

"Oh?" Harmony turned her face to him.

"Yeah, about me being better sober."

"I didn't think how it sounded before I said it." Harmony admitted.

They were quiet again and Harmony glanced over at a robin pecking at the dirt nearby.

"I didn't agree with you at first." Arrow finally said. "But then the nurse said I almost died and I realized you were right."

Harmony turned to see him looking right at her. She suddenly felt self-conscious as his eyes gazed into hers. "Oh." Was all she could muster as she quickly glanced down at her knees. "Do you want to walk around? I'm getting cold staying still."

Arrow nodded and joined her. They left the garden and began to explore the property.

"How are you doing without…booze?" Harmony asked, trying to sound light.

"It's been awful. I want it all the time but Zion is helping me. I don't want to disappoint him again. He worked so hard with me the first time."

"I don't think you could disappoint him. He seems very supportive." Harmony said earnestly. "Are you going through A.A.?"

Arrow nodded and stopped in front of the fountain to watch the water splash. Harmony looked at him through the water on the opposite side of the basin. This allowed her to truly look at him without feeling the discomfort of knowing he could catch her making note of every scar and line that make his face uniquely his. He was somebody that was hard to imagine ever being a child. He seemed like he must have always been a man.

"Why did you stay with me on the boat after we ran?" Arrow asked.

"I just had to escape my life." She said honestly.

"Why?" Arrow leaned onto his left leg so he could walk around to see her better.

"My job was boring, there's a creep at my work, and I found out my microchip had been hacked." Harmony's tone was nonchalant, but an ironic smile graced her face to show that she realized how shocking this statement would be.

"I…" Arrow laughed in disbelief. "…girl. That should have been the first thing you told us."

"I don't like to lead with the heavy stuff when I meet people while running away from something out of a horror film." Harmony laughed.

"That's a fair point." Arrow rubbed the scruff on his chin in mock thoughtfulness. He turned and began leading them down the walkway again.

She wrapped her arms around herself as they walked and tried to think of what to say next. She felt vulnerable enough already.

"Is this creep somebody that needs to be taken care of?" Arrow said suddenly as they began passing under a cluster of trees that had an unusual amount of leaves still attached to their branches.

"I don't know." She said honestly. "He seemed to give up once I talked to him. It was odd because nobody generally cared about what I felt at work. I'm not sure I really had any friends." Harmony allowed herself to feel the sadness that this introspection created. "I'm too plain. Too basic. Everybody else I worked with had vibrant wardrobes, interesting sexualities, colorful races, and interesting hobbies. I was just…me."

"What things do you like?"

Harmony thought a moment and said, "My dog. Watching TV. Earth tones. Tea. Men." She glanced over to see how this would be received.

Arrow seemed oblivious. "You sound pretty interesting and well-adjusted to me."

Her heart fluttered in her chest as the perfectly normal statement landed. "Could we go in?" She asked suddenly. She didn't want their conversation to end but she was beginning to feel the chill in her toes and couldn't walk much further.

"Of course." He led her back up to the main house and when they were in the foyer she expected him to head back up to his room, but then he said, "So, where can we go to keep talking?"

And that's when she completely fell for him.

CHAPTER 21

DURING THE DAY, IT WAS DIFFICULT to locate Zion or Rachel due to the flurry of activity going on at the rehab center. That meant that any microchip research was reserved for evenings. During the day Pat, Harmony, Clive, and Arrow were like any other volunteer at the center. They cleaned bathrooms, cooked meals, and prepared classrooms for lessons among other things.

They also were all assigned to a special project involving freshening up one of the storage buildings in preparation for remodeling. This included taking out trash and debris, scrubbing the dirt-covered surfaces, removing the items in storage, and painting. Harmony immediately grabbed the broom because this was something she knew how to do and it would take a long time to complete.

"Yikes." Arrow said as he looked around the place bright and early on Friday morning. "Zion wasn't kidding."

Harmony couldn't help but notice that Arrow was looking much healthier in clean jeans, a yellow plaid flannel shirt, and boots.

"Glad to have you back, brother." Clive said heartily as he clapped Arrow on the shoulder. "And we're ministering to their family. This is the Lord's work."

"I think you mean doing the stuff they didn't want to do." Arrow said sarcastically.

Harmony caught a glimpse of Pat and the corner of his mouth jerked into a smirk. In his own quiet way, he appeared to be agreeing with Arrow's assessment.

"They've done so much for us. This is the least we can do for them." Clive said, continuing to hold firm on his pious attitude about hard work.

"Have you done an ounce of manual labor your whole life?" Arrow demanded.

Clive didn't answer immediately, but instead turned his head away from the group to appear as though he was surveying the work that needed to be done. "I did work for a summer at my grandfather's farm one year."

"Uh-huh…" Arrow said skeptically. "Dressing the cows in fashionable boating outfits?" Pat snorted then and put a bony hand over his wide grin.

Clive's face, which had previously been expressing the feelings of a resigned martyr, now shifted to aggravation as he turned back to Arrow. "No! I helped with planting and harvesting and feeding the animals."

"C'mon, boys." Harmony said exasperated, but she secretly liked to watch people gang up on Clive. It was clear that the doctor wasn't used to being the butt of jokes. "We have a lot of work to do and it won't get done at this rate."

"Harmony's right." Arrow admitted and she glowed at the praise. She wasn't used to being "right". Everything about her was considered "wrong" in the circles she ran in.

"I'll paint." Pat said simply and went to the supply closet where the paint supplies were housed.

"I guess that leaves us to do the heavy lifting, Doc." Arrow said and Clive's attitude worsened.

"How much do we have to clean out?" Dr. Evers asked.

"Put your big boy britches on and follow me." Arrow winked at Harmony and turned to lead Clive through his first day doing manual labor as an adult.

"I have to be careful. My hands are what make me a good surgeon." Clive's voice echoed as the pair of them walked to the opposite side of the building from where Harmony was working.

Arrow was such a different person when he wasn't drinking. The apathetic and cranky person he was when they first met wasn't even close to the sober version. His eyes were bright with the gleam of a joke and his movements were strong and deliberate. She continued to glance over at the men as they worked and was amused to see how all of them worked together.

Pat was content to be alone and painted the walls immediately despite the lack of painter's tape or drop cloths. He seemed eager to just work and not be disturbed. Arrow was all about following a strategic plan to get all the objects from point A to point B and was getting very aggravated with Clive's deliberate caution to protect his hands and physical appearance.

"Just lift from the bottom. There is a gap down there where you can really grip the desk." Arrow instructed.

"I'm not sure I can lift it."

"It's light."

"But it's awkward."

THUD!

Harmony whipped around and saw that Clive had dropped his end of the desk down on the ground and a long crack ran up the side of the thin particle board that the desk was made of. It was a cheap desk, but the look on Arrow's face was frustration and disgust.

"Little Miss Priss…you broke the desk."

"I told you I wasn't able to lift it." Clive said defensively.

"Don't you lift weights?"

"I do, but…"

"I don't think Zion will be mad." Harmony offered helpfully. "I think it will be okay."

The boys looked over at her as if they had forgotten she was there.

"I bet Harmony could lift it." Arrow said suddenly.

Clive snorted in disbelief and this was a mistake. Harmony propped the broom against the wall and marched over. She edged Clive out of the way by maneuvering in front of the desk and grasped the gap under the dropped side. Arrow was already holding the other side so she took a deep breath and lifted. It was pretty solid but Harmony was determined to show "Mr. Pompous" up.

Arrow and Harmony successfully maneuvered the desk out the door and set it down with all the other furniture that had been moved outside. She dusted her hands off and grinned at Arrow.

"I knew you could." He smiled back then shouted over her shoulder, "Doc, this chick is stronger than you."

Instead of responding, Clive came out of the storage building with a heavy chair and sat it beside the desk. He went back inside with no response and continued to move furniture sullenly.

"Serves him right." Arrow muttered.

Harmony nodded and proceeded to go back into the building. As she began to walk inside, Arrow was right behind her and placed his large hand on her back in between her shoulder blades. It was a gentle touch and friendly and it sent Harmony's senses into a cascade of emotions. That split second was enough to distract her for the rest of the morning. She continued to sweep, but her gaze kept searching for Arrow going about his work.

"Don't you need to tape off the ceilings first before you start painting?" Clive asked Pat suddenly.

Pat shrugged and continued to run the roller up and down on the walls.

"Get back to work slacker!" Arrow directed Clive.

"I'm not slacking!" Clive shouted in disbelief. "I'm not even needed now. The furniture has been moved."

"We'll have to check with Zion to see what else he wants us to get done." Arrow said as he came back into the space. "We'll need to finish sweeping and painting, but we'll do that after lunch. Pat? Harmony? You ready for lunch?"

Harmony leaned the broom against the wall and nodded. Pat didn't respond but he stopped painting and placed the roller back in the paint pan. They turned the lights off and all walked to the main house for lunch. Droves of recovering addicts were swarming for the dining room, all chattering loudly. Harmony felt awkward in this group because she had never struggled with addiction or known of anybody who struggled with addiction unless you counted Arrow.

"Have we met yet? I'm Serrill!" A man came directly up to Harmony and shook her hand.

"I'm Harmony."

"Nice to meet you!" And he was greeting other people before Harmony had time to think.

"He's been here since the last time I was here." Arrow said. "He's great and pretty harmless."

Harmony felt the tension in her body ease up at the reassurance. "Wonder what we're having." She mused.

The answer was quickly answered when they entered the room and saw individuals carrying trays filled with spaghetti, garlic bread, and salad. Each of them loaded up their plates with all the goodies including Pat who usually ate sparingly. They all had low energy after the busy morning and legitimately needed the fuel to keep going. Harmony had never realized that her office job wasn't involved enough to make her feel like she truly needed to eat.

As they sat down at a table, Arrow slid his tray next to hers. Pat and Clive sat across from them and Harmony could tell that Pat was leaning as far away from Clive as humanly possible.

"So, we're having a meeting with Zion tonight?" Clive asked as everybody else dug into their meal. Pat nodded. "Did he say what it was about?"

"Just continuing to get to the bottom of things that are happening." Arrow said.

"That's what I figured." Clive twirled his spaghetti noodles around his fork and took a bite.

Harmony caught Rachel walking through the cafeteria. When she saw Harmony her eyes lit up and she waved. Harmony awkwardly waved back. Shortly after, Zion also appeared

"Howzit goin', guys?" Zion asked as he laid a kind hand on Arrow's shoulder.

"Good." Clive said enthusiastically.

"Clive got schooled in the ways of manual labor today." Arrow said.

"I didn't get schooled in anything." Clive shot back.

Zion continued to smile. "Well, good. How much did you get done?" Arrow explained what all they had done so far and Zion nodded, pleased. "Good. Good. Well, I'll join you all in the building after lunch and explain the next steps."

Arrow nodded. "Thanks, man."

When they were done eating they ventured back to the building with full bellies. Arrow helped Harmony sweep and Clive joined Pat with painting. An hour after they started back, Zion joined them and explained what else he wanted done, which consisted of mopping the floor, cleaning and dusting the furniture, and disposing of any broken pieces.

"The goal is to make this a hangout spot. Even with all the space we own, there aren't many spaces that allow people to just hang out." Zion said regrettably. "So, set this up however you think would be most inviting, and then give me your feedback on what kind of leisure activities you might think our residents would enjoy. Arrow…"

"Say no more. I have ideas!" Arrow said.

Zion gave the thumbs up and said, "I'll leave you to it. I have a class to teach but I'll see you at 8 pm for our meeting. It is in the same conference room we met before."

Everybody gave a sign of having understood and Zion left. They finished up the sweeping and painting in another hour. Pat and Clive washed up the paint supplies, Clive making most of the small talk. Arrow and Harmony threw away everything they had swept up. Harmony sought out mops and buckets and was successful in finding only one mop and two buckets.

"Which would you rather do? Clean furniture or mop?"

"Mop." Harmony said laughing.

"Of course. You're going to make me work out in the cold." Arrow said in mock horror.

"Maybe." Harmony tried to seem serious, but when she looked up into his imperfect face she cracked a smile.

"I'll help with the furniture." Pat said suddenly at Harmony's shoulder.

"Thanks, Pat." Arrow said. "Harmony here doesn't want to work hard."

"I do. Just not outside."

Arrow dismissed her with mock disappointment and led Pat outside where they began working on the furniture. In a few moments, Clive approached Harmony as she was mopping.

"Do you need help?"

"I couldn't find another mop."

Clive turned on his heel and went back to the supply closet. In a moment he was back with a mop that Harmony hadn't seen at first.

"I found another one. It wasn't immediately visible." Clive dunked the mop in the water and wrung it out. As he started mopping she thanked him. "It's fine. I won't let others work while I relax."

This was something Harmony could respect about Clive. Even though he was generally very arrogant, he was trying. It seemed like without the other guys around he was less competitive.

"So, have you noticed a difference since getting the chip?" Clive asked, suddenly in doctor mode.

"Yes, I have." Harmony said honestly. "I used to be afraid of so much. Now I can live my life."

"That's great." Clive dunked the mop again and slapped it down to scrub a particularly difficult spot. "Do you see hallucinations?"

Harmony continued scrubbing her part of the floor and thought about this question. She hadn't dealt with hallucinations when she first was being treated but had been seeing an awful lot of them lately.

"I didn't at first, but now I've been seeing apparitions a lot lately. I think it might be just what Zion told us about though. I don't think I ever hallucinated"

Clive nodded thoughtfully.

He didn't ask any more medical questions but he still seemed deep in thought as he worked. Harmony was certain he had chosen the right profession because she could tell he genuinely cared about the people he was helping. Harmony wished she knew what she was best at. She had never found a dream career to pursue and was not currently working at a place she felt was her "calling". Although, she didn't even know if she believed in having a "calling". People that generally used those sorts of terms were religious and Harmony never thought of herself as religious.

As they neared time for the meeting, Harmony realized she was hungry and had missed dinner. Cleaning the floor had taken hours and Pat and Arrow hadn't even finished all the furniture. They covered up the remaining pieces outside with a couple of tarps and closed up the clean pieces in the building, deciding that they would organize them tomorrow.

"I hope they have some leftovers from dinner." Harmony said as they all walked inside together.

"I hope so too." Pat chimed in.

Everybody whipped around to look in mild surprise at him. This was the first time that Pat had truly interjected something that could be considered small talk.

"Are you, string bean?" Arrow said with the warmth of an older brother.

"I might be the youngest here, but string bean? Really?"

"Oh-ho!" Arrow laughed in surprise. "Forgive me, Mr. Sherwood."

Clive was noticeably pleased that the teasing had shifted to Pat now. "No matter how old you are, you're still pretty skinny." Clive added.

"I realize this and no matter how old you are, you are still an arrogant…"

"Welcome!" Zion greeted them as they all entered the conference room.

Food was laid out like it had been last night and Rachel was bustling around to make sure everything was easily accessible. She was so beautiful and petite. Today her white-blond hair fell in waves down her back and she wore a yellow floral dress and a knee-length blue cardigan. There was another person there though that Harmony did not recognize.

"This is Dr. Preston Winston, President of Kimber University." The man stood and straightened his black shirt and jeans. His clothing was casual on its own but on his body they became elevated. Everything about him was straight lines and formality.

"Dr. Evers, good to see you again." Preston said kindly.

Everybody looked to Clive and it was apparent that this was not what he was expecting. He had a split second where he was unable to hide his surprise, but when he realized people were observing him he put on a mask of confidence.

"Good to see you too, Dr. Winston."

"We know you don't mean that. I apologize for our last meeting but I couldn't be myself."

"Preston has been gathering some intel for us at the higher education level so he is essentially undercover." Zion added.

"You're very connected, Zion." Arrow said, already digging into the food.

When Harmony saw this she walked over to the food and began to load up a plate. Pat was close behind her. Rachel touched her shoulder slightly and whispered "hello" and Harmony returned the greeting.

"I have to be. There is so much going on and it does us no good if we don't have people in our corner. The government may run things in an official capacity, but it is truly the schools and the hospitals that control most of our society." Zion said passionately.

"Truer words were never spoken." Preston agreed. He was directly behind Harmony and loading up his plate with food. "On the surface, Kimber University will be utilizing the data they collect for research and managing potentially violent persons. Ultimately, it is just about control."

Zion nodded in agreement. Harmony went to sit down at one of the conference table chairs and watched Preston. He was very precise and she couldn't help but notice that all the food items he chose were kept away from each other on the plate.

"So, why can't you do anything about this?" Clive asked, an edge to his tone.

"The President possesses influence and is the face of the

university, but, like the King in chess, wields very little power over decisions or strategy." He said simply.

"That's a raw deal, man." Arrow said bluntly.

"It pays well." Preston laughed darkly.

He then took his plate and sat diagonally from Harmony and across the table. As he sat, he smiled at her. She returned a somewhat awkward half smile because her mouth was full of bean dip.

"So, do I get to meet everybody before we start?" Preston asked as he picked up a baby carrot and bit down hard on it. His canines were sharper than all the rest of his teeth and Harmony was getting sparkly vampire vibes from him.

"Of course" Zion said.

They all introduced themselves and Harmony finished the introductions. Preston looked pleased and then started in on informing them all of the goings on at the higher education level. Harmony was unfamiliar with most of the names he mentioned and the concepts since she had not attended college herself. Clive, Arrow, Zion, Rachel, and Pat were all listening intently and offering comments so Harmony got the feeling that they were informed.

"So, Preston, continue to monitor how fast privacy for chip recipients will be ending. Also, try to slow it down as much as you can. We still don't truly know what's happening right now with the functionality of the chip." Zion said. "That's what we will be working on."

"Of course I will." Preston agreed. He stood and threw away his plate in preparation to leave. "Rachel, thank you for dinner." Preston bowed at the waist and then turned to wish the others good night. "I must go but I appreciate all the feedback."

"I'll walk you out." Zion said.

As Preston allowed himself to be escorted out of the room, he caught Harmony's eye and she could have sworn he winked.

CHAPTER 22

PAT WAS NOT LOOKING FORWARD TO more manual labor. He didn't want to admit this to Arrow because he was enjoying Clive being the butt of the jokes. He also wasn't sure how comfortable he felt with everybody yet. From what he knew about friendship, you were supposed to feel comfortable sharing parts of yourself even if those things were ugly. He didn't feel comfortable sharing those things with this group and especially sharing about how before coming to New Life Rehab screams seemed to reverberate in his mind daily.

These thoughts weren't far from his mind as he continued to clean and polish old furniture with Arrow on Saturday morning. Harmony and Clive were in charge of organizing the pieces in the building so he hadn't seen much of them.

"So, why didn't you come with us in the beginning?" Arrow asked suddenly as they were polishing a high-backed armchair the color of puke.

"Clive." Pat said. "He's an arrogant creep."

"Well, maybe sometimes." Arrow conceded.

"And the sailor of the vessel we would be riding in was an alcoholic." Pat added half teasing, half serious.

Arrow glared at him. "That was a low blow."

"You were in the hospital for alcohol poisoning." Pat said defensively

Arrow didn't respond to that and Pat felt a tinge of regret. Arrow was much taller and bigger than him so hitting below the belt wasn't wise. Pat wasn't comfortable apologizing though so he polished furniture harder.

"What do you think they're talking about in there?" Arrow asked.

Pat was surprised by the question. "Dr. Evers' abs?" He offered.

This made Arrow laugh and Pat felt a wave of relief wash over him. "Harmony isn't nearly that shallow."

"Clive is." Pat said adamantly.

"True."

"So, how does this manly-hunk-of-nerdiness before me bag women?" Arrow shook out his cleaning cloth and sprayed it again with the polish.

Pat shrugged. "It's mostly my money and messed up psyche. Women think I'm deep because of my problems."

"That's good. I'll have to keep that in mind. I've been out of the dating game for a long time and I don't have any solid techniques." Arrow admitted. He then mimed introducing himself to a girl. "Excuse me, miss…I'm not wealthy but I have an unhealthy addiction to alcohol and major depression. Date me?"

Pat chuckled. It seemed strange to him that he could feel close to somebody after making self-deprecating comments about each other, but he did. "Do you have a girl in mind?"

"Oh yeah." Arrow grinned secretively and marched over to the building to notify Clive that there was another furniture piece ready. When Arrow came back, he began working on a desk that looked like it had dust a quarter of an inch thick on its surface.

When Arrow didn't say anything else, Pat asked, "So, who?" If Pat had had friends in high school, this is what he imagined it would have been like. Sharing with each other about girls and life. Arrow would have never been friends with him in school, though. Guys like him ate guys like Pat for breakfast.

Arrow looked like he was about to speak, but then Harmony and Clive both came outside to take a few items. At that moment, something clicked for Pat as he saw Arrow's gaze lingering on Harmony. He looked lost and sick and Pat knew who Arrow was pining for.

***

Sunday morning dawned and Pat found himself awake at 7 am, which was highly unusual. As he rolled over he realized why he must be alert at this early hour. A cascade of red hair fell across the pillow beside him and the slow sleepy breathing of his wife filled the silence. His breath caught in his throat and he glanced over at Arrow's bed to make sure he wasn't awake. Thankfully, Pat's roommate appeared to be sleeping as well. He was twisted up in the sheets, his pillow forgotten and lying on the floor.

Pat turned back to Justice sleeping in his bed and quietly reached a tentative hand towards her to make sure she was real. His hand just kept going and his heart sunk into his stomach as he watched his love dissolve before his eyes. A sob slipped out from his throat and his hand flew up to capture it. To try and calm himself he began taking slow deep breaths through his nostrils.

Just then, a knock came at the door. Pat didn't turn around but he frantically began cleaning his face and smoothing the sheets on the side of the bed where Justice had seemingly laid. Arrow was stirring in the bed beside him as another knock rapped on the door. The large man went padding over to answer it and swung it open.

"Good morning!" Pat immediately recognized the chipper voice of Zion. "Is Pat awake, too?"

"Yes, I am." Pat said as he rolled over and sat up.

Arrow stood by the door in plaid pajama bottoms and no shirt, gesturing for Zion to come in. Zion was already wearing khaki shorts and a blue and pink polo shirt.

"I already notified Clive, but we will be going to services this morning together. I want you to see one of the most important aspects of what we do here." Zion said excitedly.

"Church?" Pat asked, trying not to let disdain slip into his tone.

"Yes." Zion said, unabashed. "Since you are staying here and working alongside us, I want you to have a clear idea of what we offer our residents."

"What time and do we need to dress up?" Arrow asked.

"10 am and no. Just whatever clothes you feel comfortable in. We'll meet in the lobby around 9:50 and I'll show you where the chapel is." Zion smiled ear to ear.

"Sounds good." Arrow said.

Pat didn't respond but studied his nails closely. He wasn't very happy about this development, but hopefully, it would just be a one-time thing. He had been around some Christians who seemed to only care about preaching at him instead of being a friend. Usually, when his mental illness reared its ugly head, they gave up. That signaled to Pat that he was too far gone to be worth saving.

The time before the service seemed to crawl by since he had been awakened so early. Showering, getting dressed, and eating breakfast barely took an hour so he wandered the grounds to waste time and played cards with Arrow. When 9:50 rolled around they all met Zion and Rachel in the lobby. Clive and Harmony were already there. It was apparent that Clive had tried to dress up his outfit despite having limited options.

"Wonderful." Zion said warmly. "Let's go to the chapel."

Zion led them outside and down the front steps. To the left through the garden and the weeping willows was a small brick building with red double doors. It was so removed from the main house that Pat hadn't noticed it before. There was no steeple like he had seen on some church buildings, so at first it didn't look like what he expected. Once they were through the doors, a man and a woman flanked the entrance and were holding stacks of paper.

"Good morning!" The woman said cheerfully. She grinned and he could see a few teeth missing and her blond curls bounced beside her face. The man said nothing but simply smiled and helped hand out the sheets to everybody. When Pat looked at the sheet he had been given, it looked as though it was an agenda for the service.

"Sit back here. That way you'll be able to see everything." Zion said pointing to a bench four rows from the back.

They all followed his instructions and sat while he and Rachel went to the front. Now that they were sitting, Pat looked around the building. Long wooden benches were in two vertical rows stopping short of a raised platform. This platform had a keyboard, drums, a couple of guitars, and a podium. On the wall behind this was a large blank white screen scrolling through announcements. He glanced up and could see the projector. Finally, on either side of the space were a couple of windows letting in some natural light. Everything in the space seemed as updated as possible, but the nicks and scratches on the furniture aged everything by a degree.

Something crawled inside him. A few congregants looked their way and it felt as though they were looking through him. He also noticed Sirona sitting with a few women close to the front of the room. He had the strong desire to shout that he wasn't here voluntarily and that this wasn't his "thing". At this stage in his life, he hadn't been very concerned with how people perceived him, but at this moment he wanted people to know that he didn't belong here.

"Welcome." Said a warm but deep voice over his left shoulder.

Pat looked around and saw a short man with spiky black hair. His eyes were deep green and every part of his face was sharp like it had been cut from stone. Everything about this man screamed strength. He was holding out his hand for Pat to shake. Pat took the hand gingerly and allowed the man to practically pull his arm from the socket. The man then reached around to shake Clive's hand, followed by Harmony and Arrow.

"I'm Misha." He smiled wide and his teeth seemed to glow in the space.

There was an awkward pause and Misha looked around at everybody as if expecting them to introduce themselves. Clive took charge and introduced each of them to this man. Pat couldn't help feeling resentment building up inside him at the nerve of the doctor thinking he wanted this stranger to know who he was.

"It's great to have you all here. Let me know if you need anything."

"Thank you, Misha." Clive said jovially. "What a nice man." Clive said as Misha made his way to the front of the chapel.

"Of course he likes you." Pat muttered bitterly.

Clive gave him a strange look but had no time to respond because that's when Zion went up on the platform and began speaking.

"It's wonderful to be in the Lord's house today." A loud cheer rose from the crowd as the residents clapped, hooted, and whistled. "Amen! I can see that worship this morning is going to be lively." Zion chuckled. "Please stand as we sing today."

The band joined Zion on stage and took their places. Rachel went to the microphone, Zion slung an electric acoustic guitar over his torso, Misha took his place at the drums, and an unknown woman with a narrow pixie-like face and long aqua-colored hair was behind the keyboard. Everybody in the crowd stood as one, including Clive and Arrow. Harmony and Pat then stood uncertainly.

The music swelled in the space and Rachel's angelic voice rang out. The discomfort in Pat's body grew as the unfamiliarity of everything assaulted his senses. Some of the people in the crowd had their hands raised and some were closing their eyes and swaying. Not everybody could sing but that didn't stop them from trying. Clive looked a little out of his element but he was trying to sing along. Arrow also seemed to be making an attempt after the first verse. Harmony was stony-faced and not even attempting to sing.

The first song ended and transitioned into another one. Halfway through this song, Pat got the feeling that each song seemed to be a love song to their God. It didn't make sense to Pat why they would sing to a God who was not here to hear the heartfelt performances. When the bridge of the song swelled into an epic crescendo the crowd sang out about how they had been brought from death to life. At this many people began sobbing and clapping and cheering. Clive smiled and clapped politely. He seemed to be the only one enjoying himself out of their group.

Two more songs later they were able to sit down but things didn't become quiet. Some of the residents were still sobbing and clapping. Clive joined in by clapping gleefully while Arrow and Harmony tentatively clapped. Pat shoved his hands in his pockets and sat. His shoulders bowed forward and he peered around looking for a quick exit. When he had mentally decided he was going to excuse himself to go to the restroom, Zion went to the podium and began speaking.

"Let's pray." Zion bowed his head. "Lord, thank you for the blessed time of worship. We owe all we have to you and humbly ask for you to move into our midst today. Give me the words to say thank you to those who are visiting with us and be with them. Amen."

Pat had bowed his head out of respect for this man who had opened up his home to them, but he did not believe the words that Zion spoke did any good. When the prayer ended, he returned his gaze to the podium and found himself unexpectedly drawn to Zion's words. The man was a gifted public speaker.

"I'm so excited to be here with you all." Zion began. "As I was preparing for this sermon, it was weighing on my heart to share with you what God says about anxiety."

Pat was sucked in at that point. He had never heard a Christian speak about mental illness. Theresa grew up in a Christian home and had always been very weird when it came to mental health. He had a feeling that she regarded it as something abnormal and to be feared. This had informed Pat about what Christians must have thought about him.

Zion expressed how anxiety can be a chronic issue that affects your mental and physical health. He explained that when people suffer from mental illness, it isn't necessarily a sin that requires a person to pray more or just have more faith.

"It's okay to go to therapy or seek treatment for these conditions. Having these struggles doesn't necessarily mean you lack faith in God." Zion stepped around the podium and began to speak directly to a few men in the front row. "You don't have to continue to suffer in silence to prove you are faithful."

A few unseen people shouted, "Amen!" in agreement.

"Storms will come." Zion said somberly. "Just because you put your faith in Jesus doesn't mean your life will be perfect. Things will still happen…"

"Then what's the point?" Pat muttered to himself.

"But when the storms come, you will have the creator of the universe in your corner. You can rely on him for all your needs and he wants what's best for you." Zion circled back around to the podium and opened a large book. "Turn with me now to Mark 4:37 in your Bibles. If you do not have your own Bible, there are a few in the seat racks."

Pat shoved his hands further in his pockets, determined to not cooperate. He still wanted to leave, but something kept him rooted to the spot. To his chagrin, Clive was dutifully turning to the passage.

"On that day, when evening had come, he said to them, 'Let us go across to the other side.' And leaving the crowd, they took him with them in the boat, just as he was. And other boats were with him. And a great windstorm arose, and the waves were breaking into the boat so that the boat was already filling. But he was in the stern, asleep on the cushion. And they woke him and said to him, 'Teacher, do you not care that we are perishing?' And he awoke and rebuked the wind and said to the sea, 'Peace! Be still!' And the wind ceased, and there was a great calm. He said to them, 'Why are you so afraid? Have you still no faith?' And they were filled with great fear and said to one another, 'Who then is this, that even the wind and the sea obey him?'" Zion stopped reading and looked out at the crowd, pausing to allow the words to settle over everybody.

It was so quiet that Pat could hear the humming of the central heating and air. No screaming. Just peace. Instead of making him excited, he felt unsettled by the change. His mind was not used to the quiet.

"Sometimes you may be led into a storm. Even if you do everything right. They obeyed God and were faced with the wind and the waves." Zion closed his book, grasped it in both hands, and walked around the podium again. "But he is peace. I do strongly believe God has provided us with treatments for mental illness to alleviate suffering, however, the only way to have true peace is through Jesus Christ."

CHAPTER 23

Harmony stood in Pat and Arrow's bedroom early on Monday morning. She noticed Pat's bed was barely disturbed like he had slept in one place the whole night. A book sat on the side table that looked like a complicated textbook about computer code that Harmony had no interest in. When she walked up to Arrow's bed with her cleaning supply caddy in one hand and towel in the other, she observed blankets were everywhere and the fitted sheet was slightly pulled off one corner. She smiled to herself, warmth spreading from her heart to her toes.

No matter how much she tried to deny it, she was developing feelings for him and this snapshot of his personality was endearing to her.

She hummed to herself as she set down her supplies on the cedar chest at the end of Arrow's bed and began remaking it. At first, she didn't notice that somebody walked into the room from the bathroom, but as they made their way around Pat's bed and towards her she sensed them. Spinning around she saw the apparition. Her blond dreads were floating in the air like she was swimming in invisible water. She looked sorrowful like her eyes were about to spill over with tears.

"Who are you?" Harmony demanded, her hands balling into fists as if ready to fight.

The woman raised her right hand and pointed at Harmony with an elegant index finger.

"Don't hurt me, please." Harmony's voice quivered.

The woman continued to keep her finger pointed directly at Harmony as she glided towards her. Goose bumps erupted all over her arms and she shook in fear. Harmony couldn't move from the spot where she stood.

When the woman was about a foot away, she pulled a wallet from her pocket and opened it to reveal her photo ID. She shoved it in Harmony's face and she saw the same sullen face on the ID as the ghostly form holding it.

"Heidi Gomez-Brown?" Harmony read aloud.

Heidi nodded slowly.

"Why are you following me, Heidi?"

The door shuddered as a key was thrust into the keyhole and turned. The sound caught Harmony's attention so she whipped around to see the door swinging open. Arrow stood in the opening. He looked mildly surprised, but not nearly as surprised as he should have been upon seeing her apparition in his room.

"Hello. To what do I owe this pleasure?" Arrow asked kindly.

"I…" Harmony glanced behind her and nothing was there. She quickly decided she didn't want to explain just now. "I'm doing my job assignment." She shrugged, unsure what else to say.

"Can I help?"

"No. It's fine. I'll be back later." Harmony picked up her cleaning supplies and rushed toward the exit

Arrow held out an arm to stop her. "You don't have to go on my account."

"I…" Before Heidi had appeared, Harmony would have been excited for the opportunity to stay here and speak with him. Now she felt scared to be in this space. "I'm not sure I'm supposed to keep cleaning when residents come back to their rooms." She said lamely.

Arrow's brow wrinkled up in confusion. " I think we'll be fine for the moment. Besides…" Arrow paused and scratched the back of his neck so he didn't have to look her in the eyes. "I wanted to talk to you. I wanted to be open with you…about my past. How Doc and I met." He gestured with his other arm to the sitting area in the room.

Harmony hesitated but once Arrow sat on the couch, she sat across from him in the recliner and set her cleaning supplies on the floor. She was curious now and could sense that this was hard for Arrow to talk about.

"I used to sell microchips. So, I was just another pharmaceutical rep to Dr. Evers. We talked now and then but we didn't get close until the trial."

"Trial for…what?" Harmony asked tentatively. She was afraid to know the answer.

"Well, I got mixed up in a dealing ring. I had hacker codes for the chips that I was selling to individual patients. I thought I was helping alleviate suffering but I just was one of the pawns aiding a bigger dealer ring. With Clive's testimony about my character, I almost got off without prison time until my fiance testified against me." Arrow rubbed his beard thoughtfully as if trying to recall more of the story, but Harmony could see that his eyes were sparkling with unshed tears.

"Why would she do that?" Harmony asked finally.

"She was scared." He shrugged. "But it was the nail in the coffin. Since I was only one of many, they gave me a deal but I still was in prison for 5 years."

She knew this fact should bother her. Harmony was trying to focus on being compassionate, but the jealous thought kept flitting through her mind, *"He had a fiance."* She finally was able to shove that out and replace it with a stronger thought, *"But he's here with you now."* She placed her hand on his knee. He stared at it for a moment and then wrapped his bigger and stronger hand on top of hers. She could feel electricity and warmth flowing from his fingertips and up her arm.

"When I got out, they had me come here to transition from prison life to the outside world. It really helped."

"Did you see your fiance again?" Harmony asked.

"No." He shook his head sadly. "I shouldn't but I miss her sometimes."

"Oh." She said simply, still trying hard to conceal the jealousy that rose again.

"That door is never going to open again, though. I am working hard to move on." His eyes then met hers. "So, what's your story?" He squeezed her hand and leaned back into the corner of the sofa to get comfortable.

She missed the warmth from his hand but reluctantly released his knee. "Well, nothing complicated. I worked in an office. My mom is Cuban and my dad is white and only god knows where." She shrugged. "But you know that already."

"Yeah, I do." He chuckled.

"Clive isn't really that bad." Harmony said changing the subject. "I wasn't sure I liked him at first."

"He's an alright dude when you get to know him better. His arrogance is just a defense mechanism." Arrow said. "But I understand why you didn't like him at first."

"How's Pat?"

"I dunno. You tell me. He doesn't talk much."

"He seems troubled." Harmony said simply.

Arrow nodded in agreement.

As silence fell between them and the only sound came from the curtains rustling as the heat began to blow into the room from the floor register. The room smelled old and she realized that this place was probably authentically old and not just manufactured to look that way. It was rare to see something that was actually old. Everybody was always striving for new.

Arrow didn't seem to struggle to be authentic. "Well, I better get back to my job and let you get back to yours."

"Oh, right." She bolted up from the couch and leaned down to grab her supplies. "What job are you doing?"

"Top secret I'm afraid. Otherwise, I'd tell you." Arrow said apologetically.

"Oh, right." Harmony felt hurt but she tried to remind herself that he had been so open with her already. This one thing didn't matter in the grand scheme of things. She bustled to the exit and was followed by Arrow whose eyebrows were knitted together in an apology.

"So, goodbye." Harmony lifted three fingers from her cleaning caddy to wave slightly and Arrow rushed around to open the door for her. "Thanks."

"Have a good day, Harmony."

She didn't want to look into his face but her eyes were drawn to his. They were crinkled in a smile that melted her insides. "You too." She mumbled and hurried away.

CHAPTER 24

THE DAY ARRIVED WHEN PAT, ZION, and Clive were going to take a trip to examine the anomaly in the skies. In spite of himself, Pat was hopeful they would find clues to finding his wife. As they waited for Clive, Zion reviewed some of the trip details.

"I wish Rachel could come with us but she is at a women's retreat this week. We'll need to record whatever we find and bring it back to show her."

Pat nodded absentmindedly. He kept thinking of Justice. The excitement that Zion had about his wife reminded him of his own joy when he got married. A lot of couples they knew complained about spending excessive amounts of time together, but Pat and Justice worked together and spent most of their downtime together. That's why her absence was felt much more strongly. His insides had collapsed in on themselves when she was taken because she filled every void.

"Where is Clive?" Zion asked finally, sounding a little put out.

"I'm not sure." Pat admitted.

"Well, if he isn't here in five more minutes, we'll go on without him." Zion said, still with a smile on his face.

Pat shrugged. "Sounds good."

Five minutes passed and he still hadn't arrived so Zion climbed into the driver's side of the car and Pat slid into the passenger's seat.

"His loss. You all aren't being paid or court-ordered to be here so I give you much more leeway."

"Of course." Pat nodded. He was relieved he wouldn't have to handle Clive's pompous attitude on this trip.

The tinkling sound of a piano wafted from the radio and cool air blasted through the vents blowing Pat's fluffy hair back off his forehead.

"If you want to turn the AC down, feel free. I tend to be hot-natured." Zion chuckled.

"Okay." Pat turned it down and closed the vent nearest to the passenger window.

Patrick Sherwood would have been fine if that had been the extent of their conversation, but he knew he wouldn't be getting off that easy with Zion who seemed to like to talk.

Once they had driven through the gate, Zion said, "So, tell me about yourself."

Pat waited for more to follow this statement, but when nothing did he said, "What would you like to know?"

Zion continued to stare at the road ahead as he said, "Well, obviously, the general public pretends to know more about you than they actually do. I just assume most of what is in the news is exaggerated." Zion glanced at Pat out of the corner of his eyes.

"You are right about that." Pat couldn't help agreeing. "I am not the sorry orphan of Owen Sherwood. I think they exaggerated the level of grief I was experiencing when he passed."

Zion did not respond to this as he turned the car onto the highway.

"I was an adult when he passed so I doubt that classifies me as an orphan." Pat laughed at his own joke but Zion was still allowing

Pat room to speak, which was not something he was used to. "So, I work at Sherwood Servers as the CEO and I live alone." Pat shrugged to conceal the lie. He could visualize the disappointed face of Justice as he denied her existence. "I barely know Zion." Pat muttered, hoping Justice would hear him.

"Do you like working in the tech business?" Zion asked, seemingly unaware that Pat had just spoken to Justice out loud.

"Uh…as much as one can."

Zion made a noise to show he was still listening.

"I am not sure it is my niche." Pat conceded.

"That's okay. You're honoring your father by maintaining his life's work."

"I did not think about it that way." Pat said honestly.

Zion smiled. "It's hard to see the positive in our own lives." He left the highway and turned right onto a small country road next. "Look." He pointed straight ahead.

Pat looked at where he was pointing and could see a slight sliver on the horizon. "How long do you think it will take for us to get there?"

"Maybe a couple of hours." Zion answered.

Pat's face didn't budge but internally he sighed in exasperation. He now almost wished that Clive was here to take the pressure off of him from socializing. As the social anxiety was setting in, Pat could hear the screaming at the far corners of his brain. This then made him do something he generally never did. "What about you?"

"What about me?"

"Do you like your work?"

"I adore what I do." Zion glanced at Pat with a smile that could melt any icy heart.

Pat's heart was made of stone.

***

Zion's excitement was noticeably growing the closer they came to the thin black line. Pat could even feel a change in air pressure as they neared. His ears popped and the left ear felt like it was draining.

"Did ya feel that?" Zion asked in an excited whisper as if his ear had just drained too.

Pat nodded but continued to stare straight ahead. At the beginning of their journey, the skies had been mostly clear and the weather calm. Now on the horizon, black clouds were steadily making their way towards them. The land on either side of the highway was barren save for a few spindly trees. After a few minutes, Zion turned right into a pitiful-looking subdivision. Each home looked like the owners had gone to no effort to maintain the landscaping or paint. The corner house was a double wide on cinder block legs and Pat worried that it would go tumbling off its foundation once the storm rolled in.

Zion drove past this home and to the end of the dead-end street where caution signs were posted. He turned off the car and looked at Pat with sparkling eyes.

"Well, I say we park here and go the rest of the way on foot."

Pat didn't argue. He began grabbing equipment and fell in step behind the excited Christian scientist. The temperature had dropped as well so Pat pulled his sweater tighter around his slim frame, but it didn't seem to help. He had always struggled to stay warm and his size did not help this issue much.

Even though Zion was slightly shorter than Pat, he was ahead by several strides. The black line they had been following was now as wide as a creek and just as fluid. Pat could understand why others hadn't noticed it before. It rippled to where the stark colors of it simply blended into the background. Somebody might have thought it was the wind or some sort of heat wave. But it was autumn and there was nothing hot enough to cause a natural heat wave to occur.

"Of course, Clive is going to be disappointed he missed this."

Zion finished, and Pat realized he had been ignoring everything Zion had said.

"Why do you say that?"

Zion smiled. "Because," He stepped over a cluster of rocks as he spoke. "We are at the forefront of this research, and…"

Pat knew that something was very wrong as soon as they were within yards of the anomaly. As if the tear in the fabric of reality had been waiting for them, three trees created a perfect triangle in the sparse grass. The black clouds billowed up in a tower behind them and concealed the black line in the sky. But what was truly sickening was the woman bent and broken on the ground in the center of the trees. Her white blond hair spilled up over her face concealing her identity but Pat knew who it must be.

"Rach…" Zion whispered.

There was no way she was alive. The unnatural curve of her spine indicated it was broken and blood seeped out onto the ground killing the grass in its wake.

"Oh, Lord God in Heaven." Zion breathed. In a state of shock, he placed his equipment down and walked in a trance to his wife.

Pat's mind was brought back to the day he had watched Justice be taken away. For a moment, the blond hair became vibrant red and Pat's feet itched to run to her.

"Patty." Justice stood beside him looking on in sadness. The wind was picking up in intensity so her waist-length red hair danced.

"I can't do it!" Zion shouted to the sky. "This is beyond what I can handle, Lord God!" Zion's sobs shook his entire body.

"How did this happen?" Pat asked Justice.

She glanced at him and placed a finger to her lips to silence him and instructed him to watch.

"Who did this to you?" Zion demanded of his silent wife. Tentatively, he reached out with his right hand and as soon as his fingertips made contact, the body dissolved into a flock of crows and flew into the black line in the sky.

Zion's gaze whipped around to look at Pat pleading for answers. Pat instantly looked at where Justice had been standing but she was no longer there. He then looked back at Zion who was now standing. All that was left in the man's eyes was emptiness.

Comfort was not something that Pat was good at so he shouted out, "Is it an apparition?"

Zion did not answer but pulled his phone from his pocket and dialed a number. In a moment, Zion had fallen on his knees and sobbed happy tears.

"Oh, Rachel Rachel Rachel."

Pat turned his back on Zion so he would have some privacy. Pat could feel a few drops of rain here and there hitting his skin but he didn't want to leave Zion behind. He didn't have to wait long because Zion had suddenly picked up his equipment and continued to talk on the phone while gesturing for Pat to go back to the car. Zion's face still looked sapped of energy, but his color had returned with the relief of being able to speak to his wife on the phone.

Once they were in the car, Zion said, "I love you, darling." And hung up. "She's okay."

"That is good." Pat said. "What do we need to do now?"

"I'm thinking." Zion said simply. "I'm rattled. It must be an apparition from when I was chipped and having my night terrors. I don't remember it but it must be from my imagination because I don't know of anybody else who would be imagining horrific things like that. My night terrors have always been terrible."

"Why do you believe in a God that lets you suffer through that?" Pat said finally.

Zion didn't answer right away. The wheels turned behind his eyes and Pat could tell he was trying to find the right words to answer the question. This was something that Pat could admire about this man — the care with which he said things.

"A good God will allow things to happen to keep us from becoming the darkest versions of ourselves. We are always being refined. He always completes the good work he has started in us." Zion bit his lip thoughtfully. "The struggle reminds me of all the goodness I've been given and the good God I serve. I am so finite but he is so great."

"That sounds masochistic." Pat said flatly. He couldn't understand Christians and their need to go through suffering to be a good person. "Humanity shouldn't need to suffer to be better. We should be allowed to figure it out ourselves."

"Wouldn't that be amazing?" Zion sighed. The emotional exhaustion seemed to be creeping back into Zion's eyes now as he started the car up. "Let's go back and take a breather. The weather is getting bad out here and I need to think and pray." His eyes were trained on the backup camera screen and he skillfully turned around to head back home. "I don't want to suffer but I know I am a stubborn human being with an inherently sinful nature. I can't fix myself."

"Pretty messed up still." Pat said.

Zion laughed. "It's the truth."

Pat shook his head. "You're going to have to work a lot harder to convince me. I'm extremely skeptical."

"You shouldn't say that kind of stuff to me. I will take you up on it."

Pat glanced up at the rearview mirror and it looked as though the storm was chasing them. It made him feel nervous because it was so dark you couldn't see anything through the clouds. It reminded him of the beast that took Justice.

"I think I saw my wife too." Pat said, suddenly changing the subject.

The teasing smile faded from Zion's face. "What do you mean?"

"When you saw the apparition of your wife, I saw my wife

standing beside me. She spoke to me." Pat cocked his head to the side and scratched the tip of his nose to partially conceal his face where a flash of despair flickered over his features.

"Was that the first time?"

Pat sucked in a deep breath. "No."

"When did she pass away?"

This question caught Pat off-guard. "She's still alive."

"I'm so sorry. I assumed about what happened from news reports." Zion said honestly.

"They say she was murdered but her body was never found. They found parts of my Father but not a piece of evidence was found for Justice. I continue to see her beside me and in my dreams. She's so real." Opening up to this man he barely knew was not like him. Pat had to use all his self-control to keep from letting tears fall down his cheeks. Even so, he sniffed slightly as his nose refused to get the memo about not crying.

"What happened to your mother?" Zion pressed on and Pat felt pressure in his heart.

"She committed suicide when I was two years old." Pat said softly. The raw truth of it tore through him like a knife. He didn't know why it hurt so much. He didn't remember his mother but the loss of her was still something noticeable whenever he spoke with other men his age who still had their mothers.

"This is a heavy burden for you to be under, Pat." Zion said. "My heart breaks for your loss and lack of closure."

"I don't remember my mom. But, Justice, I want to find her." Pat pushed on trying not to acknowledge the kindest piece of sympathy he had ever been given. "I think she might be where the apparitions are coming from."

"When we get back, let's discuss this with Dr. Evers and figure out a plan of attack."

CHAPTER 25

Clive was normally not a rule breaker, but instead of going with Pat and Zion, he decided to keep tabs on Arrow. Arrow was involved in his wife's rescue somehow and Clive suspected he would lead him to where Mayre was being kept. Another thing the doctor did that was against his personality was to wear all black. Being the fashion-conscious individual that he was, he tended to pair a vibrant tie with chic neutrals. Today, he wore black sweats and a black t-shirt he found at the bottom of the dresser in his room.

As it neared dinnertime, Clive saw Arrow leaving the dining room early. As he followed from a distance, Arrow seemed to be deep in thought and didn't notice Clive. After several twists and turns, they ended up at the back of the main house. Arrow exited and Clive followed as soon as the door shut. Peeking through the windows at the top of the door, he saw Arrow walk towards a black car that was being loaded up with supplies.

Clive's moment came when everybody loading the vehicle walked around to the front of the house. The trunk was still open, so Clive only entertained his half-baked idea for a moment before rushing out. Climbing into the trunk he pushed to the very back and rearranged the bags around him to hide the parts of his body not covered in black fabric. Just as he settled in, he heard the sound of voices. A couple more things were dropped into the trunk and then the hatch was shut, plunging the space into cool darkness.

The limited airflow inside the trunk made his heart rate speed up for a moment. It was thrilling and frightening all at once. He had never done anything like this before and he felt somewhat proud of the lengths he was going to save Mayre.

"I'm coming, Mayre." Clive breathed.

The car then roared to life and they were crunching over gravel. This jostled him around a lot until they reached the paved road outside the facility. During Clive's extraordinarily cushy life, he had never experienced something quite as uncomfortable as the trunk of a car. All the worst smells were stronger in the confined space and the feeling of being crushed by darkness was inescapable. Every time they went downhill or hit a bump his body would shift uncomfortably to one direction or the other.

The only thing that kept him going was what people would say about him when he arrived home with his beautiful wife. They would recount the great lengths he had gone to save her. He was seen as a hero by many already, but it would add to his credibility as a practitioner if he was a family man as well. Mayre would also be pleased, and this was the one thing that Clive was convinced would win her back to him.

The minutes passed at a crawl and Clive was beginning to feel like he couldn't go any longer. He was not prone to anxiety, but riding in a car in this fashion was testing his fortitude as a man and as a doctor.

Clive sensed a shift in the car's course as it slowed down and began to turn. In a few short seconds, the car pulled to a stop and the engine powered down. He did his best to pull back to the furthest reaches of the trunk and cover himself with supplies, but it was fruitless because they spotted him immediately.

"Arrow?" A young woman called over her shoulder uncertainly. She was dressed in all black and had a handgun holstered at her waist. Her hair was tied in a tight blue ponytail. Clive recognized her as the keyboard player during the church service.

At her call, Arrow rounded the corner and didn't seem surprised to see Clive curled up behind their supplies. "How's it going, Doc?"

Clive shifted and began to crawl out of the confined space. As he placed his right foot on the blacktop, he realized that his foot had fallen asleep, and he crumpled to the ground hitting his cheek hard. "It's going." He grunted, sitting up and stretching the numb leg until it began to tingle.

Arrow reached out his hand to his friend. Clive took it gratefully and stood. "I figured you'd find a way."

"It's my wife, Arrow." Clive said simply.

"Exactly. You're too emotionally invested to be here." Arrow argued.

The girl who had found Clive was standing awkwardly behind the men and trying to appear uninterested in the conversation. A couple of others circled waiting for orders from their leader.

"That's exactly why I need to be here. I will do anything to get her back." Clive's usual crooked smile wasn't present on his face but had been replaced by a firm and determined line. "Besides, I don't recall how any of you are more qualified than I am."

"What are you saying?" Arrow demanded.

"Are you part of the CIA and I didn't know it? Are you cops or Navy Seals? Are you even licensed to carry guns?" Clive waved his hand at the firearms being pulled from the trunk.

"I have a concealed carry license." Sirona said.

"So do I." Arrow said. "Everybody here except you has their license to carry. No, we're not specially trained, but the people in power who do have specialized training aren't doing anything."

The keyboardist with the blue hair whose name was Juliet and a middle-aged woman with stringy brown hair named Charlotte were instructed to stay in the car to be in charge of surveillance and communication. Meanwhile, Sirona, Misha the drummer, and Arrow clipped communication devices and first aid supplies to their belt.

"First rule…" Arrow continued, addressing the entire group. "The first rule is to only shoot if threatened or there is somebody else in danger. We do not react out of desperation or fear of failure." Arrow's eyes narrowed as they landed back on Clive. Clive nodded reluctantly. Arrow studied his friend a few more moments then said, "You will not be getting a firearm. But, since you're already here, I imagine we can't stop you from going with us." Arrow reached into the trunk and pulled out a can of pepper spray, and Clive took it gratefully and clipped it around his waist.

"Alright guys," Arrow clapped his hands together and rubbed them. "Last time we did this mission, we failed. Failure is not an option now."

"Better not be…" Clive muttered.

"What did you say, Doc?" Arrow asked a slight edge to his voice.

"I won't let us fail this time. That's why I'm here." Clive said, loud enough for everybody to hear.

Sirona ducked her head in shame and Misha stared at Clive in open disbelief. The two women handling surveillance continued to prepare the car and tried to ignore what was going on.

"This group was handpicked by me. Even if you weren't here, I would have ensured that your wife was returned with us safely." Arrow's tone was kind but firm.

Before he could stop himself, Clive's dormant anger and pain flared up as he said, "Sirona? Really? She failed the first time. And you? A drunk. An alcoholic in denial."

Everybody stopped moving. A few distant cars rushing on the highway could be heard and Sirona sniffed, but otherwise, it was completely silent.

Arrow closed the gap between him and Clive. Clive was reminded how much bigger Arrow was than him and immediately regretted what he said. "Look, if you can't show some respect and work together with us, I will make you stay behind. Sirona is here because she has comprehensive knowledge of this facility. She did not have any preparation time in the first instance. Secondly…" Arrow jabbed a finger into his broad chest. "…I know my weaknesses. I know what I've done. That has changed and I know the responsibility I have in this situation is great. I would never allow myself to be intoxicated while on a rescue."

Clive nodded, feeling an unfamiliar feeling of shame begin creeping across him. "I'll be respectful." He said simply.

"Good." Arrow nodded, then turned to Misha and Sirona. "Let's go. Stay close to me."

Clive followed and took a quick assessment of their surroundings. They were in a perfectly square parking lot with very few cars, illuminated by silent LED street lamps. The surrounding area was dotted with trees and beyond the trees was a major highway. Clive understood why they had chosen this spot. The business that used to be operational here had been closed for a long time by the looks of it. It was a small white cinderblock building with a faded palm tree mural painted on the side. It gave them just enough cover to be able to approach the doctor's office from behind without being seen.

"We will be listening to Juliet and Charlotte on the radios to give us the signal. They will temporarily disable security for us to get in the back and we will need to locate the patients. There are fewer employees working today due to our inside contact, so hopefully we will be in and out very quickly."

"Okay, got it." Clive agreed.

"Don't you dare go off on your own." Arrow said firmly.

"You're telling ME this?"

"I don't mess around when others are involved." Arrow said firmly.

Clive didn't comment. He had seen Arrow drunk and out of his mind. He had seen him in prison. He had seen him in a suit and tie. He had seen him in love. He had never seen Arrow responsible.

"The cameras will be deactivated in three minutes." Sounded a female voice from the radio.

"Good deal." Arrow responded. He flipped his left wrist around and set a timer on his watch for three minutes.

Clive did not like being a follower. He liked to be in charge and have an understanding of all aspects of a situation. In this case, all of his trust was in the hands of a functioning alcoholic, a woman who had failed before, and an intimidating-looking man he barely knew.

When Arrow's timer went off, they opened the door quickly. Once they were inside, they were assaulted by cool LED lighting and white walls. The hall before them was lined with shut doors and stretched far into the building, intersecting with another hallway going the opposite direction. Not a soul besides them was in this part of the building, but that wouldn't be for long. Clive knew from experience that medical facilities rarely stayed quiet for enough time to allow trespassers to wander around.

"Down here." Arrow said gruffly as he marched to the third door on the left of the hall.

The door opened easily and brought them into some sort of computer lab. The main lighting was off, but each computer screen glowed dimly in the gloom. Arrow gestured silently to the group to follow again and they all piled into a large supply closet at the far left-hand corner of the space. When the door clicked shut, Clive became very aware of the cologne that Misha was wearing. It was musky and strong.

"Wait until I give the signal. You may be in this closet for 30 to 45 minutes." One of the women said over the radio.

Clive nodded, but nobody could see each other in the darkness and even if the light had been on, the women back at the car would have no idea that he nodded. Clive spent most of his life being "on" and ready to socialize, so even in the darkness, he was trying to make sure he was giving off the proper body language.

As minutes ticked by, the group stood in a tight clump, elbow touching elbow, but it wasn't awkward. Business was business. However, it crossed Clive's mind that this space wouldn't have been nearly as cramped if he hadn't stowed away.

However, if they had included him earlier, accommodations might have been made in advance.

"This isn't what I expected." Clive said breaking the silence.

"What are you talking about?" Misha asked sharply.

"Not as much action." Clive tried to sound lighthearted.

Misha grunted in response but refused to continue the conversation.

30 minutes later from the failed conversation starter, they were given the signal to go. According to the women, the employees were doing shift change reports for the incoming night staff and would be gathered up at the front of the building.

"You're looking for room 101B." The voice that identified herself as Charlotte said.

"Got it." Arrow confirmed.

They all made a concerted effort to make no noise and Clive did his best to mimic what the others were doing. Clive then caught the expression on Sirona's face and was surprised by how intense and sorrowful she looked. When they reached the end of the hallway, Arrow put a cautious hand on the butt of his gun as he peered left, then right.

"It's clear." He whispered.

There was a sign on the wall noting that rooms 100-130 were in this part of the building. They had barely walked a few yards before the sign for room 101B was clearly in sight. The group paused and Clive was surprised by how easy it had been to find. His heart rate increased as the idea of Mayre being behind this door settled into his brain.

"The door is unlocked." The radio chirped.

Arrow grasped the handle and turned. The first smell was of bleach and lemons. The floors inside were laminate wood and the lighting made the space feel like they were outside, except there were no windows.

Clive's eyes immediately noticed Mayre. He could never forget her face and would always find it in a crowded space. However, in this space, it was much easier to notice. The only things in this room were a hospital bed, beeping machinery, a recliner, and a nurse kneeling beside where Mayre was resting.

"Mayre!" Clive exclaimed and rushed to his love.

The nurse at her side looked startled, but Clive didn't care. This was his wife and nothing could prevent him from accessing her.

He realized something was very wrong as soon as his hand touched hers. "What's going on?" He demanded of the nurse.

"Sir, you're not allowed to be in here." The nurse sounded absolutely terrified.

Several choice words jangled in his brain but he composed himself and said, "This is my wife. What's wrong with her?"

The nurse was thinking hard about his words. After several moments, she decided to trust him and said, "She's only here in body. Otherwise, she's gone."

The reality of what she had said settled on him like dust. His skin itched and his eyes burned. Inexplicably, all he could feel was fear. Pulling the pepper spray from his belt and standing to his feet he pointed it at the nurse's face. "You're lying!"

"Don't!" Sirona shouted and joined them at the recliner. She had her gun raised and trained on Clive.

"I just want answers." Clive said slowly, forever the diplomat.

"Dr. Evers, weren't you fired?" Said a tired voice from the doorway.

Clive turned to where the new voice had come from and saw Preston Winston there in a white coat. In the chaos, Arrow and Misha had neglected to watch the door.

"Preston?" Clive slowly lowered the pepper spray.

"Good man. Please don't burn the eyeballs of any of my employees."

Sirona lowered her gun, but Arrow continued to keep a hand on the butt of his.

"What's wrong with my wife?" Clive demanded.

"Unfortunately, she has become nothing more than a human vegetable. There is no way to get her back."

This couldn't be reality and Clive refused to believe it. She was just resting or in some sort of coma. She would be brought back to him and Preston would be sued for every inch of his life for traumatizing Dr. Clive Evers with his lies.

"Does Zion know about this?" Arrow demanded.

Preston laughed shortly, "Only what I want him to know." Preston shrugged then changed the subject. "You all are definitely trespassing, though. Except for you." He gestured at Sirona. "Glad you came back. We are pretty understaffed currently."

Clive's brain was a buzzing hive of anger now. He lunged for the man but was stopped by two security guards barreling through the door to protect Preston from bodily harm. Clive was a strong man, but not nearly as strong as these walls of muscle before him.

"You idiot!" Arrow shouted as he threw himself into the fray.

The addition of Arrow may have thrown the guards off balance, but it did not keep them from reaching for their own guns in self-defense. Clive couldn't be sure what happened next, but he heard a gun go off and the sound of a body falling onto the ground.

"Take them." Preston said, cooly.

"Yes, sir." Said one of the men.

Clive tried to fight, but the man in charge of him was strong and began to drag him away. Arrow was being dragged by the other guard. Once they were on their way, Clive could clearly see Misha lying on the floor in a growing pool of his own blood. He had seemed so strong and full of life, but now he was dead. All of his physical strength was not enough to save him.

CHAPTER 26

RACHEL WAS AT A WOMEN'S CONFERENCE, which then left Harmony to her own devices for a few days. To keep occupied, Rachel had assigned her new cleaning duties in addition to the bedrooms. This kept her much busier than usual, but she was struggling to stay motivated enough to get the tasks done. She loved having her mind occupied but hated how mundane the work was becoming.

Another reason for her lack of motivation was that her mind kept drifting to Arrow. If she didn't know any better, she would have thought that somebody had hacked her chip again and made her fall for a man who had so many issues. She did know better though, and she had done the falling all on her own.

Harmony had always prided herself on not being the type of girl to have relationship drama. She ate up all the gossip at work about the drama of others, but never her. In a way, she had been jealous of this but knew in the practical part of her brain that drama would just cause her an undue amount of stress.

She almost wished that she could see Romilda's face if she knew where Harmony was now and what she was up to. Life was exciting for the first time and Harmony was getting to experience it all firsthand. It was thrilling, frightening, and aggravating all at once.

These thoughts swirled through her mind as she made her way to one of the labs in the main house. Rachel had explained how this particular lab was generally for private research. Zion, Clive, and Pat would be utilizing it later in the afternoon, but for now, Rachel had said it needed cleaning.

Harmony utilized the master key to open the door and walked inside the very well-lit space. Floor-to-ceiling windows filled up the entire left-hand wall, but tall pine trees were blocking anybody from having a real view. On the opposite wall, there were metal shelves filled with boxes, beakers, and clutter. Spaced out across the L-shaped room were long work tables covered in books, chemistry supplies, computers, and leftover cans of soda. In the foot of the L-shape space was a tall metal supply cabinet with a door, and Harmony assumed it must be full of scientific implements of some kind.

Overwhelmed by the mess, she pinched the bridge of her nose to ease a headache that began to throb in her sinuses. "Okay, Harmony, you got this. There's no rush." She muttered to herself.

To encourage an upbeat attitude, she went to one of the computers and signed in as a guest to find a website with music on it. The first playlist she found was fun, so she let it fill the silence.

She started by throwing away the trash that cluttered the tables. When that was done, she picked up every beaker and glass cup that needed washing and went to the sink that was sitting in front of one of the windows. It took longer to work through these items because each beaker was difficult to get a cleaning rag inside. She looked under the sink and around the room for some sort of bottle brush to make the process go by faster.

Nothing was near the sink, so Harmony decided to look in the tall metal utility closet nearby. To her dismay, it was locked and none of her keys seemed to work on it. Grumbling, she walked back to the sink and continued to wash the beakers the hard way.

As she was rinsing the last beaker and turned to her right to place it on the drying mat, she caught a glimpse of someone standing nearby. With a shriek, the glass beaker fell from her hand onto the floor and her heart slammed against her ribs like it was trying to escape the prison of her body. It was Heidi.

"Why won't you speak to me?" Harmony asked, struggling to keep her voice from shaking.

The woman didn't answer. In the daylight streaming through the topmost part of the windows, she appeared to be glowing. The upbeat music in the background would have been comical if Harmony hadn't been so scared.

"Why are you following me?" The woman suddenly looked sad. "You are beautiful." Harmony said as if she had just realized this fact.

Harmony wasn't sure what made her blurt it out, but the comment seemed to please Heidi. She placed her right hand flat against her lips and moved it outward in what Harmony recognized as the ASL sign for "Thank you". Heidi then turned to leave.

"Don't go! Sign to me. I'll figure it out. I need to know what's going on."

Heidi ignored these words and continued to walk towards the metal closet, and Harmony noticed the door was hanging open. Heidi's footfalls made no sound on the concrete floor, which was even stranger.

At that moment, Harmony decided she wouldn't allow her fear to get the best of her. She stepped over the broken glass on the floor and rushed after Heidi. As her hand reached out to touch the girl, it passed right through. Harmony's skin tingled and her mind exploded into a vision of Arrow. He was in a jail cell somewhere and looked miserable.

When the vision cleared, she saw that her touch hadn't slowed Heidi in the slightest and that she was already disappearing into the darkness. "Where is Arrow?? Where are you keeping him?" She called.

She continued to run after Heidi and when she was level with the doorway of the supply closet, she looked inside and saw nothing but mist. It only took her a moment to deliberate on what she should do and then she continued to follow her. The mist quickly turned into thick fog and she was unable to see more than a foot in front of her. The temperature had shifted abruptly from the heated mansion to cold. The ground beneath her was firm earth with patches of grass here and there. The lack of visibility made the world around her seem vast and claustrophobic at the same time.

"Heidi!" She screamed one final time before her foot hit a tree limb and she went flying face-first into a creek.

Sputtering, she pulled herself up out of the cold mud and coughed up water and leaves. Up in the tree, she heard the shrill cry of a crow followed by distant rumbling. More cautious now, she pulled herself onto a large stone nearby and listened harder. The rumbling continued as if a storm was coming. She still could only see slivers of the tree that had tripped her and a creek.

It occurred to her that this couldn't possibly be inside Zion's supply cabinet. It also occurred to her that this was not outside the mansion. It was bright and sunny before and now she was somewhere else entirely.

Standing to her feet, she tried to reorient herself and head back the way she came. She was certain it wasn't very far from where she stood so she felt confident. Heidi was nowhere to be found, and Harmony reasoned that it wouldn't help Arrow if she didn't have a clue where she was.

After more than ten minutes of wandering, her confidence waned. There was no doorway and the fog continued to be as thick as ever. She was much more careful with where she stepped so she didn't fall into any more creeks, but that didn't do anything to ease the rising panic welling in her throat.

Even though she thought she was heading away from the storm, the ominous rumbling continued to echo in the space. She jumped at the cries of unidentified animals and began to see strange things lying on the path below her feet that she couldn't describe. She hoped that if she kept moving forward she would stumble across something or find someone, but she was beginning to doubt that anybody would be able to survive in this place. Heidi must have led her into a trap.

Even though she wasn't religious, she said a prayer to whichever entity would listen. As if in answer to her prayer, a figure suddenly appeared in the fog. She could not identify any distinguishing characteristics, but from the outline, it appeared to be a woman in a dress or cloak.

"Hello?" Harmony's voice quivered, but it seemed loud in this place.

The figure did not answer but continued to move towards her. Everything in Harmony's body was telling her to run from danger, but her mind was trying to reason that maybe this person was lost like her and that her anxiety was playing tricks on her.

Her instincts were right the first time though, because the familiar horrific face of the impaled woman at the gas station appeared and was moving faster in her direction. Without any concern for the tree roots beneath her feet, she ran away from the danger and off the beaten path.

***

Pat and Zion arrived back at the main house and went to the dining room for a late dinner. Pat was much hungrier than he expected. He and Zion continued to chat over their meal and Pat had to admit he was beginning to like this man. Zion's joy was contagious and Pat could feel it in his bones. Pat didn't recognize himself when he wasn't sad.

"I think we should go get Clive after dinner, then head back to the lab." Zion said happily.

"Where do you think he is at?"

"I'd say we should check his room first. Maybe he just needed a day off." Zion stood and dropped off his dirty dishes in the kitchen. Pat followed suit.

Once they had said hello to practically every resident in the place, they were finally outside Clive's room. Zion knocked loudly and called out. As they waited a few beats, the only sound they heard was distant chattering from downstairs.

"Dr. Evers?" Zion called again and rapped on the wood surface. "Maybe something's wrong." He muttered as he pulled a ring of keys from his pocket.

Once inside the room, it was apparent that Clive wasn't there.

"Maybe he's already in the lab." Pat offered.

"You could be right." Zion conceded brightly.

Clive was not in the lab either, but Pat immediately noticed that it was much cleaner than how they had left it.

"Did you leave the closet open?" Zion asked, pointing to the supply closet at the end of the room.

Pat shook his head. Zion walked around the tables and made a beeline for the supply cabinet, but before he could get there, his shoes crunched something on the floor. Pat looked down and saw Zion picking glass shards from the bottom of his shoes. For a room that had just been cleaned, the glass on the floor was odd. Zion's eyes widened and he hurried over to the closet. As Zion peered inside, Pat followed him, making sure to avoid the broken glass.

"I think we have what we were looking for in our very own lab." Zion breathed.

"What do you mean?" Pat took several long strides to stand beside Zion and peered curiously into the cabinet. As Zion moved aside slightly, Pat could see that a dense fog seemed to fill the space and a few black tree limbs seemed to be reaching for the two men.

A vicious pleasure rose inside him as he sensed this place was similar to the place from his portal at home.

"I wonder if somebody might have been taken." Zion wondered aloud.

"Taken?"

Zion nodded slowly, the wheels turning behind his eyes. Finally, he said, "Do you think Dr. Evers has been taken?"

"If he had, wouldn't we have seen this before we left?"

"He could have come down here later." Zion suggested. He then sighed and looked to the ceiling. "May the good Lord preserve whoever has been taken."

Pat felt very uncertain at this pronouncement and followed Zion at a distance as he walked away mumbling to himself.

"What's going on, sweetheart?" Rachel had returned and she was walking towards them with a wide smile.

Shaken from his musings, Zion's eyes lit up and he rushed for his wife. He picked her up by her narrow waist and lifted her into the air. She laughed loudly and smiled down into his glowing face. He lowered her slowly onto his chest and she embraced him. As they kissed deeply, Pat turned away.

Normally, he wasn't a fan of PDA, but in this instance he understood it. If he could have kissed Justice that deeply he would have. This is why he had to look away. Love that pure was something he wished he still had. As time went on, he was becoming more convinced that this lonely new life would be his forever. That he would need to wake up every morning feeling empty or feeling like an unfinished song playing on repeat. He was always striving to get better every day, but just ended up feeling incomplete.

"I'm so glad you came home early. We were trying to figure out what happened." Zion said to his wife after he had loved on her sufficiently. He explained to her what they had found and what they were theorizing. When he was done explaining, Rachel gazed at him wide-eyed and bit her lip. "What's wrong?"

"I asked Harmony to clean up in here." She said softly. She turned on her heel and rushed from the room. Before Zion and Pat talked to one another, Rachel was rushing back in, her white-blond hair falling out of her bun in stringy lines around her face. "She's gone and so are her cleaning supplies."

CHAPTER 27

HARMONY COULD FEEL FEAR RADIATING THROUGH her torso like an exploding star. With every beat of her heart, her body burned and tingled, reminding her to run. After stumbling over more tree roots and slipping across slick areas on the ground, she finally arrived in a place that had more visibility. She glanced behind her and the creature was nowhere in sight. Slowing down, she took this opportunity to catch her breath.

As she did this, it occurred to her that the air didn't smell good. The potent smell landed on her tongue first and made her spit on the ground. As she took a few more steadying breaths, she guessed that what she was smelling was a mix of sewage and rotting trees. To filter the air, she pulled her shirt collar up over her nose and mouth. Now that she could properly focus, she saw ahead of her a field covered with tall grasses. The sky was a gray canvas with barely any sunlight peeping through. Despite the dim light, she could see at the center of the field was a tall marble building with huge columns holding up the roof.

She approached the abandoned structure in the hopes that inside would give her some clue as to where she was. The rumbling was still sounding in the distance, but it seemed further away. It took longer than expected to reach the building. The staircase leading up to the front door had chunks missing from it and clods of dirt littered across what seemed to have been pure white marble. Cautiously, she navigated the staircase. One of the front doors was half hanging off its hinges and the other was still standing strong against the elements. Inside the contents of the interior spaces looked like they had been tipped upside down and scattered all over the floors. Animal feces, dust, dirt, and leaves mingled with piles of books. Even the marble staircase inside was covered in books of various sizes and even some old paintings.

Despite the sad nature of the place, it was beautiful to behold. Harmony wondered why anybody would need this many books. She also wondered who would have let it become destroyed this way. Upon inspection of one of the topmost books on a stack, she realized that most of these were so wet and damaged that it wouldn't even be worth trying to preserve them.

She had never been much of a reader, but it was something that she had hoped to get into someday. Picking her way through the mess, she ended up in what must have been the office due to the desk, lamp, and file cabinets. Every piece of furniture was swimming in books as well. Through one of the broken windows, a breeze blew in and made the brown vines hanging from the sill shiver.

Harmony turned around and decided to explore the next floor instead. Up the magnificent stairs, she climbed until she was standing by the upstairs railing and gazing out at all the books. This place appeared to have been designed to be grand, but it had long ago given up any aspirations of staying that way. Every part of it was crumbling and little animals scurried around the place. It seemed like it could potentially be full of disease, pain, and books that used to hold the answers to important questions.

She ran a finger along the dusty railing, creating a mark she secretly hoped would give hope to others like her that something living had also been in this nearly lifeless library. She had been told stories of libraries that contained only books, but in her world, this was far from reality. Rarely were the books moved from shelves unless you were in the kid's sections. The majority of people came to the library for free technology, music, and audiobooks. This place was a relic of the past and she was charmed by it.

The next room she entered had vastly tall ceilings that curved into a dome shape. One of the sections of the dome had crumbled long ago and curls of the persistent fog made its way through the gap. Bookshelves as tall as trees lined every wall and in the middle of the room were scattered tables. Some were still together and upright and others had been tipped over. The floors here were also littered with forgotten books and dried leaves.

The main difference in this room was the warmth of a living human being. A teenage girl was sitting in a far corner, head bent over her knobby knees and picking at her fingernails. Harmony didn't want to scare her so she tried to wave to get her attention first. The girl was non-responsive and continued to gaze at her hands intently.

When Harmony took a step towards her, a loud crunch sounded, alerting the girl to her presence. She didn't seem afraid but her wide brown eyes had a hunted look in them. Her hair was in multiple knots on her head that looked like a black crown. She was beautiful even though her face had scratches across its surface.

"I'm not here to hurt you," Harmony said quickly.

"Okay." The girl responded. Her voice was empty of all feeling.

"Do you need help?" Harmony asked, even though she had no idea what she'd do if the girl said yes.

"You can't help me."

Harmony began to take more steps toward the girl. When she was only a few yards away she stopped because she could tell the girl was pushing herself even further into the corner.

"Probably not, but I can listen." Harmony answered honestly.

"I don't want to talk about it."

"That's okay." Harmony sat down in a mostly clean part of the floor in front of the girl and said, "I'm Harmony."

"Lacey." The girl said.

"That's a beautiful name."

Lacey shrugged and turned away.

"What is this place?" Harmony asked, changing the subject.

"Oblivion." Lacey began picking at her nails again.

"That's an odd name for a place."

She turned back to Harmony with her soulless eyes and said, "That's just what I call it."

"Oh." Harmony tried not to indicate how frightened she was by that. This girl had obviously been hurt by something but Harmony couldn't figure out what. "Do you know how to leave this place?" Lacey shook her head. "Have you seen a woman with blond dreadlocks and a lot of tattoos?"

Lacey shook her head again. "I haven't seen anybody here."

"Okay." Harmony bit her lip and began to think over her options. She had hoped Lacey would inform her of all the things about this place. It looked like this girl was going to be of no help whatsoever. "Thank you for your assistance."

Harmony stood and the girl looked startled. "You're leaving?"

"Yeah." Harmony said uncomfortably. "I have to get out of here."

"Can you take me?"

"Oh, well…sure." Harmony was surprised by the request, but she couldn't say no.

The girl stood and Harmony was stunned by her height. She must have been 6 feet tall at the very least. Her arms and legs were very skinny and every bone stuck out. Her clothes were disheveled and she noticed that beneath the jacket she wore, her tank top was ripped in two places. Catching her looking, Lacey pulled the jacket around her body and crossed her arms.

"Thank you." Lacey said softly.

"I don't know if you should thank me yet. I don't know where to go."

"That's not it." Lacey hugged herself tighter. "It's good to have a friend here." A tear escaped from her left eye and made a track down her cheek. "I'm so scared."

"Me too." Harmony said. Feeling braver, Harmony then asked, "What happened?" And nodded towards the scratches on her face.

Lacey shook her head and more tears fell down her cheeks.

"I'm sorry, I shouldn't have asked." Harmony apologized. "Let's go."

They left the abandoned library and began walking across the barren landscape. There was a footpath leading from the library steps and heading east, so Harmony and Lacey followed it as much as possible. Spindly trees appeared out of the fog and looked like intimidating men waiting to attack them. Lacey kept her arms crossed over her chest and her pleated skirt swished over her knobby knees.

Both Harmony and Lacey stood out against the white backdrop with their dark clothes and darker skin. It occurred to Harmony that normally she had no trouble blending in but she couldn't in this pale world. She hoped nothing menacing was hiding in the fog.

"What about that?" Lacey said suddenly. "It would make it a great place to hide."

She was talking about an archway that had materialized out of the fog and was gaining more clarity as they got closer. When they were right on top of it, they could see that it was the entrance to an underground tunnel.

"I want to leave this place…not hide. Besides, it's very dark."

"But it looks like it might go somewhere important." Lacey insisted.

"I don't think…" Harmony began.

As if on queue, the roaring in the distance was getting louder and the wind had begun to pick up. Harmony hesitated because she was in a strange place with a strange girl who could have been hurt by someone or something in this place. But she wasn't sure there were any other options. The longer she was in this place, the more lost she felt.

"I'm going." Lacey said finally.

"Wait!" Harmony began to follow Lacey who was already on the second step down into the tunnel.

The pair of them made their way slowly into the darkness. When it seemed like they were at the bottom, neither of them could see an inch in front of their faces. But it was quiet and they did not stand out against the landscape like they had on the surface.

"Lacey."

"Yes?"

"Can you see anything?"

"No."

Harmony reached out her arms for anything. As she took a tentative step forward, she continued to reach out until her hand touched the wall of the tunnel. It was cold and clammy so she pulled her hand back quickly. When she felt braver, she placed her hand on the wall again to feel for some kind of light switch.

To her surprise, her hand fell on a switch of some kind and she flipped it on. One by one, Edison bulbs flashed to life on the ceiling. They were all on one long electrical cord and went off into the distance until they were just a pinprick of light. Harmony looked over and could only see the whites of Lacey's eyes in the dim light.

"Well, that's better." Harmony said.

Lacey smiled for the first time since they had met.

The girls walked through the tunnel with nothing to see except water dripping down the curves of the tunnel. "This place is so spooky."

Lacey nodded in agreement. "Maybe it's purgatory."

"What's purgatory?"

Lacey was surprised but answered, "It is something that Catholics believe happens to people who don't go to heaven or hell. It's in between I think."

"Well, that can't be right. I stumbled in here. I'm not dead. Are you dead?" Harmony teased.

"I don't think so. I sometimes wish I was."

It became so silent that you could hear a pin drop in the space. Harmony had never spoken to somebody who was suicidal. No matter how bad her life had been or how bad her anxiety had gotten, she had never wanted to commit suicide.

Lacey was now fully sobbing to herself as they walked. "I don't think I'll ever recover."

"That's not true. There's always hope." Harmony said feebly.

"I was raped." Lacey blurted out.

Harmony stopped moving and let the words settle in the silence and their implication resonated in her bones. The woman before her had been violated in the worst way possible and she was at a loss for how to handle it. All of the people she worked with had so much drama going on in their lives, but none of them talked about having sexual assault in their history. No wonder this woman looked so hunted. Harmony had heard that women who were raped sometimes couldn't remember things chronologically either, so when Harmony had first spoken with her she probably didn't even register what had happened to her.

"I keep seeing him everywhere." She whispered. Harmony felt her arms erupt into goosebumps and a shiver ran down her spine at this, which caused her to look around for the "him" that Lacey referred to.

"Who?"

Lacey shook her head. "He'd kill me if I told."

"No, Lacey!" Harmony said in an explosion of passionate anger. "You have to tell me," Lacey was already shaking her head. "If not me, you have to tell somebody. The man that did this to you must be stopped."

Tears were streaming down Lacey's beautiful face again. She opened her mouth to respond but no words came out. She pursed her lips and swallowed, wiping her eyes with the back of her arm. Taking in a long slow breath, she said finally, "I know, but he can't be stopped. He has all the power and I'm just a girl."

"Lacey, you're not JUST anything. You are valuable regardless of your gender or identity." Harmony said all this and realized she was giving Lacey the pep talk she always gave herself when she felt lesser than her peers. The image of Lyric came into her mind just then and she remembered how powerless she had felt when he had invaded her mind and made her think she was in love with him. It was embarrassing. It was scary. It demoralizing.

"I sometimes think I would be better off if I was born a man." Lacey whispered.

Just then, the rumbling started up again from where they had entered the tunnel. In the confined space, the sound felt like a physical presence. It washed over Harmony in waves and the walls appeared to be closing in on them. One of the bulbs above began to flicker erratically and it was a visual representation of Harmony's heart.

"What is that?" Harmony asked Lacey.

"I don't know." Lacey admitted.

Harmony found it odd how little this girl seemed to know about this place. If Harmony hadn't felt so bad for Lacey, she would have been angry with her for her lack of helpfulness. This place was seemingly inescapable and Harmony felt close to the edge of her sense of peace. The more she allowed herself to dwell on the hopelessness of her situation, the more she found herself spiraling into old fears.

"Let's move." Harmony wrapped her left arm around Lacey's right arm and began to speed walk down the tunnel.

Lacey was so much taller than Harmony that it was awkward to hold onto each other. Even so, Harmony held on tight. This girl was so emotionally fragile that Harmony sensed she needed the physical support. Lacey didn't complain as they stumbled their way through the semi-darkness and splashed through water that seemed to have been sitting for a while.

When the rumbling increased in volume and a high-pitched screeching chimed in, Harmony squeezed Lacey's arm tighter. "Run!"

Lacey didn't have to be asked twice. The girls ran beside one another for a few seconds, then Harmony released Lacey so she could run as fast as she could. Harmony was a few paces behind her.

Lacey reached the end of the tunnel before Harmony did and was stunned to find nothing but a brick wall. She looked around frantically and could only see the walls of the tunnel. If they went back to where they came from, it would be into the clutches of whatever menacing thing was chasing them.

Harmony began to feel her chest tightening and her breath coming out in sharp gasps.

CHAPTER 28

THE JOY PAT HAD FIRST EXPERIENCED being around Zion was slowly waning after they had worked together all afternoon, had dinner together, and continued to develop a game plan for rescuing Harmony. Clive was still nowhere to be found and Pat had realized that Arrow was not around making his usual sarcastic comments or sneaking alcoholic beverages into the house, either. When Zion had to leave one of their brainstorming sessions to take care of a conflict that had arisen between an accountability coach and his mentee, Pat used the momentary break to seek out information about the outside world.

He immediately regretted it when he logged onto the Kimber Krier website and saw that the first headline was "CEO of Sherwood Severs Still Missing: Police Have No Leads". As he continued to scroll there were other headlines like, "Hospital Unveils New Chip Implementation Plan" and "Preston Winston Accepts Award for Most Innovative College President". His curiosity got the better of him and he clicked the link for the hospital article.

A quick skim of the material informed Pat that what Clive had feared was what had happened. They immediately hired a new surgeon to head up the chip implementation program and changed the privacy policy for the patients. The article wasn't obvious about the motivation for this change, but reading between the lines Pat knew that these changes must be what Clive had alluded to earlier.

"I have to go back." Pat muttered to himself.

Theresa would just go along with whatever had been decided. Without Pat there, he knew that things would move much more quickly in the direction of making the thoughts of others public knowledge. In addition to this, Pat was one of the only people who knew about his father's invention causing private thoughts to reappear as real things. He couldn't continue to stay in this facility even though he felt safe there. He had to return to work.

Suddenly, it also occurred to him that with the guidelines changing he might be able to track Harmony by use of her chip. The only way that would be possible, though, is if he accessed the database at work and bypassed the security measures. Even though he wasn't close to her, he couldn't live with himself if he didn't utilize this information to save her.

"Sorry, Pat." Zion said as he came back into the room. "We strive for coverage across all programs here so I don't have to be hands-on 24/7, but some things just get too out of control for the staff to handle on their own."

Pat waved a dismissive hand and then said, "No worries. I think I know how to find Harmony."

Zion's face went from confusion to excitement. "Oh, really?"

"Yes, but it will require that I return to the office tomorrow."

***

The next day, Zion allowed Pat to borrow one of the many vehicles on campus to drive back to his office. When he sat in the driver's seat of the vehicle, he punched in the address to his work on the GPS and was surprised to find that it was an hour and 45 minutes away from where he was located.

He mulled over ideas for how he would explain his absence to

Theresa. He didn't want to out Zion as harboring a fugitive of the law. He had been so wrapped up in his thoughts that he hadn't noticed Justice sitting in the passenger seat. He cried out in surprise and then began tearing up.

"Patty, shhh…shhh…" Justice stroked his cheek and he leaned into her touch. This nurturing care was something Pat never remembered having as a kid. Justice was able to simultaneously meet his needs as a husband and soothe the damaged parts of him from childhood. "My baby." She cooed. "You're stressed. What's the matter?"

Gently straightening his head so he could see the road better, he said, "I thought you were gone."

"I just couldn't come see you in that place." She shrugged. "I wouldn't ever leave you."

"But you did leave. You're not real. You're just an apparition." Pat said, forcing himself to stop crying. "Zion explained it all."

"He's a religious zealot. He believes a lot of fake things." She said venomously.

"You're an apparition." Pat said again firmly.

"I'm the only thing that isn't an apparition, baby." She said.

Her voice sounded tired and Pat's heart softened. "Really? Then why will you not stay with me?"

"I can't right now." Justice said sadly as she ran her fingers through his hair.

His eyes closed briefly to just focus on her touch that was so real. "I love you. Do you remember when we first moved into our house?"

"Yes." She said. "It was so fun, but you were so particular."

"There is only one way to hang pictures and you wanted to cluster them in one spot."

"It was so wonderful to know that I was yours and wasn't leaving."

"Waking up and rolling over in the morning was my favorite." Pat's voice quivered with the beginning of tears again. "Your hair was always spread out over the white pillows in beautiful crimson waves."

"I'm trying to get back to you." Justice said suddenly, her voice shifting from the overly sweet sentimental tone to a more even one.

Pat turned to look in the passenger seat again and she was no longer there. His heart couldn't take it. He yelled into the silence and slammed his fist against the dashboard barely registering the pain through his hand. When his emotion had subsided, he sat and drove the rest of his journey on mental autopilot watching memories of him and Justice play before his mind's eye.

When he finally turned into the parking lot of Sherwood Servers, his car powered down. He slowed to a stop in front of the guard shack and remembered this vehicle did not have access to the facilities. When he got out of the car and approached the window to the guard shack, he was pleased to see a guard he was familiar with.

"Dale, it's me, Pat."

Dale's eyes bugged out of his head and he said, "This isn't your car. What happened? Where have you been?"

"It's a long story but I'm back and I need to talk to Theresa."

Dale nodded and bustled back to override the security so Pat could get in. He parked and quickly made his way through the front entrance. Before he could say anything, the secretary picked up the telephone and called up to Theresa. Other bystanders at the entrance stopped to stare at him and Pat could hear the sound of sirens in the distance.

A lump dropped into his stomach when he realized how difficult this was going to be, after all. In a matter of minutes, Theresa was power-walking in his direction. Her expression was torn between confusion and anger.

"Pat, what are you doing here?"

"My job, what else?" Pat laughed to release some of the tension.

"You haven't been doing that for over a week. I filed a missing persons report with the police department."

"You didn't have to do that."

"I checked your house. I called your phone…"

"I can explain it all later but I have some important things I have to do first." Pat tried to walk around Theresa, but she stopped him from going any further.

"I can't let you."

Before he could ask why, the front doors to the building opened, and in walked a couple of masked police officers. They came behind him and grabbed both his wrists. He struggled, but the grip they had on him was ironclad. They cuffed him and began reciting his rights.

"This is just a formality." Theresa said sadly. "It's to get you the help you need."

"I'm fine! I just have to take care of some things."

Theresa pursed her lips. "I don't think you're mentally fit to keep running this company in the same capacity, Pat. You need more help than what we can do here."

The profanity-laced tirade that he usually rehearsed in his head when Theresa was being difficult came pouring out. She shook her head in pity, which was almost worse than if she had yelled at him in return. The police took him away and he wanted to murder Theresa at that moment.

CHAPTER 29

THE SITUATION SEEMED IMPOSSIBLE BUT A sliver of darkness, barely visible, looked like it was pulling the brick wall in half. In the semi-darkness, it blended in perfectly, but it was there and just wide enough for an adult person to slip through. Harmony stuck her hand into the void and gestured to Lacey to follow.

They shuffled through the gap sideways. The roaring continued to get louder and louder, but they were moving through a gap that was hopefully able to prevent such a large creature from accessing them. When it felt like they wouldn't be able to outrun the roaring, Harmony popped out on the other side of the opening in the brick wall and fell into cold and crunchy brown grass. Lacey was right behind and fell onto the grass beside her. They could no longer hear the roaring and Harmony realized she was in a very familiar backyard.

"This is my house." Harmony breathed.

"Why is your home in this place?"

"I don't think we are in that place anymore." Harmony said slowly and stood up. "I think this is the real world."

"Real?" Lacey asked. "What was that other place? Am I not real?"

Harmony looked around at Lacey and saw sadness in the girl's eyes. "I didn't mean that. I just meant that this is the reality I know." Harmony was out of her depth when it came to being inclusive to people from other worlds.

Lacey stood up. "This is your reality, but that doesn't change the fact that what happened to me was real even if it isn't to you."

Harmony nodded soberly and said, "I understand. I wasn't trying to diminish your truth."

Lacey didn't respond to the apology but instead said, "Do you have anything to eat?"

"I can check." Harmony led the way into her home and was relieved to find that she had left her back door unlocked.

She rummaged around in her cabinets to find something that hadn't spoiled. Lacey gazed around the space in awe. Her fingers ran across the back of the couch and she then tilted her head back to look at the high ceiling. As Harmony prepared tuna salad sandwiches for them both, she watched Lacey sit on the couch and cross her legs as she happily bounced her foot. She obviously felt safe here and that made Harmony happy.

It was odd how after narrowly escaping danger, Harmony could feel completely calm and be making tuna salad as if her life was still normal. Being back in her home must have tricked her brain into thinking that life was as it used to be. The only thing missing was Rufus. The pang of loss struck her again and her movements slowed. She had a feeling she would never see him again.

"Your house is beautiful, Harmony." Lacey said, cutting through Harmony's grief.

Harmony smiled and thanked her as she walked around the counter with two plates. She handed Lacey one and set the other one on the coffee table for herself. She then went back into the kitchen to get water bottles. Once in the living room again, she sat down and handed Lacey a bottled water.

"Thank you for everything and thank you for freeing me from that place."

Harmony smiled again through a bite of tuna salad. As she looked at Lacey up close, she saw that Lacey was surrounded by a vague white glow. It reminded her of Heidi and that suddenly made her uncomfortable. Lacey had said she didn't know Heidi, but she could have been lying. There was still so much she didn't know and it frightened her to think that this girl she had let into her home was possibly against her in some way.

"So, where is home?" Harmony asked.

Lacey's eyes darkened and she said, "I don't remember."

"Do you have amnesia?" Harmony felt silly as soon as the question was out of her mouth, but it was the only thing that made sense with Lacey's patchwork memory.

"I don't think so. I don't remember very much at all. I remember him. I remember what happened." She stopped suddenly and cast her gaze to the floor.

"You don't have to talk about it." Harmony said kindly.

"Thanks."

"Do you want to go to the police?" After her encounter with law enforcement, she wasn't sure how helpful they would be, but she wanted to seek help for Lacey somehow.

Her head snapped up and she looked sharply at Harmony. "No."

Harmony nodded and took another bite of her sandwich.

In the silence, the familiar sound of the front door unlocking and swinging open made her nearly choke. Lyric stood in the doorway with a key ring in hand and Rufus at his side. He looked different from how he usually did, but Harmony couldn't pinpoint what was different. Harmony felt her throat tighten and her heart rate quicken at the sight of her boss while simultaneously feeling elated that Rufus had returned.

"Rufus…" She breathed. He bounded towards her and

immediately began licking every inch of bare skin he could reach. Some of her anxiety was diminished, but the menacing presence of Lyric was still there.

What Harmony didn't expect was what happened with Lacey. She stopped eating and craned her neck around to see who had entered. When she had taken him in, she screamed and fell onto the floor scrambling backwards across the floor until she was sobbing in a far corner.

Harmony popped up from her seat and faced him with as much fierceness as she could muster. "Please, leave." Rufus began barking as tension filled the room. He wasn't a scary dog, but his barks seemed to keep Lyric from advancing quickly.

Lyric ignored her and continued to gaze at Lacey with a perplexed expression. "I won't hurt you." He said in a gentle tone. Instead of his usually catlike qualities, he appeared meek.

Lacey shook her head violently and continued to sob. Rufus then bounded over to her and pushed his furry head under one of her quivering hands. She refused to respond to the dog's affection.

"Please, go!" Harmony commanded.

Instead of listening, Lyric walked inside and shut the door behind him. "I had been wondering what happened to you but this was the last thing I expected to find when I came over here."

"How did you know we were here? Why do you have my dog?"

"Wendy asked me to check on the house every so often. We were worried about you." Lyric sat down in the chair Lacey had previously occupied and crossed his legs the same way that she had. "Rufus was in the front yard when I arrived."

Lacey struggled to regain her composure. Her belly barely rose as she sucked in a breath and her exhales were shaky. She still looked like she was going to bolt at any minute, but she was much quieter now. Harmony reluctantly sat back down in her seat and kept her eyes locked on Lyric. Rufus, sensing that things had calmed down somewhat, ventured to his water bowl.

"Are you my stalker now? First, you hack my chip, then…"

Lyric shook his head, "No."

"Please leave. Don't hurt me." Lacey whispered.

"I'd never hurt you, sweetheart." Lyric said in the kindest tone Harmony had ever heard him use.

He uncrossed his legs and rose from his seat. He tentatively approached Lacey and she pushed herself even further into the corner. Lyric crouched and gazed into her scared eyes. Harmony was frightened to notice that they both favored one another.

"Is Lacey…your sister?" Harmony ventured.

Lyric didn't look at Harmony as he said, "No. She is me."

Harmony was proud of her open mind. She generally did not judge people based on appearance or background, but in that moment, her brain could not reconcile that the girl and man in her living room were the same person. It seemed impossible.

"I chose to forget most of my past self except certain things." Lyric said slowly and still was gazing at Lacey who looked confused and frightened. "But I guess you can't forget forever." A single tear slid down Lyric's cheek and Harmony felt unexpected compassion. "I began having memories of things I used to do as a woman and began to think that I had to transition to being a woman. The more I found out the more I realized that I had been born a woman already."

"How did you remember?" Harmony asked.

Lyric then turned to face her and said, "When I hacked your chip."

Harmony's anxiety returned and she felt the same fear that had welled up inside her when Lyric tried making a move on her. She couldn't reconcile that the person in front of her was the same as the scared girl quivering in the corner of her living room. But as she truly looked into Lyric's face, she could see the ghost of the feminine in the line of the jaw and tenderness in the eyes.

"I don't understand." Harmony said finally.

Lyric stood and ventured back to the couch to sit down. With a sigh, he said, "It's a closely guarded secret that the microchips not only manage your mental health but can help people forget too. While I had heard whispers of addicts becoming empty shells on accident, I never realized that the medical community was using similar methods on people with gender dysphoria or in cases where somebody needed to take on a new persona."

Harmony was still confused but she didn't want to interrupt. Even Lacey had taken on a less defensive stance to lean in and listen.

"My parents let me transition at 16." Lyric continued sadness in his voice. "I had all the surgeries, the drugs, and the clothes to complete the transition, but I could never forget that had been born a woman. The body I had been given had been violated and I didn't want to remember anymore."

Lacey's eyes grew wide and she looked on the verge of tears as Lyric spoke. Harmony's stomach clenched as the truth of what Lyric said hit her heart.

"The microchip was in the beginning stages but they wanted to use it to help me fully embrace the transition. I agreed and my parents just wanted me to be happy." Lyric's voice cracked. "I was deemed a success by the medical community. I have lived a life that fulfilled all my carnal desires and being who I thought I truly was born to be, but you can't outrun trauma." Lyric sighed and looked straight at Lacey. "I haven't gotten everything back, though. What happened to make you transition to me?"

Lacey bit her lip and the beginning of tears welled up in her eyes. "I was raped…" She whispered.

Something passed between the two of them and understanding flashed in Lyric's eyes. "Is it…" Lacey nodded almost imperceptibly and Lyric barely concealed a sob. "He was one of the good ones."

"Yeah, I thought so too." Lacey said.

Harmony watched as Lyric embraced Lacey. It was so gentle and something that Harmony imagined most people would love to be able to do with their past selves. If only an older version of Harmony could visit her and hug her to let her know everything would be alright.

"So, how did hacking my chip open up your own memories? Am I…did I…?" Harmony was afraid to know but there was a nagging suspicion at the back of her mind that maybe Lyric was implying she had been a man in her past life.

"I saw that you were in the witness protection program. Your past self had been hidden from you after the government relocated you. This was for your safety. When I saw that you had forgotten your old self, I started wondering if I had also forgotten my past."

Silence fell between them.

"I thought I was in love with you but it turns out I was in love with your normal life." Lyric admitted. "But you have darkness in your past, too."

"What do you mean?"

Lyric said, "Why would you voluntarily forget your past if it wasn't filled with trauma?" Lyric said matter-of-factly. "I don't know any details, but I do know your past name."

Harmony thought for a moment about if she wanted to know. She doubted a name would truly give her anything to go off of, but it could give her a small link to the past. She wanted to know what she had been running from. "Okay, tell me."

Lyric still looked hesitant, but when he finally had the courage enough to tell her, she almost wished she hadn't found out.

"Heidi Gomez-Brown."

"No, that's not right." Harmony shook her head. "You're lying to me."

This statement made Lacey cower again in fear.

"I am not lying. What reason would I have to lie?"

"You're trying to destroy my life."

"I'm not." Lyric said earnestly. "I used my appearance and authority to take advantage of many people. I'm not proud of that but I'm a new person now."

"You don't look different." Harmony snapped back.

"I've been born again, Harmony."

"Is that a fancy way of saying you're transitioning again?" Harmony knew she was being ungracious, but her whole life had been smashed to pieces in front of her.

Lyric smiled slightly. "No, but I will be embracing my biological body as much as I can. Surgeries and hormones have done irreversible damage, but with God, I will embrace who He has made me to be as a woman."

"So you found religion?" Harmony asked.

"In a manner of speaking." Lyric looked up to the ceiling for a moment then explained. "After you had disappeared, I was having a mental health crisis. The shame and guilt I felt was heavy. In the next few days, I began having chest pains and tingling running up and down my arms. It really scared me and I ended up going to the ER." Lyric sighed. "As I waited to be seen, I ended up speaking with an older lady in the waiting room to pass the time."

Harmony and Lacey didn't stir as Lyric continued to talk. Rufus had even stopped lapping up water and crunching dog food to rest on the floor and snooze.

"She shared the Gospel with me. I thought it was ridiculous at the time, but it stuck with me. I couldn't stop thinking about it and ended up going to church with this woman. God pulled my heart out of darkness on that day." Lyric began to sob. "I wasn't born in the wrong body. I'm fearfully and wonderfully made by a divine creator. He doesn't demand I have surgery to be accepted or become a slave to every passion and desire I have. He just asks me to believe in him. To come before him with all my brokenness."

Harmony didn't know what to do. She had never seen her boss cry before. She also did not have a personal understanding of Christianity. She had always assumed there was some sort of higher power but didn't think one religion was better than the other. Christianity had made a strong impact on Lyric and Harmony wouldn't deny the experience.

"Harmony, he loves me as I am. My violated body and all. I'm not worthless. I'm not damaged goods. He has taken all my sin and suffering on himself so that I could live abundantly and live eternally." Lyric wiped away the tears and patted a hand over his heart. "He offers this to everybody."

"I'm happy for you." Harmony said sincerely. "I'm glad you found something so meaningful to you. So, what pronouns should I use when speaking with you?"

Lyric looked at her like an amused grandfather. "I am a woman. I can't deny that. My name is Lacey. You can call me by who I am."

As soon as Lyric, now Lacey said this, the Lacey on the floor in the corner screamed out. "I'm disappearing! My feet!"

Harmony whipped around and saw that everything below Lacey's knees was no longer there. Her boss rushed over and began trying to feel for the missing feet, but her hands passed right through.

"I'm not ready to go!" Past Lacey sobbed as more of her form began dissolving.

"Darling, look at me." Lacey (formally Lyric) commanded. Her past self obeyed and stared into the eyes of present Lacey. "I will heal for both of us. I won't forget you again. I will always remember where I came from and be grateful for where the Lord has brought me. You will always be a part of me, but you no longer have to suffer in this form."

Harmony didn't know if what the present Lacey said was true, but it seemed to comfort her past self.

"Thank you." The form of past Lacey whispered as her torso evaporated and her thin neck began slowly dissolving into oblivion. In only a few more moments, the frightened young woman was gone from this world.

As the present Lacey stood, Harmony could see a change in her eyes. "I remember everything."

"I'm so sorry."

"Don't be." Lacey said. "This is the beginning of healing. I hope you encounter God's grace as well."

"Where are you going?" Harmony demanded.

"To find others like me. The harvest is plentiful, but the laborers are few. I want to start having honest conversations with others who suffered like I did. There is a better way." Lacey said, her voice thick with emotion. "I think your road to healing starts with you talking to Wendy." Lacey said.

"Why?"

"She's worried about you." Lacey said. "My car is in the driveway. Don't worry, I'll drive you."

CHAPTER 30

Clive woke to the sound of fluttering wings, trickling water, and howling. It felt like he had just been dropped onto the set of the ancient movie The Hound of the Baskervilles. Heavy fog rolled across the landscape, a large silver moon glowed in the black sky, and moss-covered trees sagged under the weight of the greenery. Arrow was beside him on the gravel road asleep or unconscious.

Being the doctor that he was, he checked all of Arrow's vital signs and determined he was healthy, just in a deep sleep. He shook his shoulder and managed to get him stirring. As Arrow adjusted to his surroundings, Clive stood and walked around the immediate area. There were no familiar landmarks or street signs signifying where they were. There was simply fog and more fog.

"Where are we, Doc?"

"I don't know."

"That maniac said something about a void, right?"

"Yeah." The recollection of his wife sitting unseeing in that recliner came back to him and he was angry. "That sicko did something to Mayre. She's not herself."

"It didn't look good." Arrow said somberly as he stood. "She looked like some of the addicts I sold Thought Conductor codes to."

"She's not a vegetable." Clive fiercely.

Arrow kept his comments to himself for the first time in his life and gazed around the area in silence instead.

"Let's explore that way." Arrow said, pointing at the horizon where the shadow of a building loomed.

"Why?"

"It's better than standing around. Besides, I don't want whatever is howling to catch up to us."

Clive reluctantly agreed and they began to walk towards the structure. The trees stayed thick and ominous overhead and occasionally a crow would flutter from one tree to another and caw loudly. After walking for 10 minutes, the sound of the creek trickling had increased in volume and Clive decided to step off the path to take a look at where the water was in the hopes that they could get a drink. To Clive's horror, a human skull sat in the midst of flowing crimson liquid, not water.

Clive imagined this must have been what it was like in Egypt when the Nile had been turned to blood. Seeing it before him was much more horrific than he remembered the story being in Sunday School. The quiet revulsion he felt was interrupted by the vaguest feeling that he could hear quiet screams echoing around him. When he went back to the path where Arrow waited for him, the screaming stopped.

"The water is blood." Clive said.

"That's sick." Arrow said, not even questioning the pronouncement.

"You're not bothered?"

"Not much bothers me. I'm more focused on getting out of here."

It took them a good part of an hour until they finally began seeing the detail on the shadowy structure they had been walking toward. Before them was a grand stone bridge with shadowy figures of crouching angels at intervals on the stone walls. The bridge seemed to lead to what looked like a castle.

The two men looked at one another and then back at the bridge with determination. They continued forward and Clive felt the eyes of the angels boring into his soul. When they had reached the other side there was a huge set of wooden double doors falling off their hinges and a courtyard to the left of the castle with all kinds of headstones.

"I'm going to look over here." Clive said, pointing to the cemetery.

"So, the creek made of blood is scary but a creepy cemetery isn't?" Arrow scoffed.

Clive ignored this and walked over to the first headstone in the place. It was very tall and chiseled into an intricate cross. Clive signed The Father, The Son, and The Holy Ghost. He might be somewhere unknown, but his faith was still important.

As he wove in and out of the tombstones, he felt an unusual sort of peace. A grave at the very back of the cemetery had a statue of a sleeping child encased in glass on top of a stone platform. Below this case read the Bible verse, "A voice was heard in Ramah, weeping and loud lamentation, Rachel weeping for her children; she refused to be comforted because they are no more." As he read further down on the stone, he realized that this child had died at four years old. His heart went out to the family. At the beginning of his career as a doctor, he had witnessed the tragic deaths of several children. Some were the victims of cancer, while others tragically lost their lives due to an accident. The loss of a child had a way of emptying the parents where their eyes remained open, but they no longer saw anything.

Clive said a silent prayer for the family of this child and hoped that, wherever they were, they were finding joy amidst the sorrow.

"Want to go inside now?" Arrow asked coming up behind him.

Clive nodded and followed Arrow through the castle gates. The inside wasn't much more interesting. Overgrown weeds covered every dirt surface and crumbling stone littered the rest of the space. Angels missing arms or halves of their faces stood around the areas as if protecting invisible people. The remains of a tower and a staircase stood in the very middle of the courtyard. At the base of this staircase, seemingly out of place, was a statue of an angel in prayer. Upon closer inspection, Clive saw that the angel's wings had cracked and fallen off. Intertwined in the stone fingers were the beads of a rosary.

"This place is creepy." Arrow said gruffly.

Clive nodded in agreement but continued to stare at the angel, perplexed. Arrow was walking away so Clive followed his friend. Under all the crumbled stone, dust, and dirt there was a glimmer of polished stone floors. They rounded the corner of the wall butting up against the staircase and found piles of books slipping and sliding over each other. Some of the books were relics of this place, but a few of the ones on top were beautiful leather-bound volumes without a speck of dust on them.

Clive picked up one of these new books and saw that embossed in gold on the front were the words "Holy Bible". Flipping through was enough to tell him that this was not the full Scriptures.

"This must be a Protestant bible." Clive said.

"I see." Arrow muttered, obviously not paying attention.

"How many books are in the Jewish Bible?"

"17, I think." Arrow shrugged. "I'm not a practicing Jew, but my dad wasn't either."

"I think you told me about him before." Clive said. "He sounded like a piece of work."

"That's the understatement of the year." Arrow snorted. He then stepped around Clive and picked up a dusty book from the floor. "This is also a Bible." Arrow's thumb ran across the gold-embossed title.

"I wonder why these are here."

"Maybe somebody wanted to forget religion." Arrow laughed, but Clive didn't join in.

"I'll never understand the things people choose to forget." Clive muttered. "Religion is the foundation of a good society, but I wouldn't expect you to understand that. You're a pagan alcoholic." The bitterness seeped in without warning.

"It was a joke." Arrow said defensively as he set the Bible back down in the pile.

Clive stewed in silence and gently smacked the Bible on the palm of his left hand. "I don't understand any of this." He mused. "Where are we? And what does this have to do with Preston and the microchips?"

"I don't know, Doc. You know more about the chips than I do. I just pedaled them."

"I had considered getting the chip, but I haven't struggled with my mental health. Mayre does…"

"I think she's gone, Doc." Arrow said.

"We don't know that!" Clive bellowed into his face. When he realized the overreaction, he leaned back away from Arrow and flung the Bible on the dusty pile.

"You're gonna have to calm down. We have to focus on getting out of here."

"What's the point?"

"You can't rescue Mayre if you're dead."

"According to you, there's nothing to rescue."

"If she's still in there, you might be the only one who can fix it." Arrow said, trying to be compassionate.

Clive could tell that Arrow was forcing himself to be encouraging, but Clive appreciated the sentiment anyway. It was enough to make him realize that there was always hope. The Lord wouldn't allow this to happen to him. He was a man of God and intended to make things right with Mayre. Things couldn't stay unfinished.

A shift went through him and Clive was perceptibly happier. "Let's go."

"Where?" Arrow asked.

Clive turned on his heel and began walking out of the stone structure and across the bridge at the pace he usually kept when working. His strides were long and confident. Arrow had no trouble keeping up with his long and strong legs. The glow of sunlight was breaking through the fog and illuminated the barren landscape.

"To find our way out of here, of course."

"That's what I said first." Arrow rolled his eyes.

"And now I agree with the sentiment."

"You're really not as impressive as people think that you are. You just steal other people's ideas."

Clive slowed down so he could properly look at Arrow. "Do I sense jealousy?"

"Yes, I'm jealous of your pompous…"

A loud rumbling interrupted their conversation and stopped both men in their tracks. They couldn't see anything on the path ahead of them except a few trees, but the rumbling could be felt in their bones. Lighting thrummed in the clouds above making it look like a spontaneous light show.

"We should find shelter." Arrow said, concern drawing a line between his brows.

They walked off the path and into the trees. The crimson creek was also back here and trickled over rocks and grasses. Arrow showed no concern as he walked through the blood with his boots, but Clive stepped gingerly over the creek striving to miss as much as possible.

Once past the creek, the trees began to get thicker and thicker. A surprising number of the trees had pops of red, gold, and green peeking out from the muted filter that seemed to cover this place. The rumbling started up again and they picked up the pace until they came out into a clearing with a three-story mansion. It was intact unlike the castle, so the two men broke out into a run as drops of water fell from the skies.

They barely had any time to inspect the entrance or to see if anybody was living in this place as they raced up the steps to the wraparound porch and through the unlocked front doors. Arrow quickly made himself at home by walking through the foyer and into the sitting room where an ornate pink velvet couch sat. He plopped down on the couch and flung his long arms on the back and breathed a sigh of relief.

That's when the bottom seemed to drop out of the sky and rain thundered on the roof. Clive followed Arrow and cautiously sat in a wingback floral armchair close to the window so he could look outside. It was a moot point, however, because he could barely see anything through the rain.

"Good thing this place was open." Arrow said.

But they realized why it was unlocked very quickly when another person entered the sitting room.

CHAPTER 31

PAT'S UNCONSCIOUS MIND DRIFTED IN AND out of strange dreams. They usually had Justice in them or the place beyond the portal. No matter the subject of the dream, he felt a strong feeling of sadness. In every dream, nothing was as it seemed and he had a deep sense of loneliness.

These fitful dreams seemed to go on forever, but when he felt like he couldn't take it anymore, he woke up and immediately forgot what he had been dreaming. He wasn't strapped down and he didn't appear to be in a hospital bed, but he knew he was confined by the look of the room. There were no visible doors in the space and no windows. The only thing in the room was the recliner that he was sitting in, a metal table, a couple of chairs, and a TV screen.

He tried to stand but his legs felt so weak he couldn't. It occurred to him that he hadn't eaten anything in several hours or had any water. His mouth felt like it was full of cotton and his belly full of pins. After a moment, he tried to stand one more time. Slowly walking to the TV screen, he turned it on but all he could find was static. It wasn't hooked up to anything he could access, so he wondered why in the world this was something in the room.

Walking to the table, he felt its surface and looked under it for any clues. He couldn't locate anything and felt a lump drop into his stomach. Theresa had really gotten rid of him. She must have been plotting this for a while.

Just as he thought this, a pocket door slid open on the opposite wall, and in walked somebody with a white coat, black pants, and brown dress shoes. They were wearing a mask and had short hair, so Pat couldn't identify whether they were male or female.

"Come with me." The muffled voice said and gestured to the exit. Pat was surprised about the trust they had in him, but that meant that the entire facility was probably secured, or that they knew how weak his legs felt.

"Okay. Will there be food there?"

"Later. For now, you are fasting before we do some tests."

"I'm not sure I can wait." Pat said honestly. "I'm so weak."

The person in the white coat said nothing but continued to lead Pat down the hallway. The walls were pure white and lined with silver metal doors. The bright LED lighting was blinding and the lack of decor was creepy.

They finally reached their destination and Pat was surprised to see a few more people waiting for him. There was a chair akin to a dental chair in the middle of the room and a few beeping machines around the space. With all the modern-day technology available, Pat was surprised at the sheer amount of things that still needed wires.

"Please sit." The muffled voice said again. This person was the only one wearing a mask. The other two people in the room were maskless and seemed comfortable. Pat was so weak and was interested to see what happened, so he sat.

One of the individuals by the chair began to speak then and Pat suddenly realized he knew him. "It is an honor to work with you, Patrick Sherwood." This man was sharp in numerous ways: his eyes, his chin, his nose, the edges of his lips, his attire, and his aura.

Pat was not superstitious, but this man made him uncomfortable like when a snake sits curled in the corner of a room. One wrong move, and you could be dying slowly from a venomous bite you barely saw coming.

"You can call me Pat. That's what everybody calls me, Preston."

"Pat." The man didn't seem to like it. He spoke the name like he had just eaten something foul.

"Did Theresa put you up to this?" Pat cut straight to the point. He saw no reason for formality at this time.

"Nobody hires me. I do the hiring." Preston smirked and moved to the front of the chair. He reached out a gloved hand and firmly held Pat's chin, turning it to the left and the right. "Where was your chip installed?"

"Why do you need to know?"

Preston let go of his chin and said calmly, "Either you tell us or we do exploratory surgery on your brain to find it."

Pat obediently pointed to the right side of his brain behind his ear.

"It's deep in there, isn't it? Good thing your father improved his design."

"My father figured placing the cure at the place where the sickness resided was best." Pat said quietly. He usually did not come to the defense of his fanatic father, but in this case, he felt like his father was onto something. It had been a risky choice, but it worked. Not for everybody, but it worked for Pat.

Preston waved a dismissive hand and then directed his employees with the other hand. A masked nurse approached the side of Pat's head where he had pointed and parted his fluffy hair to examine the scar. When he located it, he nodded at Preston.

"Good. That was a test. I already knew where to look, but I wanted to make sure you were being honest with me." Preston said, cooly. "Telling the truth early will make this easier."

"Are you going to do brain surgery on me?"

"Of course not. We are going to have to give you a haircut, though."

Oddly enough, this disturbed Pat more than having another brain surgery. "W-why?"

"For the sensors of course. They don't adhere properly to hair."

Pat then stood up and shook his head. "I want to know what's happening right now."

Preston seemed unperturbed by Pat's demand and instead signaled to his staff to leave the room. They obeyed and shut the door leaving Pat and Preston alone.

"Follow me."

There was a door at the back of the place that Pat had assumed was a closet, but instead it opened onto another hallway. They walked several feet and turned into another room that was much cozier. The floors were carpeted and the walls a warm cream color. The desk was sleek metal and the two chairs flanking it looked like ergonomic versions of the standard black office chair. A picture window looked out onto a small greenhouse.

Preston sat on the chair closest to the window and Pat sat in the other chair. "What's going on?" Concern was etched on Preston's face as he asked this question as if this was a completely routine situation.

"I do not know where I am. I do not know you very well. I am going to be bald. I have a lot of questions."

"We're testing the functionality of your chip, firstly."

"It functions fine."

"Then we're going to update the programming within the chip. There are some changes that have been made since you've been gone."

"Like what?"

"And we need to discover what's going on with these anomalies."

"What anomalies?"

Preston looked at him like a grandfather who had to explain to his grandson that Santa wasn't real. "People are seeing hallucinations in higher numbers since the microchip rollout started. We must determine why before we go further with this."

"What gives you the right…?"

Preston silenced him by opening one of the desk drawers and pulling out a document from within. He slid it across to Pat and he skimmed over it. From what Pat could tell, Theresa had signed something giving Kimber University access to their clients for learning purposes.

"This isn't anything that will hold up. I am the CEO. This is my Father's company."

"If we find that you are mentally unfit to run the company, Theresa can authorize whatever she wants." Preston plucked the document from Pat and placed it lovingly back in the desk drawer. "I look forward to seeing inside your mind, Pat."

It felt as though spiders had begun to crawl down Pat's spine. Despite the sun shining in the space, Preston's tone made Pat regret allowing this man to use his nickname.

"Pat, this man is no good." Justice said. She had suddenly appeared at his side and was keeping her eyes trained on Preston.

"I do not want you in there." Pat said to Preston. "I do not consent and I am leaving." He stood and Preston mirrored him.

"Oh, please don't go yet. I want to help you." Preston insisted. "I've been seeking people that are like me." Pat was still backing up but as his hand reached the doorknob, it wouldn't turn. "I locked it." Preston shrugged. "Please, sit. I'm not finished." He grinned and his canines winked.

Pat obliged, hoping that if he heard this man out, it would give him enough time to develop an escape plan before they cut his hair.

"Thank you." Preston rubbed his hands together, positively gleeful. "I just need to talk man-to-man with you."

"Okay." Pat's brain was buzzing and he was subtly trying to seek out signs that Justice was nearby. Unfortunately, she had disappeared again.

"As a schizophrenic, do you deal with intrusive thoughts?" Preston now had a pen and paper in hand ready to take notes.

"Of course."

"Good, good."

"It isn't good."

"Well, it is a relief to know that is part of your experience. I have them too, but I don't hallucinate so I doubt I'm schizophrenic." Pat was silent. "You see, I truly am the most isolated man. I have been seeking someone like me for some time and just can't find them."

"Why are you trying to find people like you?"

"Everybody is being affirmed. Where is my affirmation? Where is my 8-part mini-series?" Preston seemed like a perfectly normal man, but as he was talking about this, a manic gleam came into his eyes which transformed his entire face. "I thought for a long time that I was too different. People I opened up to said I shouldn't be allowed to live. If they can say that about me, why can't I say that about them?"

"Well, that's not nice of them to say." Pat said, his mind distracted by plans of escape. Maybe if he ran towards the window screaming it would provide enough of a distraction and momentum that he could get through.

"It really isn't, but they like to pretend that it is acceptable just because I told them my fantasies." Preston tapped the desk. "I get the greatest satisfaction out of watching people die by my hand."

"I think that is a sickness that needs to be treated."

"I thought at least you would understand." Preston said sadly.

Pat then made the mistake of glancing behind him. Justice stood there mouthing the words "run". He whipped back around and Preston's eyes flashed with anger.

"I haven't finished talking."

"I'm sorry." Pat wasn't sorry, but he was more sorry that he got caught seeking escape.

"Your hallucinations can wait until I tell you the best part." Preston straightened the collar on his shirt as he spoke, which was even more unsettling. He was acting as though they were having a simple coffee chat. "My Father died when I was young. Most people know that. What they don't know is that I killed him." Preston paused to let the revelation settle into the silence.

"That's sick."

"Your reaction disappoints me. I can't be the only one that feels this way. I'm convinced others have impulses to kill and maim, but they are just afraid to express themselves. I want to free these people from repression and societal norms."

"That isn't normal."

"Oh, it is. I argue that it is much more widespread."

"Why are you telling me all this?"

"There is a strong likelihood you won't make it through the testing we are about to do and I want to feel like I shared my story with somebody. I assumed you would be more empathetic, but I was wrong." Preston shrugged again.

"I do not empathize with homicidal maniacs." Pat said through gritted teeth.

Preston opened his mouth in mock offense. "Really? That's low. Aren't you also suspected of murdering that girl Janice?"

"I didn't murder her." Pat said. She was simply an unfortunate casualty in his search for Justice. "I think you'll find that there are less sickos like you in the world than you think. What then?"

Preston trained his eyes on the ceiling and said slowly, "If my hypothesis is disproved, that won't deter me. As the saying goes… do what makes you happy. Discovering new and creative ways to torture people makes me happy." Preston smiled his unsettling smile again and Pat's skin crawled.

Pat had always thought himself to be a severely flawed genius who did his best to treat people nicely. His flaws always made him feel like he could be trying so much harder to be better. When he was officially diagnosed with schizophrenia his world caved in and he felt like he could never measure up. He didn't feel like he fit in. When Justice came into his life, she made him feel like the dark parts could be okay and that he ultimately was good. Preston viewed the world in a way that made no sense to Pat. He seemed to believe that no matter what, he was flawless the way he was and that hurting others was okay as long as it met his needs.

"That's not what that phrase means."

"Oh, what does it mean?"

"It's to motivate people to pursue a career they love or express themselves in healthy ways. Things that build people up and not tear down. Things that contribute to society!" Pat was certain he had never raised his voice at anybody like this before. He was on his feet, hands firmly planted on the desk.

Preston continued to examine him like he was an interesting animal at the zoo. "I am making contributions to society."

"What you're doing is wrong!"

"According to who? To God? His opinion doesn't matter."

Pat didn't answer immediately because he didn't want to admit that the question stumped him. Unfortunately, his silence was the wrong response because Preston then stood up.

"As exciting as this is, we're wasting time." He pulled open a different desk drawer and brought out a spool of fishing twine.

Pat's torso straightened and he began to back up. He tripped over one of the legs of the chair he had been sitting in and stumbled into a bookcase on the wall behind him. The muscles in his back fired pain signals to his brain and he winced. Preston wasn't in a hurry, but he was striding around the desk now and coming towards

Pat. Pat scrambled to the right and reached a hand out to try the handle on the door again. It was still locked.

"I'm not in the mood to chase you." Preston said simply.

Pat continued moving to the right and quickly bypassed the corner of the desk until he was behind it and Preston was by the door. Preston's entertained smile faded and he now looked more determined. Pat's eyes darted around looking for something heavy or sharp to throw through the window. There was nothing on the desk or under. Nothing on the bookshelves. In a moment of panic, he pulled out one of the desk drawers onto the floor and the items inside went flying everywhere. One item that stayed was a pair of scissors. Pat grasped them tightly and waved them threateningly.

"Don't step any closer."

Preston froze, but not out of fear. He seemed like he was calculating. "Well, this just got more interesting." He purred as a smile stretched across his face.

"Let me leave or I will dismember you like your victims." Pat was trying to sound menacing, but it didn't feel natural.

"Please, you're not getting out of here alive. Even if you kill me, you won't get past my staff."

It took Pat only a moment to deliberate and then he spun on his heel and rammed the pointed end of the scissors into the center of the window. Spidery cracks spread across the glass and chunks fell out and onto the ground of the greenhouse. Preston was so surprised he didn't react at first, which gave Pat time to ram a bony shoulder into the remaining glass to clear the way for him to climb out.

The humidity in the greenhouse was oppressive and Pat struggled to catch his breath as he ran up and down the dirt pathways looking for an exit. A set of double doors lay at the end of the path he was on so he picked up speed to make it to them before Preston saw where he was going.

Normally, running with scissors was something Pat didn't do, but now he held to them tightly for safety reasons. Unfortunately, this security was short-lived because Preston came around a fat palm tree trunk still holding the fishing twine and an amused grin. Pat made the mistake of glancing back and was surprised that Preston was running as well. He didn't seem like a man who would physically exert himself.

When Pat burst through the double doors, he found himself in a smaller greenhouse with much smaller plants and there was no other set of doors in this room. He deflated as he heard the double doors open again and Preston was there blocking his only exit.

"Well, that was fun." Preston growled. "Time to rest a bit."

CHAPTER 32

"Heidi…" Arrow's voice almost failed him as he gazed at the newcomer.

Clive watched his friend closely and could see a change come over him. The jovial confidence was replaced by sadness. Every part of his face now showed the lines that didn't seem as visible when he was smiling and talking. His shoulders sloped downwards with the curve of his mouth. An utterly defeated man.

This was a short-lived moment, however, because the woman in the doorway pulled out a switchblade and pointed it toward Arrow. His arms flew up in self-defense and Clive's eyes widened. Not wanting to make the situation worse, Clive held himself perfectly still. Her blond dreadlocks seemed to blow behind her by an unseen breeze and she glowed with an otherworldly glow.

"Get out." She whispered menacingly.

"Heidi…" Arrow tried again. "I'm sorry."

She continued to try to bring him down with her eyes. "Get. Out. Of. Here."

"We don't know where 'here' is." Clive interjected desperately.

Heidi whipped around and stared at Clive as if she had just seen him. The knife was still trained on Arrow.

"Where are we?" Arrow asked cautiously.

Her eyes flitted back and forth between the two men. She was beginning to look like a cornered animal. If they had to overpower her, they could. She was much more petite than Clive or Arrow. However, she had the knife and that could be deadly if it sliced the wrong artery.

"Oblivion." She said finally. "Things people wish to forget get sent here."

"Why are you here?" Arrow asked.

"Wrong question." She growled.

She took a few steps forward and Arrow froze in place.

"Who is she?" Clive whispered to Arrow.

She trained her eyes on Clive again and said, "If you don't know then you might want to reconsider your friendship with this man."

Tears were making Arrow's eyes shine, but he refused to let them spill over. "Why would somebody want to forget you?"

"That's a good question." Heidi said sarcastically. In one swift movement, she grasped his right wrist and flipped it over to look up and down his forearm. Unsatisfied, she grasped what little hair he had and bent his head down to examine the back of his neck. She released her grip roughly and Arrow straightened up. "I suspected it was you, but I don't see any scarring from a chip installation."

Dejected, she lowered the knife. When this happened, Clive and Arrow released some of their tension as well.

"I wouldn't ever do that." Arrow said, hurt.

He took an involuntary step forward, but she backed away. "Don't touch me. I still don't trust you."

"Can you explain to me what's happening?" Clive asked. The pair turned and looked at him blankly. "I think we could help each other, but I don't have any idea what's going on."

Heidi glanced at Arrow and Arrow took the hint. "We had dated. We were going to get married."

"'Were' being the keyword." Heidi spat.

"She testified against me."

"You were breaking the law."

"You didn't let me explain."

"You ruined my mother." Arrow didn't respond to this. "You knew she was an addict, but you sold codes to her anyway."

Clive's heart skipped a beat. He was thinking of Mayre sitting motionless in the recliner back home. "Is your mom…gone?" Clive asked looking from Heidi then Arrow.

Arrow nodded. "Heidi's mom erased all her emotions." Arrow whipped back around to Heidi and said, "But I didn't know that would happen! I thought I was subverting the system to help people."

Tears were spilling over her cheeks now and her hand that held the knife shook. "Since meeting you, my life has been nothing but pain. Get. Out."

"We don't know how to get out." Clive reiterated. "Can you show us the way?"

Heidi wiped her face with the back of her free hand. "Why would I want to help you?"

"You seem like you care about people." Clive said, trying to turn on his charm. "We don't know how to get out of here. If you let us leave unaccompanied, we may not survive."

Heidi considered this logic and finally nodded in agreement. "Okay, I'll guide you out. But never come back."

"Can't you leave with us?" Arrow asked hopefully.

"No." She said simply. "I can only last for a short amount of time outside." She lifted her left foot slightly and Arrow could see that part of the toe on her boot was faded. "I could have disappeared completely."

"So, is this another world?" Arrow asked.

"I'm assuming." Heidi said shortly. "There are tears all over

Oblivion that seem to lead to the real world but, unfortunately, I cannot exist out there.

Both Clive and Arrow nodded in understanding. For Clive, this was beyond the realm of science he had studied. He was tempted to believe that what he was seeing was a hallucination, but everything within him was signaling that this was real. The musty air in the mansion assaulted his nose while his tongue was parched for water. The dim lighting made it hard to see details, but it all looked real. He also was able to fold his hands together and squeeze them. Things here seemed to be beyond science and instead could be classified as "magic".

"We should go now. There is a beast that roams this place but he won't in the rain."

"A beast?" Clive asked in disbelief.

"Yes. The Queen of Oblivion feeds him with the forgotten. The stronger the forgotten memory the more he craves it. He has been chasing me since I got here."

"You have a queen here?" Clive asked in disbelief.

Heidi nodded and gestured at them to follow her. Before they exited the house, she reached into a closet in the foyer and pulled out three umbrellas that were gray and dusty. Once on the porch, Clive's nostrils were filled with the smell of wet dog mixed with mud.

They followed Heidi into the downpour with their umbrellas held over their heads. They walked quickly even though they were mostly protected from the rain. Each step squished into the ground and Clive was disappointed that his nice pair of shoes were getting destroyed in this way. It was hard to see much of anything, but Heidi became their beacon to guide the way.

The trees around them danced in wavy gray patterns behind the rain and the blood from the creek began to spread like a wine stain across the trodden down grass. To Clive's horror, his foot landed hard on something firm that broke in half. As he glanced down, he realized it was the bone of some unknown creature. In all his years learning anatomy, he had never seen a part of the human skeletal system that looked like the bone before him. He picked up his pace to keep up with Arrow and Heidi.

Despite the umbrella, he still felt soggy. The puddles were so deep his trousers were drenched up to the middle of his calves and a sudden wind began blowing the rain and some drops started pelting towards his face. Arrow was soggy too, and his clothes hung off his tall, broad frame heavily. What was odd was that Heidi seemed to be just the same as she had been in the mansion, except now her hair looked like it was floating underwater. He had the mental image of a siren leading them to their deaths and this thought made him pause.

"What is it, Doc?" Arrow called out through the pelting rain.

"How can we trust her? What if she's leading us right to the Queen of this place?"

He hadn't bothered to keep his voice down, so Heidi spun around and glared at him. "The Queen and I are not friends."

"Yeah, but you and Arrow aren't either. What if you're enacting revenge?"

"You just don't like this idea because it involves people I know." Arrow argued.

"What does that mean?"

"You don't think highly of me and my friends. You only wanted to reconnect because I was useful to you. This is also the only reason why you wanted to rescue Mayre; she's useful to you. She is the key to getting your job back."

The rain temporarily forgotten, the two stood three feet apart looking at one another. They both were soaked, tired, and hungry. They didn't know how long it had been since they first invaded the hospital and were captured. Arrow's skin showed the life he had lived: scars, lines, and tattoos. Clive's skin showed youth, vitality, and perfection. Both were very different men and Clive knew that what Arrow had said was true.

"You're wrong." Clive said, unwilling to admit fault.

Arrow raised his chin slightly. "You know I'm right."

"We're wasting time arguing!" Heidi yelled finally. "When the storm ends, we'll be vulnerable."

"I am getting my wife back because I love her!" Clive said, clenching his left fist and his right hand tightening on the umbrella handle.

"She's gone, Clive." Arrow said.

Anger bubbled in the pit of Clive's stomach. If he was honest with himself he knew Arrow was right, but he didn't want somebody to tell him the truth. He wanted somebody to tell him it would be okay.

Mayre had always been the person to tell him that things would be okay. She never judged him for his feelings or dreams. She always just encouraged him, and her encouragement was genuine.

"I'm going to find my own way." Clive said finally.

Arrow looked surprised, but as Clive turned around and walked back the way he came, Arrow didn't follow him.

CHAPTER 33

Pat could feel a throbbing at the base of his skull and was surprised it wasn't the ringing in his ears that had woken him up. He instinctively reached up to touch the place where his chip had been installed. It still was healing from his last surgery, but it didn't seem like it had been messed with again.

"Good…you're up." Preston said silkily and stood from a chair that had been shrouded in shadow in a far corner.

Pat could tell they were in a different space and he marveled at how much of Sherwood Servers he hadn't seen. The walls were teal, except for one wall that had a black curtain drawn over its surface that was presumably to cover a window. He ran his fingers across the surface he was on and realized it was a hospital bed.

"What happened?"

"We just installed an upgrade to your chip. If you're ready, we need to test it."

"What happens if I say I am not ready?"

Preston grinned unsympathetically. "Then we'll have to test it while you're tied up. I don't make the rules, I just enforce them." He shrugged. "Actually, I lied. I do make the rules." Preston laughed at his own joke.

"Then I am ready, I guess." Pat lied.

"Good." Preston helped Pat up by grabbing him by the wrist and pulling. As soon as he was standing, Pat shook his wrist loose and glared at Preston. "You don't have to be so rude. I gave you options but you made things difficult. Do you know how expensive it is to fix large windows?"

"You know how much it costs to repair people? Nothing because you cannot repair people, sicko." Pat spat.

"I would be offended, but I have all the power here." Preston drawled, gazing at his nails in a bored fashion.

With that, Pat reluctantly followed a man that was more sick in the head than him. Pat had never thought that would be possible, but now that he had met Preston, it made him simultaneously discouraged about humanity and encouraged that he wasn't as bad as he thought he was.

Preston continued to make meaningless small talk as they wound through the hallways. He waved to nurses and acted as though this was simply a routine part of his day.

As they entered a new place, Pat took stock of his surroundings. This time, there were no windows or scissors that he could see. The only thing that was in there was a singular chair, a blinking metal computer on wheels, and a metal triangle standing upright that looked like his portal from home. Moments later, a few people who looked like students made their way into the space.

"Wonderful to have you all here." Preston greeted them warmly.

Pat continued to look around for a means of escape, but without any weapons or a clear idea of which part of the Sherwood Servers building he was in, he wouldn't be making it out easily. Besides, he was curious to see what he was about to partake in.

"Many of you may be familiar with Patrick Sherwood…recent CEO of Sherwood Servers." Preston said mildly. He glanced over at Pat and winked as the students were taking notes. "This will be monumental if it is successful." He then gestured for Pat to sit and reluctantly he sat in the only chair.

Pat thought that Dr. Evers was arrogant, but the pride in Preston Winston was slipping out more often now. Anytime he had read about Dr. Winston, it was always about how giving he was and the ways in which he was making space at the table for people of all backgrounds. Now Pat knew that this was simply a way for him to persuade people to give him what he wanted.

"Mr. Sherwood has graciously volunteered for our demonstration today."

"I did not volunteer." Pat said.

The crowd of students chuckled uncomfortably and Preston chortled. "All jokes aside…" Preston walked over to the machine. "We have installed an update in Patrick's microchip that has been enabled to communicate with our portal here. In some cases, the original microchips have been shown to transport resolved mental health issues to another place instead of eliminating them completely. We will now be able to trace where those things go."

Pat was even more curious now. If he ever got out, this would be valuable information for Zion's research. Suddenly Pat felt a slight pang in his chest at the thought of Zion. The trust between them had started shaky, but now Pat knew how good of a man Zion was and wondered what he would think if he knew his friend Preston was such an evil man.

"Patrick, you may feel a slight electrical pulse as we start the program." Preston informed him. "To be able to track a 'resolved' mental health issue, we must resolve one in the app." Preston handed Pat a cell phone. His first thought was to text somebody, but he saw that there were no apps except the Sherwood Servers app. He selected it and logged into his account. "Just select something you don't mind parting with."

Pat looked at the recent activity and decided to resolve the anxiety he had as he had run from Preston. As he did this, Preston powered on the portal and Pat felt the electrical impulse in his brain. For a couple of heartbeats, nothing happened and even Preston looked doubtful. Then, the portal flickered and darkness appeared before them. Cool air blew in through the entrance of the portal that had been opened and Pat watched as he saw a glowing strand curl its way from the top of his head to the ceiling. It exploded into plants and the figure of Preston appeared, racing after Pat. Nobody but Pat and Preston would know what memory was being played out. Pat suddenly felt the anxiety he had felt when this situation had occurred, and then it dissipated. The memory played out a few more times and then flickered out into the darkness beyond.

"It works." Preston muttered in disbelief.

The students had stopped taking notes and were simply staring, open-mouthed. Even though his anxiety about being chased was gone, Pat felt a new anxiety creeping up. Did this portal lead to the place that his portal at home did? Was this a portal into his mind? Whatever it was, Pat could feel nothing but fear about Preston having access to his private thoughts.

"Thank you. You can go." Preston said. He wasn't looking at his guests, but his hands flapped towards them to indicate for them to leave quickly.

They looked at each other and muttered amongst themselves, but like the dutiful mentees that they were, they left. Preston grinned wolfishly and grabbed Pat by the upper arm. Pulling a knife from his pocket with his right hand, he led Pat by blade point into the portal.

Preston was barely concealing his glee as he led Pat through a very familiar foyer. He was muttering to himself and making comments about everything they passed such as the peeling wallpaper and a dusty chandelier. Pat felt like he should have been more frightened, but the place was familiar. He was almost relieved to see it.

"This is magnificent." Preston gushed. "What is this place?"

Pat shrugged

"What if this is a different realm?"

"I am here against my will, so I am not going to pretend to be excited to be here." Pat licked his lips, bracing himself for the punishment.

Preston's eyebrows lowered and he placed the knife tip on the hollow of Pat's neck. "One more word and I'll rip your vocal chords out." Pat gave a cautious thumbs up and Preston moved the knife away from his neck, but still kept it poised nearby. Pat was pleased that he had gotten under this man's skin.

Pat then remembered the pictures of the women he had brought here and felt a tinge of fear that Preston would notice. He seemed so enamored with the spacious place that he hadn't looked at the paintings.

"Okay." Preston bit his lip thoughtfully, then grabbed some fraying rope from the floor. "I'll feel better if you can't double-cross me." He pocketed the knife and roughly grabbed Pat's wrists. Yanking Pat's arms behind him he tied the scratchy rope tightly around his wrists, forcing Pat's hands in a praying position. This would have been the moment to pray if Pat was a religious man, but instead, his mind just sang screams in four-part harmony.

The knife made a reappearance and Preston led Pat through the room, gazing at the walls, ceiling, and floor as if in an art museum. To his despair, Preston's eyes suddenly sparkled as he caught sight of the painting with Justice on it.

"Mrs. Sherwood? This must be your subconscious in physical form, then." Preston's fingers which had been stained with the blood of his many victims ran across the surface of the artwork. "She's an angel, Patrick. You did good." Pat had a strong urge to slap and kick him at the same time as shameful tears began welling in his eyes. Preston then laughed. "Easy there. I wouldn't hurt her. Destroying a work of art such as hers would be criminal."

"And murdering other people is not criminal?" Pat spat.

Preston paused as if deliberating, then continued to examine the portraits. "Janice?" He muttered aloud. "Isn't that the woman that went missing last week?" Pat didn't respond but a knowing glint shone in Preston's eyes and he said, "I may have found a kindred spirit, after all."

"I did not murder her!" Pat shouted without conviction.

"Where is she, Patrick?" The knife mirrored the look in Preston's eyes as he moved it closer to Pat's neck.

Pat remembered bringing Janice to this place but his brain went blank when he tried to remember what happened next. "I…"

"And, who is this?" Preston moved on to another portrait of a similar-looking red-haired woman. The name below her said "Candace Lane".

"She was…I do not remember."

"Do you keep a log of all your victims, Patrick Michael Sherwood?" Preston's tone was smug with a tinge of admiration. "I had no idea you were so organized and artistic."

"I did not paint any of these and Janice was just a guest in my home! I do not know what happened to her." Pat was telling the truth as far as he knew, but something felt wrong. Like he was forgetting something.

"Don't be modest." Preston growled as he adjusted his grip on Pat's arm and continued taking him through the most threatening museum tour he had ever been on. "Oh…" Preston breathed as they came to the last picture. "This must be elusive Mrs. Owen Sherwood."

Pat felt a twinge in the middle of his chest and fear spun in his brain. Curiosity won out and he looked where Preston was gazing. It felt like Pat was being introduced to his mother for the first time. She was a small, skinny woman with long auburn hair and nervous hazel eyes. Her hands were folded and a ghost of a smile played across her features. "Perdita Sherwood" was written at the base of the painting.

"Did you take your mother's life?" Preston asked, preparing to be even more impressed.

"She. Left. Me!" Pat growled. "I am not a psycho like you."

"Whatever you have to tell yourself."

"Bring him to the tree." Said a voice in Pat's mind.

"I cannot." Pat whispered.

"Who are you talking to?" Preston demanded.

"Tell him and he will take you."

"Do you want to see where I took Janice?" Pat managed to muster. Despite his anger about being accused of murder, he knew the voice had never led him astray before. He would take Preston to the place.

"Yes, lead the way." Preston loosened up his grip on Pat's arm and Pat took him through familiar doorways and outside to the stone throne below the tree.

Pat blinked a few times and as his eyes adjusted to the gloom, he was able to see the figure on the throne clearly. Her feet and hands were both uncovered. A sword was belted at her hip. The neckline of the dress was a deep v to showcase a necklace that looked like the sunbeams from half the sun. Her tall, willowy frame was dressed in strips of gauzy black fabric to create a dress. Every inch of visible skin was nearly paper white. But the most magnificent thing about her was her waist-length red hair and a tall crown that looked like it had been carved from charcoal.

The shaking began in Pat's hands and his head started to spin. Justice was in front of him in the flesh.

"Let go of him." Justice said to Preston crisply. Preston obeyed and Justice nodded in satisfaction. She then turned to Pat with a weary smile. "You're here."

CHAPTER 34

LACEY DROVE HARMONY TO HER MOTHER'S house and she felt an ache in her chest. It had occurred to Harmony that this woman might not even be her mother, which called into question everything she knew about her life.

When Wendy answered the door, her fists were balled at her sides. She looked like she was torn between hitting her daughter and hugging her. "Harmony, where in the world have you been? I thought you had been kidnapped or worse!"

"Can I come in?" Harmony asked meekly. No matter who this woman was to her, she hated making her worried.

Wendy nodded stiffly and backed up to allow her inside. Harmony paused as if expecting her mom to trip her, then she stepped up into the house. Once in the living room, she sat on the couch and Wendy sat in the chair in front of her.

Harmony took a deep breath and started explaining to her mother what had happened. When she began explaining what Lacey had said about Harmony's true identity, Wendy's eyebrows furrowed and she looked more serious.

"So, Lacey said I should come speak to you." Harmony finished, using Lyric's real name even though it felt strange. "Are you my mother?" She asked abruptly.

Wendy swallowed and looked towards the TV even though it was off. "I feel like your mom."

"That's not what I asked."

"But the only thing that matters is that I love you. I would do anything for you."

"Besides tell me the truth?" Harmony quipped.

"The truth isn't always the best thing." Wendy swung her gaze back around to Harmony.

"I need to know. There is a lot we don't understand about this new technology and if we don't get ahead of it, it could hurt others."

Wendy was chewing on her thumbnail. Harmony had never seen her mother this anxious before. She usually was comfortable with confrontation and telling the truth. This was the only time Harmony had seen her mother sweat.

"I worked for the government in the witness protection program. The way that we handled the program used to be very different before the chip implementation began. We had discovered a way to put people into witness protection and make them forget their old life so they couldn't even put themselves in harm's way." Wendy sighed. "You were so scared. You were one of the first people to volunteer. They gave you an entirely new identity and I helped by changing your physical appearance." Harmony's heart sank further and further as the pieces all came together. "I had helped so much with your rehabilitation and placement that they asked if I would take on the responsibility of being your mother. I agreed."

"Why would I agree to this?" Harmony wailed.

"You were so scared. It was such a high-profile case." Wendy said simply. "Harmony…I love you so much."

"I love you too." Harmony said honestly. Nothing could change that. This woman had stepped up when her real mother hadn't. "Who was my real mom?"

The word "real" seemed to hurt Wendy. "I don't know much about her but I was told she was an addict." Wendy was just as blunt as Harmony, which had the desired effect.

Harmony's heart sank. "An addict? So…"

"I don't think she was really in your life."

"No wonder I wanted to forget." Harmony said.

Wendy didn't respond. She was studying her feet closely to avoid making eye contact. In the silence, there was the abrupt tick of the clock in the kitchen and the sound of a pot of coffee finishing brewing. Life was moving on even though Harmony's world felt like it was spiraling out of control.

"This doesn't have to change anything." Wendy said. "I am still your mom and I still love you."

"This changes everything. Now I will always wonder why I gave up my past life. I will have no peace until I figure it out." Harmony said.

"They only gave me enough information to properly care for you." Wendy said unhelpfully. "I don't know why you chose to forget."

"Well, I think I know someone who has the connections to figure it out." Harmony said and stood up. "Could you check on Rufus for me while I'm gone?"

Wendy nodded. "I guess I can't stop you from leaving again?"

"No." She said firmly.

"Okay." Wendy sighed. "Let me give you your car. Law enforcement brought it by when they found it abandoned at the marina."

***

Harmony returned to New Life Rehab. She didn't even bother to park but left her car in the roundabout in front of the home. Taking the stairs two at a time she raced into the main house. Rachel was in the dining room preparing dinner. When she saw Harmony, shock crossed her face.

"Harmony!" She set down the tray she had been holding and rushed to Harmony to embrace her. "We thought something terrible had happened. Zion is downstairs in the lab right now."

"I have to talk to him."

Rachel didn't question this but nodded and beckoned for her to follow. Once in the lab, Zion was there examining the metal box that Harmony had entered which had led her to that other world.

"Don't go in there!" Harmony cried.

Zion turned around slowly and wore the same smile that Rachel had. "Harmony?" He walked over to her and hugged her tightly. "What happened? Here, sit." Zion pulled out a chair for her from one of the lab tables.

Once everyone had sat, Harmony started explaining the whole situation. She left nothing out. Zion and Rachel were both very engaged in what she was saying and interjected with questions for clarity.

When she had finished, Zion said, "That helps a lot. Clive and Arrow have disappeared and we are assuming it is to that other world. Pat has also disappeared."

"What?" Harmony's heart sank.

"The news reported this morning that Pat had stepped down as CEO of Sherwood Servers, but there was no press conference about it and Pat was supposed to return to Sherwood Servers to access your microchip information so we could locate you. Something must have happened when he arrived." Zion said.

Harmony suddenly felt guilty. She barely knew Pat, but he had risked his safety for her. Now he was missing.

"Arrow and Clive were on a retrieval mission to rescue Mayre Evers, but they never returned. The crew that was in the escape vehicle can no longer track them so that either means the tracking devices have been deactivated or they are out of range. Those trackers have a range of 100 miles, so it is impossible for them to go out of range that quickly unless they are in that other realm."

"I can go look for them."

"No, you're not going back in there." Rachel said. "You were close to not getting out before."

"But I am the most familiar with that place. I think I can manage it this time." Harmony argued.

"Rachel, she may have a point." Zion said kindly.

Rachel bit her lip in distress and said, "Is there any way we can monitor where she is at?"

"We can try." Zion said. "Harmony, are you okay with me giving you one of our tracking devices?"

Harmony nodded.

"For good measure, we'll give you fishing twine." Zion said. "It sounds silly, but when technology fails we must get creative."

Once she was rigged up with everything, Zion walked her over to the supply cabinet and opened the door. It still seemed to be connected to the other realm. Zion looked inside and nodded.

"Okay, Harmony. Your tracker is also a communicator. Hopefully, it works, but you just press the green button when you want to speak." Zion patted the device.

"Thank you."

"May the Lord be with you." Zion said. "We will be praying for you."

Harmony hoped there was a god and hoped he was good. She hoped he answered their prayers and hoped he would listen to her if she had to pray to him. She now wondered if she had been religious in her past life. If she had confidence in a god in her past life, what a shame to forget.

She stepped into the darkness and walked out into the fog. It appeared familiar, but she couldn't be certain because everything looked the same in the fog. It was reassuring to have a lifeline connecting her to where she came from.

She then tested the tracker. "Hello, Zion?"

"Still here, Harmony." Came the crackly voice.

"Good." She responded. She walked a few more yards and tried again. "Zion?"

"Still here." Came the voice again.

She did this for a while until she reached the creek she remembered. Instead of turning around in uncertainty like she had last time, she proceeded forward to explore even further.

When the fog had gotten thinner, she tried the tracker again. "Hello?"

All she could hear was static.

She tried to not let this scare her. Even though she couldn't hear Zion, she was still connected to them by a string. Getting back would be easy. She just had to keep going until she found Arrow and Clive. A familiar rumbling sounded in the distance. Her heartbeat increased and she stopped to take a few calming breaths.

"It's just a storm." She told herself, but she knew a storm didn't chase people down underground tunnels. Her body knew it was something much more sinister but she couldn't figure out what.

The path began to widen slightly and the fog thinned. When she reached a clearing she could see the strange library she had stumbled across before. She remembered that if she kept going straight it would take her back to her house. She tied part of the twine on a tree branch behind her so she would be able to get back here if necessary. Instead of going straight or going right to the library, she made a left and began making her way off the beaten path.

This part of the realm was dark, but not covered in mist. Tall fir trees dotted the landscape and the dirt took a deep dip into what looked like a ditch because it immediately went back up and she could feel her shoe land on hard blacktop. A couple dim streetlights lined the road and the limbs of the trees reached over the road like they were fighting to grasp the strands of dusty light breaking through the gloom. The yellow lines on the road stood out like they had been freshly painted.

Not hearing or seeing anything, she began walking along the right side hoping it would lead somewhere important. Her mind wandered while taking note of the sound of crickets, creaking branches, and the echo of her footsteps.

Like the sound of thousands of little footsteps, the rain started. A few more steps and she was in the downpour and couldn't hear crickets or her footfalls. This made it even harder to anticipate when a car came pealing around the corner. It was a brown car longer than it was tall with fake wood paneling on the sides. This was all she saw as it trundled towards her with no sign of stopping. She instinctively backed up and fell into the ditch, rolling over her head and landing on her butt.

As she pulled her tangled mess of hair out of her eyes, she was able to watch just as the car overcorrected and began slipping out of control into a hitchhiker on the other side of the road. She couldn't look away as the person was nailed in the torso by the front bumper and dragged along several feet.

"No!" Harmony screamed as she saw them go flying off into the other ditch, bloody and bent at an odd angle.

The car stopped and the passenger door flew open. Rachel Jones flew out, hysterical.

"No. No. No!!!!" She was much younger than the Rachel Harmony had met at New Creation Rahab. Her cheeks and nose were rosy from crying and the cold rain that drenched everything. A long black skirt stuck to her skinny legs and she was wearing a blue peasant top. Her hair was starting to stick to her cheeks and neck as the rain and tears mingled on her face.

A nondescript male figure left the driver's seat and came to stand beside Rachel. "It's a shame."

"A shame? A shame?? Is that all you're going to say?" Rachel demanded. Her usual calm control and joy were nowhere to be found. She hiccuped and sniffed at the same time, barely able to say, "You never gave him a chance."

"He wouldn't let me." The nondescript man said.

"Dad, he's your son." Rachel said. "Your own flesh and blood."

"That doesn't make it any easier to try to love him!" Rachel's dad was angry.

Rachel didn't respond but bent by her dead brother's side. The apparitions flickered and things shifted to now show an ambulance and police car on the scene. The rain had stopped. Rachel and her dad were being questioned.

"Why was he out here so late?" The police officer asked.

"He…" Rachel glanced at her dad. "Glen had a drinking problem. We wouldn't let him drive to his friend's house so he said he would walk." Tears continued to seep from her eyes and down her face.

"We figured we should go look for him but it was raining. We couldn't see him. I lost control." Rachel's dad said.

The police officer chewed the back of his pen thoughtfully. "This must be hard for you, Reverend Smith."

Harmony watched from her place in the ditch as the Reverend seemed to take great pains to show his sorrow by lowering his eyebrows over his eyes and bowing his head, touching his lips with his fingertips. When he had done this for a few beats he said, "It has been my cross to bear. I never understood it."

"You never bothered to!" Rachel screamed.

It all dissolved before Harmony's eyes then and the street returned to being empty. She waited a moment and cautiously peered down the ribbon of black highway. The same car came pealing back into her line of sight and the headlights nearly blinded her. She instinctively knew she was watching Rachel's brother's death scene play out again because not a single detail changed. Knowing what would happen she looked away, but she could still hear the crunch of bones breaking as the car made contact.

Running across the road behind the accident, Harmony rushed into the woods before she could hear Rachel's screams. Once she was under the shelter of the trees and the dark, she threw up. When she had finished, she wrapped her arms tightly around her torso and began to walk again.

She tried to ignore the mental image of what she had just seen, but it continued to play out in her mind over and over again. She had never imagined that Rachel had suffered so much. Her joy was contagious and she was such a loving person to everybody she came in contact with. Harmony now realized why Rachel had such a heart for addicts.

"How could she believe in a god that allowed her brother to be killed? How could she believe in the god that her father believed in?"

None of it made sense to Harmony.

It then occurred to her that maybe it was just a nightmare that had been consigned to this place by a microchip. Even so, it was a horrific dream to suffer under regardless.

"I am near. I am close. I am many."

Harmony froze mid-stride.

"I am near. I am close. I am many." The voice whispered again.

Like a chorus of snakes, the voices continued to hiss and slither through the woods. When she thought she knew where the voice was coming from, it would suddenly sound in the opposite direction.

"I feel you here." The voice whispered again.

Harmony began to move her feet. One foot in front of the other away from the voices, but no matter where she walked, it surrounded her. She whimpered and held on to the fishing twine for dear life as she continued to work her way through the woods and hopefully away from whatever was speaking to her. She felt nothing but cold in her bones when it spoke.

She broke through the tree line and fell onto her knees before the downtown of an abandoned town. In front of her was a park bench that she pulled herself up onto. She could still hear whispering behind her but couldn't make out what the voices were saying. Even though her legs were screaming at her to stop, she stood again and began running towards the dirty buildings.

Each business was a yellowish brown and covered in all kinds of grime and debris. Doors were hanging off some of these places and glass display windows were cracked and shattered on the concrete. The only thing that seemed to have life in this place was a movie theatre down at the end of the road. A couple of bulbs around the marquee were still blinking dimly. When she was level with it, she tied some of her fishing twine around a parking sign. Tentatively, she approached the doorway. Once she was close, she realized the glass had been busted out of the frames long ago. The shards crunched under her shoes as she walked inside.

Once in the lobby, she could see a few dim lights on over the popcorn machine and candy cabinet. She continued deeper into the place until she reached the bathrooms which were still lit up. She walked inside to do her business but was surprised to see Heidi standing before her in all her fearsome glory.

CHAPTER 35

Clive was motivated by his fear and righteous anger as he trudged through the sludge and the slime that covered the landscape. He also did his best to not think about the blood that mingled below his feet. Even though he handled blood in his job, it wasn't the same. There was something purifying about surgery. Eventually, the blood stopped and the wound was sewn up by surgical thread. The blood in this realm just seemed to be endless and trickled over rocks and through the grasses and the mud. The entire place reeked of death and ugliness.

Clive hated it.

In his own world, he was able to comfort himself by seeking out the beautiful things that the Good Lord had blessed him with, but in this place, there was nothing to calm his spirit or whet his appetite for beauty. Clive believed that this must be what hell was like.

He had been trudging for 20 minutes when he realized he was no longer angry and wished Arrow was there with him. There was a sense of safety Clive felt having somebody to go through this situation with, but it was too late now. Even if he swallowed his pride, he wasn't sure where Arrow had gone.

Up ahead, he could see the flicker of a candle in the window of a house. It was the first place Clive had seen that seemed cozy and still in good repair. He made a beeline for the front door, not even worrying if anybody was home. Once inside, he wiped his face off with his sleeve and collapsed the umbrella. He looked around and noticed that he was in his own home. Relief swelled in his soul and he went to his favorite chair to sit down.

He allowed himself to sink into the seat and take a few cleansing breaths. The relaxing was short-lived though because he heard some shuffling going on back in their bedroom. Standing up abruptly, he followed the sound and saw the door open a crack. He peered inside and could see Mayre sobbing on the bed.

It took all his self-control to not burst in and embrace her, but something felt wrong. His entire body was telling him to burst in their bedroom and comfort her. He was convinced Mayre could sense his nervous energy but she didn't seem to hear his heavy breathing. Using her sweater sleeve to clean her face, she stood and walked to the full-length mirror on the other side of the room. Clive watched her lift the bottom of the sweater to reveal her belly. She examined it from all angles and grabbed at the loose skin.

"Lord, why doesn't he want me?" She sobbed. She continued to look at herself for answers and was met with no response.

It was then that Clive pushed open the door and rushed to her side. "I want you. I want you so much." He tried embracing her but he passed right through her. She didn't even know he was there. "I'm right here, May." He tried again, but still no response. He glanced over at their digital alarm clock and saw it was 9 pm. Normally he was home by now. "Where am I?"

Mayre dissolved and reappeared in the bed. Clive could see a shadow of himself standing at the foot-board "Why can't I go?" His shadow self screamed at Mayre, his past self's face twisted in anger.

"Because SHE will be there! I can't trust you going alone with her!"

"Nothing happened, Mayre. I don't know what you're worried about. This conference is instrumental to my career!"

"To YOUR career. This is destroying our marriage. You said after med school things would slow down."

"They *are* slowing down." Clive argued.

"Not even slightly. Every time I ask if you want to start trying for kids you say no because there 'isn't enough time'." Mayre said bitterly.

Clive had no response.

"See. You can't deny it."

"I just don't think we are ready." Clive said reluctantly.

This scene faded and the bedroom lights turned off. Real Clive saw light shining under the door of the bathroom and cautiously walked towards it. Placing an ear to the door, he heard sobbing. His heart plummeted. He debated with himself about opening the door or not. The seconds ticked by and he didn't know when the scene would change again so he quietly cracked the door open.

At first, he was startled because Mayre stood looking in the mirror where she could see Clive's face clearly in the reflection. He almost pulled back into the darkness but remembered that she could not see him. She didn't give his face a second glance or even call out to him. She simply stared at her own tear-stained face. In her hands, she was grasping something tightly. Clive opened the door all the way and stood beside his wife. He looked at her face and hoped that these tears were not because of him.

Glancing down, he saw a glimpse of a clear plastic cap. She finally looked at her hand again and opened the fist to reveal a pregnancy test. The markers on the test strip were clearly negative. She let another hopeless sob escape her lips, then sniffed loudly. In one motion she threw the test away and started the water in the sink to wash her hands. As if nothing had occurred, she went through her usual routine of doing her makeup and styling her hair. Once done, she took a deep breath and went out into the living room.

Clive followed her and saw that the shadow of himself was coming through the front door. This past version of himself was happy.

"Mayre! Guess who got tickets to see Wicked!" Past Clive held up his phone to reveal virtual tickets to the old musical.

Mayre wore a wide grin and jumped into his arms. "I've always wanted to see Wicked!" She squealed.

Real Clive watched all this play out and remembered the day distinctly. She had never told him about the pregnancy test or about crying. She had never breathed a word to him. Clive remembered that day as being one of the best days of his life, but Mayre remembered it as painful.

This happy scene faded again to reveal Mayre sitting on the couch speaking into the phone. "Hi, Mom." She paused to listen to her mother respond. "I'm not okay. I lost the baby." Mayre placed her free hand on her belly and gritted her teeth to hold back tears. "No, I didn't tell Clive. The baby was only 13 weeks along." She paused again. "Thanks, Mom. I may go speak with Father James about it. Okay, I love you…bye."

She ended the call and placed the phone on the side table. Real Clive came and sat down beside a Mayre that didn't acknowledge his presence. He peered into her face and could see the exhaustion, but she was still beautiful. Up close, there were a few faded freckles that peppered her nose. He always remembered liking when she would scrunch up her nose when amused about something.

"I always knew you were designed to be a perfect mother." Clive whispered. "I never knew you were pregnant. I'm sorry. I'm so sorry."

Mayre faded and the side table lamp dimmed to where Clive was left alone with his thoughts. The weight of what he had done fell on his unprotected heart and he sobbed into one of the throw pillows until he felt like he was all dried up. The emptiness he had seen on the faces of countless parents was now in his own heart. He sat in silence as the rain beat upon the house and allowed the thoughts in his brain to ping back and forth without acknowledging what they were about. It felt like he had static in his brain and was unable to process everything.

He had always felt justified in seeking to meet his own needs during hard times because of the great responsibility he had as a doctor. He believed that Mayre would always be there with her joyful and quirky personality to lift him up when life got hard. But that wasn't reality. She had been suffering under her own pain for months and he hadn't known anything about it.

If he had cared sooner, she might not have been taken and might not have lost herself.

To Clive's surprise, the lights brightened in the living room and Mayre was back, but this time she was accompanied by Dr. Preston Winston.

"Of course, no disrespect for the research your husband has already conducted." Preston said smoothly. "We simply believe, at Winston Wellness, that most healthcare workers are blind to the full capability of this technology."

"Like what?" Mayre asked.

Clive felt hot coals in his belly as he noticed Mayre's knees pointing towards Preston and her cheeks rosy with excitement. She was intrigued by Preston and Clive could feel the jealousy burning through him.

"The security measures are not as robust as they need to be. There are far more victims of this technology than necessary. Hackers can bypass many of the security features and people are turning into human vegetables." Preston said seriously.

"That's awful." Mayre whispered sympathetically.

"It is." Preston bowed his head. "That's why I'm coming to you."

He grinned wolfishly and looked up into her inquisitive eyes. "Would you be interested in helping us with our research?"

To Clive's surprise, Mayre smiled and nodded.

"Wonderful." Preston said and grasped her hands. "It will be an honor to have you on our team."

CHAPTER 36

Harmony tried to find similarities between herself and Heidi, but the government had done an amazing job transforming her from Heidi to Harmony all those years ago. It just didn't seem to make any sense. The two women couldn't be more different.

"You know." It wasn't a question. Heidi said it like a statement as if she could see the truth written on Harmony's forehead.

"Yes, I do."

"Do you believe it?"

"I'm not sure. It seems impossible." They both stood awkwardly and then Harmony said, "I want to know for sure."

"That's why we're here."

"We?"

"Arrow is here, too."

Harmony's heart skipped a beat. "Where is he?"

Heidi looked sad. "Waiting for you." She motioned for Harmony to follow and she obeyed.

They walked through the dimly lit theatre until they reached "Screen 7". Harmony stepped into the room without pausing, but her heart was beating rapidly. She had known isolation, anxiety, and depression— but none of those feelings compared to what she was experiencing now. Her whole life as Harmony was a lie and the truth of her past could be frightening.

The auditorium was illuminated by warm light, which was comforting. Harmony was accustomed to the modern-day shift to LED lighting, so the old-style bulbs were unfamiliar to her. The room was filled with black, metal-backed chairs with hinged, cushioned seats. Each aisle was slanted down leading to the front of the room where a giant screen hung framed by red velvet curtains. She glanced back instinctively and saw Heidi pointing to the seats. Harmony saw the back of Arrow's head and the dark lines of his tattoos peeping above his shirt collar.

He craned his neck to see who had entered and smiled when he saw Harmony. She walked down the slanted, carpeted aisle and scooted down row "G" to sit beside Arrow.

"It's so good to see you in this place." He said and wrapped his strong arms around her. The embrace made her want to spontaneously burst into tears.

When she pulled away she said, "Heidi caught me." She glanced to the back and saw that there was a small window on the back wall with a camera poking cautiously out. Heidi was shuffling around in there.

"She found us, too." Arrow said.

"Us?"

"The good Doc was with us, but…" Arrow averted Harmony's eyes. "we had a falling out and got separated."

Before she could inquire what had happened, the lights dimmed and a clicking sound started up in the back room. The camera flickered on and a movie began to play on the big screen. It was comforting to hide in the semi-darkness and focus her thoughts on what was happening. The little girl on the screen had long bleach-blonde hair and was playing in a field full of crabgrass and wildflowers. It wasn't a very interesting beginning and there didn't seem to be any kind of plot. The girl and her parents lived an average life.

Rather suddenly, the father left when the girl turned 11 and her first day of middle school was tragic to watch. Harmony was invested now. There were many moments where the girl would be left at her school until late at night by her mother who had turned to pills and alcohol. On several occasions, she tried to have friends over and her mother was passed out on the couch. School was spent avoiding the uncomfortable stares and conversations with guidance counselors. The little girl didn't want her mom getting in trouble, so she always lied.

The girl grew up and attended community college after high school graduation. This girl was Heidi. The familiar dreadlocks and tattoos began accumulating during the latter half of high school and the beginning of college. Harmony's chest tightened as Heidi's first day of college included a very familiar face. Arrow. The two fell in love and the romance seemed to go too fast. Harmony's insides were screaming, "No!" The dread she had felt upon entering this world consumed her. It was as if she knew what was going to happen. But how could she? Arrow stiffened beside her, but they did not speak to one another.

As if it couldn't get any worse, Heidi got pregnant. The joy that filled her face was quickly replaced by fear as Arrow's past began unraveling. She found out that he had been selling codes to hack through the chip's security features. These were being sold to addicts and sold to her mom. He had told her it was for the greater good and that people in charge were preventing patients from overcoming their mental illness.

When Heidi was 12 weeks pregnant, her mother was no longer responsive. She had gone too far to numb her pain and there was no going back. To top it all off, Heidi went to her OBGYN appointment and was told her daughter had indicators for Down Syndrome.

"If you would like to terminate the pregnancy, I don't blame you." The doctor had said.

The next thing that happened was almost too much for Harmony to bear. The abortion of the child happened with no fanfare and no significant outward change, but Harmony could tell Heidi was in a lot of pain. The light had faded from her eyes.

The scenes came hard and fast at this point until they came to a screeching halt at a scene that only showed Heidi gazing at herself in the mirror. She glanced down at her arm where stitches had been sewn to seal the Thought Conductor under her skin. She steadily transformed into Harmony on screen and in that moment, the Harmony seated in the dim theatre felt a mental dam break as all her memories came back to her. She couldn't breathe and all the pain and heartbreak felt like too much to bear. A buzzing heat started at the base of her neck and began to spread up her neck and across her skull.

Harmony sensed that Arrow was looking at her, but she refused to turn her head. She gripped the cold metal armrests for support, but she felt like she was going to pass out. When she started having feelings for Arrow, the only thing she was afraid of was his addiction. Now that she had her memories back, she knew he was the man the government had hidden her from. She had testified against him in court and sent him to prison. He had been the one who gave her biological mother access to Thought Conductor codes that destroyed her. Arrow was the reason she had lost everything.

She had terminated her pregnancy because she was scared of him and scared of an uncertain future. She could have been a mother at this point, but that wasn't her reality anymore. Something inside her mourned that loss. Her baby would have been different and that difference would not have been accepted by others. She might have had medical issues. Harmony wouldn't have known how to care for her. Her decision made sense and she didn't have confidence that she could be a mother.

But all she wanted in that moment was to hold that child in her arms.

The screen faded to black. Arrow and Harmony sat in the dark as a ringing silence filled the air. Before Harmony could muster up the courage to speak, she heard little footsteps padding down the carpeted aisle. Out of the darkness appeared Haven. Her sweet smile and beautiful almond-shaped eyes were turned towards Harmony.

"You're my real Mom." Haven said simply. Her words came slowly and deliberately, but it was unmistakable the meaning of the words.

The shame and the guilt flowed through Harmony like fire. "I'm sorry…" The tears ran down her face and her voice shook.

"I'm okay now, mom. It's okay. I'm with my Creator now."

"Creator?"

"He loves you, too. He's forgiven you. Find him and we can be together."

Harmony embraced her daughter and sobbed into her very real shoulder. "You look so healthy and happy." She said through the tears.

"I am."

Harmony held her at arm's length and looked at her closely. She was different, but she also looked so much like Heidi with blonde hair and a thin frame. But she then saw Arrow's fierceness and sharp ears.

"I forgive you, Mommy." Haven said sincerely.

Arrow shifted behind Harmony and she could feel him kneel and peer into Haven's face. "This is our daughter?" He asked, his strong voice cracking with the beginning of tears.

"Yes." Harmony whispered, glancing at him.

Haven smiled at her father and leaned in to hug him. "I have an extra chromosome, but that only means I am extra fun."

Arrow laughed weakly and held her tightly. "You're beautiful." Something broke inside him and he sobbed uncontrollably. "I'm a daddy."

Harmony wrapped her arms around them both and the tears flowed freely down her cheeks. Haven simply received the hugs and patted their backs as if she were the parent comforting her children.

When they had calmed down, they detached from one another and Haven was smiling. They then noticed that Heidi had appeared and she looked concerned.

Heidi said, "We can't go with you."

"Why?" Arrow demanded, standing quickly.

"We see you both in the real world." Harmony argued.

"This is also part of the real world." Heidi said darkly. "You may not want to accept it, but this is another part of reality." Heidi sighed and then said, "We can only be on the outside for a few hours before we dissolve. We are consigned to Oblivion." She finished, waving her arms to indicate the surrounding world was "Oblivion".

Harmony felt a sinking feeling in her stomach as she remembered what had happened to past Lacey at her house. She knew Heidi was right, but she didn't think she could bear to leave Haven after she just found out who she really was.

"So, you're both stuck here because of me?" Harmony asked.

"No." Haven shook her head gleefully. "I am in heaven."

"Haven is simply my idea of what she would have been. Her real soul is elsewhere." Heidi clarified. "My soul is still alive in you, Harmony, so I am unsure how I am experiencing this horrific reality."

"I am so sorry. If I had known. If we had known…" Harmony said.

"I know. I understand." Heidi paused, then embraced her future self. When she let go, she said, "I have to get Haven to safety before the beast finds us. Leave this place and warn people. We have to stop this."

Arrow and Harmony nodded.

"We love you, Haven." Arrow said huskily.

"Love you too, Daddy…Mommy." Haven waved enthusiastically, then took Heidi's hand as they exited the dimly lit theatre.

Once the two memories were gone, Harmony let Arrow hug her. The grief she felt needed a buffer and he was big enough to absorb her pain. She did not doubt why she fell for him twice, but a small part of her brain screamed at her to remember what he had done and who he really was.

Arrow seemed to be reading her mind so he said, "I'm sorry, Heidi."

"I'm not Heidi anymore." She whispered into his shoulder.

"I'll call you whatever you want to be called if it means I won't lose you again."

"I don't know if it's that easy." She said as she pulled herself away from him. "Let's get out of here. I don't like this place."

He nodded reluctantly and followed her out of the theatre. When they were outside, she retrieved the fishing wire spool where she had placed it and explained to Arrow why she was there. They walked together quietly for some time. Harmony was still running over all the things she had remembered about her past. It was hard to motivate herself to carry on a conversation with this man whom she loved but who also frightened her.

"I don't sell the codes anymore. I realized how wrong I was." Arrow said firmly.

"I don't know how I can believe that."

"You didn't tell me you were pregnant." Arrow said.

"Because you were a criminal." She said sharply. "You are also an alcoholic."

"I'm making changes."

"I can't believe that, either." It went quiet between them again and then Harmony said, "Haven said she was with the Creator. Is she with God?"

"That's what it sounds like."

"I never believed in Jesus." Harmony said. "I just don't know why a loving God would do this to me."

"God works in mysterious ways." Arrow said cryptically. "My dad always said that, but he never believed in Jesus Christ being the Messiah. Dad always said he was still waiting for the true Messiah."

"It's too confusing. I just don't know what's right."

Arrow nodded. "Well, I could never believe in a God that allowed my father to abuse me."

They were now back in the woods and Harmony looked over at Arrow with concern. "What do you mean?"

"My father was a terrible man after my mother passed. I was a sensitive kid and when I had issues, my dad would make me drink with him." Arrow paused.

"How old were you?"

"11…I didn't realize it, but I was going to school drunk. I never did anything but I was a zombie. My grades suffered. My social life suffered."

Harmony didn't speak but focused her attention on making sure she didn't trip on any debris lying on the ground. The mist still swirled in parts of this world and everything was dim.

"I had committed to change when I was out of the house and I did change for awhile, but…then I got arrested. Once I was out of prison, it was like an old friend returned to me when I bought the first beer."

"I'm sorry." Harmony said softly. "It isn't a good friend, though. It's a toxic friend."

Suddenly, Harmony came to the end of her fishing wire and they were in the middle of a misty field. She was certain she had secured it properly which made her wonder if one of the apparitions in Oblivion had untied it. Upon closer inspection, there was no obvious tampering.

"Where are we?" Arrow asked.

"I don't know."

CHAPTER 37

"MRS. SHERWOOD?" PRESTON ASKED WITH A smug look on his face. "How is this possible? You have more of a monopoly than I thought."

Justice didn't acknowledge this comment but instead addressed Pat. "It took you long enough."

"Were you the Justice visiting me?"

"Yes."

"Why didn't you stay?"

"I can't." She said sadly.

"I love you and I miss you!" Pat was beginning to feel desperate now. "My life is falling apart without you."

"I know."

"You know?? Then, why…"

"The beast is always hungry and the only way he can be fed is with more pain and more suffering." Justice looked around as if the trees were listening. "When your father created the Thought Conductor, Oblivion was opened to accept all your trauma and pain. My very first memory was of you and your need, so I found a way to be with you in your world. It was as if I hadn't existed until you needed me and I was filled with this desperate desire to help you. But the beast was no longer receiving a steady dose of suffering as it was accustomed, so he took me home."

"This isn't your home!" Pat cried. "Your home is with me."

"I am a product of your subconscious, Patty." Justice said kindly as if she was explaining to a 2-year-old why he couldn't have dessert before dinner. "The things you've been seeing have been real, though. While your father was treating you for schizophrenia, you were possessed by many demons who influenced your actions and what you have seen."

"No, I don't believe in that. I won't believe it." Pat shook his head fiercely. "Demons aren't real...God isn't real...the only thing that's real is you and me, Justice!"

"I am near." Sounded an echoey whisper.

Justice straightened on her throne and looked up at the skies. "He is coming."

Preston looked so excited by this, but Pat's face paled. He slowly fell to his knees and closed his eyes. The wind began to pick up, which knocked Pat on his side. His hands were still tied too tight to be able to right himself.

Preston didn't notice. Jubilant tears streamed from his eyes as he shouted, "Please, take me home!" He lifted his arms to the sky which reminded Pat of the congregation at the church service back at New Life Rehab.

The branches of the tree canopy above began to wave so violently that streaks of gray light filtered through. Rumbling started, interspersed with screaming.

Pat suddenly realized it was the screams of all the women he had brought here. All the women he had led through the portal and had given as a sacrifice to what Justice claimed was a demon. These memories flooded his mind as the creature neared where they were and Pat's body was drenched in agonizing sorrow. He knew what he had done as sure as he knew his heart beat thunderously in his ears.

He had been so obsessed with finding his wife, he allowed himself to become a murderer. He couldn't reconcile how his conscience allowed him to do such terrible things to these innocent women and erase them from his memories. In each instance of sacrifice, he felt like another voice was telling him to do it and it must have been the demon.

When he thought he couldn't handle the memories anymore, a vision of his mother came to mind. It was a memory shrouded in fuzzy white light. His mom's face smiling while playing with him as a baby. As he felt his baby self shift into his father's arms, he felt increased anxiety. Something was about to happen, but he couldn't remember what.

"Great King of this realm, I will serve you in whatever way you see fit!" Preston's shouts were beginning to sound desperate, but Pat couldn't see his face from where he lay.

He fought to grasp more details about his mother, but he kept hitting a wall of white light in his memory.

Just then a human-like shadow materialized and Pat didn't like how familiar the presence felt. It was taller than a normal man with long, black branches dripping off its hands and feet. Its hair was made from briars and fashioned into a crown. It didn't walk but simply glided over the ground. Every inch of it was pitch black.

Burning that started in the place where his Thought Conductor had been installed seared across his skull as the memories came quickly. Pat and his father finding Perdita dead in her bed. An intentional overdose of sleeping pills. Agonizing screams from Owen. This memory was not something Pat consciously remembered, but it infected every area of his childhood psyche like a cancer. The pain of it reverberated over his family.

"I am ready." The demon said and Justice lifted her arms in the air.

That's when Pat knew the truth. Pat had been left to grapple with his big feelings alone during pivotal moments in childhood. Owen was his Father but did not reflect the strength that Pat expected a Father to have. Pat longed for a strong nurturing presence in his life and, when Owen created the first Thought Conductor, Pat was deeply longing for a woman who possessed the strength and the love to put the pieces of his heart back together. Justice had been conjured up in his imagination to fill that void in his life and must have been strong enough that she became part of the material world. He knew that now. That's why she was so perfect and everything his parents couldn't be for him. He couldn't explain how he knew, but the certainty filled him with despair. He wished he could keep on pretending Justice was real "until death do us part".

But that was impossible now.

Pat had real memories of his wedding day which is why he struggled to reconcile the Justice of Oblivion with Justice his wife. She had been a living, breathing human being when they met in high school. He had held her— he had kissed her. They had shared a life together. But the details of her life before him were strangely absent. When he tried to recall things she had said about her family life, hometown, or interests, he couldn't think of solid examples. She claimed to have been in and out of the foster care system. She walked down the aisle with Owen Sherwood because she claimed her "real father" wasn't a "good man". She seemed to be interested in everything and nothing all at once and Pat wondered why he hadn't questioned any of this before.

What happened next was the last thing that Pat expected. Preston's body began to pulse and then a filmy white curtain began to be pulled from him and he screamed. He began to seize aggressively and fell onto the stone path, hard. Once the filmy curtain was removed, it went up Justice's arms and into the air where the beast leapt to retrieve it. As Preston's essence flowed through and around her, she looked like a being that was half fallen angel, half human bringing pain and destruction.

Pat was so consumed by what was happening before him that he was startled to hear a voice whispering behind him. "Pat, buddy." It was Arrow holding a pocket knife.

Pat shook his head, eyes wide in disbelief and fear. Justice was so preoccupied with filtering whatever essence Preston gave her that she didn't notice his presence. Arrow grimaced and ran over to Pat, cutting his bonds and then picking him up bodily. Pat screamed, but it couldn't be heard over the demon. Arrow was strong and Pat was a very small man, so picking him up was an easy thing to do. Once up the stairs and inside the house, Pat noticed Harmony too.

"No! Justice is back there!" Pat yelled, hanging on to the last bit of his sanity. He wanted to remember her as his wife and not as Queen of Oblivion.

"Not now, buddy." Arrow said again. "We have to get out of here."

***

Harmony and Arrow had finally found their lead back to the portal at New Life Rehab— but as they did so, they noticed the gathering of Preston, Pat, and an unknown woman. As they got closer, they realized what was happening. Once they dragged Pat unwillingly to the portal, Harmony passed through first but lost her footing as she tried to slow down. She fell forward and caught herself with her hands. Before she had time to warn Arrow, he came tumbling through behind her carrying an unwilling Pat. They collapsed on top of her back in the safety of Zion's place. A quick look around and Harmony recognized that they were in the downstairs lab she had cleaned. Zion and Rachel leaned over the trio in concern.

"We were so worried." Rachel said.

"We're okay." Arrow reassured her as he stood up.

Harmony stood as well and dusted herself off. Even though they had bad news, it was comforting to be in a familiar place that was well-lit.

"Pat, buddy." Arrow said, looking down at the young man still curled up on the floor.

He reached out for Pat, but he shoved Arrow's hand away. Faster than Harmony had ever seen Pat move, he stood on his own. There was something odd about how he looked. His eyes were dark and the lines on his face pronounced. His head was cocked slightly to the side and he was sneering at them all. A sneer was not an unfamiliar sight on Pat's face, but it was usually paired with a sparkle in his eyes to signify he was being sarcastic or teasing. This time, no shard of light could be found in his eyes.

"Pat?" Zion reached out, his fingertips barely touching his shoulder.

Pat recoiled as if he had been burned and said, "Get away."

"I'm sorry. Did you get hurt?" Zion asked, still standing near to Pat.

Rachel then approached and was behind her husband, concern in her eyes. "Something is wrong, Zi." Rachel whispered to her husband. "That isn't Pat speaking."

Zion muttered a quick prayer and Pat suddenly laughed. "He will not hear you."

"He who?" Zion asked.

"Elohim." Pat hissed.

Harmony felt shivers run down her spine. She didn't know who Elohim was, but his name commanded attention. She glanced over at Arrow and she could tell that he knew who Elohim was. His eyebrows were weighing heavily over his eyes and his lips were in a firm line.

"Who are you?" Zion's voice was steady, but he shook.

"Tumultus, the author of confusion." Pat's face sneered again. Experimenting with this body he was now in, he stretched out his arms and wiggled his fingers.

"Are you a demon?" Zion continued to question this being like they were at a networking event. Harmony's heart was beating out of her chest and she marveled at how calm The Jones' were.

"How uncharitable a description." Tumultus said dryly.

"But not inaccurate?" Zion ventured. Tumultus didn't answer. "The only author of my existence is Elohim and he is not the author of confusion."

"I feel sorry for you. Elohim is exclusive, authoritarian, and a hypocrite." This voice was beginning to weasel its way into Harmony's brain and she found herself paying closer attention to what he was saying.

Zion's voice increased in volume as he said, "For God so loved the world, that he gave his only Son, that whoever believes in him should not perish but have eternal life."

"Lies!" Tumultus recoiled.

"His lord said to him, 'Well done, good and faithful servant; you were faithful over a few things, I will make you ruler over many things. Enter into the joy of your lord.'" Zion screamed. "The Lord partners with us and is not a dictator over us!"

"Shut up!"

"Jesus Christ is the same yesterday and today and forever!"

Pat's face that the demon had borrowed twisted grotesquely and he ripped a knife off one of the laboratory tables. Zion backed up a few paces, raising his arms protectively in front of Harmony and Rachel. Arrow grasped Harmony's shoulder and moved her behind him.

"Pat, don't let this creature overtake you. You are stronger than this." Arrow said.

The demon used Pat's eyes to get a better look at Arrow, "You are already mine." He hissed. "I am not concerned about you."

Arrow blinked several times in surprise but did not respond.

"Lord, please free Pat from this demon. Give him an opportunity to know your love!"

Suddenly, Pat got very quiet and his eyes began to return to their normal color. His sick grin faded to confusion. "Where am I?" He asked breathlessly.

"You're back with us. You're safe now." Zion said reassuringly. Turning his eyes to the ceiling he said, "Lord, you are good."

Zion and Rachel came near Pat, but before they could take the knife from his hand, he swung around and slashed Rachel's neck. She had no time to scream but collapsed on the floor gasping for breath. The blood was deep crimson and spilled onto the floor at an alarming rate. Arrow took his shirt off and rushed to Zion's side to staunch the bleeding but it couldn't be stopped. Harmony didn't think that Rachel could be any paler, but she was quickly becoming the color of death.

"Rach…Rach…" Zion sobbed and held her close to his chest. His lips kissed her over and over. "Call 911!" He screamed.

Harmony was frozen to the spot but her eyes caught movement and she looked up to see Pat slipping through the door to the supply cabinet and disappearing. Anger burned in her belly as the murderer escaped, but she obeyed Zion's wishes by rushing to a desk where Zion's cell phone sat. As she gave the dispatcher information on the situation, Rachel took her last breath. Harmony could feel her soul leaving the space like warmth escaping out of an open door on a winter's day. Arrow crouched over Zion and Rachel like a fallen angel with his angel wing tattoos standing out strongly. Zion continued to pray as he sobbed into Rachel's neck.

Harmony couldn't handle the grief so she turned and left the room. She ran upstairs and down the hallways until she finally found herself outside in the dried-up gardens where the wind was picking up and angry purple clouds gathered on the horizon. She didn't feel like crying. She was battling things in her heart. Zion believed in a loving God who decided to allow a demon to murder his wife in front of him. Rachel believed in that same God and died tragically at the hands of somebody she was trying to help. If what Harmony had seen in the other realm was true, Rachel had watched as her dad recklessly killed her brother who struggled with addiction.

Harmony couldn't understand why anybody would believe in God if he didn't relieve the pain. Why would anybody go to that trouble for a God that didn't care? Rachel was the best of humanity. She had been murdered by the worst of humanity.

"Sicko." Harmony grieved best through her anger. She didn't want to cry.

Harmony then saw an ambulance pull up through the front gate and shortly behind it were a couple of police cars. Realizing that this had now become much more serious, Harmony quickly made her way back inside and down to the lab. Arrow was now standing close to the sink by the window, but Zion was still holding Rachel and sobbing.

"Emergency services is here." Harmony whispered to Arrow when she was level with him.

"Thanks." Arrow said. "Rachel was an angel. When I first came here, she always treated me as part of her family even though I was messed up." He then swallowed hard. "I can't believe Pat would do that."

"What did Tumultus mean when he said he already had you?"

Before Arrow could answer, the police came over to question them. Everybody explained what they had seen and that they weren't sure where Pat had gone. Harmony knew though, and told them what she had seen. They immediately checked the supply closet, but for some reason, the entrance to Oblivion had disappeared.

These police officers looked the same as the ones that had come to Harmony's door so they did not speak audibly, but instead asked most of the questions through typing out messages. The paramedics barely spoke either, but they had the option of speaking if they chose to. Once Rachel was loaded onto the stretcher, they covered her in a blanket and began taking her out the door. Zion followed close behind.

CHAPTER 38

THE FUNERAL WAS A MUCH BIGGER affair than Harmony had expected. Rachel had so many connections to the community and beyond. Feeling obligated to attend, Arrow and Harmony dressed in black formal attire and found a seat close to the back of the sanctuary during the funeral service. The pastor talked about what a giving person Rachel had been and how God's light shone out from her. He talked about how she was leaving behind a legacy of goodness that would certainly be continued by the people she had impacted. Zion was visible in the front of the room, his eyes red-rimmed from crying.

The more the pastor spoke, the more sorrow Harmony felt. Every so often she looked over at Arrow to get an idea of how to respond, but his eyes were dry during the entire service. He had cried a lot before the ceremony so Harmony wondered if he had cried his last tear before they arrived.

When it was over, Arrow drove them both to the cemetery and they stood in the cold and blustery weather listening to the pastor share a few more words of encouragement for the grieving family as Rachel was lowered into the ground. They had already agreed that it would be too uncomfortable to speak with Zion on such a terrible day, so Arrow slipped his hand in Harmony's and they walked back to the car. Wordlessly, they climbed inside and Arrow began to navigate his way out of the cemetery before other vehicles began clogging the exit.

"Do you want to get some food?" Arrow asked.

She nodded. "Yeah."

Arrow already knew where to go apparently because he didn't ask what she was in the mood for. They ended up at a small Italian restaurant called Merchelli's and the name struck a chord in Harmony's memory.

"Have we been here before…when I was Heidi?"

Arrow bit his lip and said reluctantly, "Yes."

"Was it a good memory?"

"One of our last good memories." Arrow answered.

"Oh."

When Harmony stepped out of the car, she took Arrow's elbow and they went in together. The walls were covered in murals of old Italian architecture and white columns were at various places around the room wrapped in faerie lights. There also were potted ferns hanging from lattice work on the ceiling.

"It's a beautiful place." Harmony admitted.

Arrow smiled for the first time that day and her heart fluttered.

Once they had been seated by the host, they looked through the menu. The waitress arrived at the table and they both already knew what they wanted to order. Harmony chose the chicken carbonara and Arrow chose steak linguini.

Once the waitress left, Harmony asked, "What are we doing?"

"Having lunch together. It's been a hard day and I think we both need it."

"That's true." She bit her lip and still found herself wrestling with her thoughts.

"This doesn't have to be a date." Arrow said finally.

"But I want it to be."

Arrow was silent for a long moment. His face had no expression but his eyes seemed to waver with indecision.

"Then it's a date." He breathed and his face broke into a grin.

Harmony smiled back and grabbed for her cup of water to hide her joy. It felt wrong to feel so excited. The last few days had made her think even more about how fragile life was. She didn't want to allow things to pass her by just because she was scared. She also had seen how Arrow was now and he was such a different person compared to who he was with Heidi.

Just then, Arrow's cell phone rang. He pulled it from his pocket and his eyebrows wrinkled in concern. "It's Zion."

He looked at Harmony as if waiting for permission to answer it. "You can talk to him." Harmony said earnestly.

Arrow nodded and answered the call. "Zion?"

There was silence and Harmony's brain bounced around trying to guess what he could be calling about. His wife had just died and it made no sense that he would be calling people already. If Harmony had lost the love of her life, she would have been holed up in her bedroom watching TV and crying.

"Of course, Zion. We're just having lunch but then we can be right over." Arrow said reassuringly. After a brief pause, Arrow then said, "Of course. Well, we'll see you soon. Bye."

"What did he say?" Harmony asked.

"He wants us to come back to the rehab center. He said he has some ideas." Arrow said. "I'm surprised he's ready to get back to work, but maybe he's just making excuses to try to get us to come back. He's probably lonely."

Harmony nodded thoughtfully but didn't respond because the waitress returned with a basket of bread and salad.

***

When they returned to Zion's, they were surprised to find him waiting for them in the foyer. He was missing some of the spark he usually had but he looked much better than he had at the church.

"I've been thinking and I wanted to bounce some ideas off you all." Zion said. "Will you follow me?"

Arrow nodded for the both of them and they followed Zion to the conference room. It seemed so barren without Clive, Rachel, or Pat.

"How are you doing?" Harmony asked once Zion had shut the door.

"I feel empty." Zion answered honestly. "The Lord gives and he takes away, but I know I will see her again." His small smile faltered and he took a deep breath to compose himself. "Anyway, that's not why I have you all here." Zion sat down and gestured to them to do the same.

"What do you need us to do?" Harmony asked. "We'd love to help in any way we can."

"Well, I have a theory." Zion began. "If the other realm is inhabited by demons and darkness, perhaps we need to flush all those things out with good things. The entrance to that place that was in my lab is no longer there, so that proves they can be closed. Think of the cracks we've been finding as wounds and the infection must be pushed out before the wounds can properly heal."

"That makes sense." Arrow affirmed.

"Good." Zion scratched his nose. "Thought Conductor's have been used to help people forget bad memories but if a large group of people chooses to erase one positive memory, it'll flood Oblivion with good things In theory, if we have enough of these thoughts, they should push out the bad which will allow the cracks to heal."

Harmony nodded. "When Lacey's past self came back with me to the real world, she didn't last long. The bad things should disappear if they are trapped here long enough. How will we get enough people to delete their happy memories?"

"That I can do. I have an email list of several of the churches that support us that I can utilize." Zion answered.

"What do we do about Doc, though?" Arrow asked.

"Oh-no…I forgot." Zion said sadly. "He's still in there?"

"As far as I know."

"No, I'm not anymore."

Everybody turned around and saw Dr. Evers in much rougher condition than the last time they had seen him. His pants were covered in mud and his face had sprouted more than just scruff. His hair was matted in places and his scratched-up hands were gripping the handles of a wheelchair he was guiding. In the wheelchair was his wife Mayre. Her head was tilted to the side and her hands folded in her lap as if they were glued there.

"Doc!" Arrow rushed over and hugged his friend. He looked down at Mayre and said, "Hello, Mayre."

She didn't respond but simply stared straight ahead.

"She's in there somewhere." Clive insisted.

"Oh, Clive." Zion said sympathetically. "What happened?"

Clive explained how Mayre had volunteered for research alongside Preston Winston but they had ended up taking too much from her and leaving her like a vegetable. He also explained the other things he had seen and confessed for the first time to friends rather than a priest about his infidelity.

"I am an awful man, husband, and Christian." Clive's voice cracked and he slumped into a chair sobbing.

Zion immediately closed the distance between them and embraced Clive tightly. "Jesus Christ has already forgiven you for what you have done and what you will do. It has already been paid for." Zion said confidently. "No matter what you've done, you can lay everything at the foot of the cross and Christ will help you through."

"Is that for everybody or just Christians?" Arrow asked suddenly.

"You must choose to accept the truth of the Bible and believe in the Lord Jesus. Then repent. Once you receive that forgiveness, you will be a child of God. No sin that you have committed can ever separate you from God." Zion let go of Clive and smiled.

"I don't see how you can still talk about God when he allowed Rachel to be murdered in front of us." Harmony blurted out.

Clive stammered, "W-what happened to Rachel?"

"Something happened to Pat and he killed her in front of us." Arrow said softly.

Zion turned to Harmony, unsurprised by her reaction. He responded honestly, "I don't fully understand why he took her either, but that doesn't change the fact that he is a loving and forgiving God. I am confident that everything that happens is for our good even if we don't see it." His eyes filled with tears and his voice shook with barely suppressed emotion.

"But why would a loving God allow so much pain?" Her voice cracked as she demanded answers.

"To increase our dependence on him. If we knew all that he knows, we would very likely allow all the things that have happened to happen again."

Harmony's brows knitted together in confusion but she didn't ask any more questions.

"I'm sorry for your loss, Zion." Clive said. "Could we pray together?"

Zion nodded and smiled with all the warmth that Harmony was familiar with. He and Rachel were the only people she knew who could continue to exude joy amidst despair. This solidified in her heart that what they believe must have some merit, because how could anybody be happy after what the Jones' had been through?

***

In a matter of days, Zion had contacted thousands of churches about his plan. All volunteers in this experiment had microchips and had offered to delete one happy memory for the sake of the world.

Clive was floored by the huge network of churches Zion was connected to. Clive only connected with the members of his church, but never ventured out beyond that.

After Zion and Clive had prayed together the night before, he felt like a renewed man. He hadn't felt the urge to show others up or constantly bemoan what had happened to Mayre. Instead, he was content. He knew that his life would be harder with Mayre's condition, but he had hope that there would be a cure. If no cure was found in this life, certainly there would be one in the next.

All the local churches that had volunteered met up with Zion and Clive at the spot Zion had discovered by stargazing in his observatory. Harmony and Arrow were at the opening that had appeared in Harmony's backyard. Zion decided to livestream what was happening so the out-of-state churches were able to observe and Clive kept his phone on a Facetime call with Arrow to see if they had similar results.

The trio of trees surrounding the tear between dimensions swayed slightly with the autumn wind. The leaves had long since fallen off the branches and littered the ground they were all standing on. Zion's laptop was filled with faces and, on the presentation screen, there was a countdown clock. Once the clock reached zero, Zion instructed everybody to release one happy memory. Zion had reactivated his chip before this experiment, so he pressed a button on his phone along with Harmony and the rest of the churches.

Nothing happened at first, but then Clive could hear rumbling. As he looked at the black line, it seemed to be curling up and spreading like smoke. Even so, nothing else seemed to be happening.

"Give it a moment." Zion muttered.

Clive waited patiently but continued to watch the dark line pulse before them. Nothing was leaving Oblivion, though.

As five tense minutes passed, Clive said, "Maybe our theory was flawed."

Zion's lips pursed and he pulled out his phone again. He swiped through several thumbnails of memories. After a moment he paused, finger hovering over a spot. Definitively, he pressed on the screen and another memory was released into Oblivion.

"What did you release?" Clive asked Zion.

"The day I met Rachel" He said simply.

"What??" Clive's eyes bulged.

"The Lord asks that we give all we have. After we prayed the other night, I felt compelled to release that memory of her. If it can save others…"

Before he could finish, dark things began pouring out of the tear with seemingly no end. Clive, Zion, and every local church member hit the grass face down as Oblivion was being emptied. Flattened ghosts of the underbelly of humanity were whirling around and seeking escape. Clive was unable to move from his spot due to the force of the release.

He was able to pull his face up from the ground just enough to see other things walking, slithering, and crawling from the depths. He glanced at his phone and could see glimpses of similar apparitions appearing for Harmony and Arrow. Clive expected to see zombies, ghosts, unnamed beasts, and large spiders, but what he didn't expect was to see normal-looking men, children, priests, and grandmothers leaving the void.

To Clive's relief, these apparitions disappeared surprisingly quickly. When the stream of darkness began slowing, Clive was able to sit up. He looked around the darkened landscape as apparition after apparition dissolved into nothingness. The only figure that remained was a slim man with tousled brown hair.

"Pat?" Doctor Clive rushed for the boy and checked his vitals. Even though he knew what Pat had done, he couldn't just leave him.

"Don't touch him." A female voice commanded.

A queen stepped out of the tear and it melted behind her. She was very tall and her red hair flowed down to her waist. A sharp, dangerous-looking crown was in her left hand and she fingered it as if to say, "I'm ready to use this thing."

Clive didn't move from beside Pat, but he removed his hands from his body. Pat continued to breathe shallowly.

"I think he's hurt. Let me check him, please." Clive pleaded.

"He isn't. Tumultus has simply taken over." The Queen bent down beside Pat and stroked his still face with her long fingers. "I'm his wife, Justice."

Clive couldn't hide his surprise so he stared openly.

"What can we do?" Zion asked coming up behind Clive. The members of the local churches gathered around awkwardly.

"I fear he might be lost forever. I tried to stop this from happening but…" She swallowed hard. "…I wasn't strong enough,"

Zion nodded and then said, "Lord, you are in control in this situation and we are begging now for your wisdom. Pat is lost to us currently, but we are not ready to lose him. Please set him free. Bring him back to us and free this man from under this demon as only you can."

Clive had never seen a prayer answered in real-time, but he had never wanted something so badly before. He hoped the Lord would be gracious in this moment and bring Pat back to them.

CHAPTER 39

PAT STRUGGLED TO OPEN HIS EYES. He was enveloped in a warm heaviness that he never wanted to wake from. The screaming had ceased and all he could hear was the pleasant buzzing of silence. He would have continued to lie there if the skeptical part of his mind hadn't insisted he wake. He forced himself to drag his eyes open and pull himself to a sitting position.

He was in an indescribable place. He wasn't certain why he couldn't explain his surroundings, but no words were coming to mind. If somebody asked him where he had been, he would have simply said it felt familiar. There was solid ground beneath his body and light to see by. There must have been oxygen in this place because he had no trouble breathing, either.

He stood and began walking forward. Nondescript items passed him by and he paid them no mind. Nothing felt urgent or important in this place. He felt like he was floating just outside his physical body, so no painful sensations were felt in his flesh.

He didn't even know how long he had been walking before he noticed a black dot getting closer to him. When he was near enough to make out details, he saw a man sitting on a bench. Without a second thought, Pat sat beside the man but said nothing.

"I'm so glad you joined me, Pat." His words were gentle and the warmth reminded him of Zion.

Where was Zion?

"Am I dead?" Pat asked. It was odd how this hadn't occurred to him before.

"No, not yet."

"Am I about to be dead if I don't change my ways or give all I have to the poor?" Pat laughed at his own joke. The man didn't answer directly and Pat thought he had unintentionally offended him.

"Why do you continue to run from Me?"

"I haven't…I don't even know who you are." Pat said earnestly. He wanted to impress this man for some reason.

"I think you do, but you refuse to acknowledge Me. I know you, Patrick Michael Sherwood." The man's features suddenly made sense to Pat and he was able to describe them. The man had a thin frame with wooly, pure white hair down to his shoulders. His nose was bent as if it had been broken and was very pronounced. His clothes were simple like something Pat would choose to wear.

"I think I would've remembered meeting you." Pat said firmly and looked away into the white abyss ahead of them. His eyes were determined to find something to look at in this place, but there was nothing. "What is your name?"

"I go by many names, but all you must know is that I AM."

"I am…what?"

"I AM the strength that you need. I AM the love that you seek. I AM the stability you yearn for. I AM what I AM."

Without warning, the side of Pat's head where the chip had been installed began to burn. He winced involuntarily and placed his hand on the healing wound.

"Tumultus, show yourself." The man commanded.

The demon appeared a gruesome blot in this pleasant place. His treelike fingers seemed to spread throughout the space and eat up any available light except for the light that was surrounding the man.

"With all due respect…" Tumultus hissed. "This man is mine."

"Only because I allow it." The man stood and rays of light began to pierce the shadows of the demon, which caused Tumultus to back up slightly.

The demon's eyes now showed fear. "I humbly request to have this man and I will not ask for anything else."

"You will not have him. For I have heard the prayers of My church and am here to intercede."

The man pulled from his side a glowing sword that Pat hadn't previously seen. The demon still looked afraid but did not back down. All of the sharp black points on his body grew and the limbs on his fingers turned into blades. With a shriek, the demon lunged for the man and Pat braced himself for the impact, but in one swing, the sword sliced the creature in half and clattered to the ground.

EPILOGUE

Up and down the riverbanks the bare trees creaked in the chilly breeze and the dark blue waters lapped against the hard ground that had stopped growing things to prepare for winter hibernation. Animals ceased all noise as the skies threatened to send down a blizzard any day now. A few brave fishermen sat in the middle of their boats waiting for a bite on the line to make their efforts worthwhile.   Near the docks, a happy coupl towards the boat called Straight as an Arrow. The man stumbled a few times as he tried to carry his bride across the threshold and they could be heard laughing loudly in the stillness of the landscape.

"You don't have to carry me." Harmony insisted as Arrow grunted trying to sidle into the houseboat with both arms occupied.

"It's tradition. I want to do this right because I didn't do it right the first time around." He said through labored breaths.

Once inside the shabby houseboat, Arrow gently laid his bride on the fuzzy brown couch and shut the door behind them. She was smiling up at him and dressed in layers of white chiffon fabric covered in beading that was toned down significantly by the winter jacket she was wearing. Arrow was more dressed up than usual in a nice pair of jeans, a black belt, a white button-up shirt, and a thin black tie. However, he still looked rough around the edges. His eyes sparkled though as he bent down beside her.

"I love you." He said as he leaned in and kissed her softly.

"I love you, too."

"I'm sorry for the man I was." His eyebrows knitted together in concern. "You didn't deserve that."

"I told you, I forgive you. How can I not when I am equally to blame?" Harmony sat up and reached her hands out to cradle his newly clean-shaven face. There were more lines around his eyes and his mouth than there had been when she was Heidi, but he was no less handsome in her book.

"It'll take a lifetime for me to accept that forgiveness." Arrow said sadly.

"Remember what Zion said? God has already taken all that sin and pain and suffering on himself. We have both been forgiven." She insisted.

After all they had been through together and what they had seen, they had sought out answers from Zion. He had been very patient with them and walked them through the process of becoming Christians. While it was still an uphill battle to overcome who they had been and what they had done, Harmony immediately felt the difference and knew she was a different woman. She had seen this change in Arrow, too. He had already been 3 months sober.

Despite the changes in their hearts, Harmony still felt a twinge of shame every time she thought of Haven. Even though the girl they saw in Oblivion was a figment of her imagination, it still made her decision to terminate the pregnancy more real. She knew her daughter was with the Lord, but the loss of what could have been would always be something she would battle.

"Are you thinking about Haven?" Arrow asked as Harmony's hands fell from his face.

She nodded sadly and automatically reached a hand around her stomach. Arrow placed his rough hand over hers and squeezed. He didn't have to say anything, but she knew that he had forgiven her.

"We'll see her again." He said.

The tears filled her eyes too fast for her to stop them and she wrapped her arms around his neck tightly. She sniffed into his shoulder and whispered a garbled "thank you", which he returned by pressing the side of his head against hers.

Moments passed in this embrace and Harmony could slowly feel the pieces of her heart mending enough to be able to stop crying.

She pulled away and Arrow said, "Now, this is our honeymoon and we can do what we want, but I don't want you feeling sad if I can help it." His eyes crinkled up in a smile.

"I'm not sad now." She said honestly.

And she wasn't sad. Despite the things they had lost and the wasted time, she knew that her new life as a born-again Christian would be filled with more joy than she had ever had. Perfection wasn't the goal, but her life had much more meaning now. She and Arrow were going to grow together in their faith and build a life worth living. It was going to be different, and different was good.

She was also considering getting blond dreadlocks again.

***

Since Preston had disappeared and his employees had disbanded, the microchip installation initiative had paused for the time being. Unfortunately, those who had been receiving treatment were asked to stop immediately and use alternative solutions such as medicine, therapy, and exercise/diet until the technology could be more refined.

Healing Touch Hospital was under fire for promoting Dr. Shepherd because they had found out that he had been taking advantage of some of the nurses on his floor and several allegations of sexual harassment were being charged against him at breakneck speed. Clive knew that Tonya would have her work cut out for her defending the hospital from such bad press and found himself grinning as he read the news stories. He knew it was not the Christian response to be so gleeful at someone else's despair, but it felt validating to know that his past employer was struggling so much without him.

He put his phone down as the coffee pot beeped loudly and stuttered as the last remaining liquid dripped into the carafe. He padded barefoot across his kitchen where he had escaped police capture months ago. The charges against him had been officially dropped since it turned out Preston had been the one to press them. While Clive was not privy to the details of those charges, he was under the impression it had something to do with claims that he had been mining private patient data into his own secure database since getting fired. Preston must have wanted Clive completely out of the picture so he didn't ruin any of his plans.

When Pat had finally become himself again and things had settled down, he reluctantly filled everybody in on what Preston had told him. Clive would have given anything to get to examine Preston's mind but was more relieved the man was gone for good. He truly was a wolf in sheep's clothing.

Once Clive had poured the coffee, filled the plates with breakfast, and buttered the toast, he loaded everything on a tray and took it back to the bedroom. He quietly pushed open the cracked door with his forearm and tip-toed into the room where morning light trickled in around the curtains. Mayre was in the center of their bed propped up on several pillows and her eyes closed.

To the left of the bed was a hospital table he had borrowed months ago. The wheels rolled under the bed while the top fit directly over Mayre in the bed. He unlocked the wheels on the table with his foot and set the tray of food on the tabletop. Clicking on the side table light he was able to roll the table into position over her.

Her eyes fluttered open and she took in the breakfast, her husband, and the dimly lit room. Her eyes were blank.

"Good morning, Mayre." Clive said gently. "I made you some breakfast."

For months he had been working with another hospital in town to treat Mayre. They were more than willing to allow him to use their equipment and resources due to his stellar reputation and experience. He also knew some of the staff from his church and they loved Mayre. The treatment he had been using had been largely experimental, but he was hopeful that he would start to make inroads soon. Clive also used his influence to get Ophelia transferred under his care and get Sirona working as her nurse.

Preparing to spoon-feed his love, he wasn't looking directly at her and nearly missed a smile that spread across her face unlike it had in months. He froze and looked directly at his wife's smiling face.

"Hello, Clive."

Her hand reached out and her fingertips grazed his arm. His opposite hand flew up to his mouth as he choked back a sob.

"Oh, the merciful hand of God, I am undeserving of your grace." Clive whispered as he embraced his wife and she embraced him back.

***

The familiar winding roads gave Pat plenty of time to rehearse what he was going to say. If he was honest with himself, he had had 3 months to rehearse. Now that the day was upon him, he mentally thumbed through possible phrases or apologies like he was running a race.

"Jesus, please give me the words to say." Pat prayed aloud as he turned into the driveway leading up to a massive courtyard containing several brick buildings.

It was Sunday so nobody was outside working and the place

looked much more barren than it had last time he had been here. He parked in the roundabout in front of the rehab facility and stepped out of his car. The closing of his door echoed in the silence and he looked around to regain his bearings. Spotting the chapel, he began to walk towards it.

When he was halfway there, the door sprung open and congregants poured out all talking and laughing. One of the men holding the door open was Zion, and Pat felt his heart fall out of his body. He stopped mid-stride debating if he should do this. He was certain that Zion wouldn't forgive him and he didn't want to have to face that ultimate rejection.

Pat was about to turn around when he saw Zion's eyes fall on him. He took a moment to stare at Pat as if he didn't understand what he was seeing, then recognition flashed across his face. Zion began speaking with a man who had just walked out the door and the man nodded to accept the job of holding open the door.

Now that Zion was freed of his duties, he began to stride purposefully toward Pat and then began running at full speed until he collided with Pat hugging him tightly. Pat's arms hung awkwardly at his sides as he expected Zion to transition from hugging to strangling. When this didn't happen, he reciprocated the hug by wrapping his lanky arms around Zion's stocky torso.

"It's so good to see you." Zion said, his voice choked with emotion.

"It's good to see you, too." Pat said honestly.

Zion let go of Pat and looked into his face with a warm smile he felt like he didn't deserve. "Would you like to join me for lunch?"

"I…" Pat wanted to but he didn't feel like he deserved to be treated like a guest. "I would but are you sure?"

"Yes." Zion said firmly. "You came all this way."

Pat followed Zion into the main house and they took their meal to a secluded spot in the house with two overstuffed leather armchairs and a side table with a stained glass reading lamp on it. Pat watched Zion closely and moved his food around the plate.

When Zion seemed settled, Pat said, "I'm sorry for what I did, Zion." Zion's expression was blank as if he didn't seem to understand what Pat was saying. Pat took a deep breath and added, "What I did to Rachel. I'm sorry."

Zion set down his plate of food on the side table, sympathy in his eyes. "I forgive you, Pat."

"How??" Pat demanded. "I see what happened in my memories over and over again. The evil I did against you when you were nothing but kind to me…"

Pat trailed off and looked down at his plate.

"For we do not wrestle against flesh and blood, but against the rulers, against the authorities, against the cosmic powers over this present darkness, against the spiritual forces of evil in the heavenly places." Zion recited. "What's done is done and it can't be reversed but I don't hold any malice against you, by the grace of God."

Pat looked up and saw the ghost of a reassuring smile on Zion's face. "I'm undeserving of all I've been given. I know this now. After being freed from that evil, I haven't had any hallucinations or nightmares, or blackouts. The Lord saved me, Zion."

"Praise God." Zion breathed, his face glowing with true happiness. "What is going to happen to Sherwood Servers?"

"I signed over the rights to the company to Theresa. We had a long conversation and she wants to continue to further my father's legacy. There's a lot of cleaning up to do after Preston, but she seemed excited by the challenge."

"What happened with Preston breaks my heart." Zion shook his head. "We had been friends for a long time but I had no idea the hold that Satan had over his heart and mind."

"Nobody knew. He hid it really well." Pat said simply. He didn't want to think anymore about Preston. The memory of their conversation in his office haunted Pat and it would take some time for him to fully recover from the trauma.

"So, what's next for Patrick Sherwood?" Zion asked.

"I'm going to turn myself in. I've been running from what I've done but, the Lord has been working on my heart and I know I need to give the families of those women closure."

Zion nodded but didn't say anything.

"You may not see me for a while, which is why I wanted to come visit before I gave myself up."

"We have a prison ministry through this facility. If they do sentence you, I will come visit as often as I can." Zion reassured him. "I wish it didn't have to be this way but I know God will be honored by you coming forward. Even though God forgives, man-made law is not designed to be so merciful."

Pat swallowed hard, feeling fear fluttering in his chest at the thought of being in prison. His fear did not change the fact that he knew it was the right thing to do.

"How do you cope with losing your wife?" Pat asked suddenly.

Zion looked thoughtful then said, "The only one that gets me through it is God. I go to him every moment and pray for peace. I still cry about her often, though. I still miss seeing her every day. I miss doing life with her."

Pat tried to ignore another twinge of guilt in his heart. "I feel the same about Justice, but I guess she was never real."

On the day he was freed from the demon's grasp, he remembers waking to Justice standing over him. All he could do was mingle his tears with hers and kiss her until he was tired. They had spent an entire 48 hours together but she was gone after that. He had hoped that the sacrifice of Rachel would enable Justice to stay in his world but that was the devil talking in his messed-up brain. This final loss of Justice is what it took for Pat to finally find God.

"I think my subconscious created Justice to help me cope with my Mother taking her own life." Pat said sadly. "I don't know how to reconcile that knowledge with what I thought I knew." He set his plate of food down next to Zion's and they sat in companionable silence.

Finally, Zion said, "This is beyond my knowledge of our world but I will say this— God knows intimately what you went through even if no human being understands. You can be confident that he has his hands in every part of this situation. That doesn't change the hurt or the grief, but it does help you to carry that burden better."

Zion stood and walked over to hug Pat. Pat stood and hugged him back.

For the rest of Pat's visit, they chatted about ministry, favorite foods, and family. It was only for 2 hours but it felt like an eternity and Pat was grateful for it. When he walked out into the courtyard, the sun was still bright but low in the sky. The only sounds that could be heard were a few cars driving by and a gentle breeze picking up a few stray leaves that hadn't decomposed yet.

"It is an honor to know you." Zion said, giving him a final hug before he left.

"You might be the only one that feels that way." Pat joked.

"Even better. Everybody else doesn't know what they're missing. God bless you, Pat. I hope our paths cross again."

"Me too. You are one of the best people I know." Pat said, trying not to cry again. He had been crying more than he liked to.

It was hard to go but Pat knew that it was time. He walked around to the driver's side door of his car and opened it. Once inside the vehicle, he started it up and began to pull away from the rehab facility. Zion was waving to him and he waved back.

When he was outside the gates of the facility, he felt a sinking feeling in his soul. As much as he wished he could run away and start a new life, he knew that the Holy Spirit was pushing him to make things right. While obedience to Christ didn't guarantee happiness in this life, he knew that whatever happened to him would be for his good. It would shape and mold him into the Christian man God had in mind. It would shave off the rough edges of his trauma, sin, and pain and leave behind pure gold refined by fire. His future in this world was uncertain, but he had assurance that the monsters of this world would not follow him into the next.

ACKNOWLEDGMENTS

Before publishing a book, I never understood the necessity of an "acknowledgments" section. However, after the birth of this book idea in 2014, I realized that bringing a book into the world has so many steps that it would not be possible to see it through without the supportive community God has given me. So thank you, readers, for bearing with me as I express my thanks. If you are like me and never usually read this section, I encourage you to keep reading about the amazing people who have supported me and my writing and the ways they did what they did to make this book possible.

Jesus Christ primarily deserves all my praise and gratitude for every single person and moment that brought me here. We may make our plans in this life, but scripture says that the LORD orders our steps. In thinking back to my first steps, I want to start by thanking the author Heidi Salter who wrote **Taddy McFinley and the Great Grey Grimly**. When I discovered her beautiful book at my local library, it ignited my desire to publish a book of my own. Up until that point, I never knew kids could author books. So, it encouraged me to write all the time, which is what I did thanks to Heidi.

Next, thank you to Katie (Tillwick) Burlew who mentored me in my writing when I was a senior in high school and throughout college. She never treated me like a kid but as a fellow writer and friend. I value the encouragement and feedback she gave me on my pieces and the hours we spent hanging out. I hope you know, Katie, that I am a better writer and slightly more fashionable because of your influence.

I am also incredibly grateful for The Kentucky Storytelling Association (KSA) and all its members. I initially competed in the Youth Storytelling Showcase with no thoughts or plans that it would take me anywhere but through the careful mentoring from Don (Buck P.) Creacy and Donna Slaton, I was given the opportunity to travel, compete at the national level, meet nationally famous storytellers, be on the board of my local library and the board of KSA, record my own CD of stories, and tour the state, performing my works of original fiction. It is an experience I will never forget, and it gave me skills I have used in my professional career, college, parenting, and beyond.

To author Vivien Reis, thank you for dropping into my life when I had almost given up writing. One of the recommended YouTube tutorials on self-publishing was your work and watching it inspired me to press on despite the difficulties. I connected with authors Jenna Moreci and Kim Chance through your writing community and both ladies were instrumental in adding to my writing knowledge while spurring me on to publish books. I had the opportunity to meet Kim Chance in person at one of her book signings, which further brought me into the wider author community. I am so thankful to her for the encouragement and for the many hours she hosted writing sprints which gave me the accountability I needed to power through the drafting process.

Thank you to the Instagram author community for connecting me to so many authors from all over the world. I am continually inspired and encouraged by how God has been using these connections in my life to improve my writing and help me through challenges in the publishing process.

Thank you to my lovely Beta readers Joanne Fowler, Theresa Givens, Hannah Everett, Alex Wink, Laura Seaman, Ryan Seaman, Ron Estes, Nancy Ward, and Hannah Dieterle. You are all some of my biggest fans and it encourages me so much when you get excited about the story and the characters just like I do. Your collective feedback has helped me improve the story so much, but your praise has helped me see the gems in my writing. I know I can share writing news with all of you and you will get just as excited as I do. This story would not be what it is today without you all.

Thank you to my church family at Bellevue Baptist Church for the continual encouragement I have received. Not only am I encouraged by the body of Christ to write, but I am also inspired to go deeper in my faith which has helped inspire many aspects of this book. The discipleship at Bellevue has helped shore up the theology in my book which has been so important.

Gable Price and Friends…thank you for your music! It has become the unofficial soundtrack for my first book and if it ever becomes a movie, I will insist on the inclusion of the song "Redemption" in the official soundtrack.

To my beautiful editor and friend Hannah Haruna, thank you for taking on my manuscript (typos and all) and continuing to support my work. The way that Hannah corrects errors with compassion and provides alternative examples is such a blessing that I do not take it for granted. I am honored to collaborate with a Christian woman like Hannah and I am grateful for her hard work.

Thank you to Maja K. who designed my cover for Consigned to Oblivion. I explained to her my vision for the book, and she whipped up something for me in less than 48 hours. She saw what I envisioned and executed it professionally and beautifully. I am so grateful for her talent and creativity.

Thank you also to Sriracha who created the beautiful character art depicting all three main characters in my novel. She has been amazingly easy to work with and she is passionate about what she does. The pieces she designed completely encompass what I was looking for and it is a privilege to have her as part of this debut novel.

Author Ronald Estes deserves his very own acknowledgment for all the hours he has spent reading different versions of my novel, waiting patiently for publishing, and sharing my promotional author posts on social media. He is the first local author I befriended, and his insight and encouragement have been invaluable. He has believed in me and my work and continues to encourage me on my author journey. Thank you, Ron, for everything.

Thank you to my Uncle Mike. You always, always, always believed in me and I wish you were here to see this book come to life. I think you would have been enormously proud.

Thank you also to my living grandparents, Norma and Chancy Morgan, for saving Uncle Mike's many laptops full of his writings. Thank you for continually supporting my creative journey and checking in on my progress with the book. I have felt your love even over the miles between us and I enjoy our conversations.

Thank you to my other living grandpa (affectionately known by me as Papa Liam) for spending time discussing books and movies with me and making me feel less silly about my genre preferences. Thank you for helping me appreciate a good Irish joke and a truly well-prepared breakfast. Thank you as well for opening your home to me when I made a mad rush to Chicago to meet my writing hero Lemony Snicket (aka Daniel Handler) and on another occasion when I got to meet author Kim Chance. Your love, support, and Irish candy have helped fuel my creativity and I hope you enjoy this book.

Thank you to my Mother-in-law Ruthann who has spent many hours watching the kids for me so I could get this book done. I have felt so blessed to have her in my life and her love has been such an encouragement to me.

Thank you to my Uncle Greg for your genuine interest in my life and work. I think society as a whole gives uncles a bad rap but I have the best ones in the world. I hope you enjoy the character in this story who has a love and appreciation for astronomy like you do.

Thank you to my cousin Valerie and my sister-in-law Jessica for filling that void for sisters in my life. I am weird, but you both love me and support me anyway which makes me feel so special. If this book gets big someday, I give you full permission to tell people that you are related to me and knew me before I was famous.

Thank you to the men I grew up with…my Dad and my brothers Ryan and Derek. None of you enjoy reading like I do, but you have been some of the biggest supporters of my writing. Your collective excitement gives me the energy to keep going, and it makes me realize how blessed I am to be surrounded by God-fearing, honorable men who love me. God is so good, and I am so, so grateful for you three.

Mom, you are my best friend. You have been editing my manuscripts since I was 9 years old. I imagine this has been the craziest journey for you since you were editing my embarrassing manuscripts all those years ago without batting an eye. You took us kiddos to the library often, you signed me up for the storytelling competition, you helped me in so many of my writing endeavors, and now I am finally publishing a book! You never thought writing was silly or a waste of my time. You always encouraged me to pursue my strengths. I feel undeserving of all the love and support you have poured into me, but I am so, so, so glad I have it.

To my babies, Elliott and Bristol: I hope you love books someday as much as I do, but even if you don't, please know that you push me to work even harder at my writing because you are here. I intentionally carve out time to create, and you both have helped me focus on my priorities more efficiently. Before I was your mom, I never came close to publishing a book even though I had "so much time". Now that you are both here and my days are so full, I realize that nothing was going to get done unless I prioritized it. You remind me of what is important.

And last, but not least, I want to thank my husband, Jake. I am embarrassed to admit how many of my stories have included you but under a different name. I started writing the year we met. So, you have always known me as the weird writer girl. Even though you do not enjoy reading nearly as much as I do, you have continually encouraged me to use my gifts and to use them well. Never have you encouraged me to do something halfway. You want me to give it all I've got! This book is exactly that…a culmination of my best work. I could not have done this without you. You are the glue that holds our family together. It is through your love that I am enabled to be my wild and creative self. If I did not have that love from you, I would lack the fire to write with abandon. I love you and ours will always be my favorite story.

Emilee Breanne Ward has been writing fantastical stories since nine years old. At age fourteen she started professional storytelling which led to her placing 2 years in a row at the National Youth Storytelling competition. In 2010 she released an album of 6 original stories under her maiden name "Emilee Seaman" called "A Slice of Life With a Cup of Tea". Throughout that time, she had always had dreams of publishing a full-length novel and continued to hone her craft until publishing her first book in 2024. When she's not writing she enjoys going to live concerts, cooking food from scratch, ministering to the community through her church, advocating for people with disabilities, watching cheesy 80's murder mystery shows, and zip-lining. She currently lives in Owensboro, KY with her husband of 7 years, 2 kiddos, and a fluffy ginger cat named Henry.

www.emileebreanneward.com

www.ingramcontent.com/pod-product-compliance
Lightning Source LLC
Chambersburg PA
CBHW070608300726